RUTHLESS TRAITOR

ISBN: 978-1-956264-43-2

For the secret keepers and sisters from another mother who never let you down.

SERIES SO FAR

Savage Vandal
Vicious Rebel
Ruthless Traitor
Dirty Devil

FOREWORD

Dear Reader,

I don't even know how to start this letter. Ruthless Traitor poured out of me, a book demanding to be written and all of their stories, not just Emersyn's but all of the Vandals as well, needing to be told.

If you haven't read the first two books in this series, I encourage you to grab them and read them now before going any further. This is a series that really does need to be read in order.

At the end of Vicious Rebel, Emersyn had not only begun to trust the Vandals, but she'd begun to open up to them bit by bit. Then she and Jasper returned to the clubhouse to find out that not only had Raptor been released from prison, he was also right there.

Secrets.

Secrets.

More secrets.

While I warned you that the darkness in the dark romance of the 82nd Street Vandals would get worse in

Vicious Rebel, we go darker and deeper in this book. I don't think there will be much in the way of light for a while as we dig into the murk that makes up their history.

They are survivors though and I have my fingers crossed that will help them all through what is to come. Trust takes time. For Emersyn. For the Vandals. For Raptor. They all desperately need the time and the space to not only build trust, but to rebuild it.

The biggest question is will they get it?

Please be aware this book contains content with dark themes and intense situations intended for mature audiences only, including but not limited to: sexual assault, flashbacks of grooming, underage/childhood sexual assault, physical violence, emotional and mental abuse, as well as kidnapping, stalking, manipulation, addiction and other potentially triggering topics.

And now, as always, the housekeeping notes:

For those of you who have never read a reverse harem before, first let me thank you for picking this up and giving it a shot. Second, a reverse harem means the heroine will not make a choice in this book or any other between the guys in her life. It may take her a while to reach that conclusion, but it's the journey that drives it. There are many ways to frame this kind of relationship, currently reverse harem fits it very well.

Also, this is the third book in a series. While there may be no specific happy endings at the end of each of these books, there will be one to the whole series, that I promise you. Some of these books will have cliffhangers, largely due to the size of the story, but the happy ending has to be earned as part of the journey.

Thank you again for reading Emersyn's story and I truly hope you enjoy it!

xoxo
Heather

THE VANDALS

82nd Street Boys
    Jasper "Hawk" Horan
    Kellan "Kestrel" Traschel
    Rome "Hummingbird" Cleary
    Vaughn "Falcon" Westbrook
    Liam "Mockingbird" O'Connell
    Freddie "Unknown" Dunlap
    Raptor

Not a Vandal
    Mickey "Doc" James
    Emersyn "Dove, Sparrow, Starling, Swan, Little Bit, Boo-Boo" Sharpe

Other Characters
    Elaine "Lainey" Benedict
    Adam Reed
    Ezra Graham
    Ms. Stephanie

THEN

17 years earlier

"Milo," Mom called, interrupting me from the television. In her pen, Ivy cried, the warbling volume of her voice climbing. Sisters sucked. "Take care of your sister."

Yeah. Yeah.

I pushed off of the sofa and went to where she clung to the sides of the pen. She was on her feet, her face red as big fat tears spilled down her cheeks. The shrieking noise cut off as soon as I reached for her. Trust filled her eyes as she let go of the gate and grabbed for me. Hands hooked under her arms, I lifted her up and over. Her diaper reeked.

Oh, that explained that.

Carrying her over to the sofa, I set her on the cushion and she went to roll off immediately. "No," I told her and put a hand on her belly. She was as flexible as a monkey. That was why the pen. She walked early, did everything early. It used to make Mom happy.

Not so much anymore.

Nothing had made her happy since Dad left.

He went to the store for *milk*.

He hadn't come back.

I was almost seven. I got it.

Dad wasn't coming back.

Ivy's face screwed up and her mouth opened. Yeah, she was going to scream again, so I stuck my tongue out at her and blew a raspberry. Even though fat tears continued to roll down her cheeks, she burst out laughing.

I hurried over to the box in the corner and dug out a diaper. There were only five left. The box with the wipe things was almost empty and the powder Mom used to use had long since been gone. My stomach growled, but I just went back to where Ivy waited. I couldn't waste time, she wouldn't stay on the sofa. The commercials ended and the show started up again and I tried to watch it while I stripped her out of the diaper.

Poop was so gross.

Like really, really gross.

But if I held my breath and wiped her up real good, it was over and done with fast. I made faces at her the whole time and she giggled. It was easier when she cooperated. The first time I had to do this we'd made a huge mess.

I thought Mom would kill me, but she hadn't said a word.

Once I got her all changed, I set her down on the floor and we both stared at the TV. I liked this show. The guys had powers. They were orphans, but they had powers and they could save themselves from all the bad guys. Ivy held fast to my hand and seemed riveted, so I waited for the next commercial. As soon as it happened, I grabbed the nasty diaper and walked to the trash can in the kitchen. Ivy toddled along with me, almost running on her toes.

She had the funniest way of walking. Her face was all

sweaty and damp with tears. Her nose was snotty. Her dark hair smelled funny, but that could be the diaper. I got rid of it and then opened the fridge. I was hungry and Ivy probably was, too. There was some juice in there and I knew how to make her bottles. We also had some applesauce, so I got that out too.

The dishes were stacked in the sink and almost all the bottles were dirty. I climbed up to look in the cupboard. There were none in there either.

Ivy let out a complaint and I sighed. "Yeah, yeah." We were going to miss the show. I shoved the juice back into the fridge and got spoons for the applesauce. There wasn't a lot, just the two small containers. Wait...I had juice boxes in the pantry. I raced over there and pulled it open.

It was pretty empty, but there was a box on the shelf. I dragged it out and then grinned at Ivy. "Let's go..."

She followed me back into the living room and I put our stuff on the table, but she scrabbled up onto the sofa before I could pick her up. Her grin was infectious and so much better than her tears. I climbed up to sit next to her and then opened an applesauce.

The show came back on. Ivy let me feed her. But she had to be even hungrier than me. She ate all of the applesauce and I only got one bite. That was okay. I stuck the straw in the juice box and we split that too. That was harder for her. She wanted a bottle.

I kept waiting for Mom to come and get us and tell me dinner was ready. I was watching shows way later than normal. It had gotten dark outside. Ivy was sleepy and she still smelled funny. I needed my bath, too. I scooped Ivy up and carried her toward Mom's room.

She'd been in there most of the day after she forgot to take me to school. "Mom?"

"Go to bed, Milo."

The rasp of her voice made me sad. Ivy was heavy, but she held on to me tight so that made it easier to carry her.

"But I haven't had my bath..." Or dinner. "I'm hungry."

"You can have a bath tomorrow."

Mom didn't roll over. She was on her side, staring at the other wall. Her room smelled even worse than Ivy. "Mommy?"

"Go to bed, Milo," she repeated, and I sighed.

"What about Ivy?"

"Put her to bed, too."

I stood there for a minute and looked at Ivy again. She had her thumb in her mouth and her head tucked against my shoulder. Little sisters could be kind of cute sometimes, too.

"Go," Mom said with a croak as she rolled over and the light from the hall hit her face. I backed up in a hurry. Mom looked sick. She let out this little sigh. "Sorry baby, just—go to bed. It will be better tomorrow. I promise. You're a good big brother."

"I love you, Mom."

"I love you too, baby."

Shifting Ivy against my shoulder, I carried her toward the back of the house. I liked my bedroom with the race car bed. It was messy, but it was mine. Ivy's room was right next to mine and we shared a bathroom. I carried her into her room and set her in her crib. I had to climb up on the chair to get her in it. She complained but I dug around and found her pacifier. Mom said we had to throw it away, but I hid it.

When we didn't have a bottle, it worked.

She sucked on it and I dragged her dirty shirt off and

wiped her face. It wasn't great but I pulled a blanket over her and then headed to the bathroom.

"Night, Ivy," I whispered. I patted my hand over her hair. Mommy used to do that to me. "Sweet dreams. I love you." Then I leaned all the way over to kiss her.

That part was important. Mommy said it made the bad dreams stay away.

I trundled into the bathroom and pushed Ivy's door most of the way closed, but not all the way. It was really dark in there and I wanted her to have some light.

Wanting a bath, I figured out how to fill the tub halfway. It was a little cold, but I washed up. It was harder to get my hair clean, but I managed. After I drained the tub, I toweled off and then brushed my teeth.

I checked on Ivy. She was sound asleep. Relieved, I left one of the lights on in the bathroom and left my door cracked open, too. I didn't need the light anymore. I wasn't a baby. But Ivy did and I wanted to make sure I heard Ivy.

Clambering into the bed, I pulled my blanket up over me and then stared at the closed door to the hall. This was when Mommy would come in. But she hadn't done that in a while. I waited. When my eyelids got heavy, I reached up to smooth back my hair.

"Night, Milo," I whispered, then pressed a kiss to my fingers and touched it to my head. "Sweet dreams. I love you."

It would be better tomorrow.

She promised.

1

"**A**re you *high*?" The question slipped out before I could swallow it back as I shot a look at Doc. "I don't *have* a brother." The soft, lazy good mood from the night before vanished. Dread infused anger iced in my system as I went hot and cold at once.

What the hell was going on?

"Dove," Vaughn said quietly and I cut a look away from the pained look on Doc's face to the measured look on Vaughn's. There it was—in his topaz eyes—worry and sadness. His face, like Kellan's, was also marked up. Neither of them were bleeding though, not like Jasper.

That didn't mean they *hadn't* been bleeding.

I jerked a look back at the bruiser in front of me. He was huge. Big, like they all were, but there seemed to be something so much more dangerous about him. Dark brown eyes locked on me and I shook my head.

"I don't have a brother," I repeated slowly. "Trust me, I would have known." The only heir to the entire Sharpe fortune and empire made it a damn burden without the complicated relationships inside our family. Uncle Bradley reminded me constantly that I was a Sharpe. That no one else was good enough for me. The burn of bile scored the back of my throat and I shook my head. "So, I don't care who you are, or who you think you are..."

"Swan," Jasper said my name so softly, I almost didn't hear it as his hand brushed my arm. By brushed, I mean barely skimmed.

Raptor let out a low sound that could have been a curse or a growl or maybe just a rumbling note. But the whole world sped up as he slapped Jasper's hand away from me and tugged me to him. For as strong as his grip was, it was also gentle as hell, before he thrust me behind him and lunged toward Jasper again.

I sprang forward. Granted, the guy was twice my size, but I wasn't gonna let Jasper fight him alone if no one else would help. I didn't land on his back though. Rome caught me around the middle and pulled me back to him.

"Dammit," I swore, but Rome carried me almost all the way to the kitchen. "We have to help him."

"We are," Rome promised against my ear even as Liam let out an aggravated sigh.

"You owe me, Hellspawn," he muttered before he shot forward. It all happened so fast. Jasper was on the ground and Raptor loomed over him. Doc said something, maybe a name, then Liam was there, plowing into Raptor like a freight train. He didn't slow down, didn't sidestep but drove him forward to slam into a wall. He pinned the other man there, an arm to the back of Raptor's neck and his arm wrenched up behind his back.

The whole room stilled. Only, this stillness held way more violence than the earlier quiet had. Rome tightened his arms around me, and rubbed his cheek to the top of my head. My heart raced and I dug my fingers into his arm, more to hold on than to try and get free.

Instead of yelling or fighting, Liam and Raptor seemed to join the rest of the frozen tableau. If not for the warmth of Rome and the softness of his breath, the idea I was in some nightmare all over again might have drowned me.

Finally, Liam took a step back and Raptor stayed against the wall. Whatever he'd done or said, all the fury seemed to drain out of him. With an almost agonizing slowness, Raptor turned around and faced me. Then he glanced from me to the guys and back.

Real regret seemed to settle in his expression before all traces of emotion vanished from it. "I'm sorry, Ivy—" He exhaled harshly, then raked a hand over his face. "Emersyn. I'm sorry Emersyn."

I didn't ask who Ivy was. Considering he thought I was his sister, it seemed a safe bet that was her name.

Liam withdrew until he was about halfway between where Rome and I stood and the rest of the room. Then he leaned against the wall there, like he had nothing better to do and no care in the world.

It was Doc who finally broke the impasse as he reached out to Jasper and helped him up. Jasper staggered a little and I would have gone forward, but Rome squeezed me. Lips against my ear, he murmured, "Not yet, Starling. Raptor can't handle it. Hawk's fine."

How could he say he was fine, he was...

"They've done far worse to each other," he continued, then nipped my ear. It was the barest scrape of teeth, but it sent a pulse through my system and made me shudder. Some of the adrenaline flashed away in the wake of the action.

"He needs to process?" I kept watch on the others, but turned my head to murmur at Rome. The act made him stop rubbing his face to my hair and put his nose near mine. It was oddly intimate and comforting.

A flash of a smile tipped the corners of his mouth. It was barely there and gone again. He answered with a nod then glanced back toward the others. I settled more into him. Trembling rioting through my system now that the threat seemed to have eased.

The rub of Rome's hand along my biceps added to the soothing, but he surrounded me completely, a Rome-shaped blanket. Doc had Jasper up and Kellan moved over to help him. Freddie kept shooting me these apologetic, if worried, looks.

"I'll be fine, Doc," Jasper said abruptly. "I've bled before." Even as he said that, he looked at me. The apology in his expression, it was mirrored on Vaughn's and even on Kellan's.

Raptor stared at the guys, then passed over them to focus on me. I swore another measure of regret flickered there and he glared upward for a moment. "Rome, take my sister..."

"Nowhere because your sister isn't here and if you tell him to take me away so you can go back to being a gigantic asshole, I will scream, I will get away, and I will hit you with a brick if I have to."

I mean, I knew where the gun was in the car. And I still had the knife, even if I hadn't stabbed him with it. As if reading my mind, Rome plucked the damn thing out of my pocket.

"Traitor," I murmured, and his soft chuckle did really inappropriate things to me, considering the situation.

"You don't need to be here," Raptor said as he took

another couple of steps in our direction. Liam shifted his weight and I wasn't the only one who tracked that motion. Raptor paused and his fixed look on Liam didn't bode well. "*You* shouldn't be here."

Seemingly undisturbed, Liam shrugged. "Someone said something about donuts." The dry comment earned an actual, sharp laugh from Freddie and a snort from Doc, who just shook his head.

"Milo," Doc said. "Take a breath. This is a bit of a shock for *everyone*." His emphasis on the last word had to mean me, but before I could counter that Raptor—or Milo—or whatever his name was just shook his head once, a hard negative.

"It's no fucking surprise to these clowns, who had one job. Keep an eye on her, and keep their distance. How fucking hard was that?"

Kellan gripped Jasper's shoulder. "I told you, events spun out of control, but more than that—she needed help."

"Yes, you told me you had to get her out of a scrape," Raptor answered, but the weight of that stare stayed with me. "That was months ago. Why is she still here?" The ice in my blood chilled. "Why haven't you sent her back where she belongs?"

"Maybe because she makes her own damn decisions," I snapped out and he raised both brows. "Stop talking about me like I'm not here. If you want me to leave, I'll go..."

"Wait," Jasper said as he pulled from the others and stood on his own.

"Sparrow," Kellan murmured, and everything in his expression begged me to let him handle this, but it was Vaughn who surprised me.

"What the hell did you think we were gonna do, Milo? Pretend we didn't see what that guy was doing to her? She was hurt. *Badly*. Bad enough we had to have Doc patch her up and she had a hell of a concussion."

"Fuck," Doc exhaled as Raptor's gaze shot to him, all accusation and quiet rage.

"You didn't fucking tell me she was hurt that bad."

And I thought Jasper had anger issues, but where Jasper yelled, this guy was just...a single string vibrating so hard that it pulled the whole orchestra to follow him.

"Because she's fine now and you were struggling enough." Not an ounce of apology lived in Doc's tone. "You gonna try and kick the shit out of me, now?"

Jasper blinked one good eye at him, he had a wad of tissue to the cut over his other eye, and he flicked a look to me.

The rage that seemed to live on Raptor's surface vanished. If I hadn't caught the deep breath he took or the way he glanced down before his shoulders straightened, I'd have missed it. But the action, every scrap of it, was as intimately familiar to me as my own name.

I did that when I needed to bury something. Compartmentalize. Put it away.

Just like that, Raptor's anger erased as if it had never been there. I stiffened at the familiarity and Rome gave me another careful squeeze. Comfort wasn't what I wanted right then. It wasn't true.

This guy wasn't my brother.

I didn't have one...

"No, Mickey," Raptor said slowly. "I owe you too much and you're right. There's probably a lot I don't know." He focused on me. "A lot I need to learn, but Emersyn doesn't need to be here for this."

"Maybe she doesn't," Doc said with a shrug. "But that's up to her, don't you think?"

They both looked at me and Liam straightened. Rome did, too. He wasn't rubbing his cheek against my hair anymore and his hand on my arm stilled. But I could imagine his face. He didn't step away from me, if anything, he rebalanced my weight and I stopped leaning on him so hard. If he needed to move, I didn't want to get in his way.

"You know," Freddie announced as he held up a chocolate covered donut. "I'm calling the fifteen minute rule, and I'm pretty sure we cleaned these floors this month. Besides, the donuts are great." He took a big bite and announced around it. "But I saved the best ones for me and Boo-Boo." He held up a box with triumph. "No donuts were harmed in the making of this drama."

Kellan sighed and Vaughn stared upward, but I laughed. Even Jasper let out a sound that bordered on humor and when his chuckle cut across the tension in the room, I laughed harder.

Fuck me. This was probably the absolute worst time to get the giggles, but Freddie looked so damned pleased with himself, and I swore his eyes held their own version of a hopeful smile. He grinned wider as I giggled harder as he sailed down the hall to where I stood and he made a huge show of opening the box.

"Donut, Boo-Boo?" He took another bite of his own and made a soft moaning noise. I should have known danger was imminent the minute his eyes glittered with mischief. "I bet the only thing that tastes better is that pretty pussy, but I'll settle for this sugar today."

Rome snorted softly, it was almost the faintest suggestion of laughter. I met Freddie's gaze as Raptor stalked forward. With a sigh, Rome moved me behind him and he joined Liam in blocking the other guy.

"Freddie," I snapped.

"It's fine, Boo-Boo," he whispered, as he sidled over to me. "Get everyone pissed at me, they yell, they might smack me in the head, but then they get back to being them, and right now, all I want is to get high if they keep this shit up. The tension in here is fucking killing me." Then he paused and held out his half-eaten donut for me to bite. "And if it comes down to it, I'm Team Boo-Boo."

I groaned. "I don't think this is helping," I admitted as I took a piece of the donut he offered and tore it half.

"You'd be surprised," he said, then nodded to where Kellan, Vaughn, and Jasper had fallen in around Raptor. The only one not quite standing with them was Doc. "The guys will figure this out, Boo-Boo. I promise."

"You know how Freddie is," Kellan said, and I swore he made it sound like the most reasonable thing in the world. "Just ignore him."

"I'm supposed to ignore that you've all been shacking up with my sister? That you not only didn't do the one thing I asked, you did absolutely the worst thing possible and brought her here?" The bite in Raptor's voice wasn't directed at me but it held some of the same acidity as Kellan's had when he said I didn't belong here.

Maybe I hadn't in the beginning. Hell, I hadn't even wanted to be here.

"Has it occurred to any of you that there's a nationwide search going on for her right now?" Raptor demanded. "Her family wants her back."

"Let's talk about this later," Kellan said. "After we smooth things over."

"Man, I love your optimism," Liam said. "I've fucking missed that."

"Why the fuck are you still here anyway?" Jasper

demanded. "Don't you have some snooty boys to go hang with now?"

"You're welcome for saving your ass from a beating," Liam said easily. "And I'm here because I know how to answer my phone."

"Enough," Doc said. "You're all acting like you're twelve. Stop it. Everyone here is an adult, in theory, so let's let all the adults make decisions for themselves."

"Fine," Raptor said abruptly. "Liam had nothing to do with this... take Emersyn to your place for now. It's secure, right?"

What the hell?

"He's not my brother," I repeated, softly. At Freddie's sad look, I frowned. "Right?"

"Boo-Boo," he told me, sliding an arm around my shoulders. "I'm not going to lie to you."

So they all thought this guy was my brother?

Why?

Over Raptor's shoulder, I locked eyes with Jasper. Well, I focused on his one visible eye at the moment. The last thing in the world I wanted to see on his face and in his eyes clawed at me.

Guilt.

2

The last thing I needed was Hellspawn exploding my carefully crafted life. I'd had to half drag her out of there and I told her to get on the bike or be strapped to it. Rome followed, and my other half coaxed her into riding with me. Then he'd given me a look.

One I interpreted very well.

Hands off and take care of her.

Yeah, no problem brother mine. From the moment we arrived at my condo, she all but threw the helmet at me and stomped back to the bedrooms and slammed the door. I didn't laugh when she emerged from *my* room, still scowling and ducked into Rome's, then slammed that door.

Well, she told me.

Rubbing my eyes, I grimaced at the state of my hands. They were still bruised from the fights. There were fresh splits over old scars from dealing with Milo, and I'd had to dispose of another issue the night before, and I still hadn't been to bed yet.

Fucking Milo was out. How he pulled off getting out early after being in goddamn solitary, I had no idea. Saddling me with the Hellspawn was the worst idea ever. I ripped open the fridge and grabbed a bottle of beer. I should probably make sure she ate. I debated it for about thirty seconds, then discarded it.

Enraged Hellspawn probably only consumed and breathed fire. I downed half the bottle of beer on my way to the alarm box hidden behind the painting on the wall. I rarely used it but now, better safe the sorry. Rome knew the code if he needed in and everyone else could go fuck themselves.

The code I typed in would not allow the front door's deadbolt to unlock without a key or a code.

That would at least keep her in the apartment.

Milo wanted her safe. Rome wanted her happy and safe.

I just wanted her out of my hair and not giving me issues. Issues I didn't need to have, like the fucking boner I'd been walking around with since she put her arms around me on the bike. My dick picked today to wake up.

After draining the bottle, I dropped it in the recycle bin back in the kitchen and rolled my head from side to side. The vertebrae cracked. My eyes burned. My head ached. The plan had been in flux for years, but I was close and I didn't want another damn detour.

Grabbing a second bottle out, I headed for my bathroom and a shower. Then I was going to sleep. Maybe for a week.

I belched, loudly and with fierceness as I reached the door to my room. No way Hellspawn missed that. Old habits, however, were hard to break. "Excuse me."

Not bothering to wait for her response, I nudged my door closed, but also left it cracked. Having someone else in my space, who wasn't my brother, would make me restless enough. After I locked my guns in the safe, I stripped off the rest of my clothes and headed for the shower.

The hot water felt fucking fabulous against my aching muscles and stung where the skin had been scraped raw. One of my shoulders had taken the brunt of the hit against the metal bracing. My dick kept tapping my stomach like I'd forgotten about his engorged state.

I'd never been so tempted to flip off my own dick before. Since it was still aching by the time I finished washing up, I added some conditioner to my hand and ran it over my cock from tip to base.

Eyes closed and dick in hand, I tightened my fist and began to rub one out. The problem was nothing worked, until Hellspawn's furious face popped into my head. Whether it was the wildness in her eyes when she popped me in the alley, or the ferociousness when she got in Milo's face, holy fuck did it turn me on.

Grown men were wary of Milo. He was quiet. Easy going. Polite. But he was also dangerous as fuck and she didn't give a damn. She'd charged in there like she'd been ready to take him on and I half-thought, you know, she probably would have.

A groan escaped my lips as I could see her fierce expression as I sank into her. The bite of her nails digging into my shoulders. She would *claw* me up and I'd fucking live for it. Just the thought of the velvety heat and sinking between her thighs had me coming like a teenager. The spurts hit the wall and I let out another groan and a sigh.

That helped with some of the tension. It wasn't until after I'd dried off and finished my shave that it really hit me. I'd just jerked off to thoughts of fucking Milo's kid sister. One he put here for me to protect because he thought she was too damn fragile for the clubhouse.

Only she's not a kid. And fragile was not the word I would use for her.

Worse, she was the girl Rome was falling for. I stared at myself in the mirror and shook my head. My dick didn't get to make decisions for me. Rome wanted her and I wasn't getting in the way of that.

Fuck.

My dick twitched and I swore if the damn thing had a voice it would be saying, *liar, liar, pants on fire.*

It was official. I'd lost my fucking mind.

I was talking to my dick. With a roll of my eyes, I killed the lights and headed for my bed. The blackout curtains kept the daylight away and I could use a solid four or five hours.

Maybe I'd get lucky and manage six.

I set the phone on the wireless charge and fell into the bed. My head barely touched the pillows and my eyes closed over grit when my ringing phone jerked them open again.

Fuck me sideways. I sat up with a snarl and reached for the phone. "Knight," I answered simply with my rank rather than my name. "What do you need?"

The king on the phone was quiet, but I didn't rush him. Fuck knew he wouldn't be rushed. Instead, I waited him out like the humble servant I was. I rubbed at my tired eyes as I waited and swung my feet to the floor. If it took too long, I was going to need coffee. Chugging two beers that rapidly would hardly make me drunk, but on top of how tired I was?

"I would like an explanation," the man on the phone said. "About the current plan and why our real estate portfolio is looking rather thin compared to this time last year."

Yeah. Definitely needed coffee for that.

I stalked out to the kitchen, even as I pulled together the mental information he required. "There's been an upswing in the market here. Gentrification is well under way, but there are a lot of owners who are holding out or who aren't willing to part with their lots—not when they might profit from higher values around them."

"What are you doing about it?"

"Handling it," I told him smoothly as I got the coffee brewing. The smell penetrated my brain fog faster than anything else. "Do you require details or plausible deniability?"

It was a gamble. Pushing the king on any subject often was. The head of the Bay Ridge Royals had not earned that position by being a light hand. While I'd not met him, my rank didn't allow for it—but soon, soon I'd move from Knight to Bishop and when that happened?

When that happened, I was in the door.

"I will accept plausible deniability," the man said after an interminable silence. "But I want results. If next quarter resembles this one, Knight, you will no longer have your position."

Or my head.

Got it.

"Understood, my liege." I rolled my eyes, but only because the sick fuck couldn't see me. Who the hell wanted to be called that? The whole chess board names and favoring ranks from a royal court was fine, but it was also pretentious as hell. "Can I help you any more today?"

Another significant pause ensued as my coffee finished and I scrubbed a hand over my face. I actually checked the phone to make sure it was still connected, because the silence elongated beyond what was reasonable. Instead of chafing verbally at the delay, I filled a mug with coffee and knocked back a healthy swallow, despite the fact it actually tried to scald my throat.

"Milo Hardigan."

I didn't choke, but that was only practice coming into play. Emptying my voice of anything resembling interest, I said, "He's in jail."

"Not anymore."

Goddammit. Milo hadn't been back a fucking day.

"Approach the 19 Diamonds, secure their efforts into getting rid of the 82nd Street Vandals. Then we'll wipe out the Diamonds."

"That might be a little challenging," I admitted. "I just took one of their businesses, because their negotiator was exceptionally rude."

"Then make it work," the king said. "Hardigan is dangerous. I thought we'd dealt with him in prison, but he was like a cockroach. He avoided every attempt."

Muscles bunching in my shoulders, I glared out of the darkened kitchen toward the table I'd only ever eaten at when my parents visited—which had been all of once since I'd taken this apartment. I preferred to go to them and keep them out of the line of fire. "Do you need me to take him out of play, my liege?"

Everything was a game. Every move calculated. No sudden changes in plan. Steady. Always steady. If a loss occurred, it occurred. The boat didn't shift course for anyone.

"Possibly. Deal with the Diamonds first, then correct the real estate losses. I'll call again." The phone clicked in my ear as he cut off and I closed my eyes as I downed the rest of my coffee.

It was only after I put my empty mug on the counter that the darkness hit me. Had Hellspawn closed the blackout curtains in the living room? I didn't usually need it out here. The windows were clear, the night cityscape utterly visible.

Night.

Had I slept all fucking day?

I glanced down at my phone and it showed that it was just after seven.

Fuck.

My.

Life.

There were three missed calls from Rome. The only one who had *this* number. They knew I had a brother. But tracking him down under a different name would be a lot harder. Still. No other missed calls. Only a series of texts from Rome. A single question mark sent every hour. I needed to get my other phone.

Pivoting on my heel I stopped dead because Hellspawn just sat there on the sofa, in the dark, staring at me with those fathomless eyes.

"Hellspawn."

"Asshole."

"Well, I'm glad we had this little chat." I was too tired for this shit.

"I need to go back."

"Not my problem," I told her as I strode away and down the hall. My other phone would be in my pants where I'd left it when I stripped off. For the most part, they could wait, and Rome had this number. If he really wanted to talk to me, he'd have called.

Snagging my jeans from the floor, I scooped up the rest of my dirty clothes, only to turn and nearly bounce off the little minx. Silent little shit.

Very few people could sneak up on me.

Granted, I was tired as hell right now, but it was still impressive.

"It is your problem."

I sighed. It was still dark, darker in here than out there, but she was backlit from the hallway and the light she'd turned on out there. Her silhouette was absolutely judging me. "How is that?" I got the phone out then twisted and tossed the clothes in the direction of the hamper. The thud of the jeans hitting was enough for me.

There were missed messages from Milo. Kellan. Vaughn. Oh and look, Jasper was missing her too.

Well, they were talking to me again. Not that they were happy with me continuing to ignore them.

A hand slapped against my chest as another grabbed my phone.

"Hey," I snapped, but she danced backwards before I could grab the phone back. "Don't play with me, Hellspawn."

"It is your problem because you locked me up in this place, then passed out for hours."

"So? Are you that fucking helpless? There's plenty to do." I was more curious than irritated but fuck if I was going to let that show. Also, had she *checked* on me and I slept through it? Maybe I had been burning the candle at both ends too much.

Rather than follow her, I stalked over to the bathroom and slapped the light on so I could see her mutinous expression.

"I wasn't bored, I wanted to call them. I needed to know..."

"You need to know?" I asked, waiting.

"It's none of your business."

"As long as you're holding my phone and living in my place, it is most certainly my business. Milo wants you safe, he didn't say anything about beating your ass before I tied you up and gagged you." I'd meant it as a joke, but the deathly pale cast to her face had me. She threw the phone at me, I barely caught it before she stormed out of the bedroom.

I rubbed the back of my neck. "Fuck."

After I counted to twenty, I stalked after her. There'd been no slammed door. So she wasn't in Rome's room, but I still checked inside before I headed back to the living room. One switch turned on two lower burning lights.

She stood in the window, staring out at the city. The sense of her isolation sliced me down to the bone.

"I'd never beat your ass," I told her simply. "And I sure as fuck wouldn't tie you up and gag you."

She didn't turn around.

"Okay, that's a lie, I'd totally tie you up if you asked me." Nope. Not even a flicker. "But I wouldn't gag you. Not when I appreciate what comes out of that mouth so much."

Still no glance in my direction.

I stared down at the phone she'd thrown at me and at the girl staring out the window. I could just make out a piece of her expression in the glass. Nothing about it was calm, if anything, she looked—tortured.

It didn't even register that I was moving until I was three steps from touching her and my reflection loomed above hers in the glass.

"Don't." One word from her and I dropped my hand. Yeah, this wasn't what I had in mind.

"Here," I offered and instead of touching her, I held my phone out to her. "It's unlocked. Call whomever you want. The guys' numbers are all in there."

She didn't take the phone. She didn't even look at it.

"Please?" The word came out as gentle as I could make it, because my little hellspawn looked like she was actually in hell and it was making me homicidal.

Finally, she glanced up at me. "Will you get dressed if I take it?"

Dressed?

One glance down revealed that I was still buck ass naked and my dick was definitely vying for her attention.

"Sure," I said. "If it bothers you."

"It didn't," she admitted and that shocked the shit out of me. "Until a few minutes ago."

Until I'd made a crude joke. Got it.

"Then take it and I'll go grab some sweatpants. There's coffee in the kitchen, help yourself and then we can figure out food."

She finally took the phone and I blew out a breath before I retreated to give her some space. Yeah, I wasn't leaving her for long. I had no idea who she might call on that phone. But I'd have a log of the calls.

Even if she erased it, I logged everything in the cloud.

Sorry, Hellspawn, I told her mentally. You probably do deserve better than all of this.

No wonder Milo wanted her away from all of us.

3

I didn't move from the window until the last of Liam's retreating steps faded and there was the faintest squeak of a door. It wasn't his hall door, but probably a closet in his room or something. Only then did I look down at the phone.

It was unlocked.

He'd slept the whole day, a fact I'd been both grateful for and irritated by. There was no way to get out of the condo. I'd tried. The door hadn't budged. While Rome hadn't kept the code a secret from me, the code he used worked to get in, but there was no keypad on the door to get *out*.

Closing my hand around the phone, I moved closer to the window and stared out at the night city. After all the time in the clubhouse, this felt almost too open and exposed. At the same time, I craved the height and the breath. There was anonymity up here, too.

Liam also had a landline. I wondered if he'd forgotten

21

about that. I'd found it earlier when I'd finally stopped hiding in Rome's room. The fact I'd found comfort in there when Rome, like every single one of the others, had held their silence about this so-called relationship between me and Raptor, hit me as hypocritical. But then I didn't know what the hell to think.

I closed my eyes and pressed my forehead to the cool glass. No matter how I tried to wrap my mind around it, I couldn't reconcile the idea that this guy they all talked about in somewhat reverential tones, when they mentioned him at all, was supposed to be related to me.

How?

Had my parents gotten rid of him before I came along? Why? The Sharpe name meant *everything* to them.

It just didn't make sense. I'd almost called Lainey.

Almost.

Glancing down at the phone in my hand, all I wanted to do was call her right now. But not on Liam's phone. No, I'd wait until the next time he locked me up in here alone since, apparently, I'd just earned an upgrade on cells, and then I'd call her.

I had a thousand questions and no answers. Maybe she could help me get access to my money. Money as often as not—

"Come on, Hellspawn, put on your shoes and grab a jacket." Liam strode back into the living room, dressed this time, and a faint sneer souring his smile.

"Why?"

I didn't turn to face him, just watched his reflection in the glass. He'd turned on a light and he was as visible as if I stood in front of a mirror.

"Because we're going out." He moved to me and plucked the phone from my hand. "Don't worry, you can have this back." Then, with care, he turned me toward the hallway. "Now go. Get shoes on and a jacket. It's cold."

"I don't want to go."

"Don't recall asking," he said. "I'm going to put together another cup of coffee. Don't make me ask you a third time and I'll make you one too."

"You haven't asked a first time," I retorted and yet despite my protest, I headed down the hallway. I didn't have much with me. They hadn't given me a chance to even get my bags before Liam dragged me out.

The weirdest thing of all, the guys were clearly furious. Their argument echoed behind us as Liam hauled me toward his bike and only the closing of the door had cut it off. Yet none of them stopped us and yeah, that stung. A little.

Don't rely on others. I knew better, and yet—

I closed my eyes again before snagging the hoodie from the end of the bed and pulling it on. After I jammed my feet into shoes, I glanced at myself in the mirror of the bathroom. My hair had been pulled back with a scrunchie. The glow I'd had when Jasper and I returned to the clubhouse was gone.

Had that really only been twelve hours earlier?

I'd been in this—wildly good mood. It had been an amazing night. And I swore we'd connected. Really connected.

Then guilt.

"You'd think you'd know better by now," I reminded myself then turned away and followed the scent of coffee to the kitchen where Liam stood, studying his phone with an unreadable expression.

"Coffee's right there, Hellspawn. Two minutes and we're moving. Did you eat?"

"Nope. I starved." I picked up the travel mug with a frown. Was I supposed to carry this on the bike? One swallow had me sighing though. It was—perfect. The perfect sweetness. The perfect blend. It even had a splash of cream, and I hadn't really been adding that at the club-house, mostly because they were almost always out.

"Fine. We'll get kabobs while we're out. There's a great little Indian place near where we're going, and they have the best garlic naan bread." He clicked his screen off deci-sively then shoved it in his back pocket. The Henley he'd dressed in stretched across his chest like someone had shrunk it, and he grinned. "The boho look suits you. But I think we can do better than bag lady."

Eyebrows raised, I skimmed a look over him from his booted feet to his jeans pulling tight over his thighs to his long-sleeved Henley. I didn't miss the watch. They retailed for five thousand. His had a platinum band. It probably went for more.

"Whatever." I didn't even have it in me to argue with him. "Can we just go? I'm sure you need to pick up the ball and shackle to put on me, so I'm properly secured for the freak show."

His soft snort followed me as I turned my back and headed for the door. I wanted to know how he opened it, but he didn't even slow down, reaching around me to just twist the handle and open it.

What.

A.

Dick.

I swore the fucker laughed at me too, but I lifted my chin and headed for the elevator. Ignoring asshats was an art.

I had a decade or more of experience.

I had long since achieved prima status.

Sipping the coffee, I followed him into the elevator and took the far side, away from him. Amusement curved his lips and I could practically feel him staring at me as the elevator glided down. An eerie silence populated the empty parking garage. Despite the other vehicles present, it seemed barren of life.

Liam bypassed the beautiful dark blue bike, even as he pulled keys from his pocket and clicked a little remote. The temperatures seemed to have plummeted even lower than they'd been earlier. I had to wonder if I'd missed summer at some point here or if it was just always cold and miserable.

That would explain a lot.

Arms folded, I slowed my pace as a roll up door in the corner of the garage lifted to reveal a very fucking expensive sports car.

I didn't know cars for shit, but I knew for a fact that Lainey's nemesis, Adam, drove one of these and according to her, his investments in expensive luxuries was legendary.

The vehicle's lights turned on and the engine purred to life. Frowning, I glanced at the bike then at the car housed in the private garage. "I didn't know you had a car."

"You didn't ask, Hellspawn. Hop in, she doesn't bite." He motioned me ahead of him and then opened the door for me. The space between us seemed littered with the shards of contradictions between his behavior and his words. Even more between the image he presented, and the wealth he was clearly used to.

Sliding onto the buttery softness of the leather seat, I let out an inadvertent groan. One I failed to smother fast enough if Liam's faint smirk was any indication. The heat was on, and it chased the chill from my bones almost as effectively as if I'd sunk into a hot bath.

After he shut my door, Liam circled the vehicle and slid into the driver's seat. "You half froze on the way here," he commented as though picking up a thread of an abandoned conversation. "It's colder out there tonight. Rome said you liked the bike. Maybe we wait until it's summer and I'll give you all the rides you want."

I snorted and folded my arms again, after I'd settled my seat belt in place. The car all but prowled out of its private stall and the door closed behind us as Liam navigated through the garage to the exit. The gates to come and go were all down, but the one we needed rolled up even before we got there.

Liam didn't even slow at the corner to get onto the street, he just glided out into traffic and over two lanes, like people would get out of the way for him. Maybe he was right. The car was definitely a smooth ride, I could barely feel the vibration of the engine. Five minutes into the drive, however, Liam punctured the silence between us.

"Are you going to ask me, Hellspawn?"

"Nope."

I didn't even ask him to clarify. There were only a handful of topics he could be referring to. Nearly all of them involved the Vandals. No, I'd pass on asking for anything right now. Liam was the one I knew the least. He seemed as at home inside the clubhouse and amongst the bloody cleanup at the garage, as he did behind the wheel of his Aston Martin.

Maybe they boosted cars and worked them over and sold them to make money. We'd even watched one of those movies about boosting cars and the guys made the strangest comments all the way through it. If that was the case, I would be better off not knowing.

"Huh," Liam grunted, but left the topic alone. Music

filtered through the speakers, more instrumental than lyrical. It was Mozart. Liam listened to Mozart. The baffling new fact joined the similarly mysterious puzzle pieces, all blank and oddly shaped that didn't seem to follow any discernible pattern and yet snapped into place like they belonged there.

Twenty minutes into our drive, he pulled up to a high-end boutique. I recognized the French name. Was he for real right now? Sweat chilled along my spine. The rumbling purr of the car didn't cease as he circled the vehicle to open my door. "Come on Hellspawn, we have an appointment."

Ignoring the hand he held out to me, I slid out of the car and managed to avoid brushing against him. I was not dressed for *Le Belle Âme*.

Liam's amused chuckle chased me across the damp sidewalk to the doors, which were already being opened by a security guard.

"Mr. O'Connell," the man said as he greeted us. "Lydia and her team are waiting upstairs."

"Thanks, Gerald. Lock up and take a break. We'll be a while." Liam offered the man his hand and they shook. It was almost warm, declaring a familiarity between the two even if they couldn't look further apart. The security guard seemed generically middle-aged with a receding hairline and bit of a paunch. I swore there were carbon copies of this man in all walks of life all over the country, most of them serving as managers or security guards.

"Thank you, sir. I'll have my phone, so just have Lydia buzz me when you're ready to leave. I'll keep an eye on your car." With a nod, he left us alone. Neither my state of dishabille nor Liam's plain jeans and Henley even slowed him down. What the hell had he done to earn not only deference, but respect?

Liam cupped my elbow and tugged me out of my stupor as he headed across the parquet floor of Le Belle Âme to a set of escalators. Everything about the store promised opulence, discretion, and luxury. A boutique amongst boutiques, only the finest items and the highest quality would be featured on their showroom floors. Designers died a little when Le Belle Âme passed on their collections and fainted dead away when they accepted even one piece.

Or so I'd been reminded over and over.

The cold pit in my stomach seemed to grow heavier as Liam guided me onto the escalator itself. The machinery had to give off a hum of some kind, but I swore it was absolutely silent as the stairs carried us up. Surreal didn't begin to cover it. Music began to tickle my ears as we reached the top, along with competing scents of cinnamon and chocolate. A quiet hum of conversation seemed to come to life at our arrival, too.

"Good evening, Mr. O'Connell."

Liam let out another snort as a lovely woman approached us. She was dressed impeccably, right down to the diamond solitaire necklace featured in the open color of her button-down silk blouse. Her lips were stained a vibrant ruby, a shade that matched the hint of blush on her cheeks. Not all of that was cosmetics.

"Lydia," Liam scolded, as he released me to greet her with a careless, if perfunctory hug and air kisses to each cheek.

Liam did air kisses.

The ice forming in the pit of my stomach cracked at the display.

"What have I told you? Mr. O'Connell is my father."

"Yes, I know," she retorted with a laugh and a warm smile that bordered on very familiar. "But I love watching you get all stuffy as you get older. That wild child turning into a proper gentleman."

His scoff echoed my own, which was probably good because there were other women present and they all looked at Liam and sighed.

Wonderful. He had a fan club.

Still, was I much better? I'd been gawking for the last five minutes. The mental reminder had me snapping my mouth shut and doing my best to smooth out my expression. I didn't know these people. More, they were clearly deferring to Liam. That meant I truly needed to be on my guard.

"That will never happen," Liam said, dismissing her assertion about his status as a gentleman. "In the meantime, this is my guest. She's found herself sans luggage and quite put out thanks to a snafu. It's been quite the trauma the last couple of days, so do everything you can to relax her and get her whatever she wants."

"Business or casual?" Lydia asked as she eyed me and one of her girls fluttered over and offered me a mug of hot cocoa. "Asia, if you'd take Mr. O'Connell's guest over to the salon and get her set up. We can take care of the hair appointment, manicure and pedicure while we pull some selections for her."

"Both," Liam told her. "Also, at least two formals, full dress, and cocktail."

What was he talking about?

"Accessories?" Lydia asked.

"The works. Whatever she is going to need."

"Lingerie?"

Liam flashed a grin my way. "Whatever the lady desires, I have no trouble at all if she wants to go au natural."

"Shoes?" Lydia continued without missing a beat.

"Definitely." He studied me, still grinning. "And motor-cycle leathers. We may have to get them customized."

"She's very petite," Lydia paused in taking her notes to study me again. "I actually think she's closer to a 0 than a 2." For the first time in my life, a woman's assessment of my size and proportions didn't carry an air of judgment or criticism. If anything, there was concern. "I'm sure I'll find something that works. I'm assuming you want your girlfriend to match your colors?"

There was another teasing note.

"I'm not his girlfriend," I snapped out. Maybe I shouldn't have risen to the bait, not when Liam looked so damn pleased with himself. But I'd had enough of being talked about in the third person when I was standing right there.

"Yes," Liam said. "Work your magic for me Lydia, I'll be over here." He motioned toward some sofas. "I've got some calls to make."

With that, he sauntered off and I scowled after him. Who was paying for all of this? Not to mention, I hardly needed it. What had I done recently that required the wardrobe I had bursting at the seams back at my uncle's...

A shudder went through me. If I never wore those clothes again it would be too soon.

"Turn up the heat, Candace," Lydia said as she closed in on Asia and I. "We don't want our guest to get chilly. Now, please, let's get you over to the salon. I promise, after Asia's given you a scalp massage, you'll be a whole new person."

As much as I probably should have disputed it, I wasn't really given the opportunity as the women converged and hustled me off to their salon. A flurry of activity surrounded me, and I was still trying to fit this latest puzzle piece into place amidst the organized chaos. While I still wasn't thrilled with the idea of Liam having this woman dress me, he took no part in any of it. I caught him glancing over at us every once in a while, but for the most part he did what he said, he was on his phone.

Lydia didn't just let Liam's instructions dictate her choices, she talked to me. Not that I offered her much to work with, but I had to give her points for trying and really, after the last few months, the hair wash, trim, and blowout, followed by the mani/pedi did the impossible.

It let me relax.

WE WOULD BLEED FOR EACH OTHER

JASPER

"Yo," Milo called from behind me, but I ignored him and kept going. I wanted to be anywhere but here. In fact, I had zero intentions of hanging out at this overpriced, jacket-required, pompous, arrogant, filled-to-the-fucking-brim-with-fuckwads, country club. Liam was loaded.

Well, fucking yay for him.

I'd rather go back to Granger's and get a beer and play some pool.

"Asshole," Milo said as he caught my shoulder and hauled me to a stop. I pivoted to glare at him and he didn't flinch. Why would he? We were really fucking evenly matched. "I'm talking to you."

"I heard you the first time and my answer hasn't changed. I had a drink, now I'm going back to our side of town. The air's too fucking thin here."

Milo sighed and I dug into my pocket for smokes. The fact he pinched the bridge of his nose as he fell into step with me was the only thing slowing my pace. We followed the drive with its too perfectly manicured lawn. I'd bet money they sprayed it with some chemicals to get that postcard perfect shade of green.

What a fucking waste of money.

Cigarette lit, I ignored the disapproving and scandalized looks being tossed our way as we walked. There was a valet. But fuck that, no one drove my car but me. That meant I'd had to park it well away from their manicured lawns and white columned facing building. Heaven forbid, the smell of car exhaust and grease get anywhere near their ultra tidy and pristine establishment.

"Jas, we talked about this," Milo said in that same tone he used when Freddie was tripping or Vaughn lost it on someone abusing women or Kellan had it up to here with the rest of us. The tone that kept all of us even and on track. You chilled the fuck out and listened, because he wouldn't yell and rage.

He hadn't even raged when we'd found Freddie in that shipping container and killed the mother fucker who attacked him. He'd been ice cold.

"We did," I told him, cutting him some slack but not slowing my pace as I sucked in a deep drag. "You have a plan. I'm down with the plan and I'll happily follow it. The plan doesn't include me having to rub elbows with a bunch of pretentious fucks in a place that probably wouldn't even hire us to be the trash collectors."

Milo snorted. "Places like this don't make trash." He bumped his shoulder to mine. "And you forget fucker, the plan is to make them take care of *our* trash."

I shook my head. I hadn't forgotten that. Milo thought a dozen steps ahead. He always had. His plans took patience, an eye on the future, and the sobriety to execute them on a schedule. They weren't foolproof, but he'd never let us down. Not once. His plans had plans.

The sun beat down on us as we reached the parking lot and crossed to the far side, where I'd parked the car. It was the first one I bought. A piece of shit, but between me, Milo, and Kellan, we'd rebuilt her and last year I'd finally been able to afford a full body restore. She was perfect.

"Jas," Milo said as I opened the door. "This plan doesn't work if it's not all of us."

"Does it work if I'm not into the brown-nosing of the elite in there?" I motioned toward the main building, still visible beyond the white fencing and landscaped additions.

"We're stronger together," Milo said, then sighed. "But I get it. I'm not into pretending to be someone I'm not, either."

We shared a long look, but I cracked first. The laughter acted like a balm over the sharp edges of my temper. Pretending to be the someone we weren't, was part and par for the course. We had to fake it until we made it. It was how we'd begun to carve out a place for us before we were all even free of the foster system. Together, committed and right now we just needed Freddie to age out and we'd pick him up and he'd move in for real.

Until then...

"You still want to try and see her?" I asked, because that was later this week.

"I do," Milo said softly. "You don't have to go with."

"Shut the fuck up." I finished the cigarette and ground it out against their pristine white parking lot cement. Let them clean up after me. "Of course we're going. We'd go to watch your back anyway."

Milo grimaced.

"What?"

"Nothing," he said even as he scratched at his jaw.

"It's not nothing," I argued. "You went from trying to persuade me back into line to looking like hell. What is it?"

The secrets hidden behind Milo's dark eyes had to be legion. Not that we kept much from each other. The one area that was sacrosanct, however, was her.

"Emersyn Sharpe is a part of this world," he reminded me, and I let out a long breath. "We need to fit into it."

"Man, if you want to just tell her who you are—do it."

"No," Milo said, with a firm shake of his head, and just like that his expression shut down. "This world? Our world? No. I don't want it touching her. But when we're strong enough and we have what we need to move up? Then... then I'll think about it."

He tapped the top of my car.

"Go back to the clubhouse, have a beer, get laid. We'll finish up here and see you later." With that, he turned on his heel.

"Raptor," I said quietly and he paused. "You're more than good enough for her. You've loved her..."

"Stop," he ordered. "Don't push me on this, Hawk." Like me, he'd gone to the bird names we'd all begun to adopt. They gave us a stronger air even when we were scrawnier kids. They had freedom and the power to be free. Power we craved and we would obtain.

Power we'd already begun to accumulate.

He held my gaze for a moment, and I finally nodded. He was wrong, she deserved the chance to know him, and fuck knew, she deserved to know what he'd done for her. What he'd sacrificed. But I kept all of that out of my expression.

Raptor's sister was the one thing we were never allowed to cross him on.

He'd killed a man for her before.

I had no doubt he'd happily kill more. And I'd be right there with him.

We bled for each other.

We'd bleed for her, and we'd bleed the world for her, if necessary.

Whatever he searched for in my face, he must have found it because his tight expression relaxed. "Go get your dick sucked," he told me, before turning away. "It might fix your mood."

"Maybe you should take your own advice," I called after him. "See if you can get a taste of expensive pussy."

His laughter floated back and I dropped into the car, starting it up. Well, we'd be seeing the kid in a few days. Maybe he'd tell her who he was then.

Maybe not.

But seeing her always tore him up inside, so we'd better be ready to spill some blood after the trip.

4

The fog of tension in the room was so thick, it made breathing hard. The bruises on my ribs and face didn't help. Doc handed me a second ice pack and sat near enough to intercept Milo if necessary. It was strange as fuck to think of Doc protecting me. The day had dragged on. Every hour scraped past like a fresh injury.

He'd sent Emersyn away with fucking Liam. Worse, she hadn't wanted to go, but we'd let her. It was better for her to be away from this, until we settled the shit between us. But it didn't sit well with me that of all the people to entrust her safety to, Milo picked Liam? Was he for fucking real right now?

"I told you," Kellan said, after his last two unsuccessful attempts to explain our choices. "We really didn't have a choice."

"And I told you I didn't believe that," Milo ground out. The last few years hadn't been kind to him. The last few months must have been worse. He seemed—different was

39

too tame a word—*changed*. Like something fundamental within him had shifted. The dangerous intensity to him had always been present, tucked away, a lurking beast in the shadows that few, if any, ever saw. Milo was always the charming one, a predator in elegant disguise.

We saw him because we knew him. There was no missing the predator in him right now. No glossy surface to hide it or keep him shielded. One raw, exposed nerve.

Right now, that was my fault.

Milo folded his arms as his glare landed on me. For the last several hours, he'd avoided even looking at me. Doc had stitched the cut above my eye and checked my ribs, but there wasn't much we could do for them except let them heal. Though he'd offered me something for the pain, I declined.

"Can we have the room?" The rustle of discomfort shifting everyone in the room stilled at my request.

"Jas," Kellan began.

"I know," I said, holding up a hand to quell his argument. They were all aligned between me and Milo. Keeping us apart. Keeping him from killing me. "But we need to talk. This is between us."

Vaughn straightened. "Then I'm staying."

Freddie rose. "I'm good with leaving you guys to swing your dicks around. I love you both, but this shit is just making me hungry, horny, and desperate for a hit."

I cut a look at him. Despite the protests, Freddie's color was better than it had been in days. He wasn't hunching in on himself. But he was also not the type to dive into the conflict. Conflict between us always seemed to put him on edge. Not that I could blame him. When you came from the shattered remains of broken homes, whether they'd been good or bad, you didn't like it when *your* people fought.

"Go," I told Freddie. "But stay in the clubhouse."

"You got it, boss," he told me with a grin and then glanced at Milo. "Yeah—welcome back, man. We missed you and don't be so hard on Hawk. Boo-Boo's won us all over. We'd die for her, but I think she'd like it if we were alive long enough for her to kick our asses herself."

Fuck, he was not wrong there. The betrayal in her eyes when she'd looked at me. The gutted expression that broke through her veneer of self-control before she reasserted it. We'd done that.

I'd done that.

For hours, I'd had her in my arms and in my bed. I'd cupped fire in my palms, and she'd listened to me when I'd confessed a lot of my sins.

A lot.

Not all.

"Go on, Freddie." Milo's voice softened for the first time since Emersyn left. Kicking Freddie was a lot like kicking a dog. Thank fuck he'd remembered that.

Doc rose as Freddie flashed a peace sign and noped right the fuck out of the room and up the stairs. We'd have to check on him later. We'd already made a point of cleaning out his stashes. The only drugs left on the property was weed and I didn't care if he wanted to get stoned.

Fuck, I could go for getting stoned.

Then there were just six of us.

"I'm staying, too," Doc said after a long moment. "This involves all of us."

Kellan braced his hands on the back of the sofa behind me. Metaphorically and physically guarding my back. Considering our differences over the last few months and the fact he'd *called* it where Milo was concerned, I'd have understood if he'd refused to back me in this "I'm staying, too."

That just left Rome, who had taken a position leaning against the wall, arms folded. The careless pose was a total lie, but the stillness he could adopt often made people forget he was there. Even us. But we trusted Rome.

I trusted Rome.

Unlike his lying, traitorous and greedy fucking brother. The asshole who now had Emersyn completely to himself. Liam had a golden tongue when he wanted to, he could talk a saint into sin and seduce a thief into becoming patron. As strong and fierce as she was, Emersyn might just as easily fall for his lies.

He was more a part of her world than we'd ever been.

Then again—she didn't seem to want her world. Maybe that would protect her against Liam.

The urge to go to her and kick in the doors, then drag her off to be alone and in bed until I could earn her forgiveness, pulsed through me. I had a feeling it would take more than orgasms and donuts to win back her trust. But I'd fucking do it.

I'd fucking beg if I had to.

"Guys," I began, but Vaughn folded his arms. He stood almost directly between me and Milo.

"Shut it, Hawk. Milo's pissed at you for more than just bringing her here. He knows you guys were gone all night because we've been waiting and he's pretty damn sure you're fucking her." It came out crude, even in his voice.

A muscle ticked in Milo's jaw and I locked gazes with my best friend.

Yeah. I'd fucked my best friend's sister.

He was entitled to beat the shit out of me.

"The thing is," Vaughn continued as if unaware of the

sudden rising tension between me and Milo. "You're not the only one, and you sure as hell weren't the first."

I knew that, but from the way Milo jerked, he hadn't. He swung that furious, accusing gaze at Vaughn who didn't blink as he met him glare for glare.

"Yeah, I've had her in my bed. I'll crawl through glass to get back in hers after this shit is settled."

Same, Brother. Same.

"I'm not fucking apologizing to you, either." The bluntness of the information pulled a laugh from me. Cause—really, I wasn't going to apologize for wanting her either.

"We shouldn't have to," Kellan said, shocking the shit out of me.

"The fuck you shouldn't," Milo snarled. "You goddamn well knew *who* she was."

"Yes," Vaughn countered. "We did and we kept our part of the promise. We've protected her and kept an eye on her while you were in prison. The moment she got here, we knew something was wrong. Hawk saw it before the rest of us did."

"So we fucking fixed it," I said, refusing to stay out of this particular defense. "The call to bring her back here was mine and mine alone. Kellan and Vaughn wanted to take her to a hospital and let her people take care of her."

"She doesn't trust her people." Doc joined the conversation, and I cut a look at him. "And for what it's worth Milo, she's not a baby anymore. I don't think she's been a child for a long, long time." The words held a kind of ominous note that sent a shiver of apprehension up my spine. She'd let that dick abuse her. She'd said that it was better than the alternative.

Some fucker who raped her was better than the alternative.

So what the fuck was up with the alternative?

"Goddammit, do you all want to fuck her?" Milo demanded and I sighed.

"Yes," Rome said simply. The first thing he'd said since she'd left, and I wasn't the only one who looked at him. Undisturbed by our stares, he continued, "But it's not just sex. She's one of us. She belongs here."

As much as my dick might dispute the sex comment, the rest of me didn't. What I wanted from Emersyn was so much more than just the liquid heat between her legs or to hear her harsh cries as she came. I wanted...

"You have got to be fucking kidding me. I've killed men for less and you're all basically telling me you brought her here and are pimping her out between you."

"I love you, kid," Doc said in the most even of tones. "But make that suggestion again and I will tear a strip off you like you've never experienced. She deserves a hell of a lot more than to be referred to as a whore."

"She's not a fucking whore," Milo snarled and I was already on my feet before I even realized I was moving. Kellan grabbed me. Doc stopped Vaughn. But it was Rome who moved and blocked Milo, going toe to toe with him.

"Don't discuss her. She might be your sister, but you don't *know* her. None of us did." The words resonated and Rome poked Milo in the chest. "You put her in front of us. You told us she was valuable. You have loved her for years. You charged us with looking after her. You didn't have to. We have all protected her. We *care.* We want her here. She *needs* us."

All of that was true on more levels than I cared to admit.

"You have got to be fucking kidding me." Milo looked at each of us and for the first time since I'd known him, the divide between us seemed to be a bottomless chasm, ripped open like a jagged wound. He was my best friend...

"Guys," I repeated. "Go. Let me talk to Milo."

Milo raked a hand through his hair and turned away from all of us as he stalked across the room. Rage seemed to vibrate in his muscles, and he couldn't sit still. I got that so fucking well.

"Jas," Kellan said in a low voice and I shook my head.

"Not this time. This is between me and Milo. If we don't settle it now, we won't ever settle it." And I needed it settled. She might not understand yet. But if Milo and I were at war—it would tear Emersyn apart. I couldn't let that happen. "She needs us all. Right now—we're not on the same continent, much less the same page."

Doc frowned at me but whatever he searched for in my face he must have found, because he nodded. "Try not to rip those stitches up and no more fighting. I don't want you puncturing a lung."

I almost laughed. Fighting was what I did. "It's okay, Doc," I told him. "If I do, I've got you on speed dial."

His lack of amusement filtered through his harsh stare, then he shook his head. "You kids are never going to change."

"We're not kids anymore," Kellan reminded him.

"Yeah, I suppose you aren't." Doc glanced at Milo. "You still want to stay at my place after this?"

That stopped me dead, and I wasn't the only one. Milo hadn't even planned to stay here? How much fucking damage had I done?

"No," Milo said and it wasn't the relief it should have been. "Jasper's right. The rest of you take off, but stay close."

Yeah, that took no interpretation. He didn't want anyone going after Emersyn.

Too fucking bad, brother. That was my next stop after we got this settled between us.

Rome didn't comment, he just walked out—the door to the warehouse and not up the stairs. Doc was two steps behind him. Then it was just me, Kellan, Vaughn, and Milo.

We waited, and Vaughn shot me a look and the second chasm erupting amidst all this mess became visible. Vaughn was taking my side *against* Milo. Kellan backed me *against* Milo.

A fist bruised my heart at that realization. They were choosing me.

But they couldn't only choose me. I wouldn't allow it.

Milo and I were more than blood. More than friends. We'd been the first family the other had, beyond Emersyn for him. We'd been the first.

"Go on guys," I repeated. "Please."

That got their attention and following a pair of aggrieved sighs, they left.

Then it was just me and Milo.

He stared at me for a long moment. My face fucking hurt and so did my chest. "I'm listening," he began.

"You remember what you said to me when we turned twelve?"

Milo frowned. Maybe it was a digression, but the words fit then and they fit now. I'd had a couple of really close scrapes that year—one with a dirty cop. Milo had always had my back, but when I'd joked about a fairy tale existence, he'd said something profound. Like me, Milo was a reader. He read *everything*.

"Fairy tales don't tell us the dragon is real or that the boogeyman exists," I began.

"They tell us they can be killed." He finished the statement with a sigh. "What are you in this, Jas? Are you the dragon?"

I chuckled, even if it hurt. "I fucking hope not. Because she hates being called princess."

It was a lame joke, but Milo's harsh chuckle was worth it.

"Want to get out of here for a while? Get some fresh air? Talk?" All I could do was offer the olive branch.

He had to accept it.

EVEN IF IT HURTS

MILO

"Jasper," Ms. Stephanie said as she led another boy into the yard. He was scrawny. Bruised. His eyes, though, were hollow and suspicious. "This is Milo. Milo, this is Jasper. He was the boy I told you about this morning."

Ms. Stephanie had mentioned that she was bringing a new foster to the house today. One of the older fosters Ms. Joanie had looked after had won some scholarship to a boarding school. Ms. Joanie and Mr. Pete were pretty awesome. They opened their home to everyone, and they didn't pretend to be our parents. At the same time, they didn't pretend we weren't a part of the household.

I liked them.

They took real good care of Ivy, too. She was never dirty and always smiled. The first few days we were here, I'd changed her diapers. I'd always gotten to her first. Ms. Joanie hadn't scolded but she had told me that it was okay to let her do it.

I watched her real close, for like a week. Ms. Joanie was

really good at changing her diaper and making Ivy laugh. So I didn't mind going out to play, but only if Ivy was downstairs in the play area where I could listen for her too.

"Why don't you two get to know each other while I take Jasper's things inside and talk to Ms. Joanie." Ms. Stephanie's words pulled me back to the present and the kid eyeing me so distrustfully. He really was kind of scrawny and his clothes didn't fit. I hated when mine were too short or too long.

Ivy let out a yowl from inside and I jerked my attention to the door. Three cries. That was my deal with Ms. Joanie. Three of the yowling cries and if she didn't fix it, I would. The sobbing broke off almost as it started.

Whew.

She probably wanted someone to pick her up. Ivy liked cuddles. Ms. Stephanie was really good at them. Ivy never fussed when she carried her around.

Finally, I looked back at the new kid—Jasper.

"You want to play?"

"Not really." It was a blunt answer, so I shrugged.

"Well, I'm gonna play over there." I pointed toward the row of racing cars Mickey J had brought over a few days ago, along with his old racing set. I hadn't seen anything like it and when he said I could keep it I still couldn't believe it. Mickey was a lot like his sister. Ms. Stephanie was nicer though, but Mickey—Mickey seemed to get me. He never tried to sugar coat anything. Life sucks, kid, he would tell me. Just wait until it's your turn to kick it in the balls.

Still, the new kid watched me with so much doubt it kind of grated.

"It's better with two. But do what you want. Ms. Joanie will make us clean up before dinner." That seemed a fair warning. Ms. Joanie wanted clean hands and clean faces before we sat down to eat and if our clothes were dirty, well, we had to change. No dirt at the table.

She didn't make you starve though. But I'd rather do my own washing, she doused me but good with a bucket the first time I refused to wash up. It had been kind of funny, but my shoes squelched and Ms. Joanie had laughed so hard, I had to join in.

Jasper sat on the steps while I set up the race cars. The track was pretty awesome. The same cars didn't always win, but I really liked it when they did the loopty-loop. Mickey promised to take me to a real racetrack one day. Ms. Stephanie was inside for a while, I finished four races before she came down the steps. After she kissed Jasper on the head, she waved at me and I waved back.

Ms. Stephanie was weird. Even for an adult. She liked everyone. But she was awfully hard to fool and she never, ever got angry. When I asked why we couldn't just stay with her, she'd told me she would love to open her home to everyone, but she couldn't. Her place was small and Mickey took up a lot of room.

No matter how long I played with the cars, Jasper never left the steps. It kind of seemed like he wanted to come play, but he didn't know how. I had to learn, too. Maybe I could teach him.

When the school bus stopped at the end of the drive, I got up and walked over to the steps. Ivy and I had a visit to the doctors today, which was why I'd stayed home from school. Ms. Joanie had a lot of kids here, I liked most of them.

But Jasper didn't know them. They were loud and shoved at each other. They left me alone, mostly. So, I just watched them as they came in. New kids weren't unusual, so they just bypassed us and went inside.

Ms. Joanie would introduce Jasper to everyone at dinner. I caught him watching me and I grinned, but he just scowled.

Okay, being friends might take a while. But I'd get a smile out of him, even if it hurt. Okay, maybe not a smile—I'd settle for no grimace.

Yeah, No grimace.

That was doable.

5

The rats were scarce in the warehouse. I didn't expect to find <u>them</u> here. Kellan had more or less dismissed them all when he pulled in with Milo and Doc. Of all the things I'd thought would happen the night before, Milo coming home hadn't even made the top five.

My only warning had been Liam's arrival. Jasper hadn't answered his phone. Not once. I'd sent a message to Starling, but she'd ignored her phone, too. Likely because she and Jasper had been in bed. Fine. But they should have checked *before* walking into the ambush.

His homecoming should have been an event. Not—whatever that was when he walked in the door just burning for a fight. Liam's presence had been the one thing that cooled him. Given Milo a breath. The fact he'd calmed had earned more than one suspicious glare from Kellan. Even Freddie, who tended to keep his head down when things went sideways, had been trapped.

When Vaughn descended the stairs, Milo greeted him with a hard fist and even tougher questions. He might have been in prison for three years, but he'd lost none of his edge. If anything, he'd honed it to razor sharp and far more dangerous. I wasn't even sure the Milo we'd known was still there. This—this was Raptor. Living. Breathing. Raging beneath his skin.

All night we'd waited as the hours ticked past. Liam and I played pool. Freddie channel surfed. Doc tried to talk to Milo, but he'd been laser-focused on Kellan and Vaughn. To their credit, they were holding things back. Liam and Doc only knew a part of the story and Freddie had shards of it.

The only three who really knew what happened the night they brought Emersyn back were Jasper, Kellan, and Vaughn. Doc knew about her injuries.

All of us did.

None of us discussed it.

Not even Freddie. Freddie, who couldn't keep his mouth shut to save his life.

I didn't slow until I was in my car, and I sent Kellan a straightforward message.

Me: *No rats here on watch. You should get some in. Milo's too unpredictable and Jasper's not going to be thinking.*

Kellan: *Where are you going?*

Me: *I'll be back.*

Kellan: *Be careful.*

Me: *You too.*

Not something we would usually have to warn each other of, but this wasn't normal circumstances. It took me no time to get out of the garage and on the way to Liam's. We'd lost a huge chunk of daylight. I was still fucking tired from not sleeping the night before. I hadn't worried about Starling being with Jasper. He'd slit his own wrists before he let anything happen to her. Even if Raptor hadn't chosen the night before to come home, I wouldn't have slept until I knew for sure she was safe. Raptor hadn't allowed any of us to warn Jasper before he walked into the clubhouse and Raptor had already been on the move. An image of Starling's fierce expression when she got between Raptor and Jasper made me smile.

Fierce.

Ferocious.

Dangerous in her own right.

I couldn't let her get hurt though. Milo would *never* harm his sister. This Raptor—the Raptor who had come back to us was damaged in new ways. The fractures and cracks would need time to repair. Maybe he and Jasper would beat each other bloody until they couldn't stand.

Then they could talk.

It had happened before.

Not wasting any more time, I hit the door opener and accelerated out of the warehouse. I waited only long enough for the door to clear the roof of the car. I hit the button to send it rolling back down and only lingered for it shut fully. Too many uncertainties.

I didn't like them.

Variables caused trouble. They couldn't be accounted for.

Variables like new arrivals at the group home, workers or kids. Variables like isolating one kid for abuse. We'd all seen it. Worked to avoid it. Even I'd courted my fair share of near misses.

I didn't like change.

Except...

The dark outside had deepened and the sun was a distant memory as I accelerated away from the warehouse.

I had one destination in mind, and I didn't question it. Emersyn had been a change I embraced.

I wanted my Starling with us. From fixing the room between mine and Kellan's, to trying to make her comfortable and picking out the shoes she preferred—she wasn't a change. She was...

My people. She was mine. Ours, I supposed, but definitely mine.

The day had been brutal and exhausting, but I'd gone up to get some of her things and moved them out to the car in the quieter moments, when they forgot I was there. Raptor had seethed as he paced around, a thousand questions he asked and no one—not even Freddie—offered up the answers he wanted to hear.

Why tell him about the partner right now? The problem had been dealt with. The man was shark chum somewhere way offshore—or what was left of him. I hadn't paid that much attention to the details. Jasper and Kellan had kept some of the details to themselves.

If I'd known, he'd have died a lot faster.

Vaughn told me why later. The fact the man suffered was the only thing that mattered, I supposed. Still...

I flexed my hands on the steering wheel. The knuckles on my right hand were still scraped and bruised. The pain felt good as I stretched them. They should have told me sooner.

The drive to Liam's took forever, and no time at all. The city seemed strangely quiet, as if aware that violence streaked the storm clouds brewing. Streets slick with fresh rain gleamed and the temperatures dropping threatened ice. More likely fog. A good night to find a new canvas, a spot to work in the shadows, where the chill and the fog would keep the audience at bay.

One block from Liam's, I slowed. The hair on the back of my neck prickled and I pulled into a side street and parked, lights off and waited. This spot gave me a good vantage to the entrance to Liam's garage.

And a better vantage on the car parked across the street with two people inside of it. It was too dark to make them out. This was an affluent area. Their car didn't fit. It was missing a hubcap on the front driver's side tire. Smoke rose in a steady blue stream from the passenger side. While there were stores along this stretch, they were all gourmet or featured limited hours, often closing as soon as the business day was done.

There was no reason for that car to be there, unless they were waiting for someone.

Liam?

Starling?

Unacceptable.

Instinct had me loosening the seatbelt and sliding into the backseat. It took a little maneuvering, but I was out the back passenger door and had it closed without ever worrying about the interior light turning on. After drawing the hood up to shield my hair, I zipped up the front.

The chill in the air barely touched me. I liked the cold. Always had. This wasn't a neighborhood for lurking, but it had its own alleys and shadowy paths. I knew them all. Liam and I had used them to our advantage more than once. It only took a few minutes to circle the block and approach the car from the opposite direction and on their side of the street. There was a way to move along the building fronts where the shadows were the deepest.

The butt of a cigarette flicked out the window to join the small stack of them littering the sidewalk. A car approached from the other direction and turned into the parking garage for Liam's building. The driver leaned forward and that's when I caught sight of the camera. Long lens. No flash.

I lingered another ten minutes, but they seemed settled back in for a long evening. Time to do something about that. Retracing my steps, I slid into the parking garage through a pedestrian entrance on the opposite side. Once in, I picked up the courtesy phone and dialed the police.

Might as well let them earn their keep. I reported suspicious behavior, the make and model of the vehicle and worry that they might be armed. One of them had been pointing something out the driver's side window.

I didn't give the operator any more info, just dropped the phone after I wiped the handle. Security cameras were placed throughout the garage. The place was a fortress. But I knew where they were. The blind spots we'd created so I could come and go when necessary.

Or Liam could leave without a trail.

I followed that one back out and made it to my own car, then pulled away. It took me less than ten minutes to find a drive through coffee place that was open, and I sent a warning to Liam while I waited for the coffee.

Me: *watchers on the street.*

Liam: *How many?*

Me: 2. *Fed them to the pigs.*

Liam: *You couldn't wait for me?*

That didn't even deserve an answer. Except...

Me: *Not with Starling inside.*

Liam: *She's not.*

I frowned.

Liam: *Took her to the store.*

I stared at the last two messages. The store.

Liam: *She needs clothes.*

My eyes narrowed. Yes, they'd left without her things. It was why I'd smuggled them down to the car for her. But her dance shoes and studio were back at the clubhouse.

Liam:???

He was worried.

I sent a single thumbs up emoji, though I didn't agree with the sentiment. Liam needed to know I was all right with his decision. I wasn't. But I wasn't sure why. Shutting off the phone, I put it away and accepted the coffee before heading out again. The flashing blue and red lights were visible a block away. The men who'd been in the car were out and one of them was even sitting handcuffed on the curb.

I made for the entrance of the garage and used my remote to open it. A friendly officer waved me through and I smiled at her while pretending to rubberneck.

That was what a normal resident would do.

Once inside, I maneuvered up two levels to the spot Liam kept secured for me. We didn't hide our relationship, but we also didn't advertise it. My mirror. My brother. We couldn't hide it if we tried. That said, we took precautions. I did a quiet sweep of the garage and paused near the wall overlooking the street below. I snapped a few pictures of the car and its passengers before I gathered the bags from the backseat and headed inside.

Silence greeted me. Most of the floors were empty, their absent owners only using them when they were in town. When I reached Liam's floor, I frowned at the package sitting right outside the door.

All deliveries went by the doorman downstairs.

Getting up here required codes.

I glanced at the cameras.

Both had been aimed elsewhere.

Not useful.

Shifting the bags, I took a photo of the package and sent it to Liam.

I didn't touch it as I keyed my way into his apartment. With care, I scanned the interior. Two lamps were on in the living area and one small light in the kitchen. The layout gave me a solid view of both rooms and the hall. Setting the bags down, I nudged the door closed and went to the painting. Behind it, Liam's security system included internal cameras.

Scrolling back, I found Liam and Emersyn leaving. Starling wore a mutinous expression. I smiled. Liam looked too amused. But he was careful with her. Scrolling back further, I found her pacing the apartment, her expression hollow, alternating between fury and hurt.

The hurt cut deeper.

Enough.

Whatever the package was, the delivery man hadn't been inside. I finished with a full sweep and paused in my own room when the elusive scent of Emersyn lingered there. The imprint on the covers showed she'd chosen my room to sleep in.

Good.

I carried her bags in there and set them on the bed so she couldn't miss them. I'd brought her things, the books she'd been reading, and the bear she'd kept in her bed since I put it there. He was old and careworn, but if he brought her comfort, then with her he would stay.

Running my fingers over the too familiar stitches, the worn spots from too many hugs, and the matted bits from getting wet, I hoped he could continue to help her here. There was a row of stitches along the back of the right arm.

A repair after a fight had torn him. Another set of stitches behind a ratted ear. Those were harder to see.

Scars on the bear.

A shared life of mended wounds.

With care, I smoothed the covers and set him on the pillows to wait for her. The room here didn't have much in the way of personality. I'd not left a mark here. I should, I suppose. Particularly if it was Starling's room.

That in mind, I closed the door to the room and pulled one of the charcoal pencils from my pocket. It took no time to sketch something on the back of the door. As much as I wanted to wait for them, and to see her, I should get back. The watchers on the building, the box outside...Raptor...

No, I needed to get back to the clubhouse.

Stuffing the charcoal back into my pocket, I returned to the bed and opened one of the bags. There was a shirt inside that I'd worn the day we went to paint by the sea. I folded it and laid it on the pillow for her. Vaughn handed me his shirt when he'd seen me go for the bags. The one right off his back. He wanted her in his scent. I left it in the bag.

She'd find it, but I wanted her to have mine first.

Finished, I left the door open and headed back to the front - before I pressed my face to the pillow in search of her scent. Better that I wasn't here when they got back. Not when I needed to leave. If I saw her, I wouldn't go.

My phone buzzed in my pocket. I pulled it out.

Liam: *Leave the package. It's safe.*

It didn't need a response, so I didn't send one. The next message flashing across my screen pulled a smile.

Freddie: *Is she okay?*

How long had he fought against asking, I didn't want to imagine. He had his own struggles. I gave him a thumbs up then turned off my phone and slipped out, securing the door behind me. The package was right there, and I ignored it. taking the stairs rather than the elevator.

The cops were still out there and at least one of the car's passengers was now in the back of a black and white.

I'd reach out to one of our contacts and get that report. I wanted to know who was watching Liam's and who left the package. I didn't think they were the same person.

No.

I had a feeling there were new players on the board.

Two blocks away, I put the call through to Kellan. He answered on the first ring. But I didn't wait for him to say anything before I told him, "We may have another problem."

WHAT HAPPENS NEXT

EMERSYN

Every few months, I never knew exactly when, Uncle Bradley showed up to take me shopping. It was always amidst a flurry of business calls or meetings. He would pick me up in a limousine where we would have privacy in the back. Then he would take me to the most expensive boutiques in whatever town we were in. He preferred New York, where he could take me straight to a designer, but he always wanted to buy me a nice dress.

I had reams of clothing in the closet at his home, in the room they called mine. I tried not to chew the dried bit of skin on the corner of my nail. The last thing I needed to do was pull it until it cut all the way back and bled. Especially if I needed the distraction of the pain later. I'd been standing in the lobby when his limo pulled up to the hotel.

I'd known it was him, even before my phone buzzed to alert me. Eric was also in the lobby and he tossed me a smile as I passed him. I wanted to smile back, I really did. But he was still new and it was hard to smile about

63

anything on days I had to spend with my uncle. He hadn't stopped talking on the phone, even when I slid into the car.

Though I'd intended to sit opposite him, he'd caught my hand and tugged me to the seat right next to his. When he leaned forward, I gave him my cheek for the quick brush of his too warm lips, and then he went right back to his conversation about contracts and negotiations.

No, he wasn't satisfied with their progress. The problems were supposed to be eliminated and the fact this was still ongoing meant he might need to bring in a new company. His silence in between these ominous threats were not friendly. Even though it was quite possible to hear the voice on the other end of the phone, I tuned it out.

Uncle Bradley did not approve of my involving myself in business. From a very young age, I'd learned to be seen and not heard at any type of meeting, whether it took place in a conference room, his office, the back of the car, or when he was in bed. He settled his hand on my knee as I stared out the window. I'd dressed appropriately, but at least it was just chilly enough that I could get away with tights under the skirt.

"Just handle it," he said abruptly. "If you can't, then you will be replaced."

He hung up the call and glanced at me.

"Sorry, Princess, duty often calls." He gave my leg a squeeze. "We may not have as much time on this visit. So I've called ahead to have them pick out four dresses for you to try on for me."

I swallowed. "Four? You usually are only looking for one or two."

"True, but the season will be busier coming up and three of your shows will be in cities where I have business to attend. I need my favorite companion to attend a number of functions with me. And did you think I'd forget your birthday? You're fifteen now. Practically a grown woman." My skin crawled as he ran his fingers up and down my thigh. "We saw too little of each other last year, and I wasn't happy to hear about you drinking or passing out."

"Nothing happened," I assured him. "I made it back to my room and slept. It was fine. I know better than to drink like that again." The hangover the next morning had half-killed me.

"Hmm," was his only comment. We pulled up to one of the finer boutiques with a French name. It was one of his particular favorites because they always had exclusive, expensive clothes. "I've missed you the last year or so, Princess. Too much time apart."

He caught my chin as the car stopped and turned my face to him.

"We're correcting that this year. I don't want you to forget me." This time I had no choice but to hold still as he brushed his kiss to my lips. The rigid tension in my neck threatened a headache. If I didn't relax soon, this would get worse.

"I promise," I whispered, all too aware of how close he was. "I could never forget you." No matter how hard I tried. "I had a brutal day at rehearsals and I'm sore, do you mind if we have a little drink before we go in?"

He tilted his head.

"Just one." Licking my lips when he focused on them for a moment, I fought the sick surge in my stomach. "It'll help."

"Take us around the block," he informed the driver, after pushing the button to begin sliding the privacy shield closed. "In fact, take us for a ride around the city and let them know we'll be back in an hour."

I closed my eyes when he continued to hold my chin and then let him turn my face so he could press a kiss to my ear. Shivers raced over my flesh as he prepared the drinks. Whiskey. He made mine neat, and filled his with half as much. I knocked it all back in one long swallow.

The heat hit my system like a thermal bomb, and it sent a wave out to all the knots in my muscles, loosening everything.

"One's enough," he asked, swirling his own drink as he watched me from beneath his lashes.

I licked my lips again. "May I have one after?"

"You may have anything you want, Princess," he crooned, and I slid off the seat and onto the floor of the limo, turning to kneel in front of him. He'd already unzipped his pants. If he didn't have much time, then maybe all I'd need to do was gargle tonight.

A lot.

The drive took far longer because he canceled his meetings. The dresses in my size had been sent back to the hotel. I never got to see them and Uncle Bradley insisted on seeing me to my room.

He didn't leave until the next morning.

There wasn't enough hot water on the planet.

But I made it to rehearsals by nine, and when Eric flirted with me, I tried to find a smile for him. When I couldn't and he pulled me aside, I told him I wasn't feeling well. The last thing I expected was for him to show up at my hotel room with ice cream later and a friendly smile.

He didn't stay long, but when he left and brushed a kiss to my cheek, I didn't shudder. When I saw him the next day, I smiled for real.

6

Two days had passed without a word from Vaughn, Jasper, or anyone else at the clubhouse. Well, anyone else except Rome. When Liam brought me home from the store with my fresh manicure, pedicure, and hair styled, along with an entire rack of clothing, I'd found a present waiting for me in my room.

My bags with my workout clothes, borrowed shorts and cutoff sweats, as well as my own panties, I hadn't even looked at what Lydia had picked out when she kept insisting Liam liked lace.

I'd never wear it.

It wasn't Liam's face that chased me out of my dreams though, and I snapped awake to the room that had become mine since Raptor banished me from the clubhouse. Light edged the windows, just a bare hint of gray and pink. Sunrise. Sweat dotted my forehead and soaked through the shirt I'd been wearing to sleep in.

I'd found it tucked on the pillow along with the bear.

There was no mistaking that it was Rome's. Ridiculous that I found comfort in putting it on, when I hadn't even seen the man in question in days. I'd had a chance to call them. Liam had offered me his phone once more, but the longer I stared at their names on that cell phone, the more I realized I didn't even know what to say to any of them.

More, what I had to say wasn't for Liam's consumption. I'd searched through my bags, hoping Rome had brought my phone as well. But that had been in Jasper's car, so it was probably still there.

I flung myself out of the bed, because between flashes of my uncle's face and the rack of clothes standing on the far side of the room still sealed in their bags, there was no way I was going back to sleep. The first thing I did was yank open the closet, then drag the rack in there. Most of what was already here seemed to belong to Rome. Just a handful of clothes to change into. Nothing fancy. Everything seemed a bit worn, but not frayed. Like, why did he need new jeans when these would fit just fine?

There were shoes, too. And more shirts. I snagged one off the hook and sniffed it. Embarrassing and stupid. It smelled like laundry detergent of course. More annoyed with myself than anything else, I still took the shirt, but I closed the door on that rack of fancy clothes with the shoes and lingerie.

If I could, I'd burn it all. I had no idea how Liam had even paid for any of it. And I didn't want to know.

But I wasn't paying him for any of it in cash or favors.

The very thought sent me into the bathroom, and I heaved up bile as it burned a path up from my stomach. I turned the shower as hot as I could stand it and then stripped to get under the scalding water. I scrubbed as hard and fast as I could, I wanted any lingering traces gone. Even the memory of his fingers ghosting over me was enough to make me throw up in the shower all over again.

Once I'd rubbed my arms and legs raw, I scrubbed my face until it was stinging. Only then did I rinse and shut the water off. Wrapped in a towel, I brushed my teeth. It took three rounds until all I could taste or breathe was peppermint. Not even the hint of aftershave or cologne or foulness, that I shouldn't remember so damn clearly, and yet it was there.

I leaned against the cold counter and stared at myself in the mirror. My nails were without chips and done with a clean, french manicure, as were my toes. I hadn't really given a damn what they did with them. Painting them usually involved matching a costume. It was nice that they were all neatly rounded, I suppose.

They'd removed about a third of the callus from the bottom of each of my feet. I wouldn't let them go too nuts though, I needed those calluses when I danced. Bit by bit, I put myself back together. They'd trimmed all the dead ends from my hair and instead of falling in one straight length, they'd added a bit of layering to it.

It came down at an angle along the front then tapered back to the full length in the back. The style was not one I'd have chosen for myself, but even with soaking wet hair and red raw cheeks, it made my face seem more delicate.

There wasn't any moisturizer I could use for my face. I supposed there was some in the bags of crap they'd added along with all the things from the store, but I'd rather let my skin flake off than use it, so I just walked out of the bathroom. I pulled on dance shorts and a sports bra before I hauled a dance tank over it.

If I did nothing else today, I would stretch. Despite how long I'd been in the bathroom, the sky was still different hues of pinks and soft dove grays. Barely sunrise. I headed out of the bedroom and down the hall.

While I'd barely glanced at Liam's bedroom door, it was hard to miss that it was closed. It was only closed when he wasn't home. That much I had noticed. When he was here, he slept with it open. And he'd been here constantly the last two days, never giving me a second alone.

He'd left some time the first night, after we'd gotten back and I'd gone to sleep, because he walked in the door when I'd gotten up the next morning. The second night, I tried to stay awake to listen for him to leave so I could use the landline. No luck.

Despite the fact he went to bed, he wasn't down long and more than once his phone rang and he'd answer it.

I should have used the landline that first day when he slept for so long. It was early though, and he wasn't here, so I hurried into the kitchen. No coffee made. He'd gotten in before I got up yesterday because there was fresh coffee and he'd just showered, but he'd had a fresh bruise on his arm that he hadn't commented on, and I hadn't asked.

It was like sharing a condo with a ghost, only I was the ghost and trapped inside the walls and he could leave whenever he wanted. I started the coffee and lifted my thumb to my mouth, half considering chewing it, until I touched the feeling of the dipping powder they'd used to create the hard shell.

That was one way to keep me from chewing my nails. I started the coffee brewing and checked the fridge. He didn't keep much in it. Juice. Protein shakes. Fruit.

Though there was more in it today than had been before. Bacon, eggs, and yogurt. I stole one of the strawberry yogurts out, debated it, then put it back. After coffee maybe. I glanced at the front door. Closed.

While the coffee burbled and brewed, I checked to see if I could open it.

No luck.

On silent feet, I tiptoed down the hall and knocked on his door. I mean, I could just open it and look inside, but I'd rather not. When there was no answer, I knocked a bit louder and then checked the handle.

It turned with one twist.

The interior of the bedroom was dark, but the hall light cut across the empty, rumpled bed and the rest of the room was pitch. Even the bathroom. He had blackout curtains in the room. I listened.

No shower running.

Closing the door, I raced back to the kitchen and I'd just reached for the phone when the tumblers on the door clicked and opened.

Fuck.

Fuck.

"Fuck," I said aloud as I turned away from the phone I'd been reaching for and switched to grabbing a mug for the coffee.

Liam snorted. "No, thank you. At least not until I've showered. After, if you're still up for it let me know."

I pivoted slowly to glare at him. He looked so much like Rome and yet—

"No," he said with a smirk as he dropped envelopes on the table and walked into the kitchen. Half of his face was mottled and bruised. Even his lip was split open and bleeding. "I'm not Rome. I'm not bending over to kiss your ass, no matter how pretty it is." I was still gaping at his wounds when he reached past me and dropped a green foil and paper wrapped bouquet. "For you. I'm going to wash up and then I'll have some of that coffee."

"I don't want anything from you," I said, finally digging my voice up from wherever it had gone to hide.

"Good thing they aren't from me then, right Hellspawn?" Another smirk. "Now, be less of a pain, my jaw fucking hurts and so does my head." With that, he walked out of the kitchen, and I didn't miss the faint hitch to his step, despite how hard he tried to *not* limp.

The scent of copper lingered in the air. I glanced down at the floor. Blood drops littered the tile all the way to the door.

Fuck.

I glanced at the bouquet again and then toward the door. Dammit, I stretched up and snagged the first aid kit off the top of the fridge and dodged the blood drops as I headed back to his bedroom. As expected, the door was open and the shower was on. I headed for the bathroom but kept my head turned away from the shower.

"I brought you the first aid kit. I'll clean up the blood you left on the tile. Are you bleeding somewhere you need help patching up?" I kept my gaze firmly on the countertop, and not on the mirror which was already clouding up from the steam pouring out of the stall.

Silence met my inquiry, but I refused to turn around and look. If he wanted to say nothing, then he could figure it out on his own. I made it to the bathroom door when he let out an aggrieved sigh.

"I'm fine, Hellspawn. Most of the blood isn't mine and my knuckles were split. I'll clean up the blood when I get out there."

One hand on the doorframe, I turned his answer over in my head. "Scraped knuckles, even split open ones, don't bleed like that. Nor does someone else's blood on you, unless you were soaked in it." I could see his discarded clothes from here. They were stained, not soaking.

"I'll survive, Hellspawn. Go away now. I need to hit something or fuck it, and you aren't going to be either."

I frowned. The tiredness under the warning in his tone and words didn't detract from the actual warning. If anything, it made me want to look for a weapon. There were knives in the kitchen. I knew he had guns, but they were in a safe.

"Go," Liam repeated. "Now."

"Fine," I said. "Bleed to death, for all I care."

I was almost to the bedroom door this time when he called out. "You'd care. Bodies start to stink after a while."

"So does bullshit" I retorted. "I'd find your phone and call your brother."

That shut him up.

Or at least, I didn't hear anything else from him. Back in the kitchen, I found paper towels and spray cleaner and went after the blood on the tile. It was a disconcerting amount, and it did track all the way to the door. I wondered if it went out in the hall, but the damn door wouldn't open, so whoever cleaned the building would have to deal with it.

Back in the kitchen, I poured my coffee before I looked at the bouquet he'd dropped on the counter. There were bloody fingerprints on the paper, that was attractive. But they weren't flowers inside the paper, instead, they were finely shaped donuts, each one decorated with different sprinkles and rippled to look like roses. They were even on sticks.

Surprise rippled through me and washed away more of the shadows from the dreams the night before. With care, I peeled back the paper and found a card tucked down inside them. It also had a bloody fingerprint on it.

Nice. Liam read it before he brought them in.

Jerk.

Careful of the blood, I flipped the card open.

Swan,

These are the first part of an apology. Consider this part for not coming to see you sooner. I have a lot to tell you and I know you have questions. Call me.

J.

Call him.

"Your phone was tucked inside," Liam said from the doorway, and I nearly knocked my coffee off the counter at his sudden appearance. He was in gray sweatpants, damp, bruised and battered skin with all his tattoos on display. There was a slice along his side that he'd covered with butterfly bandages.

I pulled my gaze from his injury and looked at his face. "Where is it now?"

Liam stared at me. "In my pocket."

Of course. "I'm not allowed a phone?"

"Didn't say that," he said after a beat as he went to the coffee pot and poured the rest of the coffee into a bigger mug than I'd chosen, emptying the whole pot. After he started another pot brewing, he took a deep drink of the coffee and turned to face me.

"But you took my phone?"

"Yes."

"Why?"

"Good question," Liam said, and the weariness earlier was back in his voice and his face. There were dark shadows beneath his eyes that had nothing to do with the bruises.

"What happened to you?" I probably shouldn't care, but he looked like he'd been through hell.

"It's not important," he said, then gestured with the

coffee cup toward the donuts. "You giving Jasper points for those?"

"Do you care?"

He shrugged. "I'm kind of hungry. If you weren't, I was going to offer to eat them for you."

I rolled my eyes. "You don't eat sugar."

Surprise flickered across his face.

"You're ripped. You train on weights daily, you boil your chicken and you eat it skinless and almost no carbs except beer. Even that's not enough on a strenuous enough regimen. Your hands are scarred, and your knuckles are often split. You've had your nose broken a time or two." I ticked off the items before I took a sip of my coffee and then plucked one of the donuts out. It was chocolate covered with sprinkles. Absolutely terrible for me.

I took a deep bite and stared at Liam the whole time, daring him to deny it. The donut was excellent, but as I lifted it to take another bite, he caught my wrist. It was a gentle grip, but he held it and then tugged my hand and the donut to his mouth.

The asshole ate the whole damn thing, right down to licking the sugar off my fingers all the while his gaze held mine captive. I couldn't look away, I didn't dare. A shiver stole through me before I could stop it and I swore all the hair on my body prickled when he sucked on my fingers one last time before letting me go and leaning back to chew the donut slowly.

"You were saying?"

Not much. Especially since I didn't trust my voice or my reactions at the moment. Tingles still shot up my arm from the contact, but I refused to respond to it, I just got out another donut. He met me stare for stare, and when I tossed it at him, he caught it with a grin and then saluted me with his coffee.

"Be careful who you challenge, Hellspawn. You've got a wicked little bite, but I don't lose."

I just snorted and plucked out another donut to actually eat, before carrying my coffee out of the kitchen. I was done with the conversation. Besides, two donuts in addition to two days of just being stuck in his condo and I needed to stretch, do some pushups, handstands, and maybe even use his treadmill to run.

Eyeing the living room, I wondered how hard it would be to shove his furniture back. I had headphones. I could play music and dance, while he slept.

My skin prickled. Liam had followed me and stood behind me, but I didn't glance over my shoulder at him. The sunrise had flooded the living room with a soft dewy, pink light. It would be brighter soon.

After licking my fingers clean, I walked over to the front of the windows and put my coffee cup on a table, before sliding down into the splits to begin my stretches.

"That's it?" Liam asked on a somewhat more subdued and choked note.

"That's it about what?" I leaned over and reached for my right ankle. The stiffness went all the way down my side. I'd been lazy. I couldn't afford to be lazy.

"About your phone?"

Straightening, I switched sides and stretched toward my left ankle. "You're either going to give me the phone or you're not. Arguing with you is pointless. You're in charge of the cell and I'm the prisoner. That's how these things work. Just like you can take the donuts if you want. Or the coffee."

I swore I could feel his stare intensifying.

"You might control where I am and what I get. But you don't get to control *me*." I took three deep breaths and then released the stretch to move to the other side. Liam never left while I went through the whole series of stretches and I swore his gaze grew heavier and heavier.

Another day I wouldn't get to call Lainey.

Tomorrow morning, I wouldn't waste time.

And I was going to figure out how to set an alarm. Even if it meant sleeping on the sofa so I could hear when he left.

When I finally finished the stretches and the lunges and went to run on the treadmill, Liam snarled something unintelligible and left.

For some reason, it felt like I won that little standoff.

I wasn't sure what I won, but a glance around the room said it wasn't my phone.

Still, I'd take the win.

BECAUSE OF YOU

MILO

"You can't do this," Mom said in a voice full of tears. "You can't."

"Watch me." The snarled words made me flinch and I retreated from the bedroom door I'd been about to knock on. Ivy was awake and she was crying, but neither of them had come to get her.

"Jeff," she begged, tears soaking her voice. "Please. I can get better."

"Right, I've heard that a hundred times," he snapped. "You never do it. You can't even go take care of that brat screaming right now."

"I was just tired."

"You're always tired, or you're high, or you need to get high, or you're coming down from being high." Something crashed against the wall in the bedroom. "Do you even know how much you *cost* me?"

Dry-mouthed, I crept into Ivy's room. She was trying to stand, clinging to the rails on her crib.

"Stop," I told her as she let out another wail. The big fat tears rolling down her face made me sad, but her screaming hurt my head. I pressed a finger to my lips and shushed her. Her lower lip trembled, as another drop fell from her eyes to splash against her hands. She sat down abruptly and stretched her arms out to me. "Okay," I whispered as something crashed in the other room and I scooped her up when she flinched.

Hugging her to me, I ignored the leaking diaper and grabbed one on my way to my room. My bedroom was further away from Mommy's room, and I closed the bathroom door, but he was still yelling and Mom was screaming now.

"It's okay," I kept telling Ivy, repeating it as much for her as for me. I'd seen Mom change the diapers before and held my fingers in place to do the little tabs. The diapers were super tiny though. Sitting on the floor, I gave her one of my blocks and she immediately started waving it around as I laid her down.

I didn't have a lot of toys, but the blocks were old and if it kept her quiet, even better. The diaper took forever to change, but I figured it out around her kicking legs and snuffling. I had to use my shirt to wipe her nose though and when she threw the block and it hit me, I scowled.

"Ow. Don't do that."

Ivy grabbed her toes and laughed at me.

That just made me scowl harder and I wagged my finger at her. "It's not funny. That hurt."

She laughed again and I sighed.

It was hard to stay mad at her.

"Jeff...where are you going?" Mom's voice cut through, as she sounded like she was running down the hall.

"I'm done. I told you that before. You shouldn't have

had that second one. Milo is fine, he's a good enough kid. But I didn't ask for a girl or another mouth to feed, when all you want to do is feed your habit. You couldn't even give that shit up while you were carrying the brat and that cost more."

"I can do it," Mom pleaded.

The door to my room slammed open and I jumped, carrying Ivy up with me, as she let out a startled scream. Dad stood in the doorway and glared down at me.

"Let's go Milo, leave the brat."

I swallowed and met his hard stare. It was difficult not to notice Mom clinging to him. "Jeff please, you can't go and you can't take him."

"I can do what I damn well please," he said and shook her off. I winced when she hit the wall and her tears increased. I hated her tears almost as much as I hated Ivy's. "Now, Milo. Give the little brat to your mother and let's go."

Chin lifting, I glared at him. "No."

"What did you say boy?" His voice slowed as he stalked into the room. It took him only two strides to get to me and he loomed over me. Dad was a big man. I'd seen him beat a man once. Beat him until he couldn't walk. I was pretty sure the man died, but Daddy told me not to talk about it, so I didn't.

Shaking, I hugged Ivy tighter as she wrapped her arms around me. She wasn't crying, but she did cling to me as tightly as I did to her. I wrapped my hand against the back of her dark head as I took a step back. If he tried to hit me, I wanted to be able to turn away so he wouldn't catch her by mistake.

"I said no," I told him. "I'm not going. She's not a brat. She's Ivy. My sister."

Dad glared down at me and then Ivy, his lip curling.

"Fucking waste. Both of you. Fine. Stay here." He turned and stormed out, leaving me staring at Mom's tear-filled eyes.

"Don't worry, Milo...he's just going for milk. He'll be back." Then she was running after him, Ivy hugged my neck tighter and I stared at the empty doorway until the front door slammed.

Yeah.

Daddy wasn't coming back.

7

Despite his bruised and battered appearance, Liam didn't sleep for long. I ran for an hour on the treadmill, increasing my speed every ten minutes. It wasn't a perfect replacement for dancing, but it would have to do. Afterward, lungs burning, I went into handstands near the wall. My arms were a little buttery, but I locked them then began the relaxing down before pushing up. I bore all of my weight on my hands, nothing on the wall.

Balance was everything as I did the push-ups. Only when the sweat was running into my eyes did I right myself and swipe a towel over my face before going for water. That done, I resumed the handstand and this time, I balanced on one hand. The concentration combined with the muscle fatigue allowed me to clear my mind in a way I hadn't since Liam dragged me out of the clubhouse.

With care, I stretched one leg to the side so they were at

ninety degrees, while I still held firm on one hand. Control, like with the silks, required conscious effort with every single muscle. Still holding the pose, I dropped my free hand down until it flattened against the floor and traded the weight by lifting the opposite hand. Straightening my right leg, I dropped my left down to be at a perfect ninety degrees.

For the next thirty minutes, I alternated poses. Without silks or a dance floor, this was as close as I could get to iron-willed discipline for the muscles. I'd gotten kind of used to my routine at the clubhouse, even as varied as it had been. Maybe I wasn't spending hours every day in brutal rehearsal before performing every night, but I had fought to stay in shape, even with the weight I'd put on.

The donuts in the kitchen were not going to help with that effort, but a part of me didn't care. The rest of me wasn't sure what I would do when the time came that I left. My palms were burning, my back and biceps were feeling like spaghetti, when I straightened and stood.

My heart rate wasn't up though and while I might be sweating, I wasn't panting. This wasn't enough.

I glanced down the hallway toward the open door to his room, but there was no hint of movement. I wasn't walking down there and waking him. Though, I had to admit, the idea of dumping water on his head so I could get my phone back was tempting.

No amount of pretense would make me think the phone was anywhere but within arm's reach of him or in his hand or under a pillow.

No. Thank. You.

Tilting my head back, I stared up at the ceiling. There wasn't much else to do. I could do more stretches or run on the treadmill. He had weights, but I didn't use those as much because I worked with different equipment. The rest of the apartment had little else to offer. I usually only watched television in hotel rooms and the guys had been introducing me to movies so...

Fine. I went and grabbed a quick rinse in the shower to wash away the sweat. At least my mind was clearer, calmer. I could focus. In the kitchen, I rewarded myself with fresh coffee and donuts. I debated a beer, but the donuts were enough carbs.

Back in the living room, I hunted around until I found the remotes tucked into a cubby. Liam had lots of little hiding spaces.

I'd found a gun tucked under the sofa. Another behind the potted plant just inside the door and he had one in the fridge.

Licking the sugar off my fingers, I had to wonder if he had any more hidden around. That could be something to do. Find all of his little hidden stashes. Once I got the television on, nothing happened. There were three other boxes. That meant more remotes. One was a gaming system.

The boys had that at the clubhouse, so I looked for a player controller too. There was a slender little black box, which was another streaming service thingy. They teased my names for them, but seriously, the only televisions I ever watched were in hotel rooms and they didn't have all these little devices.

Back into the cubby hole where the remote had been. Tinier remote. No game controller. Another remote and a flash drive thing. Pfft, I checked each remote until the little black box had a blue light and the television came to life.

The first thing to pop up shouldn't have surprised me, but I had to stare at the porn that had been frozen in mid-motion. There were three guys and one girl.

The positioning was definitely interesting. She was alternating between sucking one dick and I assumed the other, based on how she was holding it. In the meanwhile, she straddled the face of another guy. I hit play more out of curiosity than anything else.

Eric hadn't been bad at sex. He just hadn't been great at it. I'd made the mistake of testing my uncle's patience at one party though. A boy, more my age, sweet, and kind, had found us a quiet corner and I'd tasted my first real orgasm.

Uncle Bradley had ruined that, too. Eventually.

Shaking my head, I pushed those memories aside and focused on the woman. She was doing a lot of work to keep all of those men happy, but the sounds she was making... It seemed like she was into it, but her eyes lacked any kind of real interest. The guys were definitely there, yanking her hair, trying to choke her with their dicks, dragging her around and the width of her asshole said they'd already been using it and I suppressed a shudder. If they started that, I was turning this off, but they weren't. She was bouncing away on one of the micro dicks, while she was sucking on the guy with the big one.

Probably should be the other way around. She wouldn't keep choking. None of them were pierced. And the guys weren't doing anywhere near as much of the work as she was. When they damn near swung her upside down, I almost choked on my donut laughing.

It was stupid.

A knock hit the door and I smacked the pause button as a doorbell rang several times and then another series of hard knocks. Whoever was at the door was not patient. No sooner did the knocking end then the doorbell began to ring again and down the hall, a cell phone rang, too.

I stood up and eyed the door warily, even as Liam

charged down the hall in nothing but the same pair of gray sweatpants he'd been in earlier. He had a gun in his free hand and a phone in the other. "Stay over there," he ordered. "And get down."

Get down?

Still, I didn't argue, crouching closer to the sofa but watching the door. What was the sofa gonna do for protection if he was answering the door with a gun in his hand? He flipped open a painting and pressed in a code before he walked over to the door and opened it. He didn't even pause to see who it was.

"I've shot people for less," was how he greeted whoever was there. "You could have called first."

"I did. You didn't answer." Raptor.

Ice slid up my spine and I stopped crouching. No way I was hiding from that mean asshole.

"Fuck, come in. You really shouldn't be here."

"I know how to get in and out without being seen." Raptor bypassed Liam and stopped dead when he saw me, and then his entire expression turned to thunder. "What the hell are you watching?"

"Whatever I want," I informed him. "Unless you've decided to add death from fucking boredom to your list of demands."

Liam dropped his chin and shook his head. I thought at first, he was just upset at my choice of words, but there was a flash of a smile as he shut the door. "You can change the channel, Hellspawn. That was just on the other night."

"Clearly," I told him with a shrug. "She's not very good at faking it, so I was trying to figure out how all three of them were gonna get their dicks in there."

"Oh, they take turns," Liam said blandly, despite the

fact Raptor turned that filthy glare on him. "Lighten up, Milo. You used to have a sense of humor."

"You used to have a fucking brain. Was I wrong to trust her with you?"

I rolled my eyes and despite the fact that I really liked the donuts, I threw the half of one I had left at him. I had pretty damn good aim. It hit Raptor in the side of the face and then bounced off onto the floor.

He swung his head to stare at me and Liam choked back a laugh, as he traded the gun to his other hand and put his phone in his right. "I think maybe you should try talking to the Hellspawn, rather than just about her. I'm going back to bed." The last he said with a flick of a look toward me and despite the bruises on his face and the fact one eye was nearly swollen shut, he raised his brows. "If you two don't need a referee."

Was he asking me or telling me?

I folded my arms and gave a little shrug.

For his part, Raptor blew out a slow breath. His shoulders squared and he was doing that thing with his anger again. I got that. Pack away all that emotion. Sometimes it was better to chain it up in the dark where it couldn't hurt you.

I hated that I got that.

"We'll be fine," Raptor said. "Just—turn off the porn cause it's fucking weird to think of my baby sister watching it."

"Then just think about it being Emersyn Sharpe who's watching it." But I turned it off, because I'd been more curious than anything else. Now, I wanted to know why *he* was *here*. "Does you being here mean I get to go back?"

"Hell no," he snapped and I swore Liam sighed.

"Man..."

"Go back to bed, you look like shit," Raptor told him. "Ivy—fuck—Emersyn and I need to talk."

Liam glanced at me again like he wasn't certain. Then again, it wasn't like he closed his door. He'd probably listen to every single word if he wanted.

"Fine, call if you need me." Then he left us alone, but he had his phone up and his finger moving. Texting the others to let them know they'd misplaced their giant jerk of a leader?

Movement pulled my attention back to Raptor and he bent down to pick up the donut. "Nice shot."

"It was a donut, not like it hurt."

The corner of his mouth tipped upward, a faint softening to the slash of harsh features. Did the man *ever* smile? Today he was dressed in a plain black t-shirt tucked into jeans and a pair of boots. Everything about him, except the tattoos along his arms, was nondescript. Well except the tattoos and the hell etched into his dark expression.

"There's coffee," I told him. If we were going to talk, words were going to be necessary.

He was still holding the half-eaten donut. "Okay." With that, he turned and went into the kitchen. I debated letting him find shit on his own, but I was still curious. Keeping my distance, I moved around so I could watch him in the galley kitchen. He was staring at what was left of the bouquet of donuts on the counter.

And he had the note in his hand. Was nothing private to these guys? He frowned down at it. "Did you call Jasper?"

"Liam took my phone."

"That's not an answer."

"It's the only answer you're getting from me," I told him. "You don't deserve anything else."

He shot a look over his shoulder and I swore a hint of a

smile was there, or maybe he had gas. As it was, he put the note back on the counter and dropped the half-donut into the trash before pouring himself coffee.

"Do you want another one, since I seem to have cost you yet even more donuts?"

"I'm fine. I shouldn't eat that much sugar if I'm going to stay trapped here anyway."

He paused with the coffee mug about halfway to his lips. "You're not trapped."

"Po-tay-to, po-tah-to, boil them, mash them, stick them in a stew—it's all the same thing. I'm locked in this apartment with my new jailer, Liam. I spent a few months being locked up in the clubhouse, then I earned my freedom. Only now you're back and I'm at square zero. It's worse than square one, because at least there I knew the rules."

He took a long slug of the coffee before he set the mug down. "Did you just quote *Lord of the Rings* at me?"

"We watched it a few days ago," I said with a shrug. "I liked it. Except the orcs and the mud dudes and Gollum." I shuddered. "He was nasty."

Raptor ran a hand over his dark hair as he stared at me. "You know those movies came out years ago."

"I didn't watch a lot of movies growing up. I was busy." I frowned. "Is that really why you came here? To talk to me about movies and donuts?"

"No," he said. "Well, yes, but no. I came to see you." He frowned. "To make sure you were all right."

"I'm assuming Jasper is all right if he left me those," I said, nodding to the donuts. "You didn't hurt him any more?"

"Let's leave Jasper out of this." A warning darkened the

underside of each word, like they were being underlined in bold.

"Sure, you're apparently the boss."

He stared upward at the ceiling. "I never pictured you like this."

"Like what?"

"Stubborn. Infuriating. A smart ass."

"Sound like someone else you know?" Liam called from the bedroom.

"Shut up," I said in the exact same moment as Raptor, and Liam's laughter carried toward us. Asshole.

"Why should you expect me to be anything else? I'm *me*." I studied him. "While you may have convinced yourself that I'm your sister..."

"You *are* my sister."

"Whatever. I have no siblings."

Any trace of humor evaporated from his expression. "Because you were adopted, and I wasn't. But you have a sibling. Me."

"I wasn't adopted." I'd seen my damn birth certificate. I needed it to get my passport and other important papers. "I know who my parents are. Sometimes I wish I didn't, but no, I know the family. I'm a Sharpe through and through." And damn, if that didn't come out bitter.

"They raised you," Raptor said slowly. "Gave you a better life."

Oh fuck, here we went again.

"I'm glad they did."

He knew as much as the rest of them. "You just think because they have money that it's the better life? Sure, okay, whatever. Are you going to ask them for a ransom?" I mean, that had been taken off the table. But Raptor seemed to be changing everything. He jerked his head like I'd slapped him.

"No, I'll drive you back myself and make sure you get there safely."

My stomach pitted and I almost vomited. "So that's why you're here—to take me back."

"Yes—no. Fuck—stop putting words in my mouth and listen. I don't want a damn ransom, but I don't want you here."

"You're the one who sent me here, genius."

Real anger burned in his eyes and I had to fight the urge to mark an imaginary score in the air. The scowls seemed to be just something he did, but right now? He was pissed. "I meant *here* in Braxton Harbor."

"Uh huh. I don't suppose I get a say in any of this?"

He blew out a breath. "You should have run the first chance you got."

"Fuck you," I responded. "I did."

He blinked.

"Then I changed my mind, and I went back. So, what's your next suggestion?"

"Do you have no concept of self-preservation? We're not safe people. You need to be... at least here, Liam can give you what you're used to."

I sure the fuck hoped not, but since he'd stayed out of my bed and kept his hands to himself, I'd call that a win. "You're unbelievable," I told him. "You, Jasper—Kellan, all of you. You want to decide what's best for me. Like you have some right to make those decisions. At least they got their heads out of their asses and stopped trying to tell me what I deserved and didn't. If I wanted to be gone, I'd be gone. Clearly, I don't want that. So, what are you going to do about it?"

Fuck, I almost wished I was adopted. Not sharing blood with any of them would be like a damn gift. As it was, I understood my lot in life. I'd learned to live with it a long time ago. Course, the tradeoff was this psycho. At least his darkness was all on the outside, right there and in your face. It was the monsters you couldn't see that you needed to worry about.

"I don't know," he snapped suddenly. "You'll stay here until I decide. You need to go back to your world." He drained his coffee and set the mug down. "Do you need anything?" He glanced down at my bare feet then the shorts. "Like real clothes?"

"I bought her clothes," Liam said from somewhere behind me. "She won't wear them."

"I have my own, I don't need to be dressed up like your doll." Or anyone else's for that matter. "I would like my phone though."

"To call your boyfriend?" Liam asked, but the jab landed on Raptor.

"Don't you start," he growled. Then he studied me. "If I asked you to not call Jasper, would you do it?"

"Try, maybe we'll find out."

"If Liam gives you your phone, will you promise to not call Jasper?"

Wow. That was an easy one to sidestep. "Why should I promise you anything?"

"Of course, everything has a price. What do you want?"

At least on that subject, we were in accordance. Everything did have a price. "My studio. I want to be able to dance. They built me one at the clubhouse and I need it."

He flicked a look at Liam then me. "If I give you access to it—how many times a week?"

"Every day would be ideal, but three or four days will do."

"If I grant you that, you promise to not call him."

"Sure." I shrugged. "Whatever." I didn't think they were gonna give me the phone anyway.

"Give her the phone."

Surprise jerked through me.

"I'll be here tomorrow to take you to the clubhouse."

"I can bring her," Liam offered. "I'm in for the night anyway."

Fuck. He wasn't leaving tonight? Did the man have to always be so difficult?

"I have something else I need you to do," Raptor said. "Walk me out." He paused. "And give her the phone."

Liam pulled it out of his pocket and handed it to me. Then he moved over and flipped open the painting. At this angle, I caught at least one of the numbers he pressed before he shut it and opened the door.

"Raptor," I said before the big man could leave, and he flinched.

"My name is Milo."

"Fine, Milo." It sounded weird on my tongue, but he looked a little pleased.

"What?"

"You keep saying I don't belong here. That I should go back to my world. Popular refrain with all of you. But if I'm supposed to be your sister—wouldn't this also be my world?"

His stare bore through me and then he pivoted and walked out without answering.

Liam dropped his chin to his chest and sighed. "Hellspawn, you'd try the patience of a saint."

"Good thing I don't know any."

He smirked, but closed the door behind him, leaving me in the apartment. I stared down at the phone in my hand and then at the closed door. Retreating to my bedroom, I put Lainey's number into the phone and sent a text, three words that she would know could only come from me, before I deleted it from the phone after I sent it.

I'd downloaded an app on the phone that would encrypt my texts and it had a vanish function. The messages were gone within sixty seconds of being read if they weren't saved. I logged in and sent a message to her saved name on my account.

I'm alive. I'm safe. For now. I might need help.

Her reply came so swiftly I almost sobbed.

Whatever. Whenever. Where are you? Let me come get you.

Not yet. I swallowed as those treasured words of hers vanished as soon as they'd been sent. *Too much to explain now. But I don't want anyone to know where I am.*

My message vanished before she replied.

What do you need?

I love you, Lainey, I whispered in my head. So fucking much.

Can you set me up an account and another ID? I can't get to my own.

Done.

The messages faded.

Will you be able to check here again?

I had no idea. The whole time I was messaging, I kept an eye on my closed door. Pushing off the bed, I retreated into the bathroom and closed that door and locked it.

I'll try. Maybe once every day or two.

It'll take me a couple of days. Lainey messaged. *Maybe three. I have someone who can help. What bank do you want me to use?*

I tried to think of the ones I'd seen when I'd been out with Rome and when Doc had driven me back to the hotel and later to the clinic.

Remmington Trust.

They had a branch here.

That'll make it easier. I hate owing that prick though.

I'm sorry.

She sent a laughing face. *Don't worry I have dirt. Holy fuck I've missed you.*

I sniffed as a tear escaped to run down my cheek. *Miss you more. Love you.*

Love you. Stay safe. I'll message you with everything when I have it set.

Just like that.

I hugged the phone to my chest, then with a pained heart, I deleted the app from the phone. I could download it again later. I didn't want them looking at it. I flushed the toilet and ran the sink like I'd been using it before I let myself back out into the empty bedroom.

Still holding the phone, I fell back on the bed and stared at it.

He'd asked me to not call him. That was the promise.

So I didn't call him.

I texted. Well, I started. I wrote and deleted a dozen different messages before I sent one.

Emersyn: *Thank you for the donuts.*

The next I sent to Rome.

Emersyn: *Thank you for my clothes and the bear.*

I considered the other guys, Doc, Kellan, Vaughn...

I scrolled to Freddie's number and pressed call.

He answered on the first ring. "Boo-Boo?" His staged, almost dramatic whisper threatened to leave me in giggles. "Is that you?"

"No," I told him. "It's a reasonable facsimile."

"Oh, cool. I always wanted to fuck a fax."

Too late, a giggle escaped.

It was like a sock to the gut, especially right on the heels of messaging with Lainey.

I missed all of those assholes.

BROKEN ORDER

VAUGHN

Life at Channing House could be worse, I supposed. The guys in my room were pretty cool and they never gave me crap about being so big. Even when some of the adults gave me weird looks, they didn't. My mom died six weeks after I arrived.

Ms. Stephanie actually came to get me in the middle of the night and rushed me over there. She kept the promise I'd asked for, that my mom didn't die alone. The nurses cleared out while I sat with her. Mom's eyes opened once, but she didn't focus too well.

I kept talking to her, telling her about the home and the boys. How I liked it, even though I wished it could be like it used to. It was okay. She'd fought real hard. While a part of me wanted her to keep fighting, the rest of me knew she couldn't. Her body wasn't all big and muscly like mine. Maybe I'd taken all her strength when she had me.

When the machines began to alarm quietly, I stared at the flatline until one of the nurses turned it off. They didn't make me leave. Ms. Stephanie sat right there with me while I held my mom's hand and fought to keep my promise to her. I didn't cry.

I didn't cry all the way out to Ms. Stephanie's car and when the first sob tore out of my throat, she wrapped her arms around me and let me cry into her shirt. It was almost as good as a mom hug, but it would never be my mom again. My eyes burned, my nose was stuffy, and my throat raw by the time we got back to the home.

All five of the boys were up and waiting when I came in. They were all silent. None of them said a word about my face. Or the fact it had to have tear tracks. Liam hopped out to go get food for us. Rome handed me a picture he'd drawn and my heart nearly stopped when I saw my mom's face. I didn't ask where he'd found the picture of her I kept, but the drawing helped more than anything else did.

The guys were like a shield between me and the others. A couple of kids made fun of me later in the day when I got caught crying. Jasper beat one of them up. Liam got the other one. They were the best friends a guy could have.

Liam wasn't there much longer. Three months after my mom died, he got adopted, but his twin didn't. I thought it was weird. We all did. Rome, however, never complained. While he didn't live there anymore, we got presents from him and mail drops. Every once in a while, he came to see his brother and the rest of us.

Milo promised Liam we would look after Rome. I took that promise pretty seriously. We were both artists, so hanging out was easy enough. Scrawnier than me and then some, Rome looked like an easy target. But he knew how to fight and he had me for backup, even when he didn't need it.

When we were eleven, some kid at school ripped his

sketchpad from him and started mocking him. I was the only one of us close enough to see the fight about to go down. Though I stepped forward, Rome caught my eye and just shook his head. I didn't like it, but I waited. Then he looked back at the other boy and held out his hand.

"Give it back." Three words were all he said. That was the other thing about Rome, he didn't talk much. It wasn't that he couldn't, he just didn't. The fool who took his sketchbook mocked him, then ripped half the pages out. Before they even began to flutter into the breeze, Rome was on him.

He laid into the bully with sharp strikes from his fists, elbows, knees, and even his feet when the kid went down. Like so many other fights, everyone present gathered in a circle to block the view and I got in there, pulling Rome off the kid, just as the teachers arrived to break it up.

When they blamed me, I shrugged. It was my turn to shake my head at Rome when he would have protested. I almost got expelled for fighting, but Ms. Stephanie showed up to fight for me and I ended up with a three-day suspension instead.

I felt bad that I couldn't watch Rome's back. I felt worse when Ms. Stephanie collected me each day of my "suspension" to spend it working with her brother. Mickey J had gotten busted for something and spent part of his "sentence" cleaning graffiti off buildings and spots where it was never gonna come off. But he showed me how to scrub and talked to me about fighting.

The one thing he commented on was the fact that I didn't have any bruises anywhere, and that sometimes covering for my friends wasn't really helping them. I shrugged and he nodded, then we went back to scrubbing. Mickey J was cool. Even Jasper liked him. Ms. Stephanie called him a rabble rouser and they'd get into some fights, but he also showed us more about fighting, weapons, and gambling than he probably should have. He also got us our first jobs as runners where we could make cash of our own.

But we'd never tell.

8

The clubhouse atmosphere was more like a funeral than it was home. No music played. No television blasted. No one was playing pool or video games. Hell, no one was down in the common room at all. When we did see each other in the kitchen, it was silent conversations and long looks.

Raptor took up every ounce of oxygen in the place. I'd given him a few days to acclimate, but I was done with not seeing Dove. Rome had taken her the phone, but we'd had no word. Fair, she may have no interest in talking to us.

The look on her face the other day had gutted me. It wasn't just the betrayal and the fury—it'd been the hurt. Then Liam dragged her out of here on Raptor's orders. Three seconds after that door closed, I was ready to slug him. I hadn't raised a single fist when he'd plowed into me over taking his sister. Nor did I back down from admitting my interest.

She wasn't *just* his sister any more and he needed to

fucking get that through his head. But until we found a way through Raptor's armor to Milo again, I didn't think any of that would go over. Frankly, the last place I wanted to be was the clubhouse today, but I'd taken too many shifts at the ink shop and my manager told me to get the fuck out of there, he wasn't paying overtime. So now I had three days with nothing to do in front of me.

You knew it was bad when even the rats were skipping out on being around. They were so silent even when they were here. Raptor had cut two of them loose the first day he'd been back without explanation or even comment, just told them to get lost and don't come back. My head was pounding but at least no one was in the kitchen this morning. Rome had been all but a ghost. Jasper I'd only seen twice and both times, his bruises looked worse than the last, but he'd also been with Raptor.

Hopefully they were talking.

Kellan had vanished to his shop. He could usually mediate anything around here, but he wasn't in the mood. The guy Liam and Kellan brought back from the shop hadn't answered one damn question and Raptor put a bullet in his head for even thinking about touching his sister.

That, Raptor had pointed out, was exactly the kind of heat we didn't need, nor did she. Well, no shit. But I kept that particular opinion to myself. Even Doc seemed warier of Raptor than normal. I'd swung by the clinic yesterday to see if he'd heard from her, but he told me no. When I asked if he'd tell me no even if he had seen her, he only said if she asked for his silence, he'd give it. But she hadn't and no, he hadn't seen her.

The worry in his eyes had been genuine.

Liam was also not answering messages. He wasn't the

chattiest person, though he also wasn't usually this much of a dick, no matter what Jasper thought. I pulled open one of the cabinets and got out some aspirin, then opened the fridge for a beer. Everything in the kitchen was nicer, there was more food stocked and we'd been using it more.

Because *she* had been here.

Now there were leftovers going bad that no one was touching, and I was pretty sure no one had cooked a single thing in days and the only thing we'd restocked was the beer.

Tossing the pills back, I washed them down with a long drink of beer and stared at the ceiling. There were cracks in it. Patches where the tiles had been broken or the paint chipped. We'd never bothered fixing it because we barely worried about cleaning up the rest of the place. But we had the last few months. Bit by bit, we'd been painting it. We'd been making repairs. Building the studio had been the biggest job we did.

Maybe we needed to do more of those.

I had time. We had paint.

Dragging my phone out of my pocket, I stared at it for a moment. No messages.

Maybe Liam had taken her phone.

That would fit with Raptor ordering him to get her out of here. And what the fuck was up with that? No one else had commented, but Liam had pulled up stakes from the Vandals right around the same time Raptor ended up in jail. So why was he suddenly all cozy again?

I wasn't a complete idiot. Rome hadn't been surprised, so he had some idea of what was going on, but Jasper? Kellan? They were suspicious as hell. Freddie?

Well, fuck. Freddie.

I should check on him. I had legit not seen him in days

and he'd been more upset than we were about Dove's absence. Not that he said a word when he learned of it, he'd just turned heel and vanished upstairs.

Fuck.

My.

Life.

I drained the beer, dropped the bottle in the trash then grabbed a fresh one, before I headed out to the hall. I'd check on Freddie then drag him out to help me with the painting. Might do him some good. He only stayed clean when he really wanted to and I didn't want him retreating back into that hell if we could avoid it.

I was almost to the stairs when a snort of familiar, husky laughter hit me like a mallet. Ahead of me, in the hall, entering from through the warehouse door came an all too sweet, slender figure that I'd been dying to see for days. She was looking over her shoulder.

"Don't tell me you plan to follow me around scowling at everything. One, it's not attractive. Two, your face will get stuck like that. Three, I don't need the company." All the vibrant sass housed in her voice lit me and I grinned. Fuck, I'd missed her voice.

I'd missed her dismissiveness.

I'd missed her confidence in herself.

I'd missed the bite in her words.

Where so many others would have been afraid of us, she'd not let that slow her down. She was so much like Milo in so many ways, did Raptor even see it?

I was still grinning when she turned and spotted me. Her eyes narrowed and her lips compressed. Still in trouble with her.

Got it.

Over her head, Raptor glared at me. "You don't need to be here."

"I don't need to be anywhere else either," I informed him, but I didn't bother letting go of Dove's gaze. The last four days had been hell. "Welcome home, Dove."

"This isn't her home," Raptor grated out and cut between her and me as if to block my view. Then he let out a grunt and swung his head around to look over his shoulder. "Did you just slug me in the back?"

"Yes," she told him. "And I'll punch you in the nose if you keep this shit up. I don't care *who* you think you are."

I shouldn't laugh. I really shouldn't. She was calling him out in the worst way. Daring him to prove to her who was in charge as fearlessly as she'd called the rest of us out. If he were still Milo, if I could *trust* he was still Milo, that wouldn't bother me so much. Milo wasn't a brutal guy.

Raptor?

He'd lost something of Milo in prison. Or maybe it had been taken from him.

Still, the absolute confusion on his face was entertaining because for a moment, Milo flickered there and it was really fucking good to see him.

"There's no point in arguing with her," I told him, meeting her gaze again. "She's twice as stubborn as the worst of us and she can hold a grudge."

Raptor's confusion turned into another scowl. "You wanted to come here to use the studio," he said, then pointed down the hall. "Go use your studio."

She was going to dance, oh fuck yes. I made it one step forward and Raptor was in my face.

"Stay the fuck away from her."

"Man, don't do this," I told him as softly and as calmly as I could. "You had a right to knock the shit out of me the day you got back. I'll take that hit because we didn't tell you. I didn't know we had no way to tell you, but I didn't even try. That was on me."

Head tilted, Emersyn studied me. But I refused to take my gaze away. I wasn't lying. Not about this.

"We didn't tell you we'd taken her and we didn't tell her who you were. It really pissed her off 'cause she couldn't figure out what we were doing either. She thought we were gonna hold her for ransom and called us kidnappers."

A flicker of a smile curved her lips.

"And to be fair, we did keep her locked in a room, but she had to recover from a lot of injuries." Injuries we'd told him about. Raptor's jaw tightened at the reminder. To my surprise, Dove just shook her head.

"So you think he's my brother, too?" The direct question were the first few words she'd spoken to me and I'd take it.

"I know he is."

"*How?*" The plea to understand occupied every part of that single syllable. "How can you know that?"

Instead of cutting in, Raptor backed off a step. Well, that was something. At least he wasn't blocking me anymore. "Because he told me you were his sister a long time ago."

"And you just believe him?" Her brows pulled together. Guilt nagged at me. She really had no idea.

"Dove," I said, softening my tone and holding out my cold beer, cause she really looked like she could use one. "Milo never lied to me. He never had a reason to lie. I didn't meet you *before*. Jasper did. I think the twins did. But by the time I came along, you'd already been adopted."

Confusion clouded those eyes of hers and all I wanted to do was pick her up and hold her until she sorted this mess out in her head. Her fingers were light as they brushed over mine, but she took the beer.

She cut a look at Raptor and while I'd rather stare at her, I glanced at him too. The hopeful look on his face *hurt*. Fuck. He might have been in a filthy mood since he got out —with good reason—but this was the sister he'd worshipped for years. The sister he'd bled for, killed for, and fought to do everything to make sure she stayed safe and out of this life.

The fact she didn't believe him. That probably cut a hell of a lot deeper than I realized.

Raking a hand over my head, I sighed and she tipped the beer bottle up and took a long drink. The motion of her throat as she swallowed held my fascination almost as much as the way she wrapped her lips around the mouth of the bottle. Raptor smacked me upside the head and the blow barely hurt, but he made his point.

"Seriously?" he demanded.

I shrugged. "You're going to have to accept that Dove is a beautiful woman. More than that, you need to get over the fact that I want her. I'm not going to pretend otherwise to make you feel better, right wrong or indifferent."

Raptor gaped at me, but Emersyn's flash of a real smile flooded me with triumph. All hope was not lost.

"Are you going to dance, Dove?"

"That was my plan," she said, but she had her attention on the bottle of beer. "I need to think."

"Do you mind if I come watch?"

I crossed mental fingers, but the minute she lifted her gaze to meet mine, I knew the answer would be no.

"Not today," she said softly. "I'm not sure what I think of all this or how you all haul me around like you get to make decisions for me. I need to dance and I need to think. Raptor..."

He sighed.

She cut a look at him. "Milo," she conceded before focusing on me again. "He agreed to let me come use the studio and that I could have my phone—the one you got me—if I promised to not call Jasper."

The grunt that came from Raptor was so Milo, I grinned and didn't bother to hide it. This little bit had snookered him and he just realized it. "So, you have your phone?"

"Yes," she told me.

"Do you mind if *I* call you?"

"Do either of you care what I think?" Raptor asked, his tone dryer than the desert.

"No," she said and patted Milo on the chest. To me, all she said was, "I'll think about it. You should look after Freddie better. I talked to him for two hours last night and he's having a hard time."

Shock rolled over me and probably crashed into Raptor, but she pivoted on her heel, duffle bag over her shoulder and headed down the hall toward her studio. Yes, I might have let my gaze drift toward her ass and exhaled a sigh. There was no exaggerated sway to her hips, just a graceful glide and having felt the power in that tiny body as she wrapped around me, I had nothing but admiration and desire for her.

"Dude," Milo snapped but it was Milo, not Raptor and I fought back a smile. Because I'd missed Milo.

"I told you," I said, not looking at him until the door of the studio closed behind her. "I want her. If she'll have me, that's exactly where I'll be. Not apologizing for it. She's an amazing fucking woman, Milo. I always thought she was pretty and kind of sexy—" I ignored his scowl. "But getting to know her?" I look at that closed door. Like us, she had her own secrets. It wasn't just the bastard partner who raped her. Something else had happened to her. Fearless and vulnerable. She was my dove, and I'd kill whoever hurt her.

I glanced at Milo again, and met his gaze. "You know Jasper and Kellan feel the same way."

I shrugged. "They're my brothers. So is Rome."

"The fuck," Milo swore. "You all want her."

"I told you, she's a remarkable woman." I clapped him on the shoulder, the first time I'd felt comfortable doing that since he came home. "Let her dance, she's usually in a much better mood and she does think better when she's letting go to the music, and come check on Freddie with me."

Leaving him to chew that over, I headed up the stairs. I didn't even make it to the third one when he swore, and I had to swallow a laugh.

"Let me guess, Fucking Freddie is crazy for her, too." I almost felt sorry for him.

Almost.

But in Milo's head, Emersyn was still that little baby, she was still Ivy. He'd had to say goodbye to her and watch her from afar for so many years. My heart hurt for him. But Emersyn wasn't a baby and hadn't been in a long time.

He'd learn.

We all had. As it was, there was a bit more pep in my step as I climbed the stairs. Granted, I envied Freddie the fact she'd called him before she'd called any of us. Freddie, on the other hand, probably needed to hear from her. Even more than the rest of us. That was on us, too.

To my surprise, Milo followed me up the stairs. He was still grumbling and muttering under his breath. Maybe we should have eased him into this. I'd had time to make my peace with the others wanting her. Didn't even bother me if she wanted them, as long as there was space for me. Space for me to look after her and make sure she was all right.

Milo needed to get used to that. At Freddie's door, I knocked. Not planning to play games, I just said, "Emersyn's here and dancing, so you should probably grab a shower and some clean clothes if you want to come down and see her before she leaves."

The rush of sound from inside the room had Milo rolling his eyes and I just folded my arms as Freddie yanked the door open. "I already showered. She said she was coming. Is she dancing?"

"Fuck," Raptor swore and stomped away.

Yeah, he really did need to get used to this.

Just wait until he found out Doc had a thing for her, too.

SOMEONE TO WATCH
OVER HER

MILO

Laughter swirled around the whole bar. It was pretty crowded and not just from the performers who'd all shared cars or cabs over from the theatre. She'd walked, granted with an older couple, who were clearly crazy for each other, but she'd still walked the few blocks, so Jasper and I paced them while Kel brought Vaughn over in the car.

It had been amazing to see her up there on the stage. I tried to catch a show whenever they came to town, ever since Mickey took me to the first one. Ms. Stephanie was never supposed to tell me the family name who adopted her. Though, she'd not cared for how hush hush they'd made it. We had a deal, Ms. Stephanie and I. Ivy's health and safety had always been my primary concern. She'd been so little when our mama died. I doubted she could remember her.

Didn't remember the three days we were alone after Mama wouldn't wake up. I ran out of food and diapers. I couldn't leave to go to school, and I didn't want to call anyone. If they called Dad, I didn't want him to take me and leave Ivy.

No, she didn't remember that, and I was happy she didn't. Some of it was a blur to me, while other parts were crystal clear with flawless clarity. The day Mickey knocked on the door. I didn't know it then, but I did now.

Mama used to buy drugs and he was a runner. I didn't get it then. I didn't understand that my father was a dealer and what Mama cost him was in the product she used. So he left her to struggle on her own. When Mickey knocked on the door, I tried to keep Ivy quiet, but she wouldn't stop.

A sharp bark of laughter jerked my attention back to the present. Emersyn was gorgeous and she looked so grown up, even if she was tiny. Watching her dance had been impressive. There was a tremendous amount of power in the way she moved. Whether she glided across the stage, flew up in the air when her partner tossed her, or danced in the silks, winding her way up only to fall.

The smile on her face right now though, satisfied that little boy inside of me who'd made her a promise.

"Rome's back at the clubhouse," Jasper said from beside me. "Freddie's there and wants to stay the weekend."

"Only if he clears it with the group home," I told him. Freddie still hadn't aged out. "I don't want them calling the cops on him again."

It had happened more than once. If we could get him out, we would. The door was always open, but just like all of us, he had to get free of the system and finish high school. I swore that kid would get his degree if one of us had to drive him there every day. We'd taken turns doing it for six weeks, so he didn't give us too much crap about it now.

"Going outside to call," Jasper said, as he slipped off the

stool next to me. The atmosphere in the bar was electric. Celebratory. They'd completed a tour, this was the last night of this show—ever. Whatever she did next, it would be new routines, new music, new challenges. I'd kept track of her travels, so many cities here and abroad. The fact they were ending this close to Braxton Harbor made it a no brainer.

I had to come and see her.

With the tour over, she'd probably go home for a while to Bay Ridge. Or one of the other houses the Sharpe's had around the world. I'd worried about her education when she started doing the tours, but I read in one article she did a lot of work with a tutor who also traveled with the show.

So, I guessed that was something.

The couple she was with had given her alcohol, a celebratory drink. Her reaction to it made me grin. Even more, *their* reaction, showering her with affection made me grin wider. She had good friends and people to look out for her.

Sometimes, when I caught sight of her profile in some of those articles when she had that distant look in her eyes, she reminded me way too much of Mom.

It wasn't long before the couple left her and she was up and dancing with other girls from the show. The music in the joint cranked it up and I continued to nurse my beer. Jasper was on his second, but I wasn't too worried about it. When he came back in, he said Freddie had squared it, so that was all I needed to know.

My heart half-stopped when she bounced up to the bar not three feet from me, sweat glistening from her brow and requested water. The bartender zeroed in on her with a predatory smile and every muscle in my body clenched. No sooner had she downed the water than he passed her another soda. Like the one the couple had brought her earlier.

"Is he fucking flirting with her?" Kellan murmured, but I didn't look at him. I was watching the bartender watch my sister.

More, he leaned in toward her.

"Yo, asshole, drinks down here and hit on the pretty girls later," Jasper called and the bartender jerked his attention to us. He glared, but some of the heat bled out of his expression when we just stared at him back.

While Jasper ordered us another round we didn't need, I tracked my sister across the bar as she downed the whole drink like it was water then ran to join the dances. Every time she took a break, the way-too-fucking-friendly bartender would send over another soda to her table. Even with the chips she ate, there was no way she could handle that much alcohol.

When she vanished to the bathroom, I gave Vaughn a nod and he moved down the back hall where he could watch it. But she came out with a damp, flushed face and her eyes too glittery and far too dilated.

Not drugs. She didn't do drugs, but when she wandered out with her friends to smoke, I followed this time. Out under the street lamps, she looked way too pale. Worse, she looked like she was going to throw up. As if she'd heard me, she stumbled away from the building and the girls and into the darker alley.

"Kel," I said. "Go get the car."

I was already moving. I barely caught her before she would have fallen over. Jasper was two steps behind me and he handed me a bottle of water. He'd already wetted one cloth and I used it to wipe the perspiration from her face. She was sweating even more than when she'd been on stage and her pupils were definitely fatter than full moons.

"Rinse your mouth out," I told her, trading the cloth for the bottle. I had one arm around her, so she didn't fall. She did it, spitting twice before she took a long drink from it. A second later, she threw all that water up.

He nodded and she groaned a little. I thought she'd swore, and I chuckled. As tiny as she was, she was fierce.

"Fuck you." Her speech slurred. "Not nice to laugh at people being sick."

"I'm laughing because you danced your ass off while tossing back rum and Cokes like they were candy and then started smoking like you do it every day." Fucking bartender was going to regret that. I'd bet money he roofied at least one of those drinks.

"How do you know I don't?" Just like when she was little, angry and demanding. It was cute.

"'Cause you're puking and you look like shit. Here, drink more, just slowly this time. Sips."

At least she listened better. She took sips. "I hate you."

"Not the first time I've heard that. You want me to get one of your friends from inside?"

Instead of answering, she tried to take a step away from me and staggered three steps before I caught her again.

"Easy..."

"I need a taxi."

She needed more than that.

"The ground is moving."

"Is it?" Nothing about this was funny, but she was fighting so hard.

"Yes."

Right. I swept her up. She weighed next to nothing.

Kel was already pulling up to the curb and I carried her

straight to the car. Great friends she'd had. Not a single one even noticed me walking away with her.

"Where are we going?"

"To your hotel."

"I need a cab."

"One is on the way."

"You should put me down." That sounded like a cross between an order and a suggestion.

"You're not heavy."

"Yeah, it's not that. I'm going to..." The gagging sound was familiar, I twisted her around so she could vomit away from both of us. "Sorry." Oh, the fight was gone, now she just sounded miserable.

"It's all right, sweetheart," I soothed. Kellan was out and opening the back door. "Get something she can use as a barf bag. We're going to get her to the hotel. You two deal with Romeo in there." I caught Jasper's gaze and jerked my head back to the bar. I wanted his eyes on the bartender. Vaughn was right behind him.

"Got it," Jasper asked. "She gonna be okay?"

"She better be," I muttered or there was going to be a dead bartender by the end of the night.

All the way to the hotel, she seemed to drift in and out. I'd seen a roofie work before. The little fucker better be glad he had Jasper and Vaughn to deal with. My phone buzzed and I could hear the distant music of the bar in the background.

"Yeah?"

"Jackass had them on him," Jasper said. "He told Vaughn he only gave her half a one to loosen her up."

"Break his fucking kneecaps," I ordered.

"With pleasure," Jasper responded.

"Ow." Ivy sounded so unhappy.

"You okay?"

"Fine. Broken kneecaps would suck. Can't dance with broken kneecaps. Be stuck at home." She shuddered.

"No one's touching your kneecaps."

"Yay."

"We're here," Kellan said, shooting me a look via the rearview mirror as he pulled into the drive in front of the hotel.

I got her out of the car and she held out her hand to me. "Thanks for getting me back here...?"

Right, she was definitely adorable. Wrapping an arm around her, I walked her inside. I already knew her hotel room. We'd cleared the hotel when we'd found out she was booked here.

"Where are we going?"

"I'm making sure you get to your room, and you're going to deadbolt the door once you're inside. Clear?" Because I wanted her safe and sound.

"Clear. If I don't remember to thank you now, I won't remember in the morning," she said in such a small voice. "Sorry about that. Never...not even sure why it's this bad."

"Well, getting hammered on an empty stomach when you can't weigh even a hundred pounds wasn't the brightest idea." I really didn't want her thinking about being drugged. That asshole did it right under my nose.

"Sorry."

"It's not your fault."

"The bartender wanted to impress me."

Fuck the bartender. But I didn't say that.

I plucked the keycard from her hand and got the door opened so she could get inside. She kicked her shoes off and headed straight for the bed. "You have to lock the door." I tried to remind her, but she was already falling on the bed.

With a sigh, I got water, and found the aspirin packets some of the higher end hotels offered. Her head was going to hate her in the morning.

She pushed off the bed. "Right. Thank you again...?"

"You can thank me by not getting drunk without having someone there to watch your back."

"Deal." Good girl.

At the door, I glanced over the room. I'd have figured she'd have a roommate. But it was a huge suite, just for her. "You're going to be alone?"

"Yeah, it's just me. I have an early pickup tomorrow, so I'm just gonna sleep." She was still swaying, and yawning now. Her eyes were even half closed.

"Put your trash can by the bed in case you need it." Then, because I couldn't help myself, I touched a hand to her head and brushed a kiss to her hair. "Night, little dancer. Sweet dreams." I damn near called her Ivy. "I love you." I whispered those last three words before I forced myself out.

I waited a beat after I was outside the door and the lock clicked into place.

I love you, Ivy, I mouthed more to myself than anything else, and then pushed away from the door. I was at the elevator when Jasper sent me a message about the bartender's kneecaps.

Good.

Kel said nothing when I slid into the front seat. He waited until we were halfway back to the bar. "You okay, Milo?"

No, I wasn't. But I'd gotten to save my sister. I'd gotten to hug her and send her to bed. That was the closest I'd been to Ivy in over twelve years. "I'm fine," I told him. "Let's get the boys and go see what trouble Freddie got into."

9

Even I wasn't prepared for how much returning to the clubhouse would mean to me. The exile to Liam's had been uncomfortable, particularly with so many open issues between me and the guys. The lies. This Raptor—Milo, he wanted me to call him Milo—was my brother tale they all seemed to believe. Secrets they'd kept from me. It wasn't like I hadn't realized they weren't telling me everything.

They'd barely told me anything until that night Jasper took me to the hotel. That night we slept together and he told me about his plans and his dreams and his ideas. He talked about stuff he'd always wanted to do...

And not once had he mentioned this particular link.

Blowing out a breath, I tried to shed the irritation and anger itching under my skin like fire ants wanting to escape. One look at Vaughn and I'd been torn between running over to hug him and popping him for not telling me why they took me in the first place. They kept saying they'd done it to protect me. They'd done it to keep me safe.

For Milo.

They'd done it to protect me, for Milo.

Eyes closed, I tried to find some internal calm so I could stretch. The studio was quiet, cold, and smelled faintly of sweat. Reaching over, I picked out one of the CDs they'd made for me, choosing *Angsty as Fuck* and almost laughed.

Apparently, they had opinions.

Music on, I moved through my stretches, but when the song transitioned to Human by Rag'n'Bone, I slid back up to my feet and turned away from the mirror. I didn't need to see the room to move to the music as it began to fill my veins.

I did back walkovers from one side of the room to the other, before rising up on my toes to pirouette back to the center. The snap of my arms out in front of me only to drag them back like it took effort pulled the buried betrayal to the surface.

Betrayal.

Lies.

Anger.

Secrets.

Brutality.

It was a part of their lives and mine. Their lies or mine. Which were worse? Metallica challenged those thoughts and they were right. Nothing else mattered. People lied to protect themselves.

Secrets?

A tear slid down my cheek as I began to spin, snapping one leg out then back in again. Milo had been in prison. Why?

He'd been furious at the other Vandals—especially

Jasper, Kellan, and Vaughn. That was an easy one to guess. They'd been the three to bring me here. I hadn't known if it was them exactly, though I could guess. They'd all played roles in my life around the show, particularly Kellan.

The silks were pulled up, but I didn't worry about them right now. I moved with the music, letting it dictate every step, every motion. I needed to think.

Betrayal?

Who had they betrayed more? Me, by not telling me or Milo, by taking me? Was there some kind of gang code they'd broken? Was that why he'd been so angry?

From Kaleo to Sam Tinnesz, I turned it over and over in my mind and I couldn't really peg who had the greater claim to it. What did the guys owe me?

But Milo?

My stomach bottomed out as I slowed my motions and went still. They were his brothers, right? I might not know how gangs worked, but they talked about Raptor with reverence. They loved him.

The anger and the brutality made sense in that context. Night Beds began to sing their mournful ballad about Even If We Try. There was truth to be found in art. In music. Even as I stepped forward to the music, awareness swept over me and I found Rome watching me in the mirror.

When our gazes locked, he followed me toward the center of the room. His steps mirroring mine as I stepped back, and when I stepped forward, he retreated. It was almost like dancing together while apart. I extended a hand to him as we began to circle slowly, not quite touching him and he didn't move in any closer.

Like me, he was bare foot. Every movement, he followed, like he'd studied it and it wasn't until I spun away and came back and he caught me with my back to his chest that I realized, I was doing an old dance.

The fact I stilled had him pausing as well. We locked gazes in the mirror. "You've seen this dance before."

A single nod.

"More than once?"

The corners of his mouth tilted upward.

As tempted as I was to lean back into him, I took a step forward and his hands fell away from me. The music continued, but I pivoted to face him. Rome studied me. He wore an unzipped hoodie over a bare chest and soft, well worn jeans. Or at least they looked soft.

Dragging my gaze up from them, I found him smiling at me again. "How many times?" That wasn't the question I intended to ask, but those were the words that slipped out.

"So many," he admitted. "I didn't count. You have a YouTube channel."

I did. I'd forgotten about that. It was a lark in the beginning, but it gained traction and fans, it was a great way to let them know where to find me on tour.

"I subscribed," Rome admitted. "I like watching you dance."

"There's liking watching me and there's learning the steps."

He shrugged again. "I like to dance."

Blowing out a breath, I walked over to where the CD had segued into some tortured blues and turned it off.

"I'll leave," he offered when I picked up one of the towels they'd begun to store in here and wiped the sweat from my face. "You looked beautiful. Freddie and Vaughn said you were here."

"I'm surprised."

"Why?"

"Because Milo wouldn't let Vaughn come watch me."

Rome grinned, a full, honest, open smile. "I didn't ask Milo."

Turning around, I leaned against the wall and studied him studying me. "Thank you for bringing me my clothes and my phone."

"Liam took it." It wasn't a question.

"If you knew he would, why did you put it in there?"

"I hoped he wouldn't."

Reasonable, I guessed. "Thank you for the bear, too."

Another smile, this one a little shyer. "You kept him on the bed, even after you didn't want to be here..."

"He was yours." It wasn't a question and he nodded. "Shouldn't you have him, then?"

"He is where he needs to be." A brief pause, then he motioned to the door. "I can still go if you want to dance."

"I have been, for a while," I admitted, not quite ready to let him leave and at the same time uncertain of whether I should encourage him to stay.

"I can go get you some water."

"Then we'll run into Milo and he'll drag me back to my new prison."

Rome frowned. "Liam's place isn't so bad, is it?"

"Sure, if you don't mind Liam sleeping all day, nowhere to dance, and no way to leave."

Paint stained the hand he lifted to scratch at his jaw. "If you want to go out, I can come get you."

Surprise filtered through me, but at the same time. "Rome, don't you get it? I came back here because I chose to and now, I'm in another cell, where I have to get permission to leave."

The tension pulling his brows together tightened then

he nodded, almost decisively. "I'll fix it." Holding out his hand, he beckoned to me. "Water?"

I really was thirsty but the minute I left this room, I had a feeling Milo would drag me out to his car and back to Liam's we would go. That was something else... "Jasper is really angry with Liam because I thought he wasn't one of you, but the way Milo talks to him and trusts him..."

"It's not my story to tell, Starling."

Oh.

Well, at least it wasn't an out and out denial. Or ignored.

"Can I ask you one more question?"

When I hadn't taken his hand, he lowered it and narrowed the distance between us. "Ask me anything you want, Starling. I won't lie to you." I appreciated that. "If I can't tell you or it's not mine to tell, I'll tell you that, too."

Fair.

"How do you know I'm Milo's sister?" Vaughn said it was because Milo told him. Why did Rome believe it?

"Because I saw you when you were little."

That answer surprised me.

"You were a baby. You smiled a lot."

I stared at him.

"It was at our third foster home."

Third.

I swallowed. "But if I was a baby..."

"You were."

"How can you know *that* baby and I are one and the same?" I had a birth certificate. I'd been born a Sharpe. Everything about my life...

"Because Ms. Stephanie told Milo the name of the people adopting you." He frowned. "This isn't all my story to tell, but it is yours. You should know. The people who wanted to adopt you didn't want Milo. They just wanted a baby. Ms. Stephanie wanted to keep you together."

My head hurt so bad, trying to reconcile what he was saying to what I knew. Like a thousand tiny cuts were bleeding me out. If I wasn't a Sharpe, then Uncle Bradley...

I slammed the door on that thought.

"Talk to Milo," Rome said. "He was like me."

"What?" I couldn't quite focus on that.

With care, telegraphing every move he made, Rome lifted his fingers to tuck my hair behind my ear. "Liam was adopted, too. He said they would take me, but I didn't want to leave the others. I wanted Liam to have that life. He would have a good life. It was worth it. Milo wanted you to have a good life. So, we're the same."

The good life.

Right. I'd almost forgotten about that part. I didn't pull away from Rome's touch, instead, I grasped his hand.

"Maybe we'll get water now?"

"Good." He smiled, then threaded his fingers with mine. "I could come get you tomorrow if you want to see the painting under the bridge."

I kind of did. I remember to grab my shoes before we walked down the hall. A shout of glee welcomed us, and Freddie swooped into give me a hard hug, pulling me away from Rome.

"Boo-Boo is here! Boo-Boo is here!" he chanted like a lunatic. "I've missed you, Boo-Boo!"

Laughter escaped me at his antics and I swatted his shoulder. "Put me down."

"No," he said with a great deal of drama. When he darted his gaze to the left, I found Jasper and Vaughn both staring at me with hungry looks, and a really irritated Milo. Rome had stuck close to us. "I think Rome can take them, then you and I can escape. Whatcha say, Boo-Boo? Wanna make a break for it?"

Hell yes, I did.

But I had a feeling if I admitted that, more than just Milo would lose his mind.

Then again...

"Why not?" I told Freddie and he jerked, his eyes going wide as he stared up at me and I raised my eyebrows. "This is the part where we run, right?"

BUSTED

FREDDIE

I ran as hard as I could. My legs burned and so did my lungs. The backpack was really heavy. If I dropped it, I'd probably be faster. At the same time, I didn't dare. One job. I had one job to do. Needed the money. Needed to pay back a debt. Needed to stay alive.

One thing about this route, I knew it like the back of my hand. My shoes slapped against the stinking water in the alley, sending up a splash. I leapt for the first box, then onto the second and caught the ledge of a window before swinging my whole body up and over the fence. The six foot drop on the other side made my knees ache.

Barely pausing to catch my balance, I took off again. The guys behind me were all bigger and stronger. My best chance was to get away. Skidding around a corner, I followed the network of alleys, avoiding the piles of trash that accumulated around dumpsters. These narrow corridors were easily blocked by the huge trash trucks. Like a pipe cleaner, when they pushed through, nothing got past them.

The beeping ahead told me I'd timed it right. Shouts came from behind me, but even around the harshness of my breathing, they were too close for comfort. Another skid and I spotted the garbage truck lifting a dumpster high above itself and emptying into the bed. It made a crashing noise as it set the metal container back down.

Ignoring the reek, I leapt into the now downed container and ducked, half-holding my breath. My eyes watered as the trash truck passed me by, it would block their view and keep them from cutting around. The blast of its horn was a warning and left me half-deaf. From this angle, I could see the grayish vehicle's tail as it passed me by.

Trusting it to give me cover, I hopped out of the trash can and raced for the street. Two blocks and I'd be in the clear. I raced out of the alley and down the cracked pavement of the sidewalk. These were mostly industrial buildings. Not a place I planned to linger alone. They were closed, shuttered by the last recession. They were more likely to house crack dens, and homeless than anything else.

Safer to stay away.

One more block.

It fucking hurt to breathe and then someone stepped into my path. A guy easily as big as Jasper and the others. The look of thunder on his face had me skidding for a halt and my hand ducking onto my pocket.

"Give it to me," he ordered. I didn't recognize his tats or his colors and I didn't care. My job was to get this bag to one person and one person only.

This wasn't the guy.

I couldn't stay here. Any minute now my pursuers would get around that truck. Fingers closing around the cool metal, I tilted my head back and squinted. He was backlit by the rising sun. It made my eyes water.

"No."

Traffic passed us at just a steady enough rate that I'd have to time my dash across the street well or I was gonna get hit by a car.

Better a car than this guy though.

A sneer on his face, he lunged for me. I tugged the knife from my pocket and flicked the switch. The blade popped out and I sliced across his palm, then his arm as I ducked under his reach and I would have caught the back of his neck, but he turned. The blade sliced across his eye instead.

Blood spurted from the wound and he roared. Instead of clapping that meaty hand to me, he covered his bloodied face and I didn't stick around to see if I'd taken his eye. I shot across the street, narrowly avoiding the traffic.

The knife had gone slippery, but I didn't let it go. The warm blood on my cheeks seemed a clarion call of neon paint, with a pointer following me, as though screaming to everyone what I did. One block later, I hit the ground and rolled under the closing garage door and then stood again.

A half-dozen guys waited for me. Their leader took one look at me, then just held out his hand silently, I slipped the backpack off and held it out to him. He glanced at my right hand where I balanced the knife. Blood dripped off my hand and splatted against the concrete floor. The guy tugged the bag open and examined the contents then looked at me again.

Doors on the far side opened, letting in my pursuers. They were pissed. Every single one of them radiated hatred, but I ignored them. I kept my eyes on the boss. He barely spared them a look then he glanced at me again. "Whose blood is that?"

"Some guy tried to stop me on the street."

I didn't know him. Didn't want to know him.

The big man with the bag nodded. He tossed the bag to one of the other guys, then held out a hand to me. I had to wipe the blood off on my jeans to shake it. "Welcome to the Daybreak Boys, Freddie. I'll have another run for you next week." He gripped my hand once, then pulled a c-note out of his back pocket and handed it to me. "You fight for me that hard every time and you'll do just fine."

I still hadn't caught my breath, but he dismissed me with a look. The other guys—all runners themselves—gave me looks that ranged from disgust to admiration. I didn't care about any of them. I went for the bathroom to wipe the blood off my face and knife, pausing only long enough for Sonny to hand me the small blue bottle with four little crushed pills in it. Not a lot, but it would take the edge off.

"Boss said you can clear your debt with the runs, taking only half-payment 'til you're in the clear." Sonny pointed to the bottle. "That's a gift for passing the test. Next dose costs and you want to put it on your tab, you can when your debt's half-paid, until then, you use the money he pays you."

One jerky nod, but I pocketed the pills. I needed them, as it was, I'd already been sweating through my clothes before I started the run. I didn't sleep without help. The wrong thing and I slept but trapped in nightmares.

After washing up, I took off. I might be a runner for them, but that didn't make me one of them. Not yet. The less time I was around, the better. I didn't even make it two blocks before the car pulled up next to me.

Jasper sat in the driver's seat and Milo in the passenger.

Fuck.

"Get in," Milo ordered and I sighed. I climbed into the backseat and Jasper pulled away. Turning in the seat, Milo studied me. "Who?"

"It doesn't matter," I told him.

"Who?" The crack in his voice said don't fuck with him. No matter how hard I tried to avoid his eyes... yeah, that wasn't gonna work.

"I owe the Daybreak Boys."

"How much?" Jasper asked.

"I got it taken care of." I lifted my chin. I was almost fifteen. I could take care of myself. They were all out. So, I had to do something.

"How. Much." We were at a traffic light, so Jasper jerked a look over his shoulder at me and the anger there was nowhere near as quiet as the fury in Milo's voice. No, Jasper was *pissed*.

"Almost a thousand," I admitted quietly. It had been bad the last few months and they'd been fronting me for a while, but jobs were hard to come by at fifteen. Harder still, when I could barely keep up at school 'cause I was so damn tired.

They didn't say anything, but they didn't take me back to the group home, either. I slumped in the seat.

"Take care of it," Milo said after a while and from the corner of my eye, I caught Jasper's nod.

"I got it," I argued. "You don't have to fix it. I can do this..."

"Shut up, Freddie," Jasper told me. "You should have come to us in the first place. You're not one of them, you're one of us."

I didn't have the ink for that. I wasn't one of anybody's. But they didn't listen to me. When we got back to the warehouse they'd claimed as their own, Milo dragged me out of the backseat and Jasper left without a word. Alone.

"Come on, kid," Milo said in a rough voice that was more concern than angry. "Let's talk Kellan into cooking so we don't starve."

My stomach grumbled at the offer. The place was a wreck, but they were pulling it together piece by piece. I still couldn't believe they'd gotten the money for a warehouse, and they wouldn't tell me how or why.

Not yet anyway.

"Milo..."

He paused with his hand on the door and gave me a kind look. One I didn't deserve. "We'll take care of it, Freddie. You're not running drugs for them."

"But..." I started to argue.

"You're not. Because in two weeks, the Daybreak boys are all going to disappear." The words froze me in place. "They won't exist. Nor will the swill they peddle. You get me?"

Then he held out his hand and waited.

Fuck.

I dug the bottle out of my pocket and handed it to him, then the one-hundred-dollar bill. He shook his head as he closed his hand around the bottle. "Keep the money, kid, and you want work, you come to us. Not them. No more buying from them either."

Sure.

No problem.

I didn't have to sleep again.

10

Freddie hadn't taken me seriously, or maybe the fact Liam walked in with Kellan behind us prevented the escape. It took a potentially awkward moment and made it funny. Talking to Freddie on the phone the night before, he'd sounded so lonely. As it was, Freddie set me on my feet and then gave me another sideways hug.

"Missed you, Boo-Boo."

"Missed you, too," I admitted, and Freddie let out a little whoop and raised his hands like a champion.

"See, she missed *me,* not you bad boys. Ha. I win." He did a little dance and I laughed. "Check me out, Boo-Boo, I got the best ass, too, right?" Without an ounce of shame in him, he bent in half and started to twerk at me. My laughter turned to a snort, and someone growled, not that I paid them any attention.

Instead, I slapped Freddie's ass. "Don't wave that thing at me. You've told me stories about where you've been."

Whirling, he stared at me slack-jawed, even as his eyes

135

kindled with delight. "That wasn't my ass, Boo-Boo, it was my dick. So, you tell me which you want me waving at you, and it's all yours."

Snorting with laughter, I shook my head. Kellan groaned and gave Freddie a light shoulder shove away, but Rome snaked an arm around my waist and pulled me toward him before Kellan could touch me.

"Starling needs some water and some food," he announced and while I couldn't see his face exactly, the way Liam's gaze tracked immediately to Milo, suggested that Rome was talking to him and he wasn't asking.

"Food!" Freddie boomed. "Food sounds great. Kel's here, you'll cook for us, right? Since Boo-Boo is here? You wouldn't make us starve?" The clowning around pulled all the attention toward him again and Kellan rolled his eyes, but smiled. Maybe in the beginning I hadn't noticed how much of what Freddie did for shock value was designed to neuter the tension around us, but there was no way to miss it now.

Still holding me, Rome turned us around and gave me a gentle nudge toward the kitchen. It meant I had to go right past Vaughn and Jasper, as well as Milo. But with Rome at my back, I just raised my chin and eased my way through the throng. This close, I couldn't miss the mottling of bruises and swelling that still made up Jasper's face. Milo's face hadn't been bruised. His knuckles? Yes, but not his face. The cut over Jasper's eye had been stitched.

That gave me a little thrill of hope. Maybe Doc had patched him all up. He wouldn't be here if Doc hadn't cleared him, right? Vaughn's bruises were less pronounced, but just a reminder that Milo had walked back in here, after however long, and just started beating on his friends. The guys looked like they wanted to touch me, but they kept their hands to themselves. They had to back up for Rome, unlike with me. Once in the kitchen, it was another blow to realize I'd missed it right down the cheap linoleum and chipped counters.

Someone had actually wiped down the fridge and the table. The only dishes in the sink were coffee cups. Instead of sitting, I just went over and started washing the cups out. I didn't want to get cornered at the table or have them jockeying for position to sit next to me.

"What are you doing?" Milo asked, as he came to loom over me. Rome might have followed me, but he couldn't stop Milo from settling into the corner where the two counters met.

"Dishes," I told him. "See, you take the cups and you run them in hot soapy water and it cleans out these nasty gunk that sticks to the inside of the cups, because the hooligans who live here haven't figured out how to not let their coffee mold on the bottom."

Liam flat out snickered.

"Fuck off, Liam." Even the rasp of Jasper's familiar snarl made me smile. "Not all of us can afford a maid."

"Apparently, you can't afford to clean out your own cups, either," Liam retorted. "That sounds more like a personal disability or just laziness."

The crash of two bodies slamming into each other had me twisting, but Rome plucked the newly washed cup from my hand and began to dry it. "They're processing."

At the reminder of the last time those two processed with their fists, I flicked a look up to find him watching me. Yes, I very much remembered that kiss at Liam's. I remembered all of them.

"What the fuck is wrong with them?" Milo snapped, as he shoved out of the corner. The fight spilled into the hallway and I tried not to flinch at the sound of flesh slamming into flesh.

"It's their love language," Vaughn called, sliding over to take Milo's spot and I stared up at him.

"Their love language?"

He shrugged and grinned. "You talking to me now, Dove?"

"Clearly."

"Does that mean I'm forgiven?" The hope in his voice was sweet, but life was not that simple. I knew better before they'd taken me, I knew better while I'd been here, and I'd still fallen into the trap of trusting too much.

That wasn't going to happen again.

"No." I resumed washing the cups. There weren't that many and I'd actually gotten pretty good at it.

"When you're done, Sparrow," Kestrel said. "I'll scrub the pot and make you fresh coffee."

I eyed the sludge in the pot. "Do I want to know how long it's been there?"

"Nope," Freddie said. "Trust me. I think it's petrifying."

Milo shouted from beyond the kitchen, but I didn't catch what he said, only that the pummeling had stopped. Hopefully, he didn't resume it.

"It'll be fine," I said. "Hand me the pot."

I glanced over my shoulder at Kellan and studied him for a moment. He was also bruised, but the sorrow in his eyes was unmistakable. "Guys," I said quietly, and Vaughn's disappointment filled the air. "Could you give me and Kestrel a moment?"

Rome passed me the coffee pot and ugh, I was sorry I'd asked for it. Nasty didn't begin to describe it.

He pressed a kiss to my temple and then motioned with his hands.

"Yeah, yeah," Vaughn grumbled, as he pushed out of the corner. He touched a finger to my cheek or would have, but I leaned away from the contact and he dropped his hand.

"What, I can't stay and watch?" Freddie complained, but the other two ushered him out. Kellan moved to stand next to me as I focused on getting the sludge out of the pot. I did my best to only breathe through my mouth. This was so gross.

"You guys haven't been having coffee here?"

"We haven't been doing much here," he admitted. "It's been a little tense."

That made sense. Doing dishes was one of the things I'd kind of learned here, though I was familiar enough with washing out my cups and bowls, still, this was a challenge. Even after I got the worst of it out, there was a ring inside the carafe.

"Let me," he said, though his tone was more asking than telling. I shut off the water and passed him the carafe. Our fingers brushed but I didn't jerk away, and he didn't linger. "There's a secret to washing these when they get bad." He went to the freezer and pulled out a tray of ice and cracked it. Then dumped the ice inside. From the inside, he pulled out a jug of lemon juice and squirted enough in there that it actually killed some of the moldier scents in the room. The last thing he did was add tabasco.

My nose wrinkled. "What—why?"

No way could I keep the disgust out of my tone.

"Trust me," Kellan invited and began to swirl the concoction around in the carafe. It was astonishing, but it ate away at the nasty ring and the stain, with just a little swishing effort. He continued to swish it as he lifted his gaze and I finally forced mine up to meet him. "I'm sorry we didn't tell you. I'm sorry we didn't prepare you. And I'm sorry I couldn't find a way to avoid that ambush for you when you got home."

Home.

How, strangely appropriate. I wasn't even sure when that happened, but the clubhouse had kind of become a home. Maybe the only one I'd ever willingly returned to or wanted to occupy again.

"Can't reach us if the phones aren't on," I said. Or left behind.

"That doesn't mean I couldn't have told you." He dumped out the contents into the sink then began to wash the carafe out. It was kind of amazing how clear the glass had become. "I thought about it," he admitted. "More than once. Argued with Jasper about it. We shouldn't have taken you in the first place, at least not back here." Then he grimaced. "While I'm pissed about it, I'm kind of glad we did. I know, that doesn't make me less of an asshole."

"It wasn't your call though, was it?" At the end of the day, it had been Jasper's.

"We didn't have to take you to Doc. We could have taken you to a hospital. He'd have been pissed, but he would have gotten over it."

I almost laughed at that. Male voices rose outside the kitchen and I had no idea who was yelling at whom. "Then I wouldn't have met all of you and... " I 'd have ended up back either with the show or with Uncle Bradley.

If I'd been admitted to the hospital, my family would have been alerted. A shudder of revulsion crawled through me.

"Fuckboy would still be dead," Kellan promised, as he finished rinsing out the carafe and shut off the water. "He would never have laid a finger on you again."

"Thank you," I said in a quiet voice, not really wanting it

to carry, even if the yelling outside had climbed in intensity. "Did you tell him? Milo?"

"Not my story to tell," he said slowly. "I gave him loose details, but not the specifics. Then—you haven't told us much about what he did."

No and I never would. "It doesn't matter," I murmured and turned away. He caught my arm lightly and tugged me back. I could have yanked away and broken his grip, but I didn't.

"It matters to us," he told me firmly. "You matter to us." The intensity in his eyes locked me in place. "You matter to me. And I don't want anything else to ambush you—so you need to know. He talked."

My stomach rolled and I closed my eyes, blocking out Kellan's face, this place, everything.

"What he said will not be shared with anyone," he continued, giving my arm a gentle squeeze. "Vaughn and Jasper both agreed with that."

"Great, so all three of you know." That just made it worse somehow.

"Sparrow," he whispered and waited. Finally, I dragged my eyes open. "I know it's impossible to ask for right now. What he said? Doesn't matter, other than he needed to pay for what he did to you. Trust me when I say, all I wanted was to get you your pound of flesh."

"But what you did was for you guys," I told him. "Not me. You needed that pound of flesh. You needed him to suffer. You needed him to confess." All I'd needed was for him to leave me alone and to go away. I didn't feel an ounce of pity for Eric. I didn't then and I wouldn't now. "Don't tell me you did it for me, when you didn't."

Kellan frowned.

"But thank you for doing it all the same," I said then

reached for a towel to dry my hands. My stomach gurgled and he was still frowning when Milo walked back into the kitchen. Whatever argument was still happening had ended.

"Time to go," he said, and I glanced over at him. "Liam will feed you when you get back, but something's come up. Kel—get the car."

"Right." He put the empty carafe back where it went then left the kitchen. Pushing away from the counter, I followed Milo back out to the living room area. Only Liam and Rome remained. Everyone else was gone. Regret tugged at me. I'd had too little chance to really talk to any of them.

"I don't have a lot of time," Liam said.

"Make time," Milo told him with the same level of understanding he seemed to pay everything else. "She's hungry, get her in and secure. Then call me later."

"Yeah, yeah." Liam jerked his head toward the door. "Let's go Hellspawn, we have our orders." He didn't wait for me, just started walking and I flipped him off.

Rome grinned, then mouthed "phone" toward me silently and I nodded before I followed Liam. I wasn't even aware of Milo following me, until I stepped out into the hum of activity in the garage. The guys were out here. Some of them were armed. The rats were back, including the one who made my skin crawl.

The noise level cut abruptly at Milo's appearance. He walked me all the way to Liam's car. This was different from the low slung sports car he'd driven the other night. It was more of a beast than lean machine. Milo opened the passenger door to the Escalade and I climbed inside.

"Ivy—Emersyn," he said, and I glanced at him as I buckled my seat belt. "I know this is hard. I'll come see you soon. Bring you back for dancing here—but remember your promise."

"I haven't called Jasper."

"I don't want you to call any of them," he admitted, and I gave him a tight smile.

"Don't take this wrong way, but too fucking bad." I reached for the door and pulled it. There was no mistaking the fact he let it go as I slammed it closed or the way his expression darkened. Liam already waited in the driver's seat and he started the engine up with a chuckle.

I ignored him, my attention out there in the warehouse as the guys moved, hurrying from trucks to cars. Something was wrong. Even Freddie was out there working. Their expressions weren't friendly. I didn't ask Liam what was going on and he didn't tell me. Instead, he just ferried me back to my luxurious cell and left me with fast food to eat and a door I couldn't open.

But I had my phone. So, I downloaded the app and checked it for messages.

Bless you, Lainey. The money and the account was set up. I'd have to give them a password to get into the secure box, but it would have my ID.

I sent back a swift thank you after I memorized the data. When she didn't respond right away, I closed the app and deleted it off the phone again.

Now I just had to get out from under the thumbs of my keepers.

RUNAWAY

EMERSYN

"I can't believe you did this," I said for what must be the hundredth time. But Lainey was here, in Florida, the absolute *last* place I thought I'd see her. My twelfth birthday was in a few days, but she was still only eleven. Her birthday was after mine.

"It's your birthday," she told me, as imperious as any of Mother's friends. "Of course, I came. All I had to do was book a train ticket. What's the point of a credit card if you don't use it? Besides, I'm supposed to be at boarding school." She rolled her eyes dramatically. "Ever since Andrea was born, Mother can't be bothered with having me home except at Christmas when Grandfather insists and over the summer, which she can't avoid."

I burst out laughing. The show was on a brief three day hiatus as they finished their set-up. This was only my second time in Orlando. My keeper—Marta—had told me to stay in my room, use room service, and finish up the assignments my tutor left for me. If I was lucky, then I wouldn't see her for three days, which was fine with me.

The fact Lainey, of all people, had knocked on my door had not only freaked me out, it filled me with delight. Except... "My birthday isn't for another week."

"Yeah, I have mid-terms that week, so...we're celebrating early. This year, *today*, is your birthday and we're going to celebrate."

I opened my mouth to protest.

"Unless you have something better to do in here..." She glanced around my hotel suite with a look of boredom. To be honest, if you'd seen one, you'd seen them all.

"No," I admitted. "I don't. But I have to tell them if I'm heading out."

"Tell who?"

I opened my mouth again, then hesitated. Technically, I had to tell Marta, but she was already gone, hence the orders to stay in my room. This brief break hadn't been in the planning, it had been rather spontaneous, because two of the leads had gotten super sick and the venue had made changes since our last performance, so our riggers were having to re-engineer some stuff.

"Nobody. Where do you want to go?"

Lainey frowned. "We're in Orlando, where else would we go?"

I waited a beat as if I had no idea and then she grabbed a pillow from the sofa and threw it at me. I laughed. Of course, we were going to Disney World. I ran to grab shoes. I had on a t-shirt and shorts, which were fine even though I considered changing. Lainey rolled her eyes.

"We're going incognito, Em, you're not a Sharpe and I'm not a Benedict, and we're going to have so much fun!"

I glanced down at myself and then at her. Other than

rehearsals, I'd always had to dress up to go out with anyone. For now, I yanked my hair back into a ponytail, before grabbing my purse that I could string cross-wise over my body. I had some cash in there, two credit cards and my cell phone.

"I still can't believe you're here." It took balls to walk off your campus, get on a bus, then a train, come halfway across the country or all the way I guess, just to surprise me.

"I'm so fucking grounded," Lainey said with a laugh. "Worth it."

Downstairs, Lainey insisted on buying the tickets from the concierge and he arranged everything. Then we trotted outside into the humidity. Even in October it was warm. The hotel offered shuttle buses straight to the parks. That was convenient. No drivers. No security. No watchers.

No...

"Hey," Lainey said, linking arms with me. "Turn that frown upside down, we're gonna be princesses..."

Ugh. "I'd rather be the wicked witch."

She burst out laughing. "Okay, you be the *evil* queen, and I'll be..." Thoughtfully, she tapped a single manicured nail against her lower lip. "Cruella."

"You couldn't be cruel if you tried." I snorted.

"Like you could ever be evil," she countered.

We stared at each other and then started laughing all over again. Because the truth was, we both had it in us. Look at our families. While I'd never confessed any of my darker secrets to Lainey, she always seemed to hear what I didn't say. When the bus arrived, there were whole families getting on together. Kids laughing and dancing. Parents hustling. Grandparents shuffling.

It was already kind of magical. No one looked at me and

Lainey twice as we filed on board and grabbed a couple of seats together. Soon as we were all loaded, and the bus rambled on. It stopped at a couple of other hotels and eventually we were pretty packed. We took the bus all the way down to the park.

The day was pure magic. We rode every ride, laughed and teased as we stood in line. We ate the absolute *worst* food. Well, worst in the fact it was utterly full of carbs and fats and all kinds of unhealthy stuff. We got flavored ice. We got ice cream. We bought each other ridiculous presents from crazy glittered ears to villain shirts so we could play our parts.

By mutual, unspoken decision, we skipped photos with any of the princesses and made bee lines straight for any villains we could find. My favorite had to be the ones we took with Gaston. He was *hilarious.* As it grew later, we stuck around for the Halloween party, the parade, the music and the fireworks.

Elated exhaustion rode with us back to the hotel on the bus. Lainey had to stay with me tonight, we were gonna order room service and she would pick some movie out and then we'd have a sleepover. It was gonna be perfect.

Except when we got back to the hotel, Lainey stopped dead in her tracks. "Oh, you've got to be *kidding* me." The snarl in her voice had me pulling up short as I stared ahead.

Two men stood there, well, men might be pushing it. They were definitely *older.* One of them was smirking, but the other wore an expression like thunder as he stalked forward.

Fear slithered up my spine at the look on his face, but I stepped right in front of Lainey. I didn't know who he was, but he wasn't going after my friend while I was here.

"Ignore him," Lainey said, moving up to hook her arm with mine again.

"Who is he?"

The guy in question barely spared me a look as he stared at Lainey. "Do you have any idea how long it took me to find you?"

"Not long enough," she told him. "And this is my mother's lover's son, or as I like to refer to him the human version of period cramps."

The guy behind him burst out laughing and Mr. Period Cramps glowered. Utterly unimpressed, Lainey urged me forward. We took two steps, and I thought the guy was gonna do something, but he just let out a snarled breath.

"If you wanted to come see your friend," he said finally, sparing me a look for the first time since we'd arrived. "You should have just said something."

"Adam Reed, I don't have to tell you anything. In case you missed the memo, let me be clear, you're like a cloud. A big, dark, ugly storm cloud and when you go away, it's a beautiful day. So, buh bye."

We continued past him and almost reach the laughing guy when Adam said, "We came all this way and we're not leaving until your ass is in the car with us and on the way back to school."

"Sorry, my ass doesn't detach—unlike your personality. Maybe you should put a bag over it or something."

All the way to the elevator, they shadowed us, and the last thing I wanted to do was get trapped in that small box with them.

"Six in the morning," he ordered. "Meet us down here and don't try to sneak off somewhere."

"Six?" Lainey snorted. "Too bad your brains don't match

your looks. I'll be down by ten." She waited until the elevator doors almost closed to add. "Maybe."

I stared at her, a little awed and she gave my arm a squeeze. I hadn't missed her shaking. "That's Adam?"

"That's Adam," she confirmed.

She'd had the worst crush on him a few years ago, but then said he'd turned into the devil and the last thing she wanted to do was deal with him. Ever.

It didn't help that her mom was having an affair with his dad.

"He must care if he came all this way."

The laughing snort she answered with didn't sound as mean-spirited as she had downstairs. "Adam lives to make my life hell. So, if he wants to wait until morning. He can wait. It's your birthday and we're here to celebrate."

Once back in my room, we both took turns getting showered and changed into comfier clothes. I'd gotten a bit of a sunburn, and I hated to tell Lainey this, but I was also exhausted. She'd ordered room service and when it arrived with an actual birthday cake on it, she looked surprised and then grinned at me.

"Happy birthday, Em."

I hugged her fiercely.

"Blow out the candle, goober," she teased and I grinned at her.

Somehow, I didn't think she'd known about the cake before and I was almost terrified to look at the card. But it wasn't from Uncle Bradley at all. When I showed Lainey the card, she just rolled her eyes.

Happy Birthday, Miss Sharpe. The cake is for you. You both look like you don't eat enough. - Adam Reed.

Weirdest birthday card I'd ever gotten, but the cake was awesome. So was Lainey. We stayed up most of the night talking and she only woke me up at lunchtime to tell me Adam had gotten tired of waiting. I hated to see her go, but I was also glad she came.

"Don't let him give you too hard a time," I told her and she just grinned.

"That would require me listening to him and I've long since learned how to tune him out."

Just like that, she was gone.

She blew in one day and out the next.

I fell back on the bed, replete with way too many calories and fun.

If there was such a thing as a perfect day—this had been it.

11

EMERSYN

It was late when I woke to Rome sliding into bed with me. For the past three nights, ever since I'd gone to the clubhouse, he'd shown up at Liam's and climbed into bed with me. It was almost always well after I'd gone to bed, no matter how late I stayed up. The first night, he'd slid in, wrapped around me like I was his personal teddy bear, and then gone right to sleep. I would have protested but it was the best night's sleep I'd had since coming to Liam's.

When I woke in the morning, he was always gone. I kind of hated that. Like I'd dreamed he'd shown up, but the depression in the pillow next to where I lay and the occasional blond hair, said I hadn't. Then one morning when I woke to the empty bed and the smell of bacon cooking, I had a sinking feeling like—what if it were Liam coming in there to sleep and I just thought it was Rome?

No. I could tell them apart. Liam was *not* a cuddler.

Still, I couldn't repress the shudder at even the suggestion he'd take advantage of the situation. He'd had plenty of opportunities and hadn't done a damn thing. In some ways, he, like Kellan, had been the most honest with me. Even Doc seemed to have known, though when...

It hit me as I sat up in bed and hugged my knees. Doc figured it out that day at the clinic when I'd gestured to the poster and said it was me. Something about it had shocked him. So he'd known then, and he also chose not to tell me.

Ugh, thinking about it just pissed me off all over again. A more reasonable side of me argued they were Milo's friends first, so of course he had their loyalty. But dammit... what about me? The minute that little pathetic voice whispered out from the dark corner, I slammed that door shut. We could—I could take care of myself. I had for a long, long time.

I also knew true loyalty. I had Lainey.

With the exception of Rome's company at night, I'd not seen anyone else. I didn't even know if Liam had come home in the interim. He certainly didn't during the day. Not bothering to get dressed, I padded out to the kitchen. Every night Rome had stayed, the one thing he'd left was a new t-shirt for me. They always smelled like him.

I'd worn Vaughn's shirt the night before and there were now two shirts on the foot of my bed, folded neatly. It was kind of funny. At this rate, Rome wasn't going to have any shirts left. Not that I minded. He certainly wasn't wearing the shirts when he came to bed. The twin working the stove in the kitchen, however, wasn't Rome.

The tattoos on his back were wrong, so I just swallowed back the sigh and went to pour myself some coffee. "Good morning, Liam."

"Morning, Hellspawn. You look like you just rolled out of bed."

"I kind of did."

"Huh." This close to the bacon, I didn't care how irritating he was. My stomach gurgled, and grumbled loudly. His snort of laughter irked, but I filled my coffee cup and then because unlike some people, I wasn't a complete asshole, I topped off his before I started another pot. Liam drank his coffee out of huge tumblers, just like I did. Between us we could empty a pot.

He was removing bacon from the pan and setting it onto a plate with a paper towel. No sooner had he added like a dozen pieces of crispy fried bacon, then he began putting fresh strips in the pan to sizzle and pop.

I cradled my coffee cup to myself and tried not to drool over the bacon. But it smelled fantastic and right now, I'd kill for a hot dog from one of the street vendors.

"If you're hungry, Hellspawn, have at it. You're not getting waited on here." The comment jerked me out of my reverie, and I glared at him.

"Of course, I'm hungry. You've been gone for three days and the only thing you have in your freezer are those prepared frozen meals."

He took a big swallow of his coffee as he twisted to look at me. Since he was basically wearing sleep shorts and nothing else, I kept my gaze up, which meant I didn't miss the speculative look in his eyes—or the fact a lot of his bruising had healed. That was a good thing.

"Right," he said slowly. "You don't know how to cook." It sounded like he was talking to himself more than to me. "You don't like the food in there?"

'It's fine, but it's way too carb heavy. I'm not big like you. I need proteins and lots of greens. Fried foods—even bacon—unfortunately aren't ideal. I can't afford the fat."

The derogatory note in his snort was an insult. "Trust

me, Hellspawn. You're a lot of things, but fat is not one of them. You're practically skin and bones."

"I'm an athlete," I reminded him. "A performer. I have to wear skintight costumes and fly. That means I have to maintain a low BMI, every extra calorie will show up somewhere and eventually..." I locked that thought down, I didn't need to share my plans.

He turned the bacon over on the pan and picked up the plate with the fresh cooked bacon and slid it over to me. "Eat."

Mutiny tightened my jaw at that command. I'd rather starve.

By the time he finished cooking his bacon and piling it on two slices of bread, I still worked on my coffee, no matter how much my stomach protested.

"Be stubborn all you want, Hellspawn," he informed me around a mouthful of food. It was entertaining that he managed to say anything at all without spitting. That took some practice. "But we have work to do today, and I don't need you fainting on me."

Work? "What are you talking about?"

"Eat your bacon and I'll show you."

He took another bite, the dare in his eyes irresistible.

"You're a jerk."

"You're a brat."

I bristled at that description. But I finally picked up one of the pieces and took a bite of it, defiantly. I would not moan at the taste of it on my tongue or how the salty meat just hit the right way. My stomach, little traitor, made all the noise for me so I just turned my back on him to eat my bacon in peace.

While it took some effort, I could pretend he wasn't there. I focused on him not being there as I worked out another plan to slip my leash and leave. The first time I took off, I had no plan. I'd gone straight to the hotel and nearly right back into Uncle Bradley's control. No, this time I *had* a plan. More, I had resources. I just had to get out of my new cell. I'd tested every single one of the windows.

None of them opened. Probably a good thing because the building didn't have much in the way of ledges. No, it would have to happen the next time Milo took me to the clubhouse. If I took my phone with me, I could get out the way I had before, straight out the roof and then down the side. Once I got the money and the IDs and got somewhere safe, I'd call the guys.

Or maybe I wouldn't.

No. Flashes of Kellan's face as he apologized to me and the sadness in Vaughn's eyes chastised me for the thought. Freddie's loneliness pulled at me. Did they have any idea how isolated he was? Or how much pain he was in? I was only guessing at it but then—I saw a lot of me in Freddie and I wanted to do for him what Lainey had always managed for me. Give him a way out of the darkness. Rome's promise without a promise to fix things, and even Liam's grudging care, were enough to remind me that none of us was happy with this situation. I had no idea where things stood with Doc, but I still owed him—if nothing else —because he had promised to help me and kept his word.

Yet despite all of that, it was Jasper's bruised and swollen eyes that called out to me. We'd had a few hours. A few hours to truly connect and I wanted to believe in it and at the same time, I couldn't shake how willing he'd been to let Milo brutalize him over me. That he'd done something wrong and betrayed Milo—but had he betrayed him because he took me or because we had sex? Or both?

That was a question I wasn't sure I wanted to ask.

A hand landed against my ass in a stinging slap and I spun, cracking my tumbler against the side of Liam's face. Thankfully, it was empty. But it still hit hard and he jerked back. "What the fuck, Hellspawn?"

"Don't you ever slap me on the ass." Embarrassment vied with rage as I glared at him. Liam had put a hand to the side of his face and there was a hint of a red welt where I'd hit him with the metal lined tumbler.

"It was a joke," he said slowly. "I asked you if you were ready a couple of times." It was only then I realized he had changed. He wore a sweatshirt with the sleeves pushed up, baring his forearms and sweatpants. He even had on running shoes. He kept his hands, palms forward as if raising them in surrender. "I thought you were just being stubborn. Like earlier."

My racing heart jabbed me in the ribs as I tried to process all that information. The bacon was gone. I'd finished the coffee. But I hadn't been here, at all. I'd been at the clubhouse, in my head, trying to sort out all these complicated feelings. Did I want answers or not? Still, Liam didn't move.

"I'm sorry," he said, his voice a notch softer and in a tone similar to the one he used with Rome. "I didn't think. It won't happen again. No one will hurt you on my watch, Hellspawn. I promise you."

Nothing about his words rang false and I nodded slowly. "I'm sorry, I didn't hear you."

"I'll knock on the counter or something next time." He mimed a knock, like he would on the door.

"Thank you..." I licked my lips as I eyed the red mark on his face. He'd been bruised up before but most that had already faded and now there was a fresh, livid reminder of me hitting him. "I'm sorry I hit you."

"Don't be," he said easily. "I totally fucking deserved it. At least you didn't try to break my nose this time."

A huff of a chuckle escaped, as I curled up my hand into a mock fist. "You offered to train me when I did that."

"Offer still stands," he said. "In fact, if you'll take that very skinny, not remotely carrying an ounce of fat on it, ass into your room and get dressed, you can go with me to one of the places I train. Get you out of here and some fresh air and maybe a workout. It won't be the dance studio, but depending on where the boys are today—I could always break you in so you can do that, too."

Break in... "You have to break in when you go there?" I was already walking so he trailed me, but kept his distance. I appreciated the lack of looming and some of the tension in my shoulders and back began to ease.

"Have to?" He leaned against the wall next to his bedroom door as I slid into "my" room and since we were talking, I left the door cracked while I hunted out workout clothes. "Not really. Want to? Hell yeah, I love getting around the shit they try to put up to catch me."

That didn't make any sense. Except... "That's how you knew I went out the roof?"

"Very good, Hellspawn. That's one of my favorite ways in. Hard for a lot of people to get to. You either need some serious upper body strength or be limber as fuck."

I tugged on a pair of leggings. The only sweats I had were the guys' and they were too big to really move in. I slipped off Vaughn's shirt, then added a sport's bra and because I was in the mood, I pulled a netting shirt over it. The white netting showed off the dark blue sports bra perfectly. I pulled the door open. "Running shoes? Or dancing?"

He glanced down at my bare feet. "Running for now, we

may have to buy you another set—but bring your dancing shoes, too in case we do break-in." A sudden grin split his face and it really transformed him. For a moment, I couldn't shake the resemblance to Rome. It was right there in their smiles. "Imagine Jasper and Milo if they get back and we're just in your studio while you rock out without anyone knowing. They'll pop their corks."

At the gleeful note in his voice, I laughed. "Can I ask you a question?"

"You just did," he retorted, but his eyes were still smiling.

"Smartass."

"Thank you." I rolled my eyes, but he just grinned and curled his fingers. "Ask whatever you want to, Hellspawn."

"The guys all act like you aren't one of them—except Milo doesn't. He acts like you're a Vandal. So—are you?" I hadn't really looked for his Vandal tattoo. I mean, I'd seen him naked a few times now, because it had taken him a hot minute to remember he wasn't here alone. Still, I had tried to respect him and not stare.

Sitting on the edge of the bed, I pulled on my socks, then shoes as he contemplated me from the door.

"That's not an easy question to answer, Hellspawn."

"Let me guess, it's not your story to tell?" Because if it was a yes or a no, that would be that. The fact he couldn't give me a definitive answer was kind of a definitive answer.

"No, it's my story," he said, as if he needed to weigh and measure each word before giving it voice. "But knowing the answers would only leave you with more questions. It's safer in some ways for you not to know. So... suffice it to say I've known those guys for a long time. My brother is one of them. I'll have their backs even when they think I don't."

"Milo knows you do." That wasn't even a question, I

pushed off the bed and stood up. I should probably pull my hair up into a ponytail, but I didn't want to break this connection we'd forged.

"Yeah? Why do you say that?"

"Because he sent me here with you."

The corners of Liam's mouth tipped down, his smile fading. The sobriety in his eyes and expression made me long for the smile to come back.

"Hellspawn, when I was adopted, Milo looked after Rome for me. He kept him safe. I owe him a debt I can never repay. Keeping his baby sister safe is the least I can do." He held up a finger before I could protest. "There's a lot of ways to answer that question you have. But all you need to know, is Milo asked me to take care of you, so I'm going to. Okay?"

I swallowed and nodded. "Rome said he and Milo were alike and that you and I were..."

"Yeah, we were the lucky ones," he said without any irony, but there was also a bittersweet sadness beneath it all.

"Were your adopted parents bad people?"

"No," he said softly. "They were much worse." I frowned and he sighed as he turned away. "They were amazing, kind, and forgiving. They deserved a much better son than they got."

That made my heart ache.

"My turn to ask you a question," he called, as I grabbed a hair band and pulled my hair up and back. I made sure to get my phone and wallet, too. If I got my chance today, I'd be better off not wasting it. It all went into a little bag with my hairbrush and dance shoes.

"Okay."

"Why won't you wear any of the clothes I got you?"

I stared at the closed closet door for a long moment

before I walked out to meet him in the hall. There was no judgment on his face, just real curiosity.

"All my life, people have dressed me to be what they wanted me to be." It was the simplest answer, stark and truthful. "I don't want to be dressed by anyone else to be their doll on presentation."

"So you didn't like anything they picked out?"

I shrugged. "They wanted me to look perfect for you, it's what they kept saying over and over. I'm sure they meant well..."

He nodded slowly. "When we get back, I'll give you some catalogs. Flip through them. Pick out whatever you want. Doesn't even have to be from. *Le Belle Âme.*"

A scoff escaped me before I could stop it. "I still can't believe your family owns those stores."

"Eh, they're pretty cool and I know way more about women's fashion than I ever wanted to, but the models are hot and watching women parade around in gorgeous outfits or even less? Not a bad life for a teenage boy."

We were out in the hallway and waiting for the elevator. "That's awful."

"I didn't mind it." He had to be teasing. "I figured you'd at least know the store, we've got a huge one in New York and another one in Los Angeles."

The cold went flush down my spine again. "I'm aware."

"Right, dressing you up like a doll. Got it." He motioned for me to get in the elevator first and I leaned against the wall as he pushed the button to take us down to the garage. "You know...if you ever want to talk..."

"I don't," I admitted.

"Okay. If that changes..." He let it hang out there and that was kind of him. The offer coupled with the hall confessions and his earlier apology all beckoned me to trust him.

But I'd already learned my lesson.

"Are you really going to teach me how to fight?" I asked.

"Do you really want to learn?" That was a challenge if I ever heard one.

"Hell yes, I want to know how to fight." I wanted to know how to make sure no one ever touched me again unless I wanted it.

"Then I'll teach you." He held out his hand and I clasped it for a firm handshake. It was kind of ironic, that for the very first time, some of the unease that had been living in me since Milo banished me to Liam's, finally settled.

He may not be my ally, but he could be an ally in teaching me how to fight.

I could live with that.

12

LIAM

The whole drive to the gym, I turned the Hellspawn's reaction to me over in my head. Granted, I had smacked her ass, but I'd also said her name twice and she hadn't even registered that I was there. It hadn't even been an especially hard slap. Had it crossed a little line? Probably. But between the mouth on her and the keen intelligence in her eyes when she retaliated verbally, I half-expected her to rip into me.

I'd have deserved it. Granted, I wanted a reaction, but I hadn't expected the hit. I should have after the whole 'princess' incident. Why she hated that nickname, I had zero clue. Not even the little bit of hunting about her and her family I'd done had gotten me very far. More than one of my sources just said to stay the hell away from them.

That was just waving a red flag at a bull. I'd been trying to arrange a meeting with her uncle, but so far, that had proven almost as fruitless as turning up dirt on the Sharpe family. Everyone knew them, no one talked about them. In a world where money shaped lives, laws, and the politics of it all—they were virtually untouchable.

Bullshit.

The uncle had put me off twice. Both times with what seemed like rather valid, if convenient excuses. He was, however, planning to be in Braxton Harbor at the end of the month. So, he was going to come to me. Right. If that didn't set off alarm bells, I wasn't sure what else would.

Emersyn's gaze remained fixed out the window and away from me. I didn't like it when she ignored me, but I also wasn't going to pick on her to get her to pay attention to me again. The ferociousness in her strike had actually hurt, but it had been the wound in her eyes that gutted me. For a split-second, the icy mask of indifference she seemed to wear around me slipped and she was that girl in the alley again.

The Hellspawn, fighting for all she was worth but she was already bleeding out on the inside, like the death blow came long before she began to fight. That thought sobered me faster than anything and I ground my teeth together.

"Do you fight professionally?"

The question came out of nowhere in the silence of the car. I hadn't even turned on the music. She hadn't questioned my taste in the classics and I hadn't volunteered how soothing I found them.

Still, I latched onto the opening while I kept an eye on our tail. After Rome pulled the plug on those guys watching my place the other day, I'd caught a couple of others either watching the place or trying to track me. If this kept up, we were going to need a different method of body disposal.

It was also why I'd been staying away from the condo and leading our pursuers to quieter locations, where I could deal with them. It hadn't really occurred to me that would irritate her, particularly considering that every time I checked the cameras, she was either watching television, stretching—fuck me I could watch her stretch for hours—or hiding in her room. There were no cameras in the bedrooms.

I should probably change, but a part of me didn't want to.

"Liam?"

"Sorry," I said automatically. "Just thinking about other stuff."

"Oh, that's fine."

"No," I retorted. "It's rude. You asked me a question. The answer is—yes and no."

She frowned and I had to bite back a smile, because I suddenly had the weight of her glare slapping me in the face. "Thanks for clearing that up for me."

"Pull back your claws, Hellspawn. I fight because I enjoy it and I happen to be really fucking good at it. I tend to stick to the underground cage matches."

"Why not the professional circuit? MMA fighters, the good ones, they make a lot of money these days. Endorsement deals and even payouts on big fights." She didn't even give me a chance to respond before she said, "But that puts your face out there and then people know who you are, and it's hard to move around quietly when everyone knows your name."

A smile tugged at my lips. There was such a forlorn note there at the end of sentence. It was sad, not funny and yet, Hellspawn vulnerable was also kind of adorable. Not that I was ever going to tell her that. "More or less. There's money in underground cage matches, too." Then, because why the fuck not, if she stuck around like she seemed intent on doing then understanding the life we led would be even more important for her. "It's also a good way to weed out those worth recruiting and getting rid of snitches and other problems."

She trailed one finger against the door. "You mean if they can take the fight, you might offer them a place? Like one of the rats?"

Fuck no. I couldn't stand the rats. Most of them would never make it to full Vandal status. Ever. They didn't know that. They took the scraps they were given for a reason. "No, rats are the ones who come looking for a place to belong. The matches are a place I can go fishing for someone who would be good for a job or a position."

"Or to eliminate them if they won't take the job?" I didn't agree or disagree to that. "Have you ever killed anyone?"

I turned at the next light and followed the road toward the private gym space I'd arranged for us. They were closed for the day. If I wasn't going to workout at home and wanted a bigger place to train, I used Phil's. It was the first gym where I'd taken my training seriously. Phil was the first coach to tell me I could go all the way.

I didn't, he didn't complain. But Emersyn needed to burn off some energy and I'd promised to show her how to fight—if she ever wanted to learn.

"Yes," I answered. No point in lying. Milo had no idea what to do with his baby sister, but she was right. She had come back of her own choice.

She knew what Jasper and the others did to her former dance partner and abuser. If that hadn't sent her running screaming...then again, she'd also been there with Rome when those guys attacked them on the playground and later the bounty hunter at the shop. She wasn't squeamish. I liked that about her.

"Were they always bad people?" The question held a note of innocence to it and I mentally apologized.

"I've never killed anyone who didn't deserve it," I answered. While that didn't mean they were always 'bad' depending on how you defined 'bad,' the blood on my hands was never coming off.

I pulled into the parking lot at the gym.

"Stay inside until I come around to your door." I grabbed my gym bag out of the backseat before exiting.

She frowned, but did as she was told. There had been no tail on us when we left, but I'd swapped the Escalade for a dark green Lexus. Switching cars kept whoever my watchers were on their toes. But I wasn't going to take risks with her.

We were alone and the lot was not visible from the street. Keys in hand, I opened her door and let her out. I swore she gave me a long look before climbing out. I touched two fingers to her lower back to move her in front of me. Then pointed toward the doors. Once there, I unlocked them and nudged her inside before following and locking us in. After I keyed in the code to the control panel, I reset the alarm.

If anyone did decide to come in after us. They wouldn't enjoy the experience. The gym itself was pretty basic, but it offered all the latest equipment, including upgraded machines. Phil didn't want my money, so I just bought the stuff and had it shipped here. Two boxing rings, one on either side, a line of punching bags, a couple of speed bags, free weights, and an open, indoor track that circled the whole thing.

"Go warm up," I told her. "I don't know what you know about fighting, but I do know what you know about getting ready to do hard work."

That earned me a wide-eyed stare for a moment, like she hadn't fully processed what I'd said. In seconds, that surprised expression turned to one of delight and a fast smile creased her lips. Holy shit. The transformation held me riveted and my dick all but stood up in smart salute.

Emersyn was pretty in the most basic of ways. Too lean for my tastes. Definitely not enough curves. She had dark hair and dark eyes. She never seemed to care what she looked like and she didn't flirt with her body at all. But the moment she smiled, like that?

Fuck.

Me.

Sideways.

"How many laps?" she asked even as she slid into a full split and began to stretch out.

I was going to die from blood loss. None of it was going to reach my brain again.

Rome's girl...Rome wants her...Rome adores...

The litany meant absolutely nothing to my dick.

"Ten," I told her gruffly. "Then five more but at speed. If you can talk while you're running, you aren't going fast enough."

One simple nod. No argument. I hadn't even set my bag down much less got my dick to even consider backing off, before she was up and that tight ass of hers flexed as she jogged over to the track.

I pinched the bridge of my nose and focused on thinking of the absolute worst things possible. It took me about five minutes, and she was on her second full lap before my dick finally got the point.

Leaving the bag next to the punching bags, I stripped off my shirt and dropped it on top of it before I started running. I waited until she was ahead of me. I didn't want to invite more conversation. Not yet. It was bad enough she was basically wearing a sports bra and nothing else.

The knit top was see-through. Not that she had much in the way of tits. But they were still tits and that as—goddammit. *Stop looking at her ass.* If my dick could flip me the finger, it would have. I picked up speed to catch up to her. Maybe then, I'd stop thinking about how that taut body would feel wrapped around mine. There wasn't an ounce of spare anything on her.

The fact she complained about the carbs made me want to belt someone. They'd fed her some line about keeping her near-starved thin. One thing I knew from training, the more fat and carbs you cut out of a developing body's diet, the more likely it was to never achieve full curves.

I'd seen it in gymnastics at school. Those girls ate next to nothing, and half of them held off puberty for years because of it. Had someone done that to Emerysn?

All at once, I was waging a war against a homicidal impulse to drag the story out of her. While she was angry at everyone for not telling her about Milo, she had her secrets, too. Like her phone, for example, which now that she had it, I never knew where it was.

Vaughn had gotten her a burner, so I couldn't track her calls if she was making any. That bugged me. More than it probably should. She increased her speed and I matched it. When she did it again, I kept pace with her. No matter how in shape she was, I had longer legs and I ran religiously. Rome might be the only guy I knew who could outrun me, and that was only because the prick barely drove anywhere if he didn't have to.

He'd been running or walking or climbing since we were kids. Still, when she slowed, sweat gleamed on her arms and there was a kind of wild joy in her eyes, and I found myself grinning as we stopped near the ring.

"You're going to teach me how to fight."

I'd do any damn thing she wanted if it put that happy note in her voice.

"Yes, I am. The first place we start is that getting away is your first defense."

"Hence, the running."

I nodded slowly. "You're tiny, but you've got power, kid." Right, insist on the kid. She's too young for you anyway. "You run first. You get the hell away from whoever is after you. If they can't get their hands on you, they can't hurt you."

She seemed to soak the words up like a sponge and I had every ounce of her attention. She *wanted* this knowledge.

Fuck me, I was going to give it all to her.

"If I can't get away?"

"Then I'll show you how to make them let you go." I took a step closer to her. "I'll show you how to make them bleed and scream. When I'm done? No one is going to fuck with you again."

Ever.

TIMES LIKE THESE

MILO

"You can be such a jackass," Liam snarled as he looked down at his suit. It was wrecked. The lapel was torn. His tie was a lost cause and there was blood on his white dress shirt. The source of his ire was no surprise.

Jasper just smirked at him as he lit a cigarette. They were both bloodied, busted knuckles and while Jasper's eye was darkening, Liam's nose was bleeding. "Don't start shit you don't want to finish," was his only apology.

Some days, my life would be a fuck load easier if they could stop competing for who could be the biggest, baddest ass around. They were both dangerous. They were both skilled fighters. Liam might have training, but Jasper was a brawler and all raw talent.

It didn't hurt that he got a lot of practice while we were growing up. He was *always* ready for a fight. Not long after he showed up at the foster home, he'd gotten into his first fight—backing me. I was looking for a way out of the fight without the violence. You could outsmart people. You could out talk them. Sometimes, you could just plain trick them.

Frankly, some people were just that dumb.

Not Jasper. No, he relished a good fight. In fact, if he went too long without one the buzz of energy around him could give me a headache. Liam was just as bad in his own way, only he went to the rich school and they had some fucking fight club. It was like taking candy from babies or so he claimed. But every dime he made in those fight clubs he funneled back to us—to Rome.

"I had every intention of finishing it," Liam snapped back at him. "Tomorrow. *After* my date."

"Ooo," Vaughn intoned as he walked out of the clubhouse. The warehouse was ours. Well, mostly ours. The money I'd invested in smaller funds using an investment banker Liam found had generated a tidy profit. The money we made cleaning out drug dealers and their stashes got funneled into the account and cleaned.

Everything was under an umbrella name, since we were sixteen and legally couldn't own shit like this yet.

The place was a wreck, abandoned for years, but once a hub for storing pallets of all kinds of shit. A great spot to hold inventory coming from the port then being picked up by trucks to go elsewhere.

It fit tidily in with future plans. But right now, it served as a place for us to secure our gear, some weapons, and beer —though I preferred it if they didn't get hammered before school. So far, we'd managed to avoid that.

"You got a girl to say yes to you for a date?" Vaughn asked, as he cracked open a soda and handed me an unopened cold one. It was Friday night, and the group home didn't pay much attention to us until bed check, unless we had jobs.

That was why we all had them, even if we didn't actually go somewhere. The last summer working at the big hotel up the coast had been the most peace I'd managed since seeing Ivy leaving with her new family.

And fuck focusing on that, or I'd be maudlin.

"Yes," Liam snarked right back at Vaughn. "A real girl. Nice tits. Great ass. She can also ride a cock like a champion. And I can't fucking go like this."

Jasper laughed and I sighed, raising a hand before Liam could take a run at him again. Or maybe for the first time. "Kellan just picked up a new suit. It might not be that fancy, but go see if he'll let you borrow it."

Unlike Liam, Kellan had saved every penny he could for that suit. While he preferred to work on cars, he could get work for driving services if he played the part. He also had the fake IDs to cover the age gap and if we had someone we wanted to scope out, putting him in place to drive them helped.

We'd gotten really creative over the last two years. It wouldn't be long before we started removing the other gangs in the area. Not that any one of them was big enough to control the whole city.

We would be.

And we'd take it with violence if we had to, but we'd hold it through legit channels. Then we'd have money and be real players.

We had a plan.

Without another word, Liam nodded and headed inside. Jasper snorted as he blew out a stream of smoke. "It's not like it's gonna kill him. How many suits like that do you think he owns?"

I wasn't having this argument again. Jasper loved Liam like a brother and his resentment over the money was the fact that Liam couldn't stay with us. Not and be part of the new family, too. Even if Rome had gone with him, I didn't think Liam would have abandoned us. Still, until we all hit legal age, we had to play by their rules.

Or at least look like we were.

"What was so urgent you two had to get bloodied?"

Pushing away from the wall, Jasper motioned to the fridge. It was the most insulated room in the whole warehouse. It didn't actually work anymore. At least, we hadn't been able to make it work, but it was soundproof, which made it useful for locking people down if we needed to hold them.

I followed him and stepped inside with Vaughn when he opened the door. Then he crossed over to the inner door and popped it open. The dude sitting in the chair was a bloody wreck of bruises. Both of his eyes were near swollen shut and more blood dripped off his face to splash against the floor.

He barely moved at our arrival. Hard to believe he could still breathe, save for the rasping of his breath. Still smoking, Jasper crossed the room and jerked the guy's head up by his hair. "Meet Marty."

I raised my eyebrows.

"Marty shot Ms. Tennebaum's dog a couple of days ago."

He what? Any worry over Liam's suit erased.

"He threatened to shoot Ms. Stephanie today."

All trace of pity this sad fuck might have earned with his condition died.

"Didn't you, Marty?" Jasper asked, blowing smoke in his face as he used his grip on his hair to make him nod his head up and down. "What was that, Marty? Why did you threaten Ms. Stephanie?"

The guy made a sound that wasn't quite human. Vaughn slanted a look at me. "Cause he beats his kids and his wife, and she was coming back with an order to remove them from the house."

"So Marty here," Jasper said, releasing his hair and slapping a hand on his back like they were friends. But he'd already broken something in there, cause the guy let out a pained moan. "He showed up at her house with a gun. Unfortunately for Marty, it was my week to mow her yard."

Oh, definitely unfortunate for Marty.

I glanced at Vaughn. "Tell Liam to enjoy his party and get laid. There won't be anything left for him tomorrow."

No one threatened our people. Shooting the dog was bad enough. This?

Fuck him.

"Get some cold water," I told Jasper as I stripped off my shirt. "Let's wake this fucker up."

His grin turned near feral. I didn't have to tell him twice.

I rolled my head around and cracked the vertebrae. I needed to work off some stress.

13

JASPER

The last week had been hell. No, I hadn't spent it in prison, not like Milo had for the last three fucking years, but this week had been an eternity and I'd only gotten a brief glimpse of her at the clubhouse before Milo sent her packing again.

I'd brought a donut bouquet over to Liam's place and left it in front of the door. Liam, the prick, wouldn't give me the code and just said leave it there, he'd make sure she got it. He better have.

Every day I'd had to wait before she sent me a message had been an eternity. Milo caught me staring at my phone and I swore he smirked. I had a feeling that he was enjoying my pain. We'd been beating the shit out of each other every day for the last week. My bruises had bruises.

And he'd learned shit in prison. He hit harder. Faster. Smarter. He was our brain. The thinker. The one who worked out the plans a dozen steps ahead. Raptor had earned his name because he always took his time in the hunt for a solution, planning all the steps out, so that when he—we—struck, it was a surgical strike.

It had built the trucking company. The network of warehouses. The shipping. The mechanic's shop. It had shut down nearly all of the other gangs in the city. The drug dealers didn't deal shit where we didn't allow it. The cut they paid us went into rehab for those hooked.

We turned profit...

"Jasper," Milo ground out my name, and I glanced over to find him glaring at me.

"What the fuck did I do now?" Because I'd taken the beating the first couple of days. He'd had every right to kick my ass for fucking his sister. But it hadn't been about fucking. Well, yes, the sex had been amazing. My interest, however, did not begin and end with her pussy. Not that I was going to have that particular conversation with Milo.

Not while he was three-quarters Raptor all the fucking time.

"They're here," he said, his expression intent and I nearly groaned. It was just the two of us for this pick-up. He'd wanted to know what had been so damn important I'd been gone as much as I'd been around at the clubhouse. Why hadn't I made a better effort to reach out to him in solitary? We had access to guards. We could have made it work.

He wasn't wrong.

But this job wasn't the only reason I hadn't told him. Telling him Emersyn was with us would have just pissed him off worse than he was right now. At least in solitary, he wouldn't know she was missing. How the fuck he got that information, I would like to know.

Guess who wasn't in a sharing mood at the moment?

We were parked off the interstate at an abandoned

weigh station. Some of them just closed over the years and never reopened. Truckers still used them to catch sleep at night. That was what we'd done when we'd pulled in here close to midnight. The drop was due at three a.m.

Not that either of us slept. I smoked and Milo paced.

Good bonding time.

"How are you running it these days?" It was the first question he'd actually asked me about the shipments, since I mentioned the hijackings that had been hitting the lines. We hadn't lost drivers—yet. But they were getting hit on the routes bringing stuff into Braxton Harbor, not taking it out. So...I'd been taking a lot of the midnight runs myself.

I wanted to find the people hitting mine, and I was going to make them bleed. I'd lost two good drivers. One to a shattered kneecap and another to the fact I didn't pay him enough to take the risks, even if they hadn't "broken" anything, they'd roughed him up.

The guy was honest, I'd paid the first's medical bills and set him up with a job when he was rehabbed. The second, I paid out three months wages so he could find another job. No, I hadn't involved the rest of the guys. I wanted security around Emersyn more than I wanted backup out here.

Besides...

"They're coming in kind of slow, aren't they?" Milo asked as the other truck approached, following the long and winding road down from the highway. This section had a lot of trees and it dipped down, away from the road. Kept casual observers to a minimum even in the middle of the night.

We were also just outside the county line and the closest law enforcement didn't leave their station between the hours of midnight and six in the morning if they could help it. Not when their sleepy little unincorporated town, population three thousand one hundred and four, were all tucked in by nine most nights.

I shrugged. "No big reasons to come in fast. You don't want to draw attention, if you're heading off the road to sleep, you take it nice and easy."

Still, I remained aware of the gun tucked securely in the holster at the small of my back and the sawed-off shotgun, I had on a strap and tucked under my jacket.

"Why this run?"

"Why all the questions right now?" We'd had plenty of time since we'd gotten here. I went early because I wanted to be in place long before the expected meet. If anyone tried to stage an ambush, they would have to do the same. The early arrival had given me time to scout the area.

I'd also set up some fall back points if we needed them. Then I'd killed a half a pack of cigarettes while we waited them out.

"Because it just seems odd that you're worried about hits only on certain runs. Those are the ones you're taking. Solo runs, no support, and no one else knowing where you are. You think about what happens if they don't just rough you up? What if they put a bullet in you, Hawk? What then?"

"Everybody dies, Raptor," I reminded him. "These are my people they're targeting. There's a pattern. It's a loose one, but it's there. If you want to hold hands and sip hot cocoa while I tell you the sad bedtime story of everything that's happened, we can do that."

The look he gave me was on par with the same dark looks he'd been giving me all week.

"But you're not ready to listen. So, we'll do it your way —but this..." I motioned to the area around us. "This we're doing mine."

I had a bad feeling about the shipments getting hijacked. The random nature of the cargo. The only commonality? They were usually coming in from a different border crossing—either airport or over the Canadian border. Once from Mexico. It had taken a while to put that together, I'd been studying manifests and companies. But they were all different.

This truck, tonight, was coming down from Canada. No stops or pickups outside of refueling. Everything in this shipment was straight up pharmaceuticals and supplies. That was the manifest. A lot of it was too expensive in the U.S. but we brought it in then distributed it to places like Doc's clinic. We took a much smaller cut on these types of supplies, but they helped the community. It worked.

If that was on board, it would take us time to switch the loads from one truck to the other. Sometimes, we just switched the hitches. But for cargo like this, I didn't want anything identifiable from their transport coming into Braxton Harbor. The shipment would just vanish into the ether.

The closer the truck got, the more the lights cut across my eyes. He could have dimmed the fucking brights, but he wasn't. The fact the driver wanted me blind was another alarm bell.

"Fall back," I told Milo. I didn't want him between me and the truck. If I were going to fuck someone over, I'd come out shooting and hit them while they were blinded.

If the lights didn't cut in the next three seconds—they shut off abruptly. The sudden plunge to darkness left my eyes dazzled. Milo had shifted his position, but the flutter of movement inside the cab of the truck told me the driver wasn't alone.

That was fine, neither was I.

The door opened slowly and the guy climbing down wasn't anyone I'd seen before. I knew most of the drivers on this particular route. When it came to prescription drugs, including oxy and other opiates, I always took the pick-up. I didn't touch that crap and I'd rather not tempt anyone else.

Following a glance back in the cab, the driver closed the door and started toward us. He was older, middle-aged, I'd say closer to fifty than forty. He wasn't overweight, though he had some bulk. His clothes were too loose on him, like he'd gone for bigger sizes to hide his build.

That and the way he *walked* told me more. I didn't reach for either gun, but I also didn't walk forward to meet him. I let him come to us.

"H and H Trucking?" The driver glanced from me to Milo then back. The way his stance shifted gave me a few ideas. He was trying to figure out which of us was the bigger threat.

This wasn't my contact.

But they were using my connections.

"Depends on who's asking," I answered finally.

"Jasper Horan." It wasn't a question.

"I wasn't the one asking."

"No," he said. "But I just wanted to confirm. My employer will be happy with this delivery."

A flash from inside the truck. Hint of light. Either from the movement or the interior lights, but it gleamed off something metal. We needed answers. The shotgun popped up into my hand. One pump and then I squeezed the trigger.

The driver went down swearing, his knee a bloody ruin. Milo was already at the truck on the passenger side. A gunshot split the night and my heart stopped. I kicked the driver in the head on my rush to get to him.

We didn't just fucking get him back to lose him.

I circled the truck, shotgun at the ready, but Milo had the other guy down and unconscious on the ground as he stripped the gun. It wasn't just a gun, it was a fucking sniper rifle. I glanced back at the downed driver then this guy.

Kneeling, I flipped him over and then patted him down. No wallet. No ID. Nothing in his pockets. Not waiting for any comment from me, Milo was in the truck searching. Pulling zip ties from my back pocket, I secured this one and then went back to the driver. He was still alive.

So, I tied up his knee with his shirt. There were tattoos on his arms, nothing I recognized, and he didn't have any ID either.

Fuck.

After securing him, I glanced at Milo. Raptor stared back at me with cold eyes. "Nothing in the truck. I'm guessing this is what you've been waiting for."

"Yeah," I said. "Pretty much. Got the keys?"

He held them up and I lifted my chin gesturing to the truck. We made our way to the back and he unlocked the chains. Only when I had the shotgun up and ready did he swing open the door.

The stench hit us first.

Feces.

Urine.

Sweat.

Fear.

It wasn't until Milo turned on a flashlight that we saw what we were dealing with.

People.

Men. Women. Children.

All of them shackled and chained to the walls inside the trailer.

All of them.

The urge to walk back to our downed captives and put a bullet in their heads damn near overwhelmed me.

Fuck.

"Keep it together, Hawk," Raptor said as he studied the people inside. Most of them shied away from the light. Most of them looked half-starved, sick, and ill.

Someone was using my supply chain to bring in people. Who the fuck knew what else...the pharmaceuticals had probably been hijacked above the border and the whole truck replaced.

We had problems.

Big problems.

I glanced at Raptor as he went to the first person in the truck, a man—guy had to be in late sixties. He was old. Who the hell would do this to him? With care, he got the chains unlocked and then gave him the keys and motioned to the others.

With shaking hands, the man nodded and shuffled his way down to the next person on the line to unlock her.

Some of the fear in the truck eased as Raptor retreated toward me.

He jumped down and pulled out his phone then handed me the flashlight so I could keep the back of the truck illuminated for them.

"I need everyone out on Highway 41, just pass mile marker 219—the old weigh station. Bring extra cars, blankets, clothes—and Doc." He shot a look back inside the truck. "And be fast. We're gonna need water and food, too."

Call ended, we stared in silence into the back of the truck.

"Hawk,—Jas...look at me."

I cut my gaze away from the house of horrors inside the trailer and met his gaze.

"We'll help them. Go secure those two jackasses in our truck. I want them alive—one of them—preferably both. We need answers."

I nodded, handing him the flashlight.

"They might get bruised on the drag."

"As long as they're still breathing."

I grinned. "They can't hurt if they aren't breathing."

He nodded.

"And Jas..." I stopped but didn't turn around. "After we sort this shit out, we're going to have some liquor and you're gonna tell me a bedtime story."

A snort escaped me. "Do I have to hold your hand?"

"Fuck off." But there was almost a smile in those words. Almost.

GUYS LIKE ME

KELLAN

I didn't know how old I was when I realized I'd already been "adopted," but that I wouldn't be leaving the system. Having friends like Milo, Jasper, the twins, and Vaughn when he came along balanced nicely against a system that seemed to be weighted against us from the beginning.

Alone? We'd probably have vanished. Become a statistic. We'd seen it happen. Fought back. Without Ms. Stephanie? We'd likely have been even worse off, because we were stronger together and she fought to keep us together. When Liam was adopted, she fought like hell to get Rome to go too, but Rome hadn't wanted that.

In the end, that separation had at least been a choice. The only thing that really changed was Liam had a different address and often as not brought supplies and presents with him. It was how Rome got better paints and Vaughn got new ink to do some of the more stylized stuff.

For Milo, Liam often as not brought news, whether it

was magazines or papers, but also books for him and Jasper. Jasper was the most voracious reader. More so than Milo. When e-readers were the thing, Liam got us each one. It was weird to have him spend his money like that, but he said it was our money. Some of the gifts were expensive, so we got better at building stashes and cubbies to keep the other kids out of our shit.

We also developed reputations that kept people in their own lanes and out of ours. Liam paid for me to get driving lessons, and he even offered to buy me a car. I thought he was kidding at the time, but when he proved serious—I took him up on the offer. More, so he could help me store it somewhere I could work on it.

I haunted junkyards all over town to rebuild the wrecked Charger I'd gotten for a song. It took time to find the pieces and something of a game with the guys. It took me a year and a half to build her out fully the way I wanted her, the interior was pristine, all original parts.

Granted, the car wasn't that old, so it hadn't been that hard. When it came to detailing the exterior, Rome and Vaughn were all in. Vaughn had already started apprenticing to a tattoo artist. The guy paid him under the table and Vaughn practiced on himself where no one could see.

Still, he and Rome helped me paint her the sweetest cherry red and when I sold her—much to everyone else's shock, I walked away with close to twenty-five grand. I could have done a lot with that money, but what I did was turn around and buy another wrecked car. Then I rebuilt it the same way. The profit left over went into the fund.

Milo's fund. The fund for the plan he'd been working on his whole life. The plan to take the city and make it ours. To elevate us from the back alleys to the gilded elite. He wanted to be a power broker, not that we really understood the term. Or at least I didn't. Because I didn't care about the money.

I just wanted to build cars, work on cars, and take care of my friends. I liked having grease under my nails. But an early driver's license and a skillset made taking jobs as a driver for some of the companies in town an option.

One Milo encouraged, so he splurged from the fund and I got my first nice suit. And a rather odd addiction to wearing clothing that cost more money than my entire childhood. Plenty of times, teachers and counselors tried to redirect my interests. They said guys like me had to have goals, we needed to impress with our scores, and make a real effort to improve our lives. Guys like me didn't have the kind of options I might have had if my parents hadn't died in a car accident.

Guys like me. The only guys like me were my brothers. We came from the worst and the best. I didn't know much about Milo's past. I'd been there when Ivy left though, when the wealthy couple cooed over her because she was adorable and had the best smile. I'd been there when they brought her new clothes and a whole family, including a nanny, to collect her that last day.

I'd been there when Milo said goodbye to his sister and right alongside him, I'd studied these people who chose his sister and not him. Milo never once complained. He cut Jasper off every time he tried to argue that they shouldn't take one without the other. Ms. Stephanie had done the same. Argued for him, but Milo hadn't been remotely bothered.

This was for Ivy. This rich family wanted her. They'd give her the best. They'd take care of her. Ivy would be loved.

For Milo, that was everything.

Guys like me and Milo didn't need that.

Not anymore.

He told me that once, about a father that had tried to take him and leave his sister behind. That father was out there somewhere. When he admitted it, I wanted to know why his father didn't have him and Ivy now?

"Because I never told them who he was," he said, his gaze so distant it felt like he'd left me to go into the past. "Because he would have abandoned Ivy to this life and taken me."

"What a prick." I probably shouldn't have said that, but Milo grinned.

"Yeah, he is and someday—I'm going to make him pay for that."

I'd help. Cause that was what guys like me did. We helped our brothers—and sisters. We looked after them. We put their needs first.

Then I met my sperm donor. Tripped over him. The guy who looked exactly like me. A guy who peddled flesh and traded in people.

How could I look like this guy?

It didn't make sense. I had a hard enough time remembering my parents. I remembered the scent of Mom's perfume and the way she laughed. I could remember my dad's booming voice and the way he would lift me in the air. I even remembered my grandmother's breath always smelled of peppermints and that she always had them in her pocket. So much else about them was a blur.

I didn't want this man's face in my head. This mirror image of me. Liam hired someone to dig for me and got a name. Once I had that, we began to pull at threads. Eventually, the horror I uncovered made me wish I'd never looked in the first place.

Guys like me should hold onto the best memories and let the past die.

I took too long to learn that lesson. Ms. Stephanie listened to me rage one night, drunk off my ass, about the whole sordid story. She listened without judgment, then wiped my tears when I sobbed about the fact I couldn't remember my mother's face anymore. Later, after I puked in her bathroom, and at least I made it to the bathroom, she sobered me up and sat with me while I calmed.

Eventually, she pulled out a photo album and she flipped through it. There were so many kids in those pages and so many of those albums on her shelf. But she came to the page that she'd made of me. Pictures of me, year after year, at things big and small. There was a great shot of all of us together—the Vandals—that was who we were now, after Freddie. After we killed that bastard.

But there were three other photos on that first page of mine.

Mom. Dad. Grandma.

I stared in shock.

"Whenever one of you has to go into the system and there is no family, the state takes care of boxing up all personal items and storing them until you're eighteen. Everything else of value is sold off—like cars and homes— so the money is invested in you and sometimes it's also put into a fund for you when you turn eighteen. There's not a lot in your fund, Kellan. But there are several boxes from your family home and all the pictures."

She tapped the photo of my mom and it about killed me because just seeing her face brought so many memories swimming to the surface. Memories I'd half-forgotten somehow.

"Not all of my kids come from good places, but you did.

This woman right here loved you. She loved you more than anything, and this man? Your father? He adored you and your mother. I can't say for certain he knew about her past or any of the rest of it, but I know love when I see it. It was in every photo of him where he looked at you or your mother."

Fuck.

It hurt, ripping that wound open through dense layers of scar tissue, but I hadn't realized how infected seeing that son of bitch had left me.

"I promise you, when you turn eighteen, I'll make sure you have everything. If you still need answers, I promise I will help you find them."

I looked up into her kind eyes and shame crawled through me. Ms. Stephanie was the best. And I'd kept her up all night with this, but she just smiled.

"Kellan, I know what they tell you in school and how much everyone beats the drum of success. God knows, Milo is determined. All of you are in your own ways. But don't try to just become a man of success. Success can cost you more than you might be willing to pay."

"We have a plan." I wouldn't tell her what it was. If Milo had, then that was his call.

"I know you do and I'm so very proud of all of you. Nothing," she said, emphasizing that word sternly which suggested she knew so much more than I realized. "Nothing any of you could do will ever change that. But if you want my advice, Don't try to become a man of success, be a man of value."

I didn't get that. She ruffled my hair, which should have been patronizing considering how much taller than her I was now, but it wasn't.

"You'll get it someday." She rose and pressed a kiss to the top of my head. "Get some sleep. I'll deal with the group home tomorrow."

Guys like me? We were damn lucky to have a Ms. Stephanie in our lives.

14

It was two days after the cluster fuck with the trucking situation, and we had far more questions than answers. Thankfully, Doc had connections and used some of those to help the people Milo and Jasper found being transported. They were a range of ethnicities, mostly Eastern European, and only a handful spoke the most basic English.

Not ideal.

Still, Vaughn had gone to fetch one of the tea ladies from the shop on 84th. As old as Mrs. Ivanova appeared, we knew to mind our manners whenever we stopped by the shop for anything. She ran the place with her sister. They were a pair of merry old widows, having disposed of their own husbands decades before we were born. Or so they liked to joke.

They'd been born in Eastern Germany long before the country reunified and when the Iron Curtain had been firmly closed. They were sassy, sometimes crude, always bold, and to a bunch of hooligans such as ourselves? Absolutely adorable. Mrs. Ivanova came out, took one look at the victims and fired off a series of questions. She switched languages so fast, I couldn't keep up. With Vaughn acting as her shadow, she managed to find a couple willing to speak to her and they spoke enough Polish between them—apparently—to communicate.

Unsurprisingly, they were all here as part of paying off debts. Some of the kids had been sold. Some of the kids had their mothers with them, both having been taken as part of a debt repayment, while the older men were failures of some kind or taking on the servitude themselves to spare their families.

Those men got my respect. They had to know this kind of life would kill them, but unlike the fuckers who sold their kids and wives, they'd taken the burden themselves. I'd like a list of names.

We all would. But they were willing to only share so much and we couldn't exactly press them for more. They'd been through enough. Doc reached out to a safe haven project and with a little finagling we got them to some human rights lawyers, doctors, and advocates who would take the mess on from there.

As for the driver—he bled out before Doc could get to him. For once, he didn't give a damn. Save for the fact we needed some answers, I couldn't say I gave too much of a damn either. We still had one prisoner and he was currently dangling from a meat hook in the freezer.

Stubborn fucker hadn't given up anything yet. He'd break.

They all did.

For now, I was away from the stench of it and standing in the garage. The medical supplies that were supposed to be *in* that shipment still hadn't been found. Something or someone in our transportation network had been compromised. Maybe multiple somethings...

"A year," Vaughn repeated. He wasn't one to hang onto these things, but Jasper had been chasing this shit down for the last year and it explained a lot about his moods. A lot.

"We've covered that," Jasper replied in a tone that was far more exhausted than it was irritated. "I didn't have enough evidence and we've been shorthanded."

I took a sip of my coffee and ignored the argument. They'd broken back into it a dozen times in the last forty-eight hours. None of us had slept. Everyone was cranky. The five minutes we'd gotten to see Emersyn hadn't seemed like enough and now, I couldn't be happier that she was at Liam's—far away from the stain of this.

Because this was a stain. How many of these *hijacked* shipments had been human trafficking? How many people had been funneled into Braxton Harbor and elsewhere, using our trucks? Our people? Our *system?* Jasper got points for wanting to solve the problem, but he lost them for not involving us.

Freddie, who shouldn't be anywhere near this mess considering his past, had actually helped cooler heads prevail. He and Rome both kept the rest of us steady. Milo was a damn stick of dynamite left in the sun too long, with nitroglycerin leaking down the sides, and you never knew when it was going to combust.

Vaughn had grown more short-tempered than I'd ever seen him. His normal affable nature kept him cooler when Jasper or Liam would have long since blown up. The one that worried me the most, to be honest, was Jasper. He wasn't arguing. Not once had he snapped back, no matter how hard Vaughn shoved or Milo growled. Liam had swung by for a brief visit and the only thing Jasper had done was ask how Emersyn was, despite Milo's hostility on the subject.

"You should have told us," Vaughn repeated.

"We know," Freddie said, snapping his fingers. "Jasper should have told us so we could help. But we've all been dicks and measuring dicks, and throwing our dicks around like a bunch of dicks. So, for fuck's sake, let it go."

I glanced over to where Freddie gesticulated wildly. I wasn't alone in staring, he had gotten all of our attention, including Rome's. Rome, who had just walked back in shortly before dawn from wherever he'd been going at night.

While I could guess, lucky prick, I refused to ask. Not until we sorted some other shit out here. At least if he was there, she had someone looking after her. As glad as I was that she wasn't *here*, goddamn did I miss her.

"Seriously, Vaughn. Get another song. It's bad enough Raptor can't carry a tune in a bucket with the lid welded on that doesn't sound like some bad 80s rocker screaming after too many cigarettes and booze."

I didn't laugh.

Barely.

"But nobody needs that shit from you. You're the nice one—well," Freddie said, pausing as if for dramatic effect. "You're not the *nice* nice one. That's Kellan. He's the respectable one here."

"Gee, thanks," I drawled, so glad to be included.

"Are you saying that I'm not nice or respectable?" Vaughn asked, the corners of his mouth betraying his amusement, even if he still frowned.

"You're not as nice as Rome," Freddie announced. "Because he's the super nice one."

The one in question flipped Freddie off. The young smartass just grinned.

"You're also not as respectable as Kel."

I rolled my eyes.

"What does that make me?" Jasper asked, grimacing as if he couldn't believe he was asking.

"I'd have said the grumpy bastard, but Raptor came home." Everyone had a sense of self-preservation. Or at least, everyone except Freddie. Apparently, when they'd been handing that part out, he'd skipped out on the line. Probably distracted by a hot girl.

It fit.

"Tell me how you really feel," Milo said, as he finally walked over to join us. He and Vaughn were both splattered in blood, or their shirts were. They had washed their hands and faces. Jasper hadn't bothered. His knuckles were a wreck, split open, busted and a couple looked like they were gonna get infected. He hadn't cleaned the spatter off his neck either.

"Thank fuck you finally asked me," Freddie announced, as he spun around to face our illustrious leader and missed brother.

"Freddie..." Jasper began, but Milo cut him off with a shake of his head.

"Let him speak. He has the right." He flicked a look at all of us. "You all do."

Rome snorted. Instead of just ignoring us, he settled in and leaned against Jasper's car, arms folded. We were alone, for the most part, in the warehouse. The rats all had tasks or jobs to do. Two of them had been cut loose by Raptor the first day he was back. The minute he kicked them, the others had all embraced an attitude adjustment.

Well, not all of them, but JD and his buddy were still

doing their jobs and not causing trouble for now. They also hadn't shown up in the clubhouse again.

Squaring his shoulders, Freddie put his hands on his hips. While he was probably the leanest of all of us and a good two inches shorter than Milo, he lifted his chin and stared at him.

"Let's start with how you're treating Boo-Boo."

Oh. Fuck.

Instead of blowing up, like he'd done just about any other time Emersyn had been mentioned, Milo just stared at him as he sipped his coffee and waited.

"She belongs here, not at Liam's. She belongs with people who care about her—not saying Liam doesn't—" Right on cue, Jasper let out an exasperated growl and Vaughn ground his teeth. Rome snorted again and when he caught me looking at him, he just gave a shrug. "The point is," Freddie pressed on, ignoring the responses he'd gotten so far. "Boo-Boo is one of us. You may not like it, but that doesn't change facts. You didn't want me to be one of us either, but look how delightful I make life."

Milo held up a single finger and Freddie paused. "I've never said you weren't one of us. The only thing I ever wanted for you was for you to be safe and to make safe choices."

The silence grew taut for a moment, then Freddie relaxed a fraction and spread his hands.

"Fine, I'll accept that. But there were plenty of times when it felt like you didn't want me." That was news to me and apparently to Milo, but not Jasper, who just pulled out a cigarette and lit it. The flame illuminated his bruised face. Fuck that made me hurt for him. He and Raptor had fought every single fucking day, until the last two.

If nothing else, having someone to torture seemed to be

bonding them again. Maybe we should pick up a spare, in case we needed it after this one expired.

"Boo-Boo has been alone for way too long and fuck knows Liam is not the most entertaining guy. No offense, Rome," he said over his shoulder and Rome just shrugged.

"None taken."

I couldn't help it a chuckle escaped me.

"See," Freddie said, pointing at me. "I'm entertaining. *Vaughn* is entertaining. Even Jasper, when he's not being a grumpy puss, is entertaining. Liam's just a dick. No offense, Rome."

The twin in question just flipped him off, but there was a hint of a smile around his mouth. A door creaked open on the far side of the warehouse and Doc stepped in out of the sunshine.

"The point is, *here*, Boo-Boo is with more of us. She's not stuck locked up all by herself, which for your information she hates. She hated it here. She's going to hate it there. For a second thing, we were getting her up to speed on movies. Do you have any idea of how many movies she hasn't seen? Dude, she didn't even know what *Lord of the Rings* was until we watched it. She doesn't like horror movies, but she will watch them if we warn her about the bloody parts." Freddie made a face then grinned. "Though, I don't think it bothers her as much as she says it does."

"No," Vaughn said, agreeing with Freddie. "She always peeks between her fingers or hides behind one of us and watches over our shoulder."

Jasper huffed a laugh. "Or uses one of our hands to hide her eyes and then peeks around it."

"Exactly," Freddie said. "And when she's here, there's real food and she's trying to learn to cook. She's absolutely horrible at it."

Hey... "She is not," I argued. "She's never had anyone *show* her how before. She grew up with servants. What the hell do we expect?"

"A really prissy bitch who couldn't be bothered to do dishes," Freddie countered and he faced me instead of Milo when he said that, and it was a good thing. Cause at the words 'prissy bitch' Milo's face turned to the thunder. "But she's *not*. She likes trying to figure things out."

"Yeah," I admitted with a sigh. "She does. She almost had scrambled eggs down." Which had been kind of cool. I liked that she listened when I showed her how to do things. She didn't argue that there had to be another way. "It was the same when she came to the shop. She's never seen the inside of engine before."

Her excitement had been a delight.

"She likes painting," Rome admitted and that pulled everyone's attention. "Not doing it. She liked watching me do it. She doesn't ask a lot of questions, even when she wants to. She adjusts to the people around her. Like she doesn't need me to tell her I prefer it quiet when I work, she's just peaceful."

Milo frowned.

"She is curious when she has questions though," I said. "If she thinks we'll answer, she'll ask."

"And she's fun," Freddie pointed out. "Boo-Boo works hard even here, she trained in the studio every day after her bruises and broken bones healed. She watches what she eats. A little too much, but she's not fussy if we don't have what she wants. I mean, we'd get her anything, but she doesn't ask."

"Except when there are too many carbs," Vaughn grumbled and Jasper snorted, then even he nodded.

"I swear to fuck—if it has too many carbs, and she adds

an hour to her workout or more. It makes me fucking tired watching her."

"Liar," Freddie said, calling Jasper out. "You're a greedy fuck about watching her dance. You don't want to let the rest of us, but you went in there all the time."

That was true.

"Do you blame me?" Jasper retorted.

"Nope," Freddie said. "Just like I loved the fact she read to me."

I hid a smile, because not everyone knew about that.

"While I was detoxing and in hell, she sat outside that door on that cold floor and read me books through the door. Crazy series, chick ends up with all these guys, who form their own gang."

Milo made a sound and Freddie spun to face him.

"I didn't buy her the book, I don't even know where she got it. But it's a cool story. We're not done with it yet, Aaron's missing and we haven't gotten him back."

"Who the fuck is Aaron?" Doc asked.

"Guy in a book," Jasper said, before Freddie could go off on a tear.

"Exactly." As if that summed it all up, Freddie faced Milo. "We know Boo-Boo. We care about her. She belongs here, with us. So why won't you bring her back?"

"Because she doesn't belong here, Freddie," Milo answered him in a soft voice. "She belongs to a better world."

"Well, the one she was in wasn't better," Doc said before any of us could interject. "If it had been, they wouldn't have brought her to me all busted up and broken."

I held my breath, and I had a feeling I wasn't the only one.

"You can tell yourself all you like that world is better for her, Milo. But she didn't want to go back to it. She had the chance. She asked me to help her and I said I would, but she got out of here on her own."

That was news to a few people, Jasper's entire demeanor changed and he glared at Doc, but didn't move.

"I found her walking, in the cold, just away, and I picked her up. Took her all the way back to her hotel...and at the last minute, she walked away from there, too. So, I brought her back to my clinic so she could think."

Doc had everyone's attention. I got it. I knew she'd left, she'd admitted as much. She'd also told me she chose to come back and if we were where she wanted to be, then I wouldn't fight her on it. Even if I wanted her somewhere safer. Her choice.

"She chose to come back here. To these fuckers." He gestured to all of us, and Rome wasn't the only one who flipped Doc off at that statement. Not that he gave a damn. "If she wants to be here, Kid. You gotta stop pushing her away and punishing her."

"I'm not fucking punishing her." Anger flashing over his expression, Milo took two steps toward Doc. "You know what I've done for her to have that life. That's all I ever wanted..."

"It's not about what you want," Doc said.

Man, that hurt. It was like the knife dug right between two ribs and severed muscle.

"It's also not about that life," I said. "Milo..." Because if everyone was going to have their say then fuck it, so was I. "That life. This life. You're assuming a lot. We all have. For a long time. That life partnered her with someone who was hurting her—a lot."

"And she stayed with him because it was better than

the alternative," Jasper said slowly. If that wasn't a sickening thought, I didn't know what was.

"You love her," I continued. "We know that. You always put her first. You taught us to do that, too. To protect her and keep an eye on her, always from afar. But I think—and I may be wrong—but I think we've been too far. The one time we got up close, what did we find?"

I didn't have to draw him a map. That bartender had gotten her drunk and roofied her. A fourteen-year-old kid. If we hadn't been there? Yeah.

"You can't change the past," I said. Fuck knew we'd tried. All of us in our ways. "You can't undo what's happened to her." While I didn't mean to emphasize the her part of it, I had to. Because we didn't know. She didn't trust us enough to confide in us. What ground we'd gained, we'd turned around and lost.

"You can change the future," Doc offered. "You can get to know your sister instead of running away from her and locking her up in the name of keeping her safe."

"You can bring her home," Freddie said. "To us. Where she belongs."

"And we can teach her to trust us for real," Jasper said. "With everything out in the open, then maybe she can tell us what that alternative was..."

"...and we can fucking kill it." Rome finished.

"That's a plan I could live with," Vaughn agreed and all of us focused on Milo. "What about you?"

SHE CAN FLY

MILO

"Are you sure this is okay?" I asked Mickey, for what had to be the hundredth time. He was home on leave for such a short stint. It was the first time I'd seen him in a couple of years. While Ms. Stephanie insisted that the military was the best place for him, I wasn't too proud to admit that I missed him. Not that I planned to say it aloud.

"It's fine, kid," he told me in that rough voice of his. "Seriously. Steph has home visits tonight so she wouldn't have seen me anyway. You said the show was only a couple of towns over, so we can get there, you can watch, then we'll get back."

Something that felt like real excitement burbled in my stomach. "It's stupid."

"What is?" He shot me a look. But instead of meeting his gaze, I looked out the window. It was stupid and embarrassing. "Yo, kid," he pressed and snapped his fingers. "Earth to Milo."

"Ha," I scoffed and then slouched in the seat some. The

other guys had been jealous, but the tickets to the show were expensive and they'd thrown in some money to help me buy one, then Mickey just paid for it without letting me pay him back. "I'm—I don't know. It's stupid that I'm this excited. I don't even know *why* she's in some show. Isn't she supposed to be away at school?"

"Been keeping an eye on her?" While he didn't glance at me this time, I swore he wasn't judging. Mickey J was pretty cool on that front.

"Yeah, mostly what I can hear, but—there was an article in the newspaper." Her name had popped right up at me. Her new name anyway. I liked Ivy better. Emersyn sounded snotty.

"You still reading those every day?" He sounded surprised.

"Can't make anything of myself if I don't know how the world works," I reminded him. "I like to be informed."

He chuckled, but there was nothing derisive about it. "If only I'd been that smart when I was your age, kid. I might not be where I am."

"I thought you wanted to go in?" Now it was my turn to study him. Jasper had been mad at Mickey since the day he enlisted. Talk about dumb choices—Jasper's not Mickey's. I got it though. The judge had given him a choice—enlist and get his act together, or jail. I probably would have chosen the military, too.

It was only a couple more years and then he'd be back. We could handle the runs until then.

No sweat.

"It's better than jail," he admitted. "I'm learning a lot. I have my shit together now." Still, Mickey shook his head. "I made some bad choices, kid. Took some of you with me and I want to fix that."

"Mickey." Shifting in my seat, I looked at him now. While I might admire the hell out of the guy, love him like a brother, and owe him my life and more, some things were still my call and not his. "You didn't take me anywhere I didn't want to be. I get it. Your choices put you where you are. Not saying that's good or bad. We have a plan and the jobs we're all doing right now? That's just another stepping stone on the path of it."

I had it all worked out. We could have everything we wanted and more, if we played our cards right. Some of it was a gamble, but most of it was just plain, hard work. We could do it.

"Just—be careful," he said with a small shake of his head. "I don't want you to pay for my mistakes, too."

Then we were at the arena where the show was being held. Mickey sprang for drinks and popcorn. We had shitty seats, all the way in the back and up, but it afforded a decent view, and I didn't need to be too close. I just— wanted to see her. The pictures in the magazines had been one thing.

It was hard to believe that poised little girl had been that snotty, baby with her toothless grins, and terrible diapers. Mickey ducked out part way through the show with a girl who'd been sitting a couple of seats over. When he came back, he was a lot more relaxed and she was flushed and grinning.

"Your zipper's down," I warned him, glued to the action below. The performers were acrobats, dancers, and more. There was some story being told through the whole perfor- mance. I didn't pay much attention to it. I thought I'd seen her a couple of times, but we were too far away to tell.

The lights went dark all of a sudden, and the roar of applause from the last performance ended. Was that it? I tried to curb the disappointment burning through me but...a spotlight cut on and a gasp rippled through the crowd.

The light focused on a solitary ring descending bearing a little girl in it. She balanced easily, like she wasn't sitting in some inch wide circlet with nothing between her and the ground over a hundred plus feet below her. All the moisture in my mouth dried.

Then the music started and she began to dance, weaving in and out of the ring, sometimes only spinning from one leg or one hand. She flew—almost effortless in her grace.

I forgot how to breathe.

Ivy.

15

Training to fight with Liam was not what I thought fighting would be. In fact, we hadn't fought at all. I ran a lot. A lot. He complimented me on my speed, but he was right, he was faster than I was. No matter how hard I ran, I could not get away from him.

So, the next thing he taught me was to be a dead weight if someone grabbed me. "Even a little bit of fluff like you can be as heavy as ox if you try."

I wasn't sure whether to be insulted or amused. Particularly when I understood the principle of shifting my center of gravity and not helping him in the slightest. Then he proved he could deadlift me whether I helped or not.

"What the fuck is the point of telling me to do something so you can then prove to me how useless it is?" This was after the third such attempt at evading and dead-weight, only to find myself over his shoulder and staring at his ass.

"There's the fire I've been waiting for." The asshole

actually sounded smug and for a moment, air swished past my ass and I twisted. Maybe he'd remembered I didn't like having my ass slapped. Or maybe he was just screwing around. But the one thing Liam needed to remember was, I understood bodies.

I went from being over his shoulder to straddling it and I arched backwards like I was doing reverse cartwheel and my legs pulled the startled jackass with me. I hit the mat with my hands and let go of his torso as I completed the full flip back to my feet.

My so-called teacher landed hard, the only thing keeping his head from hitting the mat were his long arms. I'd give him credit, he tucked and rolled right back up to his feet and then grinned at me.

Like a fucking psycho.

"That," he said, still grinning and his eyes positively dancing with glee. "That's the energy I want from you Hellspawn. Not the little 'yes, sir' 'no sir,' robot you've been all week."

Robot?

I slapped a hand against his chest. "I was being a good *student*. Listening to what you said. Soaking it up. Repeating move after move."

"Aww, does Hellspawn want a cookie?"

Asshole. I flipped him off. "Wow, I suddenly understand your brother so much more."

Liam laughed. A full-throated, head back, laugh and the warm masculine sound of it filled the gym. I didn't know how he got us the empty space every day, but he did. We only worked out for a couple of hours, but there was never anyone here with us.

"Right. Now, we're going to do all of that again, Hellspawn. You're gonna run, I'm going to chase you. You don't want me to catch you." I swore, his smile grew on that last sentence. "But when I do," the cocky asshole continued. "You have to get away from me. No holds barred."

"This is your idea of teaching?" I raised my brows.

"It worked, didn't it?" He spread his hands. "You got away from me."

I had. "But why didn't you tell me to fight back to begin with?"

Arms folding, Liam stared at me for a long moment. "You're serious with that question, aren't you?"

"Yes."

"Dancer. Choreographers. Have you always had someone tell you every move you have to take when you're on a stage?"

Well... "No. But some shows were more stylized than others. Particularly when working with a partner."

The crinkle of lines between his brows deepened. "Your partner called the shots." That wasn't a question.

"If I stepped wrong, or shifted something. I could hurt him." I shrugged. That had been Eric's excuse the first time he dropped me and I'd sprained a wrist. Later, he didn't need excuses.

"Right." He nodded once. "That's dance and your partner was a fucking bitch who's dead, so anything you learned about working with a partner from him—throw it out the window."

"Okay."

"This," he said, unfolding his arms before gesturing to the two of us. "We're not the same *kind* of partners. In dance, you work your bodies in harmony with each other. In fighting, the harmony you need, you find here," he continued, pressing a hand over my heart. I swore it sped up at the brief touch. "And here." He raised his hand to cup the side of my head. "You need to trust everything you know, to keep you safe."

"Do I get to ask questions?"

While he hadn't taken his hand away, I hadn't withdrawn either. "Could I stop you if I tried?"

Right.

"I know how bodies move and where soft points are. You're not teaching me how to hit them, you're teaching me to go for them on my own."

"Sure," he said with a chuckle. "Let's go with that. In a straight on fight, Hellspawn—Emersyn. You're a tiny fucking thing. I've got a much longer reach, I'll hit you way too hard and I could break your arm without trying if I wasn't careful." There was no braggadocio in his words. This was all facts. "Most men are going to be bigger than you are. They're going to have one thing on their minds—subdue you any way they have to. Which means they won't hold back."

"What if I end up really hurting you?"

"I can take it," he assured me. Course, he probably counted on the fact that I wouldn't be able to hurt him. "Trust me, Hellspawn. I can take a beating as well as deliver one."

I frowned at the choice of words.

"Now, no more playing. I really am going to try and get you and if I do, I'm going to pin you. Your job—don't let me." He gave me a long intense stare and I swore my heart beat a path straight to my throat and the sweat dotting my skin went ice cold. "Run."

He said don't let me catch you.

So, I kicked him square in the balls before I raced across the gym. His low, hissing groan carried across the open space, and I glanced back to find him staggering to his feet.

"Sucker. Punch." Each syllable rode a pained note.

"You said get away," I called. There was at least thirty feet between us. "I got away."

A wheezing laugh escaped him. He stood, half folded, hands on his thighs as he caught his breath. But when he glanced up at me again, there was definitely the promise of mischief on his face. Yeah, I had a feeling I was going to pay for that.

"Besides, you promised to teach me how to hurt someone so they could never hurt me again."

"I know."

"So why aren't you teaching me that?"

"Because I teach you to survive first, then I teach you to maim."

I couldn't help it. I laughed, "If I didn't know how to survive, I wouldn't still be here."

Something akin to pain and understanding flashed through his eyes, but he shook his head and looked away too fast for me to grasp it. "Let's make a deal, Emersyn." It was so fucking weird when he said my name. I'd gotten used to Hellspawn. "I won't smack your ass and you don't kick me in the balls."

I probably shouldn't have laughed at him, but c'mon... "That's a soft point on the body."

"Oh, trust me, Hellspawn. There was nothing soft about that target." The red flush staining his neck and face eased and I didn't think it was a blush. On the other hand, at his suggestion that the target hadn't been soft, I glanced at his crotch.

The flicker of movement had me jerking my head up as he raced toward me.

Oh shit.

Heart hammering, I pivoted and ran flat out. The only

rule was we couldn't *leave* the gym itself. The rest of it was wide-open. I cut across the floor, swerving around the equipment and hoping that my head start and speed gave me just a bit of an advantage. I could turn faster than he could.

Nearing one of the boxing rings, I hit the edge of it and vaulted, up and over the ropes to land inside the ring. I had four directions to choose from and a glance toward him found him slowing as he eyed my position.

A hint of a smile turned up his lips. We were both panting, but I wasn't really that winded. Or at least not as winded as he was. I shouldn't find that so amusing, but I did. He asked for it. Still, my next move was based on what he did. I was pretty sure that I could catch a metal bar that was about halfway up the wall and from there, flip up onto one of the support girders that ran the length of the gym.

I'd noticed them our first day in here. They were roughly a foot wide, but that was more than enough space for me to balance and run. I didn't look up. Not once. I had it all mapped in my head, the speed, the trajectory and the leap. If he got to me, I could actually use his height to my advantage.

That said, it would be preferable if he didn't close the distance between us. The calculating look he wore unsettled me. I swore he was trying to read my mind as he began to ease his weight onto his right foot as though he were going to make a rush in that direction. But I didn't think so. I didn't shift my weight at all.

I wouldn't answer his body with mine. No. The goal was to get away. I was going to win this damn game.

As expected, he didn't go right or left. He charged right at the boxing ring, I was in. He vaulted, much like I had, but I was already halfway up the wall and gripping the bar. I pushed my body upward, balancing on my hands as my feet touched the girder.

Liam slowed below me and we locked gazes. "Woah, Hellspawn." Genuine fear flashed in his eyes. "Let's not get crazy."

"Not crazy," I told him as sweat dripped down my forehead. This was a strain, but I was warmed up enough to handle it. I hooked one foot onto the girder, then the other.

"Fuck me," Liam whispered. "Hellspawn..."

I let go of the bar and curled my whole body up while holding onto the girder with only the strength and balance of my feet and then I grasped the girder and pulled myself up and over until I straddled it and gazed down at him.

Eyebrows raised, I waited.

"How do you get away from there?" Curiosity filled his eyes, and I checked the girders. "What's your next step?"

"There's a window. I could break the glass and get out that way..."

"Maybe, but those windows aren't just kick the glass out."

I studied the roof. There was no hatch like I'd found at the warehouse. "You could wait me out."

"Yep, and if I had a gun, I could shoot you.."

I glared down at him.

"So think, what's your next step. You're up there. I can get up there, but that's not my best approach."

"The next step should have been to get up here faster and run. I could have been over by the doors while you were still gaping and then outside."

He grinned. "That's definitely one way."

"But not the way you were thinking?"

He eased out from between the ropes and jumped down from the ring. "I just wanted to know what you were thinking. You had that step planned for your getaway, so what was the next and the next...always keep thinking what can you do to save yourself. The worst thing you can do when a threat is present is to freeze."

For a split-second, the moment in the alleyway when he'd grabbed me, and his hand had covered my mouth flashed through my mind. I'd fought like hell, damn near knocked myself out to get him to let me go.

But I hadn't had any other thought than flee. When it came to my uncle...

"You won the round, Hellspawn," Liam beckoned, derailing the thought before it could take hold. "Come on down." He clapped his hands and held them up. He was right below me. "Just drop. I'll catch you."

"You promise that I won and this isn't a trick?"

His smile grew and it was another of those real ones that lit up his face and his eyes. "Excellent question, Hellspawn and because you thought about it, I'll give you the full marks."

"Great—still didn't answer my question." Because I wasn't giving myself up unless he well and truly threw in the towel.

Holding up two fingers, he said, "Scout's Honor, you win."

I didn't know much about the Scouts, but... "If this is a trick," I warned him, swinging to dangle from my hands. "I'll kick you in the balls again."

"Noted." It wasn't that far of a fall and he was right below me, hands upward. I met his gaze and then let go. His hands clamped on my hips, catching my weight and my momentum and taking a step back before he set me down. "Thank you."

"For what?"

"For trusting me."

I had. "Well," I said slowly. "So far, you've been honest. When I've demanded you stop something, you have."

"You mean when you deliver your message with explicit violence?" The teasing note robbed the statement of any sting. "I might be thick-skinned, but I'm not an idiot. And today was good. You're thinking now. Multiple steps. Next time, I'm going to show you how to break someone's grip on you and how to make a grown man cry with just his thumb."

Everything about that statement sent a wild swirl of tingles through my system and I grinned.

"Blood-thirsty, aren't you?" He sounded almost thoughtful as he said it, but you know what...

"Not even going to deny it." I skipped away from him to grab a towel and dry my face. I snagged the hoodie I'd worn inside. We'd already worked out how to slide out of over-sized clothes if they grabbed at it.

Liam snagged his bag and handed me the thermos with water in it, before we headed to the doors. "You did good today, kid."

Pleasure suffused me at the compliment. He didn't say much else as we walked out to the SUV. He walked me all the way to the passenger door and it felt very much like he was covering me from the street, but I didn't say anything as I climbed inside.

There were sunglasses and a hat that I put on once in the seat. It seemed a lame disguise, but Liam pointed out that people were still looking for me, and since we didn't know exactly who these people were, and if they were good or bad, we would assume bad.

Right. If it was my family looking for me? Definitely bad. As much as Liam made me think I could trust him, so had the other guys, and look where we all were. How did I even begin to tell them my story? I didn't want to think about it, much less recite it. I wanted Emersyn Sharpe to disappear for good, or at least, disappear until I had the money to stay away.

To keep him away.

We passed a Remmington Bank on our way back to Liam's place. I'd caught sight it on our second trip. He didn't take the same route each time, so it was hard to mark the distance. But I'd gotten the cross streets and I had my phone. If nothing else, I could look up their number and call them for their address or Google it.

All the way back to his place, we were both quiet. It smelled like sweat and hard work in the vehicle. Weirdly, I'd missed that scent. Despite his offer, Liam hadn't taken me to the clubhouse so I could use my studio, but the gym every day had definitely been a workout.

It wasn't until we were in the elevator that I glanced over to find him studying me. "What?"

"Nothing," he said. "Just thinking that you're a lot tougher than you look. I told them you were, but I think you might be even tougher than I thought."

For some inane reason that made me feel good. "You'd be surprised." I grinned as the elevator doors opened to his floor.

"You know, Hellspawn, you might be right."

I stopped two steps out of the elevator as Raptor straightened from where he leaned against the wall next to the door. His forbidding expression tracked past me to Liam. "I said keep her fucking safe, not take her out on a damn date."

SINNERS

MILO

The trip to see Ivy might have been a mistake, but it wasn't one any of us regretted. Not after the thing with the bartender. Kel was on my ass to talk about it for months afterward, but he wasn't my shrink, Ms. Stephanie or even Mickey, so no I'd pretty much keep the thoughts to myself.

Besides, we needed to be focused on what we were building here. Everyone had taken on a task or a job. Kel worked at the shop and apprenticed himself to a master mechanic while he also took classes. He was self-taught for the most part, but between rebuilding cars to sell and going to school at night to get his license, he'd been putting every ounce of that knowledge to work for us.

The trucking company we were in the process of taking over had a lot of broken down rigs. Kel spent a lot of his downtime working on those, while Jasper got his business degree. Liam took care of the paper trail, building shell fronts and LLCs to hide the ownership for the trucking company. Vaughn lent a hand wherever he was needed and donated more than fifty percent of his income from his work at the tattoo shop to the overall fund.

Still, even with everything we had coming in, there were a lot of threats all around us. Smaller, more feral gangs we had to deal with, and deal with in such a way that it couldn't be tracked back to us. No one was going to trust a group of nineteen somethings with their business. Not even if some of us were twenty or almost twenty-one.

By society's standards, we weren't good enough, trustworthy enough, or even pretty enough to trust much less invest in or respect. Not that it mattered to me. I didn't need their trust or their respect. Their money on the other hand? Well, there were plenty of ways to acquire it.

Investments went both ways. Amazing the dividends one could reap, with a little judicious application and inside information. Liam had cultivated a lot of resources at that expensive school of his and those resources, in turn, provided him with some quid pro quo. We'd handled some jobs for them, quietly and off the books. Busted some kneecaps or fingers. I drew the line at dropping bodies for anyone that wasn't us.

As if summoned by the thought, my phone rang and it was Liam's number. I only listed the guys by their bird call signs. If the phones were lost, no one had a compromised identity, and as ridiculous as it sounded when we'd first discussed it, those names had saved our lives more than once.

Mockingbird flashed across the screen before I hit the green answer button. "I thought you were visiting the O'Connells in Florida." That had actually been one of Liam's first actions after he and Rome hit eighteen. He'd talked his adoptive parents into retiring to a warmer climate. His adopted mother had a heart condition, one of the reasons they'd wanted to adopt in the first place.

As it turned out, the couple were very nice, but maybe too nice. They really would have taken Rome if he'd agreed to go. They'd even fixed up a second room in their house—let's not lie, mansion—just for him if he ever changed his mind.

Rome spent exactly one night there and said no. Hopefully more politely than that, but knowing Rome? Probably not.

"Leaving for the airport in fifteen. Rome decided to come, that's the first reason I'm calling."

I laughed. Liam had been after Rome for three weeks to go with him, but Rome had just shrugged it off. I'd bet a week's salary he showed at Liam's place with a backpack ready to go. Liam still spent part of his time at an apartment in the city when he didn't crash here. He had to walk a fine line between their world and ours.

"That's cool. It's two weeks, right?"

"Who the hell knows?" Liam's gruff voice held both aggravation and affection. "He could get bored and steal a car then be back in a few days."

Grinning, I shook my head. "He's flipping you off right now, isn't he?" I headed inside the clubhouse. The warehouse was our base of operations for everything. We'd been growing what we could do out of here slowly, easing into it as it were. Mostly to keep the other gangs from showing up to try and take what was ours.

"Pretty much," Liam answered. He wanted to invest in a high-tech security system, but that would tip our hand to how much money we had in our pockets and there was still an old rule of thumb we played by. If it was valuable enough for someone to lock away, then it was valuable enough to steal.

Believe it or not, leaving the warehouse unlocked had actually reduced the interest of others poking around. That, and the conveniently placed traps and junk barrels we set up. We'd considered using storage containers from the docks, but with Freddie hanging with us more and more, no way in hell were we doing that.

"That's fine. Rome is gonna Rome." I'd long since given up any pretense of giving Rome instructions. He did jobs. He helped out. He followed his own beat. The only thing we did, was make sure we covered his back. Though, he made that difficult at times by just disappearing.

Liam was the only one I knew who could reliably find him, most of the time.

Chuckling, Liam said, "You have a point. Look—" he dropped his voice and while the twins rarely kept secrets from each other, there were still some things about his second life Liam preferred to protect Rome from, or at least keep isolated away from his twin. "I got a call today from a guy, about you."

Eyebrows raised, I grabbed a cold soda from the fridge and popped the top on it before responding. "A friend?"

"Calling him a friend would be stretching it. That said, he's... reliable."

Not trustworthy. The choice of words intrigued me. "Go on."

"Just wanted to know if I knew you."

"Which, of course, you don't."

"Right?" Liam scoffed. "When I asked him why he wanted to know, he got cagey." Dislike licked that word. "Then told me there's a possible bounty out for you."

Me? I didn't say that out loud but that didn't make any damn sense.

"Which sounds a little fucking weird," Liam commented. "One, that he would reach out to me about you on a subject like this."

"Fishing expedition?" I took a long swallow of the soda.

"No. The one thing about Reed, he's a fucking dick about a lot of things, but he's always been straight with me. He was the first one to offer me an in with the Royals."

They'd smoothed a lot of Liam's way through school, made things easier for him. But he'd never committed, no matter how hard they tried to recruit him. The only reason he didn't openly wear his Vandals colors was because he was our guy on the other side of the line. Not his first choice and I respected that, but for now, we needed to keep that profile solid a little longer.

"So you think he had a reason for asking, a solid one?"

"Yeah, I do," Liam admitted. "I just don't know what. I'm friendly but not in, if you know what I mean."

I did. "Tell me what he said. Word for word. Exactly."

16

"**G**reat," I mumbled. "Captain Killjoy is here."

Liam choked on what sounded suspiciously like a laugh. "Been waiting long?" he managed as my so-called brother took a step toward us. While I refused to be intimidated by him, I didn't necessarily want to be caged in between the pair if another fight broke out.

As if reading my mind, Liam stepped around me and cut off Raptor's line of sight. "Should have called. "If the sudden appearance by the leader of the Vandals bothered Liam, he didn't show it.

"Long enough. Why did you take her out?"

"None of your fucking business," I retorted in the same breath that Liam said, "Because I fucking felt like it." When our words collided, Liam glanced at me over his shoulder. His expression seemed equal parts amused and "shut up."

It took effort on my part. Effort and biting down on the inside of my lip to keep from laughing at his expression.

"Anyway," Liam said, dragging out the syllables as he

229

faced Raptor—no Milo—right, he wanted to be called Milo. I'd respect that. He'd made sure I'd gotten my phone back and he'd taken me, all of once, to use my studio. So, I could show him that respect. Maybe he could do me the same courtesy. "Move and I'll let us in."

"First, you tell me where you took my sister," Milo said, grinding out each word as if at great personal effort.

"We went to the gym to work out, so she doesn't go stir-crazy. The condo is nice. But a cell is a cell and you of all people should understand that." The whip of words cut at me they were so sharp. Milo had just gotten out of jail.

Jail.

My brother had been in jail.

The two men stared at each other, neither moving, neither backing down, and I was willing to wait, but my bladder? Not so much.

"Could we put a pin in the pissing contest so I can go inside and actually use the facilities?" I cut between them and then around Milo, since he'd left distance between him and the door. "Or just give me the key to get in."

The silence elongated for one more moment, then Liam nudged me to the side and unlocked the door himself. "Go on, Hellspawn," he said. "I'll talk to Milo."

"Yeah, you're damn right you'll talk to me."

I rolled my eyes and walked away from them both. Let them sort out their secrets. Course, if Milo decided I couldn't stay here anymore, there was a slim chance he would make me go back to the clubhouse. I was in the bath-room with the door closed as I weighed that idea.

I wanted to go back, right?

But going back would mean leaving Liam, and as tired and sore as I was from today, I had learned.

Been learning.

Liam didn't treat me with kid gloves or like I was breakable. He respected me. Well, at least enough to not keep calling me that wretched nickname or to slap my ass again.

I stripped off my clothes and turned on the shower before I sat down to pee. The sweat had dried on my skin, but now I was itchy. It wasn't long before I pulled my hair out of its ponytail and climbed in the shower. The hot water felt great on my muscles. I'd started stiffening some in the car.

Fighting, running, even twisting his weight and countering it used slightly different muscles from what I was used to. Also, despite going every day for the last few days, we hadn't really been pushing me. I couldn't push it here at the condo. Even if I ran full out on the treadmill, running wasn't dancing, or silks or acrobatics.

The more I thought about it, the more aggravated I grew. Maybe I should tell them I would go back. A shudder crawled up my spine at the thought. But telling them and doing it were two totally different things. Not even scrubbing my head more vigorously could quite chase that shadow away.

If I called Lainey, she'd come out to meet me. I could pick up the stuff from the bank and be out of here. I trusted Lainey. There would be no way she'd take me back to my uncle or even clue him in on what was going on. At the same time...

My stomach bottomed out as I poured conditioner into my palm. Leaving would mean not seeing the guys. Leaving them wasn't high on my list. Ditching Milo was definitely climbing. I was still chewing over the whole thing after I changed into one of Rome's many t-shirts that he'd been leaving, and a pair of dance shorts.

After just running a comb through my damp hair, I

debated pretending Milo wasn't out there or just hiding in my room until he left.

Hide in my room until he left? How fucking childish could I be? Shaking my head, I checked my phone was where I'd hidden it, before leaving the room. Liam's door was open, but the shower was on in his bathroom. Okay, maybe Milo had already left.

I padded out to the living room and paused. No such luck. Milo stood with his arms folded as he stared out the windows toward the city. This was really the first time I'd been able to study him without him being aware. From this angle, I could make out the slope of his jaw and the way his neck muscles shifted as though he swallowed.

The fact he wore only a muscle shirt and jeans left his tatted up arms on display and they really were huge. His biceps had to be bigger than my thighs. My thighs were nothing to sneeze at. Jail. He'd been in jail.

Whether he was aware of me or not, he didn't say anything. I could wait him out, ignore him, or... "I guess this doesn't look like a cell to you, huh?"

"No," he said slowly, without turning around. He hadn't jumped at the sound of my voice. So, I guessed he'd been waiting for me to make the first move. Fine. I'd done it. Folding my own arms, I walked out to the living room slowly.

"A cage is a cage," I told him. "Some of the worst cages don't even have bars." They look like a spotlight on a stage or a beautiful silk dress on a red carpet while dozens of cameras flashed and twinkled. Both could leave you blind to the world beyond their circle and served to remind you that you weren't allowed to leave that circle.

"Yeah," he answered with a sigh and finally faced me. The man's expressions were damn hard to read, but the way he stared at me should make me uncomfortable. Those dark eyes drilling into me as if he could see right past the skin and muscle, to the core of who I was. While it should be discomforting, it wasn't. It only made me more curious.

At the back of the sofa, I paused and leaned into it. "If I asked you why you were in jail, would you tell me?"

"Maybe," he said. "If you were to ask." The words were on the tip of my tongue, but he continued before I could ask, "I'd rather you didn't. Or at least, if you would wait to hear that story."

"Why?" There were plenty of questions I didn't want to answer, so it seemed only fair that I gave him his privacy. Still wanted to know.

"Because you already don't like me," he said slowly. "None of this was how I planned to meet you. We got off to a rocky start and I'd prefer it if you didn't hate me—even if you never like me."

Those words made my heart ache for him. There was a lonely vulnerability housed beneath the gruff, rough tone. "Telling me why you were in jail would make me hate you?" What had he done?

"I don't know," he admitted, dropping his arms and spreading them wide. "I don't know you like I thought I did." The last words were a whisper. "In my head, I've had this conversation with you a thousand times, in a thousand different ways—and in none of them did you push back or get so angry with me, that you were willing to fight me over one of my brothers."

"I hate to break this to you, but all the imaginary conversations in the world wouldn't prepare you for the real thing. Not really."

"Well, think of it as a rehearsal..."

"...on a stage you don't know, with sharp edges and cue

points no one tells you about, lighting you don't control, to a song you've never even heard, and using a style you've never studied." It wasn't a question. Even if they had told me about Milo... "You don't know me."

"I know," he said and raked his hand through his hair. The grief littering those two words cut at me. "I know that, dammit. I know you're not Ivy. I know you don't remember me or Mom or the life we had. You don't remember stinky diapers or throwing toys at my head. You don't remember crying and the only thing that would make you happy is if I sat with you and let you climb all over me." The intensity in his eyes and his voice rose with each word. He took a step towards me. "You don't remember *me*."

Oh, the rawness of that anguish. I'd have to be dead not to feel it. "I'm sorry," I whispered. "I wish I did. I wish... " I closed my eyes at the sudden warmth of tears and swallowed before my own emotions could escape. There were things Sharpe's didn't do, and break down in front of strangers was top of that list. "I wish your story was true."

I sniffed and blinked until the tears were gone and then met his gaze again.

"But I can't imagine my parents abandoning a son. The Sharpe name means everything to them..."

"Because *they* aren't your biological parents, and they aren't mine. They didn't want a boy who was almost eight to take with them. They wanted a baby." Frustration tightened his expression before he rubbed his hands over his face. "Look..." He continued forward and whipped out a wallet. He flipped it open and then held out a photo to me. "That's us."

The care he took with that single thin photo made me show it similar care as I took it. It was an old photo. The corners were worn until they were soft, like fabric at the edges. The picture itself wasn't the best quality but there was a young boy staring up at me with the most solemn eyes. He had his arms around a baby. She had a fistful of his shirt and his hair, and a grin featuring just two teeth.

"It's the last one I have of us. Ms. Joanie gave it to me after you were adopted." Behind the kids in the photo was a sofa covered with toys and school books. The baby's hair stood straight up on one-side and her face was red and there was an impression of a blanket. "I remember that day like yesterday. I didn't know it was the last day we would be together."

I dared a glance at him, but he wasn't looking at me anymore, his attention was on the windows and the city beyond it.

"I came home from school and you had just woken from a nap," he continued, a trace of humor entering his voice. "You were *pissed off* about something. Ms. Joanie and I had a deal. I had to let you have three shrieks before I went to you. She worried that I was always hovering over you. I mean, I'd been looking after you so long, it was my job, right?"

I had a feeling he wasn't talking to me anymore.

"But she wanted me to be a little boy and a brother, not caretaker. So, three shrieks. If she didn't make it by then or if you hadn't calmed down, then I could come. We'd just gotten off the bus and it was cold outside. Kind of gloomy. It was supposed to rain but it hadn't, and the air was thick and muggy, like even the water in the air was waiting for it all to just let go. You were screaming from the second I got off the bus. I gave you the three shrieks, but you just got louder and louder."

Glancing down at the photo again, I traced my fingers over the two little kids. The baby could be me, I supposed. We had the same shape face, but there were none of my more pronounced features. Then again, babies *changed* as they grew, so this baby could have grown up to be Freddie.

Yet, despite all that, Milo wasn't lying to me. He believed I was his sister like it was a fundamental part of him.

"I raced inside, and you cut off mid-shriek as soon as you saw me." He laughed, but it was one of those one chuckle sounds that escape but don't bring real humor with it. "All at once, you had your arms up and demanding and you were glaring at me... a lot like you were a little while ago." Air escaped him in a sigh as he scrubbed a hand over his face. "But as soon as I picked you up, you laughed and cooed and started to babble like we'd been in the middle of some conversation. You were so red-faced, you were almost cherry-colored and sweaty."

I guess the baby did have a bit of a sweaty forehead and a runny nose. "Where was Ms. Joanie?" I asked after Milo went silent.

He shook his head and faced me again. "She was coming, just—she was in the bathroom when you woke up. But as soon as she saw us like that, she took a picture. You were yanking my hair and my shirt, cause I'd tried to put you down and you didn't want to be put down. Course, you were already climbing everything by then. It was hard to keep you penned in if you really wanted out."

That was good to know. Even if it wasn't me.

"Anyway," he said. "The guys came in and we all got cleaned up and changed. Rome took you for a bit so I could wash up and change, cause you still weren't letting me put you down. Then after dinner, Ms. Joanie sent the boys upstairs and told me that the Sharpes were going to pick you up in the morning. She'd gotten the call. We'd talked about it, you see. Me, Ms. Joanie, and Ms. Stephanie."

"Talked about me being adopted?'

He nodded. "They'd come to see you a couple of times. I met them once. She smelled like lilacs or something. Really floral, made my nose burn."

Mother did prefer her Chanel.

"He seemed all right. He didn't complain when you threw something at him and when he was holding you, you got snot all over his expensive suit, and you kept trying to bite his watch." Milo shook his head. "He was good with you though. I guess she was, too. But they had a lot of money, nice things, nice places...and they wanted you."

They wanted me.

I continued running my finger over the kids in that image.

"I just didn't know it would happen so fast. I thought, you know, there would be time. Ms. Joanie said I could stay home from school the next day so I could see you off."

"They didn't want you?" I asked, because if we really were siblings... "Don't they try to keep siblings together in the system?" Granted, I didn't know much about it, but it seemed that way in the handful of news pieces I'd seen on something similar. Like the cop who adopted the five kids of a woman who'd overdosed and he'd found them. He'd adopted them to keep them all together and there was a baby and a much older kid in that grouping.

"Yeah, they try," Milo said. "Doesn't always work out and most people—they don't want older kids. We have issues. Hang-ups. Trauma. They want babies."

"Clean slates," I murmured.

"More or less," he said with a shrug. "And I didn't want you to go, but I also didn't want you to stay there. The simple fact was, sooner or later, I was going to age up into a group home with the guys and you'd have been in a different one, maybe or at another foster home."

I swallowed at the bleakness in that statement.

"One way or another, they'd have taken you from me. At least this way, I got to say something. I got to say yes to you getting a better life."

Better.

Life.

"Ms. Stephanie wasn't supposed to tell me their names, but they had. Then she told me what name they'd picked out for you—Emersyn—it's a lot fancier than Ivy. Sounded important. Rich. Successful. Not—little Ivy Hardigan—whose mom was too strung out on drugs to look after her kids and shot up on some crazy house cleaner cause she was desperate for a fix."

Nausea swam in my stomach.

"Ivy Hardigan is the kid you feel bad for. She's a statistic—like her older brother Milo. But Emersyn? Emersyn Sharpe, she's a star, a debutante, a wealthy woman from a wealthy family and the whole world is her oyster."

I swore my heart shattered for him.

Because if he really believed that was my life—he would never understand the truth of it. I couldn't even swallow around the lump in my throat. He ripped his shirt off and showed me a tattoo on his side, it went all the way up his side to curl around his pec over his heart.

It was a vine, twisting and growing. Weaving and curling with the vine were images of a girl growing. Vine and leaves.

Kellan had one.

So did Vaughn.

And Jasper.

"Ivy," Milo told me. "I kept you with me, this piece, we all did. You're my north star. The goal I was chasing."

The tattoo held me riveted. I'd seen a similar ivy-wrapped mark on Kellan. I didn't know about Liam or Freddie, I hadn't really examined their tattoos. "I don't understand," I whispered.

"I wanted to see you again," he said and that dragged my gaze up to his. "To meet you on your level. To be someone—you would be proud of, not some random street thief who got really good at the con and could plan a heist and just about anything else. To be important, and not just the orphaned kid of a junkie and her dealer. A guy who couldn't even be bothered with his own kids."

I think I died a little inside.

"That was always the plan. You were going to have a good life and I was going to walk up to you one day and introduce myself and you were going to be so damn happy to meet me. Then—we'd talk and you'd tell me these stories about who you were and I'd have to make up some shit, but, we'd be brother and sister again. A family, again."

Yeah.

I died a little.

Looking back down at the picture, I stared at those kids. I really wanted to be this little girl and at the same time, I didn't. Because the truth—it was so far from Milo's dream it might as well be on another planet.

"I can prove it," Milo offered quietly. "I mean we can do DNA testing and all that—or you can come with me to see Mickey."

My heart leapt at the idea of seeing him. "Why Doc? I mean—I guess he can do the blood tests"

"Yeah," Milo said. "He can do that. But he can also tell you the truth."

"What truth?"

"That you're Ivy. That you were in the system with me until you were placed and they changed your name legally."

I shook my head. Wait—the poster in the clinic. The stunned shock on Doc's face when I told him that was me. All the moisture in my mouth dried up.

"Mickey's the one who found us after Mom died. He's the one who took us to Ms. Stephanie in the first place."

A nasty thump began to pound behind my right eye.

"He found us?" Was I really buying into this? "I mean—he found you?"

"Yeah," Milo told me. "He also took me to your show so I could see you. It was the first night you danced in a ring coming down from the ceiling. It terrified me, but you were so amazing and so tiny and..."

I was going to be sick.

I dropped the photograph and turned away. Milo said something. At the end of the hall, Liam stood there, staring at me with a grave expression, but I couldn't.

I just couldn't.

I barely made it to the bathroom before I threw up.

MATCHED SET

School days all went the same. We got up early, ate breakfast, then hustled out the door to get on the bus. It was like when we were at Ms. Joanie's only without Ms. Joanie. The group home had a lot more kids, a lot more beds, and way less room. That was okay. Milo, Jasper, and Kellan were our roommates. We had one empty bunk in the place, but no one else had been put in with us.

The day before, we hadn't been able to go to school because the people came to see Liam again. They wanted me to visit as well, but I just sat there and drew. I didn't need to get to know them. Liam said they were really nice and they wanted to get to know me too. When I asked why, he said because they might offer us a home. They could be our new parents.

I didn't need new parents. We had one set. They were gone. Now it was us. But if Liam wanted new parents, I was okay with that.

The whole afternoon we spent with them had dragged.

They took us out to lunch, then to a park. The woman—Mrs. O'Connell—came to sit with me at one point.

"That's a very nice drawing," she said.

I nodded. It wasn't my best work. But Mr. O'Connell was easy to draw. He had very square features. Mrs. O'Connell was harder. I'd figure it out.

"Do you want to be an artist when you grow up?"

I shrugged. Growing up was a long way away. I'd decide when I got there.

"You know, Rome," she said my name with a lot of care. "Liam loves you very much."

Yep. I knew that. But he'd probably get mad at her for being mushy about it. He hadn't even been mushy with Mom. Though he endured her hugs a lot better than I did. I paused to think about that. He had endured them or had he liked them. He used to joke that he got twice the number of hugs because I always let him have mine.

"We're very serious about taking both of you home with us—if you'll have us."

No, Mom's hugs were fine, but she always wanted to cuddle us and I couldn't do that. Brief hugs were fine, cuddling hugs not so much. That was right. I could remember her face now. The smile she would give me when I let her squeeze me. Only once. Never more. She never asked me for more. Sometimes when I didn't feel like it, she didn't make me.

Liam would give her two hugs to make up for me not being able to do it. I went back to Mr. O'Connell's face and shaded around his eyes. He'd had on a funny hat when they came to pick us up. I liked the way it made the light do weird things.

"Do you think you would like that?" Mrs. O'Connell asked. "Coming to live with us?"

I glanced up to where Liam was playing. He was showing off for Mr. O'Connell and was all the way on top of the jungle gym, walking across the monkey bars. We did that a lot. Climbed high, got up where no one could reach us.

"No," I said, without looking at her. Then remembered Ms. Stephanie reminding me about manners. "Thank you."

"Oh," she exhaled the word and it sounded like she might cry. Twisting my head, I studied her. She wasn't looking at me anymore. She was staring at Liam. The look on her face was so sad. Suddenly, I understood how to draw her. How to ease the curves around her cheeks and to soften the lines of her eyes and the slope of her nose. While Mr. O'Connell was all hard edges and big features, hers were far more delicate.

I patted her hand, and she gave me the most startled look. "Liam would like to live there. He needs new parents. I don't."

That should make her feel better. Liam was better with people anyway. Returning my attention to the drawing, I went back to it. If Liam went with them, then I'd stay with our friends. I liked them. They never asked me for hugs or tried to touch me. They never expected me to do things.

And they never asked me so many questions.

"Rome," Mrs. O'Connell said. "Liam doesn't want to leave you."

Oh. I looked at my brother. "I'll fix it."

Then I went back to the drawing. Mrs. O'Connell tried to talk to me some more, but eventually she went to join them on the playground and I finished my drawing. Liam wanted to go, so I would want it for him, too.

At school, though, Liam and I didn't get every class together. The teachers thought it would be better if I took a different set of lessons in the afternoon. I was fine with that. Afternoon classes meant a room with a special counselor and a lot of drawing. She was good at asking me simple questions and accepted my answers.

Like Ms. Stephanie, she told me manners were important. When you talk to someone, look them in the eyes. I didn't care about that so much, but I practiced it when I was with her. The same with drawing, I should pause when people spoke to me. If I kept drawing, they might think I wasn't listening.

It depended on what I was drawing, but I tried to pause when I remembered. Every day, we would repeat the lessons over and I wondered if she needed the practice. So, when I headed out to wait for the bus after the bell rang and ran into another boy, I did what she told me to do.

I looked him in the eye and said, "Sorry." It was an important word to say.

"What did you say to me, dummy?" the other kid asked as he shoved me. I went back a couple of steps and glanced at the ground.

I was pretty sure I'd said it right. I looked up at the kid again. "Sorry."

He hit me.

The force of his fist cracked into my face, and I tasted blood on my lip as I stumbled back. Still, I didn't fall down. My backpack was secure.

"Dummy says sorry," the kid said, and a bunch of the others laughed.

I hit him back. Only when I hit him, I came from below and cracked my fist against the underside of his jaw. He bit his tongue and landed on his ass. The blood that sprayed everywhere was kind of funny. Especially when the other kids started screaming too.

His friends yelled and rushed toward me. I smiled. This I understood.

I also wasn't worried.

Liam was just there, wading into the fight with me. Just like I knew he would be.

We were a matched set.

17

The elevator traveled too slowly up from the parking garage. Liam's text message had been blunt and to the point.

Hellspawn needs you.

I packed up my stuff and ran. I didn't have a car with me, but I made it to the stop in time to hop on the midtown bus. The bus wouldn't make it all the way to Liam's place, but it got me within ten blocks.

Running the rest of the way left me breathless and sweating in the elevator. I should have taken the stairs. As soon as it stopped and the doors started to open, I sprang through them. Not knocking, I typed in my code and unlocked the door with the key. Inside the apartment, it was quiet and the air electric with tension.

Liam stood near one of the floor length windows with a drink in his hand. Milo sat on the sofa with his head down. A quick scan of the room didn't reveal Starling. "Where?"

Was she not with him? If they'd taken her back to the club-house, he should have told me.

"Your room," Liam said and stepped into my path when I would have gone straight to the closed door. "Easy, cool off a second."

"You said she needed me."

"She does but..." I dropped the backpack and walked around him. Behind me, Liam sighed but he didn't follow. At the door, I knocked and then listened. No sound came from behind the door. After a moment, I said, "It's Rome."

A soft sigh from inside. Then a sniff. "Give me a minute."

"All right." I turned and sat down. The wall was cold against my back, and it felt good after the run. Liam was still visible down the hall, but he made a point of not looking this way. If he and Milo were talking, their voices were far too low to carry. The two had been deep in each other's pockets where secrets were concerned, and still were, or so it seemed.

The water turned on in the bathroom and I closed my eyes while I waited. If she needed me, then right here was where I would be. The soft click of the door unlocking pulled me from the light doze. Though she didn't open the door, the fact she unlocked it was an invitation.

I let myself in. Night had fallen at some point and the interior of the room was dark, save for two pools of light. One was at the open bathroom door and the other from a small lamp on the bedside table.

Honestly, I wasn't sure I'd ever turned it on. The lamp was very dim, almost too dim for reading or drawing. Prob-ably needed a different bulb.

"Hi." The soft murmur of her voice had me hunting around for her. She sat on the bed, arms wrapped around her knees. At least she was in my t-shirt. I liked that. "You look—sweaty."

"I ran," I told her, then lifted my arm to sniff.

The corners of her lips tipped upwards. "You can take a shower if you want. You have clothes here—and even if you didn't, you've left a lot of yours for me."

That was true. "Did you like them?"

She let go of her knees and sat back against the pillows, tugging the bear to her chest. The whiteness of her knuckles said almost as much as her body language. "Yes. I do."

"Do you need me now or can I shower?"

She frowned.

"Liam said you needed me."

"Oh." Surprise flickered across her expression. "And you ran here?"

"Yes."

I waited as she stared at me. Sometimes, Starling needed to think things through before she responded. I didn't mind the bouts of silence. Taking my time when I wasn't sure of an answer was something we had in common.

"Please, go ahead and shower, Rome. I feel bad that you ran all the way..."

"Don't feel bad. I wanted to." I started to tug off my shirt, then paused and locked the door again. She'd locked it for a reason. If she wanted Liam and Milo to stay out, I wouldn't leave it unlocked for them. "Five minutes," I said, then finished stripping the shirt. The musty smell of body odor, sweat, dirt, and paint all hit my nose at once. It wasn't pleasant. I glanced at her. "Ten minutes."

For a split-second, she smiled and I grinned.

"I smell."

"Okay."

"Bad," I promised.

She laughed. "I actually like the smell of sweat but go take a shower. I can wait for you." As I turned away, I caught her wiping her face. The shift let more light from the bathroom hit her and there were tear tracks on her cheeks.

Inside the bathroom, the sink and shower were wet, but there was another sour smell. This time, not me. I looked around before stripping off my clothes and turning on the water. It heated up fast here, so I stepped under the cold first. It sluiced away my run.

The shampoo and conditioner were in different places, and there were new soaps. New things in the shower like a blue and white loofah, a black file, and there was a jar of something. I ducked my head under the water before lathering it up with shampoo.

It smelled like Emersyn. This wasn't my stuff. My stuff was still here, but it was out on the counter. I shrugged. I didn't mind smelling like her. The little jar smelled heavily of wintergreen and menthol. My eyes watered and my nose stung.

Heat rub for muscles. Was she hurting for real? I hadn't seen new injuries. After returning the jars, I borrowed the soap and scrubbed away the sweat and dirt. There was paint on my fingers and different colors embedded around the nails. It never all came off and I didn't worry about it.

It was less than ten minutes when I finished rinsing and shut off the water. I hadn't bothered with closing the door, but I did snag a towel and run it over my arms, chest and legs before I wrapped it around my waist to step out of the shower.

Snagging my dirty clothes, I walked out of the bathroom. Emersyn still sat on the bed, hugging my bear. "You forgot something," she murmured.

"I did."

Glancing around, my laundry hamper wasn't where I expected it to be. It had been moved to a different corner. Probably because her suitcases were still out. One was on the dresser and the other on a chair.

After depositing my clothes, I opened the closet door and stared at the huge rolling rack of clothes.

"Sorry," she said with a sigh. "Liam bought all of that. I didn't want it, but it was out here taking up all the room, so I shoved it in there out of the way."

"I'll fix it." With a shove, I pushed it further back and then walked in to grab a pair of sweats off the shelf. Stripping off the damp towel, I pulled up the sweats and tightened the drawstring before returning to the bedroom. I would pull the rack of clothes out and get rid of them later, for now I closed the door before taking my towel into the bathroom to hang up.

Shutting off the light, I paused. "Do you want the light on?"

It had been on when I came in.

"No, it's fine," she murmured. She'd opened the curtains that I never bothered with when I was here, and stared out at the city. I climbed up onto the bed as I had the last few nights and slid an arm around her shoulders. Normally, I'd just tuck up to her back, it was what I did when she was curled up on her side.

But I wouldn't pull her to me unless she wanted to come. When she burrowed back against my chest, I wrapped both arms around her and held her much like she held my bear.

Though she smelled far nicer than my bear.

Quiet filled the room, growing more peaceful with each breath she took. The rapid hammer of her heart slowed and so did the faint raggedness to her breathing. She'd been crying, but she didn't offer an explanation and I didn't ask.

Content, I waited for her to tell me, or not. I'd half thought she'd fallen asleep when she hadn't moved in so very long, but then she let out a sigh. The world suddenly pressed into this soft bubble surrounding us.

"Milo told me about Ivy today."

"You."

"He believes it."

"So do you or you wouldn't be upset." It seemed straightforward enough. Why else would Milo be here and she would be so sad? The sadness bothered me. I wanted to fix the sadness, but I wasn't sure how.

"He's held on so tightly to the idea of me," she whispered. "Like it was this one truth that he has, and he believes with everything in him that I'm her."

"Yes."

"When Liam was gone—did you miss him?"

"Yes."

She twisted to look up at me. "Why didn't you go with him?"

"I didn't need new parents. Liam did. I was happy where I was. He wasn't. But when he left, I didn't lose him."

That was a lot of words but they all fit. "That actually makes sense." Even if she sounded puzzled about it. "When I left, Milo lost me."

"Yes," I agreed. "But no." Because he hadn't. None of us had. "We never forgot you. Milo always had a plan." For as long as I could remember, he'd had a plan. Ivy had always been a part of that plan.

"Oh." Another soft breathy escape and she settled back

against my chest again. I tucked my cheek to her hair and waited. "I don't remember him." The lost note creeping into her voice twisted my insides into knots. "At all. He has this —bond—with me."

Understanding crystalized.

"But you don't have one for him."

"No," she whispered, and a teardrop landed on my arm. I stared at the droplet of water as it quivered for a moment before sliding down my skin to fall away. "I've never had a sibling. I've always been alone."

No. I wanted to tell her. You haven't. But if she didn't know we were there, then she wouldn't know she wasn't alone.

"And I struggle to believe that I'm who he says I am."

"Why?"

A humorless laugh escaped her. "Because it would mean I'm not Emersyn Sharpe."

Now it was my turn to not understand. "You said names were important." Months ago, when she'd been struggling with the concussion and her injuries.

"I did," she said with another weighted sigh, and I wasn't sure why that knotted my guts even tighter, except something was hurting her and I didn't know what it was.

"Starling," I said. "Tell me what's wrong so I can fix it."

"I don't think you can."

"I can fix a lot of things. What I can't, the others can." My brothers had never let me down. We could find a solution.

Her head settled against my shoulder, and she caught one of my hands in hers. The bear still sat in her lap, but she held my right hand with her left and traced her fingers over the different splotches of paint.

"If I'm not Emersyn Sharpe, then...everything I was raised on was a lie."

Yes.

"But if I'm not Ivy—" She hesitated.

"Hardigan," I supplied, if it was the name she needed.

"Hardigan, yes, thank you...Hardigan. O'Connell. They both sound Irish. Not very WASPy at all."

I wasn't sure what insects had to do with it, but I shrugged. "Cleary is Irish, too."

"Cleary?"

"That's me—Rome Cleary."

"But Liam is..."

"He took his adopted family's name, but he's still a Cleary too."

"That's weird. I can't imagine having a twin and having them be somewhere completely different."

"But we were never apart. Even when we were in different places."

She turned my hand over and the light graze of her nails against my palm sent tingles up my arm and soothed at the same time. "Still—you knew about each other. You still talked. I didn't know about Milo—fuck." Without banging her head, she mimed it against my shoulder. "Rome, I want to believe him—but I've seen my birth certificate. Name and pedigree is everything to my family."

I shrugged. "If you want a dog, we can get a dog."

My starling stilled, even the petting motion of her hand froze, and she sat forward and then twisted to look at me. As much as I missed holding her, I loosened my arms and focused on her gaze.

It was important to meet the other person's eyes. Especially if they were important. Staring into her eyes wasn't hard.

"What did you just say?"

"I said, if you want a dog, we can get one. Just tell me what kind. I'll find it. Liam will hate it getting hair everywhere. That would be funny." I grinned. Liam liked everything orderly. We were alike in that respect, but when I was creating, I didn't need order—I craved chaos.

Dogs were chaotic, right?

"Why would you even bring up a dog?" Tilting her head, she studied me as though there would be an answer on my face and then her gaze dipped to my chest, and she let out a whoosh of breath. "You have one, too."

I glanced down as she hovered her fingers over one of the swirls of pattern Vaughn had inked into my skin. I'd drawn it, and he'd done the work. There were birds escaping from some of the pattern. There were droplets in other places—for blood and for paint. There was a twist of two fingers, one for me and one for Liam. He had a similar one on his arm, hidden among his other ink.

But she was staring at the leaves sprouting from one of the waves where it dipped toward my spine.

"Ivy," I told her. "For you."

That was what she meant. "Does it make you sad?" If it did. I'd find a way to get rid of it. Seriously, I could ink a starling on myself for her. It would be more appropriate anyway.

Especially now.

"No," she said with a slow shake of her head. "It's just— all these years, you guys have been out there, out here, watching me. Knowing me. Thinking I was her."

"Knowing."

"You believe." It wasn't a question.

"I know," I told her. Then traced a single finger along her jaw then up to her eye. "This face—I would know it anywhere. Your cheeks were ruddier when you were a baby, and fuller, but the jaw and the shape of the eyes. They are the same. The tip of your nose. The way you flatten your lips when you're angry or how you curl your toes when you're concentrating on something you're trying to learn."

She immediately relaxed her feet, but it was too late

"It's okay if you don't know what to believe. I know the truth."

"You make it sound so easy."

I shrugged. "It is that easy. You're one of us. You always have been—even if you didn't know." Since I was still touching her, I cupped her face and she leaned her cheek into the contact and I had to fight the urge to kiss her. I liked kissing her. I liked how dazed she looked when I kissed her.

I liked it even more when she was pressed up against me and I could feel all of her while I kissed her. But I wasn't here to kiss her. I was here to make her feel better. To fix what was wrong. If she was missing the others, I'd get them over here. One at a time maybe—

"Rome?"

I focused on her again.

"Why did you ask me about a dog?"

"You said names and pedigrees were important to your family."

Her lower lip trembled faintly then slowly dropped open.

"Dogs have pedigrees. That's not what you meant?"

Her laughter filled the room as she clutched the bear to her chest. It rose and fell, and even though tears slipped from her eyes, I grinned.

Told her I could fix it.

RANDOM ACTS

VAUGHN

The year we turned fifteen was a shitty one. It was the year we killed someone for the first time. It wouldn't be the last. Between them, Jasper and Liam took out three more pedophiles over the course of that next year. I didn't think too much of it. Killing someone changes something inside of you. We'd always been tough. I may never have liked fighting, but I wasn't exactly afraid of it either.

My size always seemed to freak people out, when I hit puberty, I just got bigger. The guys had all thought it was funny when they hit before me. Rome and Liam shot up one right after the other. Pissed Jasper right the fuck off when Liam got taller. For six months, we had to listen to those two snarl and snipe at each other like a pair of rabid dogs.

Considering that I was usually taller than all of them, I didn't care. Milo even got sick of their arguing, and Rome actually dumped a bucket of water over them once to get them to shut up. Then one right after another, Milo and

Kellan grew over the summer. It was funny, suddenly they were all a little bit taller than me and it was nice.

For the first time in forever, people weren't trying to pick fights with me 'cause I was the biggest. It didn't take long for any of us to get a reputation in high school. Even at the group home, the other kids tended to let us be.

Then Liam found his first fight club.

Though, maybe it wasn't his first one, just his first *lucrative* one. The kids at that fancy prep school of his were a vicious bunch of bastards. They hosted a fight club every weekend. Apparently, you had to have a buy-in to qualify, but you could bring in ringers if you wanted.

Liam invited me because brawling was something I did better than all of them. When it came to strict fighting, I could take more damage and dish it out. Liam *loved* fighting. Like it was in his fucking blood. He craved the violence and the blood, even more, he thrived on the mind games he played with his opponents.

If one didn't know him, you might call him a borderline sociopath. But Liam had a conscience, even if he kept it hidden under fancy uniforms, expensive gifts, and pricey cars. The couple who adopted him were wealthy as sin and they showered all of it on him. He, in turn, showered it on us.

"Why?" I asked when Liam approached me about the idea. No, I didn't miss that he came to ask me when Jasper wasn't around. "Jas would probably enjoy it as much as you do."

"Yeah, but he has a hard time pulling back," Liam answered. "Once he's in it, he's in the fight. Knocking them out is fine, not really looking to kill them."

Yet. While he didn't say it, the word sat there bright as

day. Like I said, you might mistake Liam for a bit of a sociopath. "Yeah, sure, not gonna do it every week. And I'm not taking a fall either."

"Brother, I would *never* ask you to do that." Liam's eyes glittered when he said that, and his grin was downright devilish. "I'll swing by and grab you on Saturday. They always move the club, we don't know where it'll be until the day of, usually an hour ahead of time and we have to make it by cut-off, or we can't get in."

"Whatever," I told him. "I gotta go finish my math homework. Milo said he'd help me with the numbers."

"You still having issues?" Liam's frown turned fierce.

"Nah, not since they figured out the dyscalculia thing. Milo just checks the numbers over to make sure I didn't write 'em down wrong. Turns out I'm not stupid when the numbers are in the right order."

"Let me know..." he began, but I waved him off.

"I'm fine. Go away."

He laughed but I caught that flash of worry in his expression. Inside, I found Milo in our room. Rome was somewhere. Kellan and Jasper were both working. They had after school jobs, pretty much taking anything and everything they could get their hands on. Freddie was sprawled on Jasper's bed doing homework. He was too young to share our room, but he hid in here most of the time.

"Liam's gonna call you," I told Milo as I dragged my backpack out and pulled out the math text. Our school hadn't invested in tablets for all the students, so we still got real books.

"Yeah?" Milo glanced up from his book just as his phone started to buzz.

"Uh huh. He wants you to tell him I don't need a special tutor or something."

Milo laughed. "Right, I'll be back a few." He was already talking into the phone on his way out the door. "If you wanted to talk to me, you could have just come in..."

"Why don't you let him pay for a fancy tutor?" Freddie asked. "He could probably make the school do all kinds of stuff for you. They'd probably want to suck his dick because he smells like money."

"Pretty sure no one needs to get their dick sucked because numbers dance when I try to write them down," I told him. "And Liam doesn't need to feel guilty because he's got all that and we don't."

As soon as I cracked the book, I began to write the numbers down slowly. It was painstaking work. Once I had them in the right order, I could do most of the functions. But getting them to go from one place to the other—it took more concentration than drawing a detailed work with varying textures.

"Man, I'd kill to have that kind of money. I bet they even have fancy dope at his school. Fancy pussy. Fancy cars. Fancy drugs."

I glanced over at him, even if it meant I'd have to focus again to get the numbers right. "It's a school. Just like ours." We had drugs, pussy, and cars at our school too.

"Yeah, but ours aren't fancy. You think fancier drugs make you feel better than regular drugs?"

A part of me wanted to shake him. Drugs were just bad news. But could I blame Freddie for wanting to forget the shit he'd gone through? Milo tried to get him to talk about it. So had Jasper. Not once had Freddie said a word. Not one word when we killed the guy. Not one word when we took him to a doctor.

At least we knew a guy who could stitch him up without asking any questions. It cost, but Liam had paid it without blinking. So would we, but he actually had a roll of fucking cash.

"I bet their drugs just come in prettier packages," I said after a long moment. "Same shit, different box."

The kid grunted and flopped onto his back, but not before I saw how dilated his pupils were. He was already tripping on something.

One of these days, he was gonna do too much, and then what? I ran a hand through my hair and looked back at the paper—

"Well, well, well..." A cutting voice said. "Look who's here, Freddie the fucking thief."

The owner of the voice made it exactly one step into the room. Freddie rolled off the bed and had a knife in his hand, but I stood up and the voice's owner backed up hurriedly. Without a word, I walked across the room to the open door and stared down at the kid.

He wasn't alone. But none of them had the balls to even meet my gaze. "Freddie the fucker isn't any of your business, got it?" I said.

Silence stretched out and I cracked my knuckles.

"Got. It."

One word after another I punctuated with the pop of bone and suddenly four gazes pivoted up to me with jerky nods. "Sorry, Vaughn," the youngest of the four said. His voice had already begun to crack. "Didn't know you were here."

"Clearly. But understand me—we're here, even when we're not."

They nodded again and took off. Closing the door, I looked over at Freddie who white-knuckled the knife. "I—"

"Don't lie to me," I said, holding up a hand. "I'm not asking what you took, unless it's cash. Give it back. Don't do it again."

The arm he wielded the knife, which lowered a fraction.

It was money.

"How much?"

Fidgeting, Freddie scratched at the back of his neck with his free hand and tried to turn away. I folded my arms and waited. I already had a headache of numbers waiting to figure out. But if Freddie stole someone's money, they were gonna be looking for him. Those little rats were nothing.

We could handle them, but if he aimed higher.

"It was like twenty bucks," he mumbled, and I almost missed it.

I sighed. "From who?"

"Darin."

I nodded. "Do your homework and put away the knife. I'll get the asshole his money and you'll leave their shit alone, Freddie."

"I needed it." Again, he didn't look at me but the twitching in his hands and the dilated eyes were a dead giveaway.

With a sigh, I dropped back onto my own bed and went to work on the numbers—again.

Ten minutes later, Freddie said, "I'm sorry, Vaughn." His voice was real quiet and low, the sadness in it gutted me.

"Don't worry, man," I told him. "We got your back."

And we would. One of these days, he'd believe us and maybe we could get him off that shit.

"Next time you need money..."

"Even if it's—"

I sighed. "Yeah, even if. Come ask, don't take it."

The guys would kill me. But I'd rather we had a chance at saving him, before he stole from the wrong people.

Unfortunately, it turned out Darin wasn't the only guy Freddie took cash from. The other guy? He was bigger. He was meaner.

And he turned out to be the second guy I had to kill.

18

Rome stayed. He curled around me and answered me if I asked anything, but for the most part, we just sat there in silence, staring out the window. The company brought me far more comfort than I was prepared to admit.

At one point, Liam knocked on the door and Rome answered it to bring in the food that Liam had ordered. After setting it on the bed, he grabbed the big rack out of the closet and dragged it out to the hallway.

"She doesn't want them," he told Liam. "Put them in your room."

Then he closed the door.

Guilt gnawed at me. Enough that I climbed off the bed and opened the door to find Liam still there, staring at the rack. I'd told him I didn't want the clothes. I didn't want other people picking stuff out for me.

Rome was right behind me, but he didn't try to intervene and when Liam lifted his gaze from the clothes to me, a fresh wave of guilt hit me. "I don't hate them."

"I know," Liam said slowly. "You just want to pick out your own things."

He had heard me, more he'd *listened.*

"I just liked spoiling you," he murmured, more to himself than to me. The corner of his mouth kicked up into a self-deprecating smile. "Thought you'd like me more."

"Because you bought me clothes?"

"Yeah, I get it. I'm stupid. You grew up with more money than I did, I suppose, and for a lot longer."

The warmth of his listening to me, froze in the tundra of that statement. "It's never about things," I said, and he frowned.

"Hellspawn, I didn't mean anything by it."

"No, I know. It's me, I'm cranky and I have cramps." It was an excuse. I mean I was sore and achy, those could be cramps.

He grimaced. "You need something special for it?"

"No," I said slowly. "Though I wouldn't say no to a heating pad and maybe a glass of wine or a beer?"

"I got beer," he said, then frowned. "What kind of wine do you want?"

"I don't care. Alcoholic preferably." Getting drunk would be a terrible idea, but one drink might actually let me relax again.

He chuckled, then shook his head. "Hellspawn, you confuse me."

"Right back at you—what did they call you—Mocking-bird?" I could have sworn that was his name, He rolled his eyes, but it was Rome who snorted a laugh behind me.

"Yeah, I'll tell you the story someday," Liam said. "Maybe when I'm good and plastered."

"Or not."

"Or not," he agreed. He looked above me, his gaze fixed on Rome. They were doing that thing again. I swore the air around us pulsed whenever they did that silent communication. What would it be like to be so close to someone you didn't even need to hear their voice to understand what they were saying? What they needed? What you could offer? Whether they would accept it?

When I was little, I'd always wanted a brother or a sister. Someone to play with who was my age. Eventually, I grew to be glad I didn't have one. Could I have ever worked it out to perform and escape like I had, if there was a younger sister there to take my place?

All at once, my appetite fled and I turned away from Liam to look at the rack. I snagged one of the shirts off of it and carried it back into the room.

"Um—Hellspawn?" Liam never sounded uncertain.

I glanced back at him. Raw. I was too raw to have this conversation, I should have just let Rome shove the clothes out there and leave them. The guilt didn't make any sense except—so far Liam had kept his word to me and the training at the gym...it helped more than he might realize.

"I think they put that shirt on there for me." He motioned to the shirt in my hand and I glanced down at it. The color was damn near the blue of their eyes. The sleeves were long and it was a button down. It was definitely way too big for me.

"Good," I said slowly as I studied it. "Do you mind if I steal it?"

"Asking isn't stealing," Rome said as he shut the door on his twin and then locked it. "Now it's stolen."

A laugh escaped me as I ran my fingers over the shirt. It was super soft. It really would look amazing with their eyes, but that said—I wanted it and I wanted him to feel like he'd done something for me.

Yeah, Emersyn, I said to myself silently, you keep telling yourself that. I hung the shirt up and then retreated to the bed.

"Do you think Milo is still out there?" I moved the bear over to sit on the nightstand, while Rome slid onto the bed and pulled the tray up to us. Even with my appetite gone, I could appreciate the scent of the meatball subs that were under the lids.

Rome grinned at the sight of them.

"You like these?"

"My favorites," he said. "Liam always orders them for me. And no."

"What?"

"Do I think Milo is still out there? No."

Oh. Maybe he was giving me time. Rome offered me a plate with half a sub on it and he looked so damn happy, I took a bite.

"Good." He nodded, then ate his so fast, I was worried he might choke.

Despite the speed, he was extremely fastidious, not letting a single drop fall onto the plate or his bare chest. In fact, he kept his fingers clean, too. And I found myself watching to see how often he had to suck the meatball sauce off his fingers. About halfway through his second sandwich, he paused and returned my stare.

"I'm sorry," I said, and jerked my gaze back to my own food. Why was I staring at him while he ate? Way to make him feel self-conscious.

"It doesn't hurt when you look at me."

"Has anyone ever hurt you while they looked at you?"

He seemed to turn that idea over in his mind, considering it. "Most people who look at me want something or want to hurt me because they don't like what they see. I don't really care what they see."

"Liam would never let anyone hurt you," I said, absolutely certain of that. "Not to mention, I've seen you fight." And kill. But I didn't need to add that. The faint smile on his face held secrets—not secrets from me but secrets we shared.

"I like when you look at me," Rome said. "I like looking at you."

From any other guy, that would be a flirty comment. Rome just said it like it was a fact. "How are the others?" I picked at the bread on my sandwich. When Rome nudged my plate, I made a face at him before I took another bite.

"Kel works to avoid everyone. He and Milo are angry at each other. Vaughn is the same, but he can't take any extra hours because he is maxing out. Jasper..." On the last, Rome shrugged. "He kept more than you secret, and they are trying to clean up the mess."

I frowned. "What mess?'

Rather than answer me, Rome rose when Liam knocked on the door. He opened it to his brother, who stood there with a droll expression. "The lady requested a beer or some wine, I brought us some."

He held a bottle in one hand and three glasses in the other.

Rome grunted. "I don't like wine."

"Then go get yourself a beer." Not waiting to be invited, Liam walked into the room and set the glasses on the dresser before he began filling the first of two. He'd picked out a red. Yes, my wine knowledge extended to colors, no matter how much my mother and father discussed wineries and grape seasons like that should mean something.

Rome glanced at me. His expression didn't change but I swore I understood the question he didn't voice. Was I okay with him leaving me alone with Liam?

I nodded. After the torrent of emotion earlier, numbness was all that remained. He gave my sandwich a pointed look and I had to pick it up and take a bite before he vanished up the hall.

Liam passed me a glass of wine before he motioned to the bed. "Do you mind if I join the two of you?"

More curious than anything else, I had to ask, "If I did?"

"Well," Liam said with a sigh. "I'd bitch, probably make rude remark or at least a bit of a cutting one, then leave you two alone. I will never get in Rome's way."

"Thank you," I said slowly, before shifting to sit cross-legged against the pillows. I still had my plate and now the glass of wine.

"For telling you I'd complain?" Liam asked, his tone epically dry.

I just rolled my eyes. He knew what I meant. But he still didn't sit until I motioned to the end of the bed. Rome walked back in as Liam took a seat more on the side of the bed, closer to me than the foot of it.

Not only did he have a beer in hand, he had two more wrapped sandwiches that looked like the huge subs he'd already consumed.

"They're his favorite," Liam told me.

"So he said."

Rome moved to sit next to me, with his back against the pillows and he stretched out his legs. "I'll share," he offered, but glanced at my only partially eaten sandwich.

"I'm working on it," I promised. "I just don't usually eat this much."

I had no idea why I said it, but I had, and the lie seemed far more palatable than all of the earlier discussions, and thoughts about my family left me sick to my stomach. I took a swallow of wine instead. Maybe it could unknot the muscles in my neck and back.

Liam stared at me and I caught his gaze over the rim of my glass. "Why lie?" he asked. "You're not going to offend either of us if you're just not hungry. Besides...if you're not, then I can just..." He reached forward as though he was going to take my plate, but Rome was that much faster and snapped it away.

"Starling's," he said with a hard, almost savage note. "You can get your own."

The direct echo of Liam's earlier statement had me biting the inside of my lip to hold back the laughter. Because while Liam had been teasing, Rome definitely wasn't.

The "see what I put up with" look on Liam's face didn't help me suppress the laughter. "The point," he said. "He doesn't share unless he's worried."

"No," Rome said simply. "I'm sharing because I like her."

Offense filled Liam's tone when he asked, "And you don't like me?"

If not for the twinkling in his eyes, I'd have believed he really was upset. Instead, he just sipped his wine as Rome washed down another bite of meatball sub with a long pull of beer.

"Not really, no," Rome said. "You're letting Milo lock her up here. She doesn't want to be in the cage."

The world tilted from humor and play to sober tension

that seemed to crackle in the air between them. It kind of reminded me of the static building when a storm was coming. You could just feel the pressure against your skin.

Not answering immediately, Liam took another swallow of wine before he said, "Would you rather I had told him no, and he locked her up somewhere at the clubhouse? Or just sent her home?"

Ice filled my veins at the last option.

"No," Rome said. "Starling should decide where she can be."

At that, Liam looked at me. "Do you want to stay here or go back?"

Right now, going back absolutely meant dealing with Milo. The anguish in his eyes and the depth of emotion he wore like this aura of pain and certainty would haunt me. Going back meant seeing the others. Seeing Jasper—we had so much that needed saying. Vaughn. Kellan. Freddie.

Then there was Doc. The man Milo said found him and his sister.

Me.

I turned that over in my mind, trying to test the weight of it. It didn't even *feel* right. Not for the first time, I wanted to call Lainey. That wasn't happening with these two in here.

"I don't know," I finally said when they both watched me with their identical eyes. Despite how much they resembled each other, and they did. There were differences. Liam never flinched about meeting my gaze. Rome didn't either, except he also didn't need to hold it like Liam wanted.

Liam pushed and challenged. Rome was there, willing to drift with me. The regiment of schedule dictated Liam's training. He used every bit of the equipment in the front room. I didn't think I'd even seen Rome work out once, but he was exceptionally fit. They both were.

And they could both fight.

"Why?" Rome studied me, and I tried and failed to find a smile for him.

"Because—Milo. Jasper. Vaughn." Those were just three. "I do want to see them—I need to talk to them. Freddie..." The phone calls had helped but... "He's struggling. Then there's Kel and Doc. All of you had your reasons for not telling me about Milo or why you took me. I need to hear those reasons—at the same time, I still don't believe it and Milo needs me to believe. I don't want to hurt him."

I'd managed about half of my sandwich, but I didn't want more so I passed the plate to Liam. He studied me with the most bemused expression. Rome didn't say anything about me giving him the food. When I drained my wine, Rome took my glass and went to the dresser to fill it with more.

"What?" I asked Liam, because he hadn't stopped staring.

"If I had any doubts about you being his sister, what you just said would have proven it."

"What?" Maybe the wine had been a mistake, on the other hand the warmth suffusing me and my muscles began to gradually ease the tension locking me up stiff. That and Rome's gentle look as he brought me the glass— far fuller than Liam had poured—and encouraged me to take it.

The red was dry, but with a kind of smoky flavor, like it had been around something burnt, but in a good way. Even if I swished it around my tongue, I couldn't identify all the flavors. I just knew I liked it. Liam kept watching me and I swore I could feel his gaze stroking over my skin. Which was ridiculous, he wasn't even touching me. The only times he touched me were to train or to slap my ass. Though he stopped that.

"Are you going to answer me?" I asked when Liam didn't respond, beyond taking a swallow of his own wine.

"You're just like him," he admitted slowly. "Tough as hell. Never show the world a single vulnerability. Always thinking. Planning. I bet you have a plan, Hellspawn. Don't you? A plan to get out of here. A plan to go back to the clubhouse or to leave Braxton Harbor altogether. Something spooked you at the hotel."

The ice assaulted my veins again, invading the warmth the wine set to glowing in my stomach.

"It's a good thing you're pretty," I told him. "Because I'm seriously tempted to hit you."

That wasn't what I meant to say, but Rome shrugged. "I'll hit him."

"Woah." Liam pointed a finger at Rome. "You get one free shot, brother mine. If this is what you want to use it for, remember what you owe me."

The twins contemplated each other, and I pushed up onto my knees and got between them. Not that I was going to be able to do much if they started fighting. Also, balancing a wine glass while trying to knee walk on a bed sucked.

"I said I was tempted," I told Rome firmly. "But I can hit him if I need to. I've done it before. Right in the nose."

"And the junk," Liam muttered. "Trust me, she's not some fragile little bird with a broken wing."

"That was a kick," I corrected him, as I twisted to meet his gaze. The fucker was laughing at me. The merriment in his eyes was right there. That annoyed me for some reason, so I flicked his nose with my finger. "You're mean."

"Sometimes, Hellspawn," he agreed, then caught my hand before I could pull it back. Holding it, he didn't look away as he lifted my hand to his lips and pressed a single kiss to my palm. That was almost worse than when he sucked the sugar off my fingers when he ate the rest of my donut. A quivering mass of butterflies threatened to launch in my middle, but I tugged my hand away.

Thankfully, he let me go.

"Movie?" he asked as if nothing had happened, only he wasn't asking me, he was asking Rome.

Oh shit. Rome had just seen him kiss my hand. I glanced up but found no judgment in his eyes. Only thoughtfulness. "Starling doesn't want to be alone."

I opened my mouth to protest, but nothing came out. Seriously—nothing. I didn't want to be alone. Alone, I'd have to think and face those demons...

"Grab the girlfriend, I'll get the wine. And the plates," Liam grunted as he rose and before I could ask anything, Rome scooped me up like I weighed nothing. Was I supposed to argue this or what? I wasn't sure.

I managed to not spill the wine, that was a good thing.

Turning on his heel, Rome carried me out of his room and right into Liam's. "What are we doing?" Oh look, there was my voice.

"Liam's bed is bigger." Not even slowing, Rome walked right up onto it and carried me to the head of the bed, where he sat me down gently. I hadn't been in here since the first day and I really hadn't paid attention to the bed. It was definitely bigger than Rome's. He was so relaxed as he settled next to me and then when he took my hand, I interlaced my fingers with his. "You're not alone," he assured me, and I swore some of the bruises on my soul eased.

It wasn't long before the scent of hot popcorn invaded

the room and my stomach rumbled. I really hadn't eaten all that much. But I didn't usually need much. Liam returned with a fresh beer for Rome, the bottle of wine for us and a bucket of popcorn. My mouth was watering, even as Liam walked up onto the bed just like Rome had. He passed the drinks and the popcorn to his brother, then stripped off his shirt and sent it flying into the corner.

Like Rome, Liam was also just in gray sweatpants, and now they were both shirtless and warm and when he settled on my other side, I was cocooned in heat. Before I could say anything embarrassing, I took another drink of the wine. They really were both very beautiful and so alike, and yet so different. Not opposites, not at all, but not the same either.

"What are we going to watch?"

"Rome's turn to pick," Liam said as he handed him the remote. "So brace yourself. He likes weird shit."

I elbowed Liam. "Don't call him weird."

"I would never call him weird. I just said he likes weird shit."

Wrinkling my nose, I scowled at him. "He likes me."

Liam grinned. "Thanks for proving my point."

"Ass."

"Brat."

I stuck my tongue out at him and he burst out laughing. Jerk. I scooted a little closer to Rome, though in truth there really wasn't much space, Liam seemed to have no problem spreading out into it. Both of them had a leg pressed against me and that ice from earlier cracked. I was not gonna be cold at all, even if we were on top of the sheets.

Really wanting popcorn, I reluctantly let go of Rome's hand to grab a couple. As soon as I popped them into my mouth, I sighed. Holy crap that was good. In the meantime,

Rome had turned on the huge 80-inch monster television on the wall. Why they needed such huge televisions, I really didn't understand.

I also didn't much care except... *I want to understand them all.*

Instead, I read the titles Rome scrolled through. I didn't know most of them. When he finally picked one, the title left me skeptical.

Nightcrawler.

"This isn't going to be a horror movie or something is it?"

"Don't worry, Hellspawn. We'll keep the monsters away."

"It's not a horror—it's a thriller. I like it." Rome looked at me as he caught my hand. "Okay?"

And he'd change his choice, just like that, if I didn't want to watch it. "You've seen it before?"

He nodded.

"You really liked it?"

Another nod.

"Then, okay."

His smile lit me up as he grinned. Then he pressed his lips to my forehead in a kiss. "Watch." And while I knew he meant the movie, what I wanted to do was watch them. Without facing him or turning my head, I was sure Liam watched me. Watched us.

That made me tingle from my scalp to my toes. Maybe I needed to focus on the movie. Yes, that was exactly what I should do.

In between bites of popcorn, that ended up being in my lap where they could both reach it, and finishing the bottle of wine with Liam, we watched the movie. I really couldn't take my eyes off it. The horror of what unfolded, the ethics of it, or lack of ethics. The scene where he pressured her for sex turned me right off, but Rome gripped my hand and Liam settled a hand on my leg, and just like that some of the disquiet left me.

By the time it was over, I was in awe and exhausted. But they started another one. It was Liam's turn. He picked a movie called *Atomic Blonde*. The music was amazing, but holy shit the woman could fight. I barely made it to the end of the movie though, before my eyes were closing. A yawn stretched my jaw and I swore the guys were doing that talking without talking thing. They cleaned up the food and the glasses and then I was tucked under the sheets with Rome behind me and his arm around me, while I faced Liam who lay on his side looking at us.

Oh, we were staying in his bed.

"Shh, Hellspawn," Liam whispered, and brushed his fingers down my face as though telling me to go to sleep. "You're safe."

"Not alone," Rome whispered, then pressed a kiss behind my ear. It was like they were magical words, my eyelids went heavy and I let them close. When Liam hooked his fingers around mine, I sighed at the contact. Probably shouldn't hold hands.

Probably shouldn't sleep between them.

Rome tucked his face into my hair and the soft sound of his breathing lulled me.

Probably shouldn't do a lot of things.

But they were right. I wasn't alone. Not here.

So right here was where I wanted to stay.

With them.

RICH BLOOD

LIAM

The worst part of school was the uniforms. My parents, because I'd spent three steady months practicing that and not the O'Connells, had done me the favor of having all of mine tailored. My growth spurts had come at random times, but not once had I ever had to go to school in pants that were too short or with sleeves that didn't reach my wrist.

A lot of the clothes I outgrew, they donated. At least the ones I didn't set aside for the boys. They'd also stopped interfering with my need to see Rome and the rest. If anything, their quiet unspoken approval resonated in the fact that our family driver would take me anywhere—no questions asked.

Something that had proven quite useful prior to my getting a driver's license. Since I had to drive to and from school, I qualified at fifteen. Not bad. I was one of a select few who showed up with an expensive car and attitude. I knew them. They knew me. By the time I turned seventeen, we'd done quite a bit of business and I'd cleaned them out at fight club more than once.

For months now, they'd had their eye on me. I'd practically smelled them in the hallways, caught them peeking in classes, and more than once at a party one or more of them would "end up" in a conversation with me. My awareness of their surveillance meant I wasn't remotely surprised when a pair of them stepped into the room while my dick was down Christine Brewster's throat.

Fuck she had a mouth like a hoover. I'd already gotten her off and now she was returning the favor. Ezra Graham leaned against the door, almost like he had all the time in the world. His best friend folded his arms and settled with his back against the wall. I fisted Christy's hair, choking her a little as all the tension in my balls loosed.

She swallowed like the champion cock sucker she was, and then leaned back to look up at me. A drop of cum at the corner of her mouth. Her eyes were shiny and I ran my thumb over her lower lip, then caught that drop and pushed it in. She let out a little sigh and I had zero doubt that her soaked cunt would welcome me if I bent her over a desk.

Alas, I had no condoms and I'd been waiting for these fuckers to get off their ass for a while. "Later, babe," I told her, and she pouted prettily but then she let out a breathless little giggle at our audience.

"Oh," she practically sighed the word as she looked from Ezra to his best friend and back. I took my time about stuffing my dick back into my pants. One, I'd been here first and two, let them understand that they were coming to me, not the other way around. "I'll see you tomorrow," Christy called over her shoulder as she collected her purse and book bag. She slowed on her approach to the door, her hips rolling just a little as Ezra gave her a long look.

There was no doubt in my mind that she was flirting with him. Hell, if he'd pulled out his dick, she'd have gone to her knees right there. Christy Brewster might come from a family as wealthy as mine, with all that entailed, and been raised into this life of privilege, but this girl also had a very healthy appetite for sex, casual hookups, and zero strings.

Needless to say, that was a pussy I plundered often.

Without a word, Ezra pushed open the door and Christy pouted again. I swore the girl could do it with her whole body when she was in the mood.

"Fuck off," Ezra told her, almost politely. "Now."

"You're such an ass."

"And you're a slut. But we all have our crosses to bear." He didn't even stop smirking when she slapped him.

I had to bite back a laugh as her flounce turned into a stomp and then she was out and gone.

"Goddamn if she couldn't suck dick like a pro," Ezra commented as he stared after her. "I'd have to be offended."

"Shut up," his best friend said. "Watch the door. I don't need to know who you're fucking this week."

"Blue-balled bastard," Ezra said with a wicked grin. "Stop panting after the... little..."

My eyes narrowed, but whatever Ezra had been about to say he swallowed. The look on his friend's face was far from "friendly." Apparently, even smartasses had a sense of self-preservation.

"You two want to get a room where he can kiss and make up, or you wanna tell me why the fuck you're bothering me?" The question worked to snare their attention off each other.

"Watch your fucking mouth, O'Connell," Adam said as

he pushed away from the wall. "You know damn good and well why we're here. Get cocky and you can go back on the waiting list."

I laughed. Honestly, I liked the guy most of the time. He was pretty straightforward. Brutal at times, but straightforward. "Damn, and here I thought you were going to sweet talk me into it. Maybe cozy up and court me."

"You just had your dick sucked," Adam said. "Pretty sure you've been sweetened enough."

"Fair. Fine, let's do business." I folded my arms and waited. The ploy was a deliberate misunderstanding, but from the tight frown Adam wore, he wasn't certain. This was where being me paid off. Brutal but direct, was a similar game I'd played. But I could lie without a twitch in my expression. It was how I glided between two vastly different worlds.

Contrary to what these guys might think, my loyalty was not, nor had it ever been, for sale.

"This is an invitation," Ezra said when Adam stayed quiet. "You've been tapped."

"For?" C'mon guys, spell it out. I didn't have all day. That was what I wanted my body language to communicate.

"Don't be such a dick," Adam countered. "You know what for. The Royals only choose the best. You've been tapped by the King. You complete his three tasks, and you'll earn a place."

"Three tasks? What is this some Dungeons and Dragons shit?"

"No," Ezra said in a bored tone. "It's a loyalty test."

'And a test of skills." Adam shrugged. "It's also nonnegotiable. You're in or you're out. You won't get invited a second time."

"Secret society shit," I muttered, hiding some of my inner glee. Five years in school with these guys. I knew them pretty well. They were untouchable, but for an entirely different reason. The Royals. Gang? Corporation? Both? Whatever they were, they had their eye on Braxton Harbor and Milo had plans.

I had connections.

It was time to put those connections to work.

"Well, since you obviously can't live without me," I told him and grinned at Adam's dark look. "When do we start?"

It was Ezra who pushed away from the door. He held out a phone. "Keep this with you at all times. Don't give the number to anyone else. Don't mess with the settings. When it rings, you answer."

The phone was just like any other burner. Blank. Untraceable.

He didn't let go of the phone when I took it. "It rings, you answer. I don't care who is sucking your dick. Clear?"

"Yep." I gave the phone a jerk and pulled it out of his grasp. "I got it the first time you said it."

The pair glanced at each other, then back at me.

"Am I not playing hard to get enough?"

"No," Adam said slowly, locking his gaze on mine. "But you should know the king doesn't tolerate mistakes. Once you're in, there's only one way out."

"Blood in. Blood out." Rich blood. Poor blood. It was all the same. Only my blood oath began in the womb, so this shit was nothing.

"You might be better off turning us down," Adam said, almost by way of suggestion, and Ezra shot him a "what the fuck are you doing" look that his friend ignored.

"I might be better off doing a lot of things. But I

wouldn't have half as much fun." Rich. Talented. The world at my feet. I played my part well.

"Right. Your funeral."

With that, they left. The phone stayed with me for the next three weeks, about as useful as a brick.

Then it rang.

19

Awareness slipped over me slowly, like a sunrise in the desert. One moment it was dark, and the next pink and purple hues began to crest on the horizon. The light followed rapidly, like the sunlight rushed in to fill the void. Only in this case, it wasn't sunlight—it was the gentle stroke of fingers over my hair and the steady thrum of a heartbeat beneath my ear.

Wine.

The twins.

Right. We'd all slept in Liam's room.

The featherlight touch glided along my hairline to my cheek. I didn't want to open my eyes. The minute I did, I had to let the world back in. The memories. The questions. The...

"I know you're awake, Hellspawn," Liam murmured, and I flicked my eyes open to meet his almost apologetic gaze. "You look beyond peaceful, and I let you sleep for as long as I could. But I really have to pee."

The admission pulled a reluctant laugh from me. I groaned as I lifted my head. Oh, I'd somehow managed to curl right up on top of him and I'd trapped one of his arms. The heartbeat had to be from where my ear pressed against his chest.

With care, I disentangled myself. I really had scooted almost on top of him. "Sorry," I finally managed to form coherent syllables. I ran a hand over my face, all too conscious of the fact Liam watched me with a faint smile. Somehow, I managed to get back to the middle of the bed before I realized Rome's side was empty.

My disappointment must have shown, because Liam tugged my hair lightly. "Don't worry, Hellspawn. He'll be back. He just likes to paint when it's early and quiet."

Then Liam left me alone in the middle of his bed while he headed into the bathroom. I debated getting up and then I flopped onto my back for a moment to stare up at the ceiling. The world had already rushed in to fill the gaps.

Milo Hardigan.

My brother?

The more I thought about it, the truer it felt. But was that because I wanted it to be true? The expression on his face when he talked about the good life he'd wanted for me had me backpedaling. No, if I was Milo's sister and he... just no.

Like a torturous water wheel, my thoughts went around and around in a circle. The best thing I could do for all of them was go away. Almost ironic, considering the last time I'd left it had been to escape them, but then I'd gone back. Now I just wanted to protect them. They were...

"Hey," Liam said so close to me, I jerked. Adrenaline dumped through my system and sent my heart racing. He raised his eyebrows at my abrupt inhalation of breath, that sounded more like a gasp than I was comfortable admitting. "It's okay," he soothed. "You're still safe."

I tried to steady my breathing, because he really shouldn't have to assure me of that. Yet, he'd taken the time to do it. There was a softness in his eyes that hadn't been there before.

"You good?" he asked as I sat up. I guess after the night before, we were having a moment. "Those were some pretty deep thoughts there, Hellspawn. Let's not hurt ourselves."

Moment over.

I flipped him off and scooted down the bed even as he chuckled. "C'mon, I'll make us coffee and breakfast. Then show you the code for the security system."

The words froze me in the doorway and I glanced back at him. "Wait—what?"

"I said I'll show you the code for the security system. How to let someone in. How to let yourself out." He still stood by the bed, looking even better all rumpled from sleep with his hair disheveled. "Rome's right. If you can't come and go when you want, this is a cage. But—"

Of course, there was a but, I swallowed as I pivoted to face him.

"But, I'm going to *trust* you to use good judgment. Let someone know if you're going out. I'd rather someone was with you because..." He hesitated.

"Because someone was trying to kill me?"

Not a subject we'd really discussed but it was still out there. I'd been "missing" for months, one could only hope that person or persons had given up. My uncle was the one who wouldn't stop looking for me and he wasn't trying to kill me.

No, what he wanted was far worse.

Except, I was eighteen, fuck almost nineteen in a few

months. I rubbed my hands against my face. I had options. Lainey had set up other options for me too.

"Well," Liam said slowly. "That and whatever it is that makes you not want to go home. Then there are people who would very likely use you to get to them."

Right. The gang.

They did things, not always stuff they were proud of, at least according to Jasper, but they had plans. More—they had dreams.

"Then I guess it's good I'm here and not there." I met him stare for stare and the corner of his mouth kicked up.

"I'm not going to tell you someone could use you to get to me. You already know that. Rome cares about you." He gave with one hand and took away with the other. "He would do anything for you."

The last carried a worried note.

"Don't hurt him." That was a request.

"Liam...I don't want to hurt anybody."

"That's not true, Hellspawn." One corner of his mouth pulled a little higher. "Everyone has someone they want to hurt. Your ex-partner for example."

I made a face.

"See?"

"Are you *trying* to piss me off?"

"Is it working?" I swore I couldn't tell what he was doing now. He'd been so sweet when I first woke and now this...

"No," I told him. Just to piss him off. Particularly if he wanted *me* mad. He was the one holding the cards, right?

I padded across the hall to my room—well my "borrowed" room—and made use of the bathroom, too. After washing up, I got dressed. The deep blue shirt won first pick, even if I had to roll up the sleeves, along with a pair of workout capris.

I actually liked the look and headed out to the kitchen. The scent of coffee curled invitingly in the air. Liam was still just wearing the same gray sweatpants he'd slept in, but he'd also pulled his shirt back on.

Pity.

He stood at the stove with the phone at his ear. At my arrival, he put a finger to his lips.

"Yes, sir, I understand," he said, in the most carefully neutral tone I'd ever heard from him.

Well, that wasn't true. He'd been that careful with the call he took the first day of my incarceration. There was sausage frying in a pan, alongside what looked like eggs and the oven was on.

"No, sir," Liam replied, still all neutral, no emotion. I eased past him and retrieved the coffee tumblers. With care, I fixed both of our coffees. When I handed him his, he paused, staring at it like he didn't know what it was. The chill look in his eyes had me hesitating. Maybe he really wanted his privacy for the call.

Right. The minute his gaze shifted off me and his attention back to whomever was on the phone, I grabbed my coffee and went for the exit. I didn't make it two steps before he snagged the shirt and halted my progress.

"I said I would take care of it. Patience." The barest hint of a clipped tone. "Have I ever let you down?" A pause. "Then trust me, I won't now. I have to go." Then he ended the call.

"I was just..."

"I know, you were going to give me privacy. It was fine. The call wasn't anyone I wanted to talk to anyway."

He released me to go back to the food and I leaned

against the counter. "Jasper?" It was a guess. The two of them really didn't get along.

Liam chuckled. "No," he said. "Him, I would have enjoyed sparring with. Don't worry about it, Hellspawn."

Enjoy...? "Why does Jasper hate you so much? Cause that doesn't feel like play."

He sighed.

"Or is it because you and Milo are close and Jasper doesn't trust you anymore?" Milo was Jasper's best friend. All the clues were there. The things Jasper had said about him, without saying it was him.

"Nah, it's not jealousy, Hellspawn. It's kind of complicated and has more to do with keeping a safe distance while taking care of business."

"Secrets," I told him. "Suck."

"Yeah?" He plated the sausage and the eggs before shutting off the stove top and popping open the oven. There were huge fluffy biscuits in there and he only put one on my plate before adding three to his. "You tell me yours and I'll tell you mine."

The gauntlet slammed to the floor between us and I stared at him. Could he handle my secrets? Probably.

Could I handle him knowing?

I cut my gaze away and he said, "That's what I thought. Here." He held out the second plate and I accepted it then followed his ushering to the table. We didn't normally eat out here, but he dragged out a chair for me then one for himself.

Saying nothing for a moment, he dug into the food then washed it down with coffee. I was a lot hungrier than I realized. I cleaned the plate before he was down to his last biscuit. Without missing a beat, he split the biscuit in half and set it and another sausage patty onto my plate.

I could argue or I could just eat them. My stomach won the argument before it even began. He waited until I finished before quirking a brow. "You want more?"

"Probably," I admitted. The truth kind of hurt. Except, we had a massive workout the day before. "But I'll wait. I was a lot hungrier than I realized."

"You burned a lot yesterday and didn't refuel. You barely ate the subs, then filled your stomach on popcorn."

An indelicate belch escaped me and I just barely managed to cover my mouth. "Excuse me."

He chuckled. "Your stomach is tattling on you, Hellspawn. You need to up your calorie intake. All right..." He stood. "Let's do this."

By this, he meant his system. He flipped open the painting revealing the security pad. I stared at that for a moment then at him. "That's kind of secret agent Batman of you."

Snorting with laughter, Liam just shook his head. "This is the code to disarm the system, that will let you open the door and let someone in. It will re-arm as soon as the door is closed."

"If I want to go out?"

"I'm getting there Hellspawn, keep your pants on." He paused a beat and looked me over "Yeah, definitely keep them on. You with bare legs in that shirt and my good intentions would all die a grisly death."

"Clearly," I teased. "You can't take your hands or eyes off of me."

"Hmm," was his only response. "If you want to go out, I'll give you the spare key for the door, you put in the code, unlock the door, lock it on the outside then the system will re-arm on its own."

"Okay, Rome used a code to get in the elevator or a keycard."

"Each system is separate. There's one code to enter to get back in and one to enter to get out."

"Why make it—" I didn't even finish the question. Of course, he made it complicated. I was here and he was keeping me inside. Except... "You want to keep the extra security in place in case someone tries to get in while I'm here."

"Exactly. Also why I would rather you let someone know you're going, or get one of the guys to pick you up."

"What about you?"

"Oh, you'll still see me. We have to train, but that will have to be tomorrow. I have something to do today. But until we're done with the fight training, do me a favor—don't disappear, okay?"

Not a difficult promise to want to make. Not sure about being able to keep it.

"If I want to go out on my own, like do my own..."

He took a deep breath then exhaled it. "Like I said. You have a plan. Leaving on your own to do things on your own indicates you don't want to be observed. Take Rome. He will keep your secrets. From everyone."

"You won't?"

With a smirk, he reclaimed his coffee cup. "Didn't say that, Hellspawn. Now I have to get dressed."

He was halfway up the hall when I realized what he hadn't done. "You didn't give me the key yet."

"You're right," he answered. "Said I'd give you the code. I have to get you a key made."

Right. He said he had a spare. "Why don't I believe you?" I called.

His laughter was the only answer. Fine. At least I had

the code now. I took care of the dishes and the pan. There were still two more biscuits, so I threw caution to the wind and ate one while I brewed more coffee.

I had gone to get my phone when I heard the front door open. "I'll see you later, Hellspawn." Liam was leaving? "Make good choices today."

The door closed and the sound of the locks clicked into place just as I made it back out there. I hurried over to the painting and popped it open, then entered the code before grabbing the door to open it—only Liam was gone. The elevator must have been right there.

Well... fuck.

"Asshole," I muttered to the empty hallway then shut the door. The locks clicked and because I'd left the painting open, it showed the red meaning the alarm had engaged.

My phone buzzed and I glanced down to see a message from a number I didn't know.

Don't be too mad, Hellspawn. Baby steps.

Liam.

I sent him back a middle finger emoji, even if I was already fighting back my own smile. Fine. Baby steps. I could open the door.

There were messages on the phone from Jasper, Vaughn, Kellan, and Freddie.

Guilt sucker punched me. Hiding the phone meant I didn't check it as often as I should. Worse, after we got back yesterday, I'd been too off center to think about the phone.

Jasper was worried. So was Vaughn. And Kellan. Freddie was bored. I answered them all in vague terms. Then asked one by one if anyone was free.

Kellan answered first. He was at the shop, but he could pull himself away from work if I needed him. Jasper took a minute longer to answer, but he was on the road. Tomorrow, he promised. We needed to talk.

Yes. We did.

Freddie hadn't answered his text, but he might still be asleep. Vaughn hadn't answered either. A knock on the door, the first since I'd been in the apartment, made me jump.

My phone buzzed.

Vaughn: *Let me in, Dove.*

CONFINED

MILO

The cell was supposed to be roughly eight and a half feet by eight and a half feet. It took me a little less than three steps to cross from one side of it to the other. Pacing was out of the question in such a confined space.

Fortunately, I could read. There wasn't much in the library cart that I hadn't already devoured. I asked for any newspapers or magazines, and occasionally I got one. We had a couple of guards in this place, but I didn't want to exercise those options.

Every once in a while, I'd come back to my cell from a meal to find a letter from one of the guys and a new dance magazine or the latest article printed out from the internet.

They kept their eye on Ivy for me. They let me keep my eye on her, too. She was growing up so damn fast. Every day in this place seemed to either drag or blur together.

Hell, sometimes they did both.

One hour, each day, the inmates on my cell block lined up and headed out to the yard. There was weight equipment. A basketball court. A track. As crappy as it all looked, it was roughly the same quality, if not better than, the school I had attended.

As soon as the whistle blew, marking the beginning of our sixty minute period, I would move away from the others, stretch and then begin walking the track. Always walking before I ran. I needed to loosen up my muscles and I didn't care how short the circumference of the track was, it took a lot more than three steps to circle it.

By the end of my second circuit, I picked up speed. Jolly was on watch today with a guard I didn't know. They'd had some turnover at the prison. As long as my guys were secure, I didn't pay much attention. Jolly, however, had come up in the system, just like us. We slipped him some extra money and kept a lookout for his younger brother who hadn't quite aged out.

It worked well for all of us. His brother was going to college and getting a real degree. Jolly didn't care what he had to do to make that happen. So, it worked out for all of us. I kept a wary eye out on the others. Most of the cell block I knew, and they didn't bother me.

Well, not anymore.

The first year in here had been hell. It was like being dropped into the group home without my brothers at my back. I'd fought and won every inch of the respect I controlled.

That hadn't stopped the occasional newcomer from trying to shiv me. Just three months earlier, a guy transferred onto our block. Call it a sixth sense, or native awareness forged from over a decade of having to watch my own back, but the guy clocked my every move.

When he came for me, I was ready. Two things kept my hands. I didn't start it and I never moved out of the sight of the guards or a camera whenever I was out of my cell. I wasn't a fan of being watched on all sides, but I didn't want any years added to my sentence and I'd grown fond of breathing.

I grappled with the guy, twisting him and getting his arm in a lock until he let go of the shiv. I didn't try to retaliate or break his neck. If he hadn't struggled so much, I wouldn't have broken his arm or dislocated his shoulder.

The minute the guards were on us, I released him and went facedown on the ground and kept my hands clear of where the shiv had fallen. The vulnerable position made my skin crawl. But I didn't get any penalties and Mr. Shiv disappeared from the cell block and transferred to another prison.

It wasn't the first time someone had gone for me. Nor had it been the last. The first time, I landed myself a six-week stint in solitary because I had almost killed the guy. But their investigation determined I'd been defending myself, so that had been my only punishment. After—I'd taken damn good care not to get caught if I needed to eliminate a threat.

That had been my last two and a half years in this place. It was cold outside, winter was firmly here. I had 195 days left on the sentence I'd negotiated, with the help of a court-appointed attorney. Pleading down had given me more control over sentencing. That, and a show of solid contrition when I made during my allocution, had persuaded the judge.

It didn't matter if the words tasted like ash on my tongue, as I claimed responsibility for the crime I'd been charged with, or that I'd broken out in a sweat when the judge agreed to accept my plea and the terms of the deal the district attorney offered. Three to five years of my life.

It was better than risking fifteen to twenty-five, but when the judge came down on the lighter end and said three years with good behavior. I locked onto it. My hands had to stay clean. Then in one hundred and ninety-five days, I could walk out of this place.

I'd just finished my last circuit when Jolly called my name. I diverted immediately to approach him. He did a finger twirl for me to turn around and I gave him my back, and immediately put my hands behind me.

Even the looseness he left in the cuffs when he put them on, didn't change the way the feel of cold steel on my skin left my flesh crawling. "You have a visitor, Hardigan," Jolly said as he led me to the doors. He still had yard duty, so he couldn't go all the way with me. In a lower voice, he added, "Don't know him. But he paid a lot to see you. You'll get your cut."

Someone *paid* to see me? The only time that had happened before was when Liam had made arrangements to see me privately to discuss the plan. It was the one and only visit he'd made to the prison outside of normal weekend visiting hours, and even then, he limited those visits.

The guard inside wasn't one of ours. In fact, I didn't know him at all. That kept me focused, and I did my best to keep my muscles loose and my expression neutral, as he guided me from the block to the room where we were occasionally allowed visitors without a glass divider between us.

The only occupant, a man, stood on the far side with his back toward us. He wore a suit that probably cost a small fortune, just based on the cut and the material. Inside the room, the guard removed my handcuffs before he stepped out, closing the door and leaving me alone with the suit.

Rubbing my wrists absently, I moved toward the windows to glance outside. No one was focused on this room. All nearby guards were focused elsewhere.

"Mr. Hardigan," the man in the suit said and I pivoted to face him. He was older, maybe in his mid to late forties. Dark hair. Dark eyes. Clean-shaven, and as I'd already noted, dressed in an expensive suit. Even his cufflinks were gold.

Everything about him screamed wealth, power, and privilege. Folding my arms, I leaned back against one of the tables and kept the distance between us. At least he hadn't offered to shake my hand. "You are?" I asked.

"A potential friend," he said.

Right.

When I said nothing, he nodded. "I was given your name by a friend of a friend. He explained your—circumstances and your history."

"Well, good for him." I didn't like that I couldn't quite pin where this was going.

"I'm not going to dance around the words. There are no cameras or recordings right now. This is the most privacy I could get us, and these fifteen minutes cost a great deal." Fortunately, the man's pause was only to make sure I was listening before he continued. "I've made arrangements to transfer a prisoner to your cell block next week. I will be obliged if you would make sure this is his last stop. I don't care how you do it, he can slip on soap in the shower and crack his head open. I just want him eliminated."

"Why would I do this?" Because I didn't do hits. It was the one thing I'd insisted for all of us. We could steal, blackmail, assault, break bones, or vandalize, but we didn't kill unless it was an absolute last resort.

Well, that or the person in question deserved to die.

"One, because I will compensate you handsomely. However, I am very aware that money doesn't attract you as much as power and influence. I can provide all of the above. Two, I will make sure no consequences wash back on you. You will be provided an opportunity and privacy to deal with him."

Still not convinced, I flicked a look at the clock on the wall. We still had another eight to nine minutes, easy.

"Third," the man said as he crossed the room toward me and showed me a picture on his phone. "He tried to rape my daughter. When that was prevented, he came after her again as soon as he was on bail. She has a broken wrist. Fortunately, her friends prevented anything worse from happening. He's a serial rapist. Doses girls, then rapes them while they are unconscious."

I memorized the guy's face then looked at the suit again.

"He got too light a sentence," the man continued. "He'll be out in a year with good behavior. I know his type. He'll go after her again. He blames her for this..." He exhaled a harsh breath.

"Why me?"

"Because you have a reputation, Mr. Hardigan. You killed a man and got a sentence of three years for manslaughter. What was done to that man wasn't manslaughter." Lifting his chin, he tucked his phone away into his inner breast pocket. "I'm a very good friend to have, Mr. Hardigan. I'll also provide you with any other compensation you might require."

Right.

"How many?"

"Excuse me?"

"You said he dosed and raped a number of girls. How many?"

"Only five came forward. But the prosecutors believed the number to be much higher."

Five was five too many.

"Any message you want to send him?"

"Goodbye," the suit said. "And good riddance."

Fair enough. I studied the man for a long minute, and he didn't shy from my gaze. I had a feeling, if he could get this guy alone, he'd do it himself. Protecting his daughter.

"Thanks for the visit," I said as I headed toward the door to knock for the guard. "Let's not make this a regular thing."

"Don't you want to know who I am?" the man asked.

I chuckled. "I don't need to know who you are." I glanced over my shoulder. "You don't need to know me later, either."

I'd kill this dick for free. Rapists and pedophiles.

They could all burn in hell.

Whatever the man read in my eyes impressed him. "Thank you, Mr. Hardigan. I'll keep my word."

I believed him. But I'd still have done it for free.

The fact it landed me a six-month stint in solitary had been a small price to pay. It was safe there, no one else came for me and I hadn't had any years added to my sentence. But solitary was boring as fuck, none of my guards were on this wing and I was cut off.

No word about the boys or my sister or anything else.

Still, there was one less rapist in the world. Even as confined as I was, I could take pleasure in that.

20

The moment Rome sent me the text that Dove needed to see me, needed to see all of us, really, I completely dipped out of work. The guys at the shop were bitching about how many hours I had anyway. No one who had appointments with me were specialty clients, so I passed them all on and headed uptown. Her texts arrived not long after his, including an apology for having not answered my last two messages.

Frankly, I didn't care about that. If anyone owed an apology, it was me. One I wanted to give her in person. The phone contact had been both balm and temptation. A balm because it truly did soothe me to know she was all right, but a temptation because I wanted to *see* her.

Milo had brought her back to the clubhouse once. The last two weeks had just...had it really been two weeks? It seemed like we'd all been busier than ever and yet time had practically ground to a halt without her there. I hadn't realized just how much I'd come to rely on her being present.

Her absence was an agony.

I'd parked a block away, then checked the street before following Rome's instructions on how to get into the parking garage and on the elevator without being observed. The text message had also included a code to get me up to Liam's floor.

Everything about this place screamed quiet, almost restrained, opulence. It had been a long time since I felt out of place anywhere. Whether for my size, my tats, or even the clothes I wore. This ride in the elevator succeeded at what few had managed to do in years.

It made me feel small.

When the doors opened, I followed Rome's instructions. There were two large apartments on this floor. One to the left and the other to the right. The left was Liam's, still I glanced to the right to check the silent door on the opposite end. I knocked with an uncertainty I hadn't felt since Ms. Stephanie walked me into that room with five strangers.

She didn't answer it immediately. But could I blame her? They had her secure in there, but Rome said to go, and I had a code if I needed it. I dragged my phone out and opened her message.

Me: *Let me in, Dove.*

Hope shouldn't gnaw on a person like sand in an open wound. The grit stung and chafed. The tumble of the locks added the first dregs of real relief that I'd experienced since seeing Dove's wounded expression that morning everything crashed down.

The door swung inward, and I had to grip the doorframe to keep from launching myself at her. Three things assaulted me at once as I locked on to the rich, brown of her gaze. She seemed even tinier than I remembered, a powerhouse fused into the slender, fragile frame. The wounded look in her eyes seemed to have been erased but lost had replaced it and anger flooded me.

"What happened?" I asked, giving in to the temptation to sweep forward and lift her right off her feet. Even as I tried to keep from swooping her up like a hostage and tearing out of here to get her back to the clubhouse, I couldn't fight the need to *touch* her. To know she was real. To feel her heat pressed against me. To taste... I barely shoved the door closed before my mouth closed over hers.

I honestly couldn't have said who pulled who in for the kiss. Every single intention I'd had to apologize, explain, and hopefully begin to put right what had deepened the gap between us, went up in the flames of her kiss. Her lips parted on a soft humming moan that sent my pulse straight into my cock.

A half-thought of her could give me a semi, the softness of her lips parting to let me invade her mouth with my tongue and I was stiff enough to ache inside my jeans. Her phone fell and mine followed it. She tasted of coffee, sausage, mint, and the sweetness that was all her own.

"Missed you," she whispered against my lips as I tried to drag in oxygen as though I needed to breathe for both of us. I slid my hands down to cup her ass, even as she locked her legs around me.

"Missed you," I admitted, not too proud to confess how much or how desperate for her I was. Every moment I'd been away from her had dug into me like a form of torture. Now, it didn't matter. I could survive anything if I knew I could get back to her.

Knocking loose my cap, she fisted my hair and half-pulled me down, even as she arched up and then she fused her lips to mine. The roll of her hips ground her cloth-covered cunt against my abs. I started moving. The sofa was closest, and I dipped her down until her back hit the leather.

Her thighs tightened even as I pulled back, but I wasn't going far. I went for the buttons of the man's shirt she was wearing. The fact she had it on was like her wearing some other man's mark. Before I could rip the buttons though, she covered them with hands before hurriedly undoing them.

"I like this shirt," she admitted on a breathless laugh.

Fine. But all I managed to express was a grunt. I slid my hands along her thighs and under the shirt while she wiggled out of it, and peeled down the tight little capris she wore. They gave her just the faintest hint of a camel toe and my mouth was watering before I stripped them and her panties right off.

She had to part her legs to let me go and I left the pants dangling from one of her ankles as that proud pink pussy came into view. Slick, damp, and ripe like the best summer fruit. I was torn between dipping my tongue into her until I'd satisfied this wild craving to have her and....

Before I could even decide, she tossed the shirt off and peeled off her sports bra. Her breasts were even more beautiful than I remembered. There was a shadow of a bruise on her side and on her hip. I stared at them a moment as she undid my jeans.

"Who hurt you?" I loved Liam like a brother, even if I didn't get whatever the hell he was up to, but I would put his ass in the ground if he hurt her.

"Don't fuss," she warned, and I jerked my gaze to hers as her slim fingers wrapped around my cock. Holy shit, it was hard to think when she did that. "Liam is teaching me to fight."

Fight...? The word raced around my brain and collided

with the hot, sweetness of her mouth closing over my cock. Fuck my life. I discarded thoughts of anything that wasn't my dove. She worked her hand against my base, pumping me, even as she stretched her jaw to try and take as much of me as she could

My hips surged forward in demand, and I bumped the back of her throat. The gagging sound worried me, but then I locked on her teary brown eyes as she kept hollowing out her cheeks and sucking.

Fuck.

Fuck.

I was not going to come in her mouth like some teenage wimp who'd never had his dick sucked, but the combination of her hand caressing me and the suction as she pulled me deeper, taking me into her throat each time, and I had to grip the sofa to keep blowing my load right there.

When she cupped my balls and began to massage them, I swore. I hadn't even taken off my fucking shoes.

"Dove," I said and the strangled note in my voice had me digging the fingers of my right hand into the back of the sofa and the other I used to cup her face. She slowed her swallowing motions and met my gaze. The sight of her, mouth locked around my cock was probably one of the most beautiful things I'd ever seen, save one.

When she rode my cock and I was balls deep in her pussy as she came. That was hands down the most beautiful.

"I need your cunt," I managed to push the words out, but it was effort. "Please."

I needed to feel her come around me, the spasming of her inner muscles as the sweet velvet heat locked me to her. I needed...

With care, she pulled off my cock and licked her lips as she continued to stroke me.

"You can have me any way you want," she offered, and I swore to fuck, the information flooded my dick because two more pumps and I came. The jets of hot cum splashed against her chest and chin. Then she dipped forward to suck the head back into her mouth and I closed my eyes as my whole soul seemed to rush out of me and into her.

Fuck.

Only my grip on the sofa kept me from collapsing. The pleasure gleaming in her eyes, and the flush on her cheeks as she studied me, filled me with a kind of inescapable joy. I just came like a fifteen year old boy with his first woman and she looked so fucking delighted, like I'd given her a prize.

"On your back, Dove," I ordered. Though, arguably, the ragged notes of my breathing didn't sound very commanding. She ran her finger along her breast where some of my cum clung and scooped it up. When she sucked that finger into her mouth and licked it clean, I swore my whole cock throbbed.

"Now."

She smiled around her fingers, perfectly aware of what she was doing to me. I shucked my shirt and toed off my shoes before yanking down my jeans, as she lay back and spread those sexy fucking legs. She balanced the toes of one foot against the coffee table and the other over the arm of the sofa.

Flexible as fuck.

So perfect.

Falling to my knees, I slid my hands under her ass, dragged her slick cunt to the edge and then buried my whole face in it. The dampness of her cream beckoned to be consumed and I thrust my tongue deep into her channel, swirling it around as though I could sample it all. Her hips bucked as my nose brushed her clit. I kept my gaze on her as I went to town, licking, nipping, and sucking. Up and down the slit of her cunt, dividing my attention between the hard nub of her clit as it swelled up at the attention, to the fresh rush of dampness slicking her further.

"You're soaking, Dove," I admired as I alternated between long, lazy licks and hard pulsing thrusts with my tongue. I kept shifting from one to the other, refusing to give her an ounce of quarter. She'd sucked my fucking brain right out of my cock, and I planned to devour hers right here. "Play with your breasts. Show me those gorgeous tits."

Her nipples went taut and pebbled at my words and her hips rose and fell to the rhythm I set with my tongue. She worked her fingers over her nipples. Sticky with cum, she traced over them like she marked herself with me, and that was all my dick needed to power through his recovery.

Ready to get off the bench, I worked her clit furiously and speared two fingers into her and stretched them wide. She came on a scream, arching upward as she ground her cunt to my face and I lapped up every bit of sweetness. Slicking up my dick with her juices, I rose to scoop her up and then I turned us both so it was my naked ass sitting on the sofa already dampened with her release and she gripped my dick, her thumb playing with the piercings.

Each touch sent a pulse through my system and then she was stretching around me as she sank down. Head thrown back, she let out a low cry. I knew I was big and I worked her down slowly, but she sped up and then slammed me home. I grabbed her hair and pulled her to me.

This time, when we kissed, it was a collision of teeth, lips, tongue, and need.

She dug her fingers into my shoulders as she began to ride me. There was no hesitation in her, nothing but pure, hot, unabashed, sex and desire. The drag of my cock pushing and pulling inside of her as the piercing amplified my own need and hers, fuck my life, I'd never been so happy to have pierced the fucking thing as I was when she lost it.

Another orgasm hit her and another, but I wasn't going to come like some two-pump chump this time. Fuck no. I caressed her ass, squeezing with each lift as I took over for both of us. Sweat gleamed on her skin and she cupped my face. Kissing me until the only air I received was through her.

"Harder," she demanded, and I twisted to put her back down on the sofa and powered into her. She dug her heels into my back, twisting her hips as she writhed up to meet me. Every fucking thrust seemed to drag my balls up tighter.

One more time, I needed my dove to come one more time. I traced a finger between us to find her clit and I barely touched it before she went off, screaming, and it dragged my orgasm right out of me. I came so hard, I swore I saw stars and my muscles turned to pure liquid as I collapsed against her.

We lay there, clinging to each other in a hot, sweaty, mess of sticky cum and need.

"I really missed you," she said softly.

"I'm really sorry," I said, forcing my head to get up. "We should have told you. Warned you both before you got there, or at least told you the truth before it fell on your head."

The fact she'd been as hungry for me as I was for her fed the hope in my soul that it wasn't too late, that we hadn't lost her.

That *I* hadn't lost her.

"I don't know how you kept it from me," she admitted, and my heart sank. "Then again, I don't know how you could have told me. He's told me and I don't—"

She hesitated, a troubled look sweeping into those eyes that had just been filled with pleasure.

Finally, she swallowed whatever she had been about to say. "I'm not mad at you," she said softly, and it was too easy. My guilt shouldn't be absolved so simply.

"No? You have every right to be furious, Dove. Furious that we kept it from you. Furious that we haven't gotten you back to the clubhouse. Furious that we're letting Milo dictate where you are." The last came out angrier than I intended, but just when I thought we were getting through to Milo, he shut us all out again.

"Well, those all sound like fine reasons to be mad, but I just don't feel that way. You did—what you believed to be right and whether I believe it or not, it only matters that you all did."

I frowned.

She closed her eyes for a moment, and I swore it was like I could feel her collecting herself, despite the fact she was still impaled on my cock.

"Dove?"

"I'm okay," she said. "I don't want to fight, not when we're like this and I've missed you and been worried about all of you...is Freddie really all right? What about Jasper? I know Milo seemed intent on killing him. Kellan sounds— distant in his messages. Is he okay?"

Real concern echoed in her voice, and I curled my arms

around her so I could trade places and lay with my back against the sofa while I cradled her to my chest.

"They're all right, Dove. Want me to tell you about how Freddie has been giving Milo hell? Not backing off on him for coming home a dictator? Or that Jasper and him seem to be finally mending some fences? Kel's okay, he just misses you and doesn't want to fucking admit it. Freddie though? He's started singing about you every time we're trying to eat."

Her eyes widened and I grinned. Because the darkness in her eyes had gone away again, leaving behind delight.

"I'll try to record him for you," I promised her. "And we're fighting to get you back there...you know, if that's where you want to be."

Because no more clipping her wings. Not anymore. As much as I wanted to keep her with us, I was more than willing to follow her, too.

"You amaze me," she murmured, and I quirked a brow at that. Spreading her fingers against my chest, she traced the ivy wrapping the Celtic cross on my right pec. The ivy I'd inked on all of us for her.

"You take my breath away," I confessed. "To be honest, I never want it back."

"What do you want?"

That was easy.

"You."

PROPOSAL

EMERSYN

I slumped onto the bed in the hotel room. The show would move on to the next city and the next venue the following day. We'd get a break *there* but not here. For that, I was grateful. I honestly couldn't even remember where we were at the moment. Exhaustion had dogged my every step since the brief trip I took to meet Lainey.

"You need time to recover," she'd scolded me. Even the doctors had said I needed to take it easy. But I couldn't let any weakness show. I didn't dare let word get back to anyone that I might be ill or need assistance.

Fortunately, I was well-practiced at masking my true feelings and well-trained enough that my body obeyed me, even when it wanted to collapse. The most difficult challenge had been avoiding Eric. It was my own damn fault that he pursued me so vigorously.

I'd thought that his interest meant more than it did. That having sex with him would take back something stolen from me. In the beginning, it had been fun. Yet fun turned possessive and dark so quickly, what little oxygen I'd been able to find on the road disappeared. Booking my hotel away from the rest had been my own choice. A perk of finally turning eighteen. I didn't require permission from anyone. I needed something that was mine.

The knock on the door made me groan. I didn't want to get up and see who it was. Maybe if I ignored it...

Three more knocks and I got the picture. Whoever was there wasn't going away. Pushing off the bed, I paused at the door to look through the peephole.

The last person on the planet I would have expected, stood on the other side of the door.

"I need to speak to you, Ms. Sharpe." Adam Reed's cool tones were unmistakable. As was the fact that Lainey hated his guts.

"Why?" I asked without opening the door.

"I would prefer to have this conversation face to face, rather than shouting through a closed door."

I almost laughed. Of course he would, but... "I don't even know how you found me and I'm not asking." Not removing the safety bar, I cracked the door open. One habit I'd taken to doing in any hotel room I stayed in. That safety bar went on. It meant no one could sneak in just because they had a key.

Adam stood in the hallway, dressed in an expensive suit with no tie, which was probably the most casual I'd ever seen him, save for the time he'd shown up at the Disney World hotel looking harried and pissed.

"Miss Sharpe," he greeted me.

"Mr. Reed." I raised my eyebrows. "What do you want?"

"I thought we were acquainted well enough that this wouldn't be an issue."

"Well, when you tell me what *this* is, I'll let you know if it's an issue." Seriously, I had cramps, my insides hurt, my chest hurt. My bruises had bruises and I just wanted to crash and sleep until the wake up call came in the morning.

The barest hint of a smile graced his lips. "This is business, I assure you and has absolutely nothing to do with a certain person of our mutual acquaintance."

I snorted. "Right. Then you can wait and I'll come out and we can go downstairs..."

"I'd prefer this meeting didn't get back to your uncle."

I tilted my head back and stared at the ceiling. I'd prefer this meeting didn't get back to him either. Frankly, the last time he'd seen me talking to Adam had left me in pain for more than a week.

"Miss Sharpe, I give you my word I mean no harm to you or to Lainey." The fact his voice actually softened when he said her name convinced me more than anything else. I pushed the door closed, then flipped off the safety bar, before I opened it again. "Thank you," he said, though he waited until I stepped back and held the door open for him to enter.

The hotel offered me a small suite and I didn't need anything fancy. Most of my gear for performing traveled with the show. The rest of my clothes were already packed, save for the outfit for tomorrow. So, while a small space, it wasn't cluttered.

He paused after I closed the door and I swore he assessed me with that cool gaze of his. "Do you require assistance in removing a problem?" His gaze had moved to my chest with the question, then flitted back up.

I glanced down at the bruises visible over the v of the shirt I was wearing. Turning away from him, I snagged the robe off the bed and pulled it on. I rarely wore it when I was alone, but I was in sleep shorts and the loosest t-shirt I owned.

"I'm fine," I told him as I faced him once more and tied the robe. Like I said, I had perfected the mask. "Now, what did you need to talk to me about?"

He slid a hand into his pocket as he studied me, and I swore he was trying to peel back a layer of my skin to look beneath it. I didn't hesitate or flinch. Stay away from the Benedicts and Reeds. That was my uncle's advice.

"I have a proposal for you," he began, his tone considering. "Do you have an hour to listen?"

An hour?

"Why? Do you need to compose it as an epic poem in iambic pentameter or something?"

He chuckled. "You and Lainey share a singular wit."

"Right, you said this isn't about her."

"And it's not," he conceded, then gestured to the small sitting room with its one hard chair and one slightly less hard love seat. "Shall we sit? If you'd like to order up anything, I will happily cover the expense."

"If you're hungry, you can eat on your own time," I said before moving to sit on the loveseat. Let him have the chair of pain. "There's water in the mini fridge if you're thirsty." Not that I planned to offer it to him. "I need to sleep soon, so let's just cut to the chase. What do you want?"

Removing his hand from his pocket, he crossed to the mini fridge and removed two bottles of water. He brought one to me and didn't release it when I went to take it. "I want you to marry me."

21

EMERSYN

Vaughn's arrival had soothed me on many levels, not the least was unleashing all this pent-up desire I hadn't even realized was there. He spent most of the day, we even made it back to the bedroom eventually. Unfortunately, we didn't pick up the clothes from the living room, a fact we discovered when Liam shoved the door inward, Vaughn's shirt in his hand and a thunderous look on his face.

"Really?" The harsh judgment and demand in his voice irked me.

"Baby steps," I mocked his earlier farewell and glared right back at him. His gaze dipped briefly to my bare chest, since I was sitting up with the sheets pooled around my waist.

"I said steps, not make a baby," he snarled, the curl of his upper lip dismissive. He threw the shirt at Vaughn. "Get your ass dressed and out of here before Milo gets here."

Milo was coming over?

"Why?" Vaughn asked, having caught the shirt easily and then without slowing, tugged it over my head so I had to slip my arms through the sleeves. It smelled just like him and it had been a while since I'd been surrounded by his scent.

"Because I said so, they have enough issues to fix between them besides who she is fucking, or should I say, who is fucking her."

Shoving out of the bed, Vaughn rose and blocked my view of Liam. The lines of Vaughn's back had gone taut and that ass of his tensed. "Watch your mouth, Liam."

"Put some clothes on, Vaughn."

Instead of being offended, Vaughn chuckled. "My dick bothering you, man? I thought you got over that with your—"

"I could care less about your dick or the shrapnel in it. What I do care about is not having Milo flip his shit when he gets here. They need to talk. You need to go."

With that, he stomped away from the door. Well, maybe stomping was hyperbole, but he certainly didn't sound very happy. Rubbing the back of his neck, Vaughn turned to look at me. "Dove..."

"It's okay," I said, pulling my knees up to my chest. "You already got in trouble with him once, it's fine..."

"No," he said sharply. "It's not okay. We made our feelings clear to him. I'll get dressed, but I'm not just taking off. I'm not apologizing for caring about you or being here." When he bent toward me, I lifted my face to meet him and the soft kiss he dropped on my lips. "I am, however, going to shower."

"Okay."

"And as much as I want you in there with me," he muttered, and I had to laugh.

"I do believe a shower is where this all started."

"No, Dove," he whispered, caressing my cheek. "A shower is just where we let it all out. It started well before then."

My heart did a little squeeze as he brushed another kiss to my lips.

"I'll be out in a few minutes."

The little sigh I released as he closed the door made me laugh, more at myself than anything else. What had been an awkward start of the day had bounced from infuriating, to peaceful. Until I'd seen him when I opened the door, I hadn't realized how badly I was missing all of them. It was there, constantly, in the back of my mind, like some constant buzzing I couldn't quite turn off.

It wasn't just the sex, but the affection and the warmth —and yes, even the safety they offered. I'd grown addicted to it during those few months. While Liam and I seemed to take two steps forward and one step back, it wasn't the same. At the same time, he offered a different kind of safety, even when he worked so hard to piss me off.

Speaking of Liam, I decided to just deal with that right now. I pushed out of the bed and padded out to the living room. He stood next to his sofa with the blue shirt in his hand. The one I'd taken from him and that I hadn't wanted Vaughn to rip.

"Tell me you took this off before you fucked him on my sofa." But before I could open my mouth to say anything, he thrust the shirt at me. "Actually," he said. "Never mind, I really don't want to know."

"Liam," I began as I took the shirt. He didn't let go of it though, instead, the moment I gripped it, he pulled me to him. The distance between us closed and then he dipped his head. My pulse thundered in my ears at the sudden nearness and the way he invaded my space. The rich spice of his aftershave, something that made me think of leather and the woods tickled my nose.

"Hellspawn," he whispered, a ragged note in his voice as he hovered his lips just above mine. "Stop me if you don't want this..."

My free hand was against his chest. I could shove him back, not that I could move the wall of muscle he presented. But I had a feeling if I did push him away, he would go. Instead, I fisted his shirt and rose up on my toes to close the last few centimeters of space separating us.

Liam kissed like he fought. Or at least, like he trained me to fight. Slow, gentle, and almost without moving, he began to massage my lips with his. The first taste was like a teaser, not quite connecting. The hesitation had me pull back some to flick a look up and find him watching me. The ice from his earlier glare had melted and so much blazed back at me from within those blue eyes, I let out a gasp.

It was all he'd been waiting for, apparently, because he hauled me to him as he locked his mouth on mine and claimed it like a prize. His tongue swept past mine and my feet left the ground as he lifted me. I lost the shirt as I slid my arms up and around his neck. The demand in his kiss set my nerves on fire. The cataclysm of it started somewhere near my core and radiated outward.

The languor in my body transformed to desperation, and I moaned as he sucked my tongue. Every move demanded a counter move and when he clamped his hand over my ass, he seemed to freeze. The warmth of his fingers on bare skin invaded the tempest storming through me and I opened my eyes as he released my lips.

Our pants mingled our breath together, and the seam of his blue jeans dug into my skin where I had hitched my thighs to his hips. "We shouldn't do this," he said finally, but he didn't move his hand from my ass. If anything, his fingers spread out as though he wanted to cup the whole thing. "You were just in bed with Vaughn."

"I know," I answered. It wasn't exactly the pithiest of responses, but I didn't let him go either. "I—"

He pressed his lips to mine before I could finish the thought, and this kiss held far more scorching power than the first. I swore he was devouring me, and I arched my hips, grinding against him as he nipped, licked, and sucked at my lips and tongue. He squeezed my ass so tight as he ground into me, that the heavy weight of his erection and the roughness of his jeans lit me up.

He sank his free hand down, gliding it along the part of my ass cheeks and then a heavy, blunt finger rimmed the puckered hole of my anus. The kiss went from scorching to terrifying. From raging inferno to a plunge in ice water, I ripped my mouth from his as wildness clawed its way up through me.

Pain flashed in my memory like a red and black strobe light and I twisted my legs, even as I struck his jaw with the heel of my palm.

"Fuck!" The curse exploded out of him as we went from upright to hitting the floor. There was no time to save myself from having the wind knocked out of me, even if he managed to get his hand cupped to the back of my head. I didn't give him a chance to pin me, twisting again and then tumbling free.

I raced for the bedroom and slammed right into Vaughn's hard chest. I fought against the grip of his hands on my arms and tried to yank away. He loosened his hold and I stumbled backward, catching myself with a hand on the wall. His lips moved and he said something, but no sound penetrated the swarming sound of sobs and cries echoing in my ears.

Flattening my back against the wall, I jerked my look back at the living room at my—

Liam knelt on the floor, one hand braced on the back of the sofa the other stretched out palm forward. His expression was so full of tension and concern, I let out a harsh exhale.

Liam was in the living room.

Liam.

Not...

I closed my eyes and sank down to the floor as I tried to get more air into my lungs. A thump of sound next to me finally broke through the past and I dragged my head up to find Vaughn kneeling there.

"Hey," he said carefully, holding a hand out. "You with us again?"

The words sounded so far away, and I closed my eyes again and pressed my forehead to my knees. Not yet. I wasn't ready yet. I needed to put the broken pieces back into place. Every crack, every splinter, it threatened everything. The cracks outnumbered the solid pieces, and I wasn't sure there was enough glue in the world to put it all together again.

"What the fuck did you do?" Vaughn asked in tense voice that did rise above rasp.

"Kissed her," Liam admitted and the anguish underscoring those words made me want to drag my head up. I had to tell him it wasn't him.

"This isn't kissing her," Vaughn argued. "What else did you do?"

"What the fuck, man? I just told you I kissed your girlfriend, and you don't think that's enough to upset her?" He was so harsh on himself. Why did he do that? This wasn't Liam's fault. The words wouldn't come, nothing could get out past the debris left behind when the past collapsed in on me.

That was then, I tried to tell myself over and over. But even those words couldn't dislodge the rubble. Breathe, I had to breathe. Vaughn's hand was on my back, gentle and sure. He just rubbed slow circles and I concentrated on the contact.

"She can kiss whoever the hell she wants," Vaughn said. "If you're telling me you kissed her against her will, I will *kill* you."

He hadn't.

"No," Liam admitted. "Not against her will. I'd *never* fucking do that."

"I know." Vaughn sighed. "She's got—pain man. A lot of it. Locked away. What did you do right before she flipped?"

No, I didn't want to hear this. I jerked my head up and shoved the words out as forcefully as I could, "He didn't do anything. I need a shower." I shot to my feet, using the wall to balance me. "It's fine. Leave it alone."

"Don't," Vaughn ordered, catching my hand when I would have staggered away, and it would have been staggering. My legs were like jelly and every muscle trembled as if I'd just put myself through a brutal workout. "Don't lie to us, Dove."

I made myself look at Vaughn, to meet his eyes. "I'm not lying," I told him, and I wasn't. "It wasn't him. Leave him alone. Please."

Vaughn searched my eyes, the green compelling me, almost begging me to confide in him. Some things never needed to be seen in the light. This—this least of all. They already pitied me. They all wanted me to be this Ivy so badly. Maybe not as badly as Milo did. But that girl they held so beloved was so far from who I really was that—they would probably hate me if they knew the truth.

Or worse, they'd just feel sorry for the poor broken rich girl.

No. I needed to get myself together.

"Hellspawn," Liam said in a voice I barely recognized. "You can trust us."

As much as I wanted to grasp those words and wrap them around me like a security blanket, the problem wasn't Dove's or Hellspawn's. She probably could trust these guys.

But Emersyn Sharpe?

I knew better.

Nothing in life was free. Even protection could extract a cost in blood and tears.

I wouldn't let any of them pay that for me. Not if I could help it.

"Then you can believe me when I said it wasn't you," I told him without looking at him. "Let me go, Vaughn."

I wouldn't yank my hand free, but I needed some time to fix all the jumbled and broken bits. I had to rebuild myself and those walls *before* Milo got here. He was a singular raw nerve, vibrating at such a high frequency that this—this could break him if he discovered the truth.

Bile burned at the back of my throat, but I swallowed it. I couldn't afford another episode, and the last thing I wanted was Liam summoning Rome again. Rome—fuck. I closed my eyes. Rome had come the day before and he had been safety. The second I realized, I wanted him there. Or Jasper. Or even Kellan. Someone to hide and shield me, I shoved those thoughts away.

This was all spinning violently out of control.

With an aggrieved sound, Vaughn released my hand

and I moved toward the bedroom. "I'll be out in a few minutes," I said from the doorway. "Thank you."

It took every ounce of effort I had to close the door gently, then make my way over to the bathroom. I didn't vomit. Barely. I got the shower on and I stripped out of Vaughn's shirt. I stepped under the icy spray and shuddered as it slapped my skin like dozens of needles burrowing into my flesh.

The cold brought me to the present. To the now. To the fact I wasn't back there. The pain was a part of the past. I'd survived it. Survived so much. It wouldn't beat me now. Then, all too aware they were probably clocking me, I shifted the water to hot and chased the chills with warmth. I was almost coherent by the time I'd finished washing up.

When I came out of the bathroom, I found the bed had been remade—right down to fresh sheets and a comforter. The blue shirt I'd abandoned, along with my dance pants were on the bed. The bra and panties were missing, but I didn't worry about that. Instead, I moved to the suitcase and pulled out all fresh things.

My things.

I slid them on, one piece at a time, like I needed them to hold the jagged edges in place. The shirt I chose had the name of one of my shows on it. It was ragged around the edges and there was a tear in the sleeve. Eric, I thought, but even that wasn't enough to remove the comfort the familiar top offered.

The yoga pants covered all of my legs, and the socks hid my feet. I finally pulled on a hoodie. It wasn't that cold in the apartment, but after the icy shower even the hot one hadn't been able to warm up the frozen cube at my core.

Pulling the wet hair out from under the collar, I squared my shoulders. This would have to do. The clock said I'd taken twenty-two minutes. Not the best time, but enough. When I emerged, however, I wasn't prepared to find not only had Milo arrived, but Jasper was with him.

All at once, my heart ping-ponged against my ribs at the sight of him. There were still some bruises on his face. They were a lot lighter than they'd been before. His grimace turned to a smile as we locked gazes and then he strode across the room to sweep me up into a hug.

As bad of an idea as it was, I returned the hug fiercely, even as I met Liam's concerned gaze and could practically feel Vaughn's laser-focused attention.

"Missed you," Jasper whispered against my ear and I managed a smile so that when he set me down, he hopefully wouldn't read anything into my reactions. "You look even more beautiful than I remembered."

"Oh, for fuck's sake," Milo said. "We get it. I don't need to fucking listen to it."

"Then stick your fingers in your ears, jackass," Jasper said over his shoulder. "I get to tell my girl she's beautiful, especially after her asshole brother kept us apart for weeks."

Milo muttered something about Jasper's head and tying his balls in a knot, but Jasper just grinned wider at the threat. My fake smile took less effort as real humor invaded. "I don't think that's biologically possible." While it wasn't quite as light as I was aiming for, there was amusement in my tone.

"Trust me," Milo said, folding his arms. "I could make it work." Despite his bravado, echoes of the previous day's concerns shone in his eyes. "You better, now?"

That question was so loaded, and he couldn't even begin to understand why. Jasper shifted to face him with me, and he hooked an arm around my waist so I could lean on him if I wanted. No matter how much that was true though, I kept my feet on the ground.

"Yes," I answered. "Much."

From the corner of my eye, I caught Liam's slight head shake. I had averted disaster for the moment.

The only question was, how much longer would it last? Well, one of the only questions was that. The other was, "Are you here to take me to Doc?"

HOMECOMING

JASPER

When Doc came back to Braxton Harbor, he did it quietly and without any fanfare. In fact, he did it without saying a word to anyone, except maybe his sister. The fact he turned up bare months after Milo's sentencing and didn't come to see *us* was more than a little suspicious. Vaughn and Kellan thought I was overreacting. Still, Milo had *just* been sent to jail for three years.

Three years where *I* had to make sure we stayed on target and followed the plan. Milo's words to me the day he decided to plead guilty in order to get a reduced sentence, rather than fight the charges, echoed over and over. *"Watch who you trust. Verify everything. Keep an eye on my sister. I don't know what is going on, but someone is making moves against us. Trust your gut."*

Two days after he pled guilty, Liam moved out of the clubhouse permanently. He had to focus on his life, his contacts, and his future. Making zero apologies, he wished me luck. I punched him in the face.

Bastard.

Then we get word that a new doctor had opened a clinic, but the whispers carried notes of approval and, in some cases, genuine surprise. Mickey J was back. The original 82nd Street Vandal, and he was a doctor. Would you look at that? The place he'd taken over was on our list of acquisitions back in the day, but we'd never done anything with it.

Kellan swung by the clinic to check the rumors out. If this was some imposter, we'd be evicting him, with prejudice. A part of me looked forward to kicking some bastard to the curb. It would be a definitive move in our defense. Particularly since Freddie had fallen off the grid—again. I hadn't found him yet and we were still trying to get our trucks up and running. So many demands in so many directions.

Then Kellan confirmed that the "Doc" everyone had been talking about was Mickey J. His silent arrival and seeming indifference to the rest of us stung. This, after years of hearing *nothing* from him, not even the occasional letter or card like he'd sent previously, added insult to injury. I had zero intentions of seeing him, beyond evicting him from our property.

Only, Milo stayed my hand. Turned out that of all of us, Doc—because fuck him he didn't deserve the name Mickey J anymore—had gone to see Milo upon his return. He'd also visited every two weeks or so.

"He's a mess, Jas," Milo said via the phone that we had to use to communicate, because of the solid glass separating us. "He wanted to set up a clinic. He's basically using a grant to pay his expenses and he's donating his own time."

"So we're apparently donating an entire building to this

effort?" Don't get me wrong, I approved of the idea of getting a clinic with more services in our area, fuck knew the closest hospital was fifteen blocks north. A lot of people avoided services and just suffered if they either, couldn't get to them, or couldn't pay for them.

"Yes," Milo told me. Damn his soft heart sometimes. He and Doc had been tight forever, I got why. At least he'd come to see him though. "Don't fight me on this?"

"I won't." Didn't mean I wouldn't give Doc shit for it. "Just because he's back doesn't mean he's in." There were some things I wouldn't give in on.

"Fine," Milo said with a sigh, but he didn't argue Doc's case anymore. That handled, I filled him in on Freddie's current situation—including the fact I hadn't been able to track him down. "Focus on him. Let's see if we can get him into one of those thirty day programs. Get him started at least. Break into the emergency fund for that."

Agreed. "I'll do my best."

"You'll find him." I appreciated Milo's confidence, but I wasn't as certain. Freddie had backslid so fast this time. Faster than any other time previously, and I had no idea why. What the fuck had I missed? Though, the most likely culprit remained unspoken. Milo's incarceration forced Freddie to deal with yet another change. Still, he'd *seemed* okay for a while. But apparently not.

We had less than ten minutes left on the visit, so I spent the time filling him in on Ivy's newest show. The launch of it had been all over social media. We'd downloaded some videos for him. Even if he got internet time in here, he wouldn't do searches on her. All of that was recorded. I'd get him any articles or magazines with the latest smuggled in as soon as possible.

As soon as our visiting time was up, they were already

coming to escort Milo back to his cell. I hated watching them take him away. Worse, I hated that where he was going, I couldn't follow. None of us could. It wasn't the first time one of us was out there alone, but it was the first time we wouldn't be able to back him up.

And that? *I loathed.*

The trip in and out of the prison wasn't all that fun either, but one of us would make it weekly. The fact that it was a drive wouldn't stop us. As soon as I was back in the car and on the road back to Braxton Harbor, I called Kel.

We needed to pay a visit to Doc. He had Milo's permission. But there would be rules.

22

Milo didn't answer me immediately. If anything, he looked wearier at the question. Rubbing his eyes, he finally nodded. "Yeah, I can do that."

"Why do you need to see Doc?" Jasper asked, concern in his eyes as he gave me a once over.

"Because Milo said he's the one who found us as children," I answered. "Or at least, found him and his sister." I had to distance myself. Stop trying to cling to a role that wasn't mine. The fact Liam's gaze bored into me grew increasingly more difficult to ignore.

Vaughn, on the other hand, just stood there, arms folded while he rubbed his lower lip with his thumb. It was distracting as hell. Honestly, all of them were distracting. Jasper gave my side a squeeze and I covered his hand with mine. The fact he immediately threaded our fingers both offered comfort and assurance. It had been so crazy and beyond a few texts, we'd had no time to talk since that one night.

"You think Doc can convince her if you can't?" Jasper asked, his attention on Milo, even as Jasper stroked his thumb along the side of my hand. "I can tell you when I met you, too," he offered without waiting for Milo's response. "You were still a baby, but you were his whole world."

"Jas." The quiet order in Milo's voice silenced Jasper, and I met Jasper's gaze searchingly for a moment before I looked over at the man who wanted to be my brother. "I can't make you believe me. I can't make you believe any of us. This—none of this—is how I would have chosen to tell you."

"By none of this, do you mean the fact they kidnapped me?" I had to know. "Or because I'm having sex with them?"

I swore, he growled an exhale and Jasper's arm tightened around me. All the gravity in the room seemed to shift and pull toward where Milo stood. Like he controlled the orbital arrangement, and the flash of his temper and frustration magnified the effect. "Do me a favor..." He pinched the bridge of his nose before he squared his shoulders and met my gaze.

There it was again. Burying his real reaction under one more *acceptable*. I recognized the body language. Even the way he tilted his head and raised his chin. More to the right, as if he needed that extra bit of control.

"The fact you have sex at all is not really high on my list of things I want to know," he said in a tone that was as much aggrieved as it was worried. "The idea that my sister is fucking my brothers is not something I'm all that comfortable with. I didn't like it when I thought it was just one of them. I like it less now that you're letting yourself be passed around..."

"Milo." His name lashed out at him from three different directions. Each one of them offered varying levels of violence. His expression, however, turned into more of a dark smirk than it was chastised.

"First, don't ever refer to me as being passed around again." The ice licking those words startled me. I hadn't even meant to say them, much less want to cut him for even suggesting it. "Second, get over what I do or don't do. No one owns me. Not anymore."

Brother or not—just no.

"Third," I continued, peeling Jasper's hand off my hip before I took a step forward. "Why are you so against me with them? In theory, these are the guys you trust with your life and clearly you trusted them with mine. What? Are they good enough to fight for me or get hurt for me? But not good enough for me to like myself?"

"That's not what I meant," Milo said, the anger in his tone turned way down from where it had been. "At all."

"Then *what* did you mean?" I glared. "Think real careful like, I've had it up to here..." I raised my hand to my nose. "...with people telling me what to do or how to do it and who is good enough and who isn't."

No one was good enough for the Sharpes. A Sharpe couldn't have a roommate or a friend or a boyfriend or a life...

My heart slammed even as heat burned my face. What the hell was I doing? When Milo opened his mouth as if to respond, I held up a hand. "You know what? Never mind. This is an argument neither of us is going to win or agree on. I want to talk to Jasper for a couple of minutes, then we can go see Doc."

It would be good to see him, too.

I didn't miss the looks the other guys shot me as I turned my back on Milo and headed down the hall to my room. There was a faint murmuring of voices behind me and then Jasper finally followed.

He actually entered the room with a cautious expression. "You okay, Swan?"

"No, I'm not," I said with a shrug, then folded my arms. "I'll get there. And no, before you ask, this isn't something you can fix."

"How do you know?" A hint of teasing crept into his voice. "If you don't tell me, I can't help. Maybe I know more than you think."

I studied him for a long moment. Sadness swelled up inside of me. There was a simple joy in just having him there again. "I missed you," I said softly. "And I don't know whether we're coming or going or what's going to happen—"

He closed the distance between us and pulled me into the fiercest of hugs. Eyes closing, I clung to him and buried my face against his neck. Cupping the back of my head, he shifted just enough to press his lips to my forehead.

"I missed you, too," he assured me and then pulled back enough to meet my gaze. "Talk to me. What's wrong? Liam giving you issues? Vaughn stir up shit cause he was here? What?"

A laugh escaped me. "No, Liam is great. He annoys me, but I annoy him so that works. He's teaching me to fight. That's pretty cool. I loved having Vaughn here today. I can't believe you're back—I thought you wouldn't make it until tomorrow."

"Fuck that, my girl sounded like she missed me," he said, his whole expression softened. The resting Jasper face he wore most of the time was nowhere in evidence. Instead, this was the man who teased me and played with me at the hotel in the little cottage on the bluff. "I know this has been hard on you. That we should have told you...but it was never ours to tell."

"Why did you keep me?" This one question bugged me. "After everything was said and done, you got Eric, you took care of him and you got me medical care, but—then you kept me. And it wasn't just for a few weeks. It was months. Months where you changed everything at the clubhouse including adding the dance studio, cleaned the place up, and that also meant the rest of you had to shift your schedules to look after me, too."

"There's an easy answer," he said slowly. "And a much more difficult one."

"Well, easy answer first then."

"Because I wanted to," Jasper admitted. "Once we had you there, I wanted you to stay. I wanted to know you were safe." He pressed another kiss to my forehead before he let me go and walked away a couple of steps, before turning and leaning back against the door. It didn't seem so much a blocking maneuver as needing a reasonable distance.

"The much more difficult one?"

I sat on the edge of the bed as he rubbed his hands over his face, before he smoothed down his beard. "I've loved you for a long time."

My heart fisted.

"I loved you when you were this glittering, shining star that made my best friend smile. The first time I saw you perform, everything about you called to me. At first, I told myself it was because you were Milo's sister. You were Ivy. You were important to us. You were part of us." He licked his lips. "Then later, I just loved you for being so fierce and fearless. Everything about you was so graceful and ephemeral. You were a light we could all warm ourselves by...then some asshole roofied your drink when you were fourteen and all I wanted to do was pound him until he was nothing but meat left over."

I frowned. "Fourteen?"

"Yeah, you were just finishing a show, it was the last one on the tour. You were three hours away, so we all drove there to see you. Got tickets in the nosebleeds just to watch you. Never seen anything like it. Then, when you all went to that club, we followed."

"I..." What he was saying pulled at a memory.

"We kept an eye on you. Your friends gave you a drink before they took off and you were dancing with some of the other girls. But the bartender," he said the last part with a snarl. "He kept it up. He damn well knew you were under-age, and he was getting you good and drunk, then he flirted with you."

I barely remembered the bartender. "I got sick."

"Yep, you went out and bummed a smoke from one of the girls, but you were not steady, and Milo caught you before you fell into the damn street."

Surprise zipped through me.

"It was the first time I think I realized just how fragile and perfect you were." He spread his hands. "There you were, right in front of us, delicate as hell and so tiny by comparison. Fuck you're still too damn tiny. It pisses me off every single time I think about all those bruises on you, or how you looked when you realized I was putting a lock on that door and not giving anyone else the key."

Licking my lips, I nodded slowly. "There's a lot of power in a locked door."

"Security is behind the door, the power comes from being able to lock it." He got it and I appreciated that. "I told myself, everything we were doing, we were doing for Milo," Jasper continued. "It started out for him, because he's our brother. I would die for him."

That made me cold even thinking about it.

"But I'd die for you, too. Emersyn—the complicated answer is, you belong here with us, even if we're not the best or have all the money or the fancy standing. Even if we can't give you a swanky apartment in a high rise or fame or even all the stuff you're used to...but we protect what is ours and we always have each other's backs. I'll have yours in everything. Even if it comes down to letting you go, because you decide."

That reality crashed down on me like a bridge collapsing. Before I could respond, a swift knock hit the door. "Milo's getting agitated that you guys have been in there this long," Vaughn said. "Take your time, but if you are getting naked, don't get noisy, Dove. I don't think he's up for that yet."

I swore my eyes rounded and the laughter exploded out of me before I could stop it. Even Jasper chuckled, and I swore Vaughn was laughing as he walked away.

"He's such a dick," Jasper said, but he was smiling.

"But you love him."

"All right, let's not get too touchy feely. I'd kill for him. I'd die for him. Let's leave it at that."

Another wistful chuckle escaped me. What would I have been like if I'd grown up with all of them? If I'd had seven or eight older brothers, instead of one fierce, angry one who'd just gotten out of prison, and guys who I didn't have an ounce of fraternal feeling for? Who would I be?

Who was Ivy Hardigan supposed to be?

Had I already decided to agree with him? There was one way to find out. A simple blood test could give us the DNA match or not. But what did that mean? Why had they never told me I'd been adopted? Particularly when they put such emphasis on how much better we were...

It made my head pound and I closed my eyes.

"Hey." Jasper was suddenly there, closing his hands over mine and cradling them. "What just happened?"

I shook my head, more because I didn't want to answer the question. "I'm still trying to wrap my mind around all this." I sucked my upper lip between my teeth and scraped it hard enough to sting. "Jasper..." I opened my eyes to meet his gaze. "All of this started because you all thought I was Milo's sister. What if—what if we get blood work or a test done, and it turns out I'm not this Ivy you all love so much. What then?"

"I have zero doubts that you're his sister." The ferocity of his belief seemed to echo with Rome's unfaltering faith. "But let's say for the sake of argument, you guys take a blood test, and it says you're not brother and sister."

"Right."

"I'd still love *you*," he told me simply and I swore a chill wrapped around me like an icy north wind. "Because *you* are the girl I've watched over from afar for years. You, Emersyn Sharpe. My swan. The fierce dancer who fights back with not only her body, but her mind. Who doesn't let anyone control her, no matter how right they might be or how much they may have her well being in mind. You are probably one of the toughest people I've ever met, and I adore you. It's really that simple."

That... simple.

"You love me."

I was still back on those three words.

He gave me a smile that was half-secret, half-teasing. "Yes, I do." Lifting my hands to his lips, he kissed each palm before he fixed his gaze on me again. "I love *you*. I don't need a test to tell me that."

Pain flickered through me, it was like trying to hold a guttering candle up against a relentless dark and there, at the end, was a flare of light like there really was a way out.

"You don't have to say the words to me," Jasper said. "I've never needed to hear the words. I always believe that actions speak a lot louder than words. And I was one of the first people you texted—even if you called Freddie."

I winced. "The deal with Milo..."

"It's fine, Swan, really. I'm just teasing. I know what Milo wanted you to agree to, and I loved how you walked right around that restriction while still keeping your word."

"The devil's in the details."

"Yes, he is." Another kiss to my hands. "Now, I can smell the sex in here and the fact that you must have come a few times today for it to be this strong. So, before I strip you down and see how many times *I* can make you come, let's get you out there so you can go see Doc."

He made a face.

"You still don't like him or Liam and..."

Two fingers pressed against my lips. "I'll tell you, but not right now. We can talk about all of that later, when there's time for you and me. Since we're alone, there is one thing I do want."

No question existed within me about what that something was. When he leaned in, I mirrored the action and we tilted our heads at almost the exact same moment. Not once did I close my eyes or look away as his lips brushed mine. It was a teasing taste, a sampler of what was to come. The next was a more nuzzling kiss. The softness of his beard tickled my face and then his tongue swept along the seam of my lips, asking permission.

I launched myself off the bed, arms around his neck as he stood. Our mouths fused together in a kiss that was every bit as much about desire as it was about reconnecting. Somewhere in the last few weeks, I'd forgiven them all. Even for not telling me about Milo.

Losing myself in the sensations his kiss conjured, I clung to him and only whimpered a little when he lifted his head and broke the kiss. "You really did miss me."

Smugness filled his tone and I laughed as I stroked the back of his head, feathering my fingers through his hair.

We allowed ourselves one more kiss, this one far too brief, before we returned to the living room. The guys were more or less where we'd left them. Though Vaughn had taken a position at the end of the hallway, leading to the bedrooms. It registered that he'd been guarding it when Milo latched his gaze onto me and his lips tightened a fraction before his whole expression relaxed.

"You ready?" The gruff way he asked said he was trying, so I didn't snap back at him. The poor guy didn't deserve to be snapped at anyway.

"Yes. Will I be back tonight?"

"Maybe," Milo said. "Let's figure this out one step at a time." He took a deep breath. "Please."

I glanced around at the guys. Liam quirked a brow. "You got your phone?"

Patting the pocket of my hoodie, I nodded. "But I don't have a key."

He let out an exasperated sound, before crossing over to hold one out to me. "Baby steps."

I curled my fingers around the key in his palm and read his expression. "If I get stuck, I'll call."

He nodded once. Then stepped back. Turning to Vaughn next, I rose up on my tiptoes to brush a kiss to the corner of his mouth. "I'll talk to you later?"

He chuckled. "You're playing with fire, Dove."

I shrugged. "Just as long as he doesn't burn you."

"Don't worry, I can handle Milo."

The key emphasis was on the Milo part. They all seemed fine with Milo, while Raptor worried them. I filed that away for later and then slid the key into my pocket before I headed to the door. Milo opened it and I paused before going through it to look back at Jasper and Liam, who for once were in the same space and *not* glaring at each other.

"Could you two try not to beat each other up while I'm gone?"

"No promises," they said in the exact same sarcastic tone.

Milo snorted. "Leave them alone, they'll figure it out."

"Have they *always* fought like that?" I asked as I headed for the elevator. I swore Jasper said "hey" and Liam grunted something while Vaughn laughed, but Milo closed the door on them.

"Yes," he said. The elevator was already open and he motioned for me to step in first. "As hard as it might be to believe..."

"They are too much alike," I said. "No, it's not that hard to believe. They are both putting the weight of everything on themselves."

His gaze settled on me and then he gave me a nod. "That's part of it." When the elevator let us out into the garage, he made no bones about cutting me off to step out first, then held out a hand to me so I would join him. The car he led me to was another SUV. How many did they own?

Opening the passenger side door, he waited until I climbed in before he studied me. "If you're going to be making out with Liam like you are Vaughn and Jasper, be ready for that to infuriate Jasper."

Yeah, I'd already figured that out.

"But not Rome?" I asked, more curious than anything. Milo bounced his head gently against the door before he looked at me again.

"No, not Rome—I—Emersyn—do something for me?"

"If I can." And I meant it exactly that way. If I could.

"Be careful with them. They're all... decent men. Good men. Some of them are the best. But they are also the worst. You can't do what we do and not be both."

That made sense.

"So just—be careful, that's all I'm saying for now. Also, if you could never have sex again, that would be great, too." He shot me a weak smile, then closed the door and I couldn't help it. I snickered.

I waited for him to get behind the wheel before I asked, "So does this mean you're a virgin?"

"What the fuck?" He shot me a startled look. "No, I'm not a fucking a virgin—why would you ask me that?"

"Just wondering if I got the same rights over your sex life you seem to want to take over mine."

He glared at me, but there wasn't an ounce of meanness in that glare. He shook his head slowly. "You're still a brat."

For some reason, that pleased me almost as much as Jasper telling me he loved me. It was also a lot easier to believe. "Thank you."

With a groan, he started the car. "Maybe Doc can get through to you."

"Well, he is cute," I admitted. Milo swore for the next four blocks.

I laughed until I almost cried. I probably shouldn't torment the guy, but I'd never had a brother before. This was...kind of nice.

Probably wouldn't last, but for as long as it did? I wanted to enjoy it.

FIRST GLANCE

MICKEY J AKA DOC

The last thing I expected to see when the boys called me in for an emergency near midnight was them arriving with an unconscious girl bleeding from a head wound, and quite literally black and blue from a series of beatings—or what looked like beatings.

The striations of the bruising was deep, there were new bruises over old bruises. Her feet showed heavy calluses and bruising, particularly around the soles and on her toes. The x-rays fucked with my head at the signs of the old fractures that had healed.

A road map of abuse embedded into her skin and bones. Stripping off the clothes had just revealed more and more damage. Pulling the rape kit bugged the hell out of me, but I did it anyway. The boys wouldn't have brought her here if it wasn't important. The damage visible suggested a recent attack, but the scars told a far worse story.

A colonoscopy would be needed to confirm what I'd already found, but I wasn't putting her through any more invasive procedures without her explicit permission. Someone had done a real number on this kid. From pelvic development, to the slight formation of her breasts, to her height, she couldn't be more than fourteen or fifteen. Barely into puberty.

Malnutrition seemed evident in the way the injuries had healed. I kept her covered with a sheet as much as possible to preserve her privacy. Her absolute lack of response to my physical manipulation was also a cause for concern. Pulse was steady and breathing even.

Jasper stepped back in, radiating hostility. The kid had always had anger management issues. They'd gotten worse in my absence. The fact he flat out fucking hated me hadn't escaped my notice. But there wasn't much I could do, beyond being the guy I'd always been.

"It's going to take some time," I told him, before he could say another word. "I'm getting her on an IV, antibiotics, and pain meds. Then I need to treat these breaks."

"How many breaks?" Jasper demanded.

"Easily three or four," I explained. "Look..." I pulled the images up on the screen. I'd already fired them to Cam at the VA. Not only would he keep the request private, there were no names attached to the file, only numbers. I needed his confirmation. He was on the team that helped put me back together.

The broken ribs included bruising and minor fractures. Other than making sure they weren't about to impale her lungs, I couldn't do much for those. They had to heal on their own. "I'm not an expert, but I can read these well enough and I got a friend looking at them right now..."

Unsurprisingly, this just pissed him off more. I rolled my eyes. I had neither the time nor the patience to cater to his resentment today. At some point, he'd either get over it or just have to live unhappy because I wasn't fucking going anywhere again. "You can trust him."

"We don't trust anyone, Doc," he told me in a cold voice. "You had to earn it, too."

It took everything I possessed not to snort at him. "Pretty sure that shit was the other way around, kid, but whatever helps you sleep at night. Now look..." These boys were family. Family did stupid things or as my sister had once told me, *I love you in spite of your shitty choices, Mickey, but someday, it would be great if you would learn to appreciate the chances life has given you, rather than trying to make more of a mess.*

Steph had been damn right. It only took damn near dying in the middle of fucking nowhere, halfway around the world, and my skin on fire, for me to realize that life had been generous with me.

I survived, for one.

Kellan and Vaughn joined us and I walked them through the patchwork of injuries, while I got the medications ready. I wanted to do an MRI, with that much soft tissue damage there was no certainty I hadn't missed *something*. Still, she reacted to all reflexive stimuli to fingers and toes.

"Why the fuck is she naked?" Vaughn demanded suddenly. I'd added a blanket to the sheet to keep her warm. So far, I hadn't found any signs of shock, but I'd rather avoid them.

"Because I had to do a full exam." Simple question, simple answer.

"If you—" Jasper started, and with that, I'd had enough.

"You finish that sentence, kid, you better do it with a bullet to my brain, because I've beaten men to death for less charges. She's a fucking child. Not to mention an abused one. She's barely got tits."

That shut him up.

"What she does have, are bruises over three quarters of her torso. How the hell she performed like that, I don't know. But she's got cracked ribs, that had to be impeding her breathing. She's broken every single one of her toes, some of them multiple times. She's had broken fingers. A broken wrist. Twice on the right. Old healed fractures to her arms and both legs." The dance clothes were the only clue I had to the fact she'd been performing, but still... this kid was a mess.

And if they weren't aware before, they needed to know *now*.

"Someone is beating her."

Kellan's neutral expression gave away to pure fury. Vaughn, probably one of the most laid back guys I'd ever known, wore a stony expression. Jasper's raw anger vibrated in the air.

"And you better make sure he doesn't lay a finger on her again."

Not that I needed to give these guys encouragement, I understood the road they'd followed. A road I'd once walked and invited them to join me on. They'd blazed farther down that trail than I had ever imagined. But some things weren't forgivable.

Whoever beat and raped this girl deserved a grisly and painful death. I might work to heal people now, but some things healed the soul, killing monsters was one of them.

The boys talked amongst themselves, but I ignored the conversation while I finished getting the antibiotics ready. I'd give her the morning after pill, but I wanted to wait until I *spoke* to her before I made that decision for her.

"What about her head?" Vaughn asked, the belligerence in his voice absent now, and I gave him a considering look.

"Concussion most likely. Contusion from where she hit the stone, looks like she caught a corner. I'll do a couple of stitches, but I'm not seeing swelling yet. Need to get her to wake up and check her cognitive functions, but she's probably wiped, poor thing." I'd seen worse in the deserts and the mountains. But not by much. "Gonna put her on an IV, get some fluid into her and do a couple of other tests. Then I'll get you some scripts. You taking her to the clubhouse?"

All three nodded at once. Good, at least I could keep an eye on her and check in.

"All right, get out then while I do this. Give me an hour." I needed to keep myself focused on the task. Jasper and Kellan left, but Vaughn settled in, arms folded. The fact he didn't interfere or ask questions as I went to work, helped. I spared him a look and there was no mistaking the anguish in his eyes. This kid was either important to him or he blamed himself for her injuries. "I know it looks bad," I told him. "But we'll get her through the worst, then help her with the rest."

He met my gaze for a moment and then nodded as he let out a heavy sigh. "I shoulda been faster, Doc."

"You were fast enough to get her here," I offered what comfort I could. "Focus on that for now."

23

Leaving her alone all day hadn't been high on my list. Oddly enough, guilt had been my companion as I headed to my various appointments, including a meeting her uncle was supposed to attend.

He sent an emissary—an attorney. The man was a cold mother fucker with an icy tone and even icier presence. It served to both piss me off and incite a deeper curiosity about this man who was supposedly doing everything he could to find his "niece" and yet, couldn't be bothered to meet me himself? Right. That wasn't suspicious at all.

As it was, the attorney made no friends with me. I stayed at the meeting for exactly ten minutes. He wasn't going to tell me shit. The fact I didn't bother to hide my disdain, nor my dismissal when I left, didn't earn me any points.

It did earn me a tail though.

These fuckers would never learn.

Ever.

My phone rang a block away from the appointment. "What?" I answered it without a glance at the screen. For one, only a very specific group of people had this number. If it was the king, I'd apologize. He liked it when I had to grovel.

"Well, you sound like you need to get laid," a familiar voice snarked at me. "That or whoever you're fucking isn't very good at her job."

I rolled my eyes. "Ezra, not everything is about sex."

"Nah, just the good parts. *Anyway,*" the wealthy prick continued, blowing past any objection I might have. "Tell me you've sorted out that bullshit in Braxton Harbor. I do not want to field another call from his royal jackassness."

That did pull a smile from me. The king might hold all the cards, but none of us really cared for him. It took a long time for Adam and Ezra to *trust* me with that information, and I didn't blame them. How could I, when the king had, more than once in the past eliminated one of the Royals for questioning him. More often than not, that job fell to Adam or Ezra. Though I'd done my fair share.

It also didn't escape me that I'd likely been filmed or recorded, because blackmail material would keep us all in line. As did potential threats against my other half. Though I informed the king from the get go, Rome was not negotiable. They touched him and I would burn them all down. Whatever issues he had with me, he would take up with me.

I had no idea what he held over Adam or Ezra. They'd never told me. Just as I'd never confided mine. Though, I suspected, based on a handful of conversations—it was a woman.

Shoving that information to the side, I simply said, "I have it handled. I can't move any faster and still keep it low-key and untraceable. If he wants it to be brutal, bloody, and very noisy—I can do that, too."

"Fuck." Ezra snarled the word. The guy seemed to be in possession of dual personalities, and ping-ponged back and forth between them. The sex-crazed dilettante vied with the raging asshole for dominance.

"Let me guess," I said, keeping my eye on my tail. I was taking him for a nice little drive. "You're tasked with my reprimand if I fail." It wasn't a question.

"It's nothing personal," he grumbled.

But he didn't want to do it and that made it personal—at least in the right ways.

"Don't sweat it. Remind his majesty that patience is how we've gotten this far. If he wants to risk the attention a rush job would bring down on our heads, I'm game for that, too."

The dark laugh echoing down the phone made me smile. "You're a such dick," he commented. "But point taken. We both know he wants speed and silence. He also thinks you're playing both ends against the middle."

"Maybe I am," I said. "Maybe I'm not. Take me out of play and you'll never know. Course..." I wasn't above bragging when it was fact. "You have no one who can do what I can."

"Don't I fucking know it." Another aggrieved note escaped him.

"You got a problem you need help with?"

"Yes," Ezra admitted. "But there are others who would beat me unconscious if I bring it up, so thanks for not offering."

"Any time."

He didn't waste time hanging up. By others, he meant Adam. The call itself was a step outside the norm, because it was a warning. One I hadn't really needed but appreciated all the same. Our reputation had been cultivated more because of their work and mine, than any other member of this so-called "elite" society.

Society my left ass cheek. It was a fucking gang. They just dressed in more expensive clothes, bought more expensive cars, and fucked more expensive pussy. At least that was how I'd always seen it. Then again, maybe the Vandals were coming up in the world thanks to Emersyn's...

I wanted to punch myself in the face for even going there, however briefly, in my head. She deserved a lot more respect than being valued for her pussy, no matter how pretty or sweet it might be, and just like that I had a cock so hard I could probably drill wood.

Fuck.

My.

Life.

Time to get rid of my tail. I cut through the business district then headed down to the interchange for the highway that would take me out of the city. There were a half-dozen switchbacks and exchanges. The barnacles on my ass did not have a vehicle with half my speed or maneuverability.

Thirty minutes later, I slid into my garage and checked the cameras in the apartment. It had been a dick move to give her the code and not the key. Baby steps, sure, but a part of me liked knowing she was secure in the apartment. Anyone trying to break in would not only set off the security system and alert me as well as Rome, but it would also alert a security team.

I was playing a long and dangerous game. The best way to survive those things was to prepare for the worst. She was as safe as I could make her, without taking her to an isolated and private island. Not that the thought hadn't crossed my mind since Milo dumped her safety in my lap.

Clothes were scattered all over the living room. I checked the various angles and I wasn't wrong. Shirts—a t-shirt and the blue one she'd taken from me—along with those sexy fucking dance pants she'd had on. Lace panties peeked out from inside the pants and my temper, already aggravated, began to boil.

Who the fuck...

Rolling it back, I went to an earlier timestamp—like *right* after I'd left. There she was, glaring at the door before she'd gone to get her phone. Not for the first time, I debated the wisdom of not putting a camera in her room. Again, I reminded myself, she didn't deserve any more invasions of her privacy. I just hadn't figured out *where* she was hiding that phone and until I could clone it, I had no idea who she was talking to or what she was saying.

Then she stared at the door for a really long time, before she went over and keyed in the code.

Vaughn.

Fuck.

What the hell was he *doing* here?

I got my answer to that seconds later. While very little in this life shocked me, the speed at which she shed her clothes and then had his cock half-down her throat had me so hard, I thought I would come just from watching.

God, she was gorgeous. Even prettier than I'd imagined. From the faint curves I'd had in my hands when I was training with her, to the peaked nipples on her breasts. There was a careless abandon to her, like she had no idea just how beautiful she was...and then Vaughn blew his load on her chest and I laughed.

Fuck my life, I probably shouldn't have. But goddamn.

You couldn't even get undressed or do something about *her* before you came like some randy kid?

Not that she seemed to mind. Before I realized it, I was still staring at the screen after he'd buried his face in her cunt and she was so close to coming... I wished like fuck I'd added sound so I could hear it and that was when I killed the feed and leaned my head back against the seat.

I checked the time.

That had happened *hours* ago, and their clothes were still on the floor in *my* fucking living room. That meant somewhere in my place, they were still fucking.

Slamming my palm against the steering wheel in three rapid hits, I ignored the sting of pain on my hand. Nor did I look too closely at how pissed off I was. I'd ignored it all the way up the elevator, into the apartment—which reeked of sex. There was a damp mess on my goddamn leather, too.

If anyone should be fucking her on that sofa, it should be...

Don't finish that thought. Not that the order could strip the image of her head thrown back as she spread her legs wide, while Vaughn ate her out. Then my phone buzzed and I dragged it out, more to distract myself than anything else.

Milo: *Heading your way. Be there in fifteen.*

Oh, the day had just gotten better and better. Walking into the bedroom, I wasn't ready to find her and Vaughn just enjoying their intimacy in a bedroom that was more sex scented than anything else. No, we'd never be able to cover this up. My cock was a stone by the time my gaze landed on her, sitting there without a care in the world, bare breasts and flushed nipples just begging to be sucked and teased.

It pissed me off.

All of it.

I would never have taken it out on her. No, just—needed a minute to get it together. Then she walked out in his t-shirt and smelling of sex, lips puffy and beautiful, looking more relaxed than I'd *ever* seen her and what did I do?

I fucking kissed her. It was a thousand times better than I ever imagined and left me hungrier for her than I thought possible. She wasn't for me or Vaughn or Jasper. She was supposed to be Rome's. The only girl he'd *ever* shown even an ounce of interest in, and I was toying with her ass and imagining filling her with my cock. Her mouth. Her cunt. Her ass. I wanted to fill her and mark her and stamp her with my claim so the whole goddamn world knew.

The freakout had been the biggest bucket of water on my libido. The fear in her blown pupils, the sheer, raw panic as she struck. It was a damn good hit, too. The air she knocked out of me as she took us to the ground and I barely managed to shield her head from bouncing against the hard floor.

Everything I'd been drumming into her, she'd executed beautifully then...

"We should go," Jasper was saying to Vaughn, jerking me out of my musings. Milo and Emersyn were gone. Jasper wanted to put distance between us. Hardly surprising...

"Go ahead," Vaughn said. "I need to talk to Liam."

"About what?" Jasper demanded, and while Jasper's attitude chafed as usual, I was curious about what Vaughn wanted to talk about, even if I have an idea.

"Dove." Vaughn never was one to pull his punches. "She had a moment when Liam kissed her."

I saw the fist coming and I let it hit.

Honestly, I did it more for Hellspawn than anything else. Also, belting Jasper back felt pretty fucking good, too.

The next two days were an entirely different kind of hell. One, I'd tasted her lips and her passion and it half-dominated my thoughts. Two, she was not in the best of moods when her and Milo's trip to see Doc had been aborted by a medical emergency Doc had to deal with.

Instead, they'd ended up back at my place and they'd argued. Again. I wish they could see themselves the way I did. How fucking alike they were. Thank fuck for Rome, his presence each night kept me from making a damn fool out of myself.

They didn't sleep in my bed again, and as much as I wanted to extend the invitation, I kept my fucking distance. Rome noticed. He didn't comment, but he did study me and I had a feeling my guilt was written all over the black eye I sported.

I just met his gaze blandly and waited. Especially since he told me that *he* had been the one to suggest Vaughn come see her. She needed Vaughn and Jasper.

Yeah. No fucking comment on that one, bro.

Still, she was aggravated because though Milo had tried to take her to see Doc, he and the others had all gone quiet. Based on her stomping around after her stretching and run on the treadmill, I had to imagine no one was answering her messages.

Or if they were—they weren't telling her what she wanted to hear.

The final nail in the coffin of her mood though came when

Rome didn't show up that night. Plenty of times he came in after she'd gone to sleep, but he'd texted me and said he wouldn't be. He had something to take care of, and that was it.

The very real and visceral disappointment in her eyes cut. While I wanted to ask her about the freakout and a host of other questions, most of which was none of my business, I kept a lid on it. We had enough problems. I didn't need to be digging into her psyche if I had no idea what landmines were waiting there.

Vaughn and Jasper had only agreed they thought it was lingering trauma from her rape. Apparently, the bag of dicks they'd dealt with hadn't raped her once, but repeatedly. Just the kind of thing I needed to hear to put me in a killing rage.

On that issue, we were all in lockstep. Even Jasper mumbled a half-assed apology about hitting me, when Vaughn said he'd run up against a similar barrier with her. Then Jasper confessed she'd done the same to him. At least it hadn't been me kissing her.

She was definitely fucking the pair of them, so maybe there was hope. I shoved a pin in that thought as deep and as fast as I could.

The wealth of sadness wreathing her as she shared a wordless breakfast with me unraveled all of the duct tape and chains I'd put around the desire for a deeper intimacy with her. It apparently also slit the throat of my good sense along the way, even if I had managed to get my ego to sit down and shut up.

"I know we haven't had a chance to hit the gym for another session," I said, watching her carefully for any reaction. "I've got a couple of things to do this morning before I can go over there."

The blank look she sent my way didn't give me anything.

"So," I said slowly. "Feel like getting out of here and coming with me? The errands aren't anything exciting, but you can stretch your legs, look at different stuff and then we'll hit the gym for a proper lesson in making grown men cry."

Her soft snort made me smile. "You're inviting me to go out with you?"

"Well, it'd be a working date. Like, I work and you get to hang out and be a little bored while I do things. But then I promise to show you how to hurt me."

Not entirely sure why I phrased it that way, but it made her laugh and it was like winning the lottery and getting picked by the O'Connells all at once. They'd *wanted* me and that feeling had been hard to express. Same thing here.

"Well, with an offer like that, I don't see how I can turn you down."

"Then don't."

She smiled. I hadn't realized how much I missed her lighter expressions or how her eyes would soften. "Okay. Do I need to wear anything fancy?"

"Fuck no," I told her. "I'll be in a suit, doesn't mean you have to be uncomfortable."

That earned a genuine snicker.

An hour later, when we arrived at the store, she made a face and I glanced over at her. "Do you really not like the store?"

"It's hard to explain," she admitted, as she stared out the window. "Let's just say it takes me back in time to far more unpleasant days."

"They say talking about it can help."

"Is that what they say?" She slid me a look like she didn't believe me. Fact was, I didn't believe me.

"Well, we could always try, and see how we do."

"Hmm." She studied me a beat. "You first."

Right. "And on that note..." I let myself out of the car, but her laughter echoed inside the vehicle. She wore a fun little cap and sunglasses along with a flirty little outfit she'd put together out of her dance clothes and my shirt. It actually looked almost swanky, but I said nothing about it. Instead, I scanned the lot.

Emersyn Sharpe was still in the news. A subject the majority of us had not been talking about, including her. While I trusted my staff to keep their mouths shut if they figured it out, I still kept picking up random tails and we hadn't identified who they were.

Yet.

There were a few potential sources. The king could be checking on me, in which case, fuck him and his people following me. The private investigators and bounty hunters looking for Emersyn Sharpe had already turned up once in Braxton Harbor. Twice, if you counted the guys watching my place. Then there were the 19 Diamonds. Meeks was still pissed at me for taking his club.

I'd be taking quite a bit more here, soon.

Finding nothing out of place, I opened the door and let her out. She went in with me and instead of hanging out with me in the office, she asked if it was all right to wander the store. I motioned to the screens I had and asked her to *stay* inside the store and she agreed.

It took me the better part of an hour to go over everything that I needed to review and sign off on deliveries and orders. During that time, I glanced at the monitors to track her path around the store. She'd taken her time, moving from one section to another, by the time I finished with paperwork she had vanished into a changing room.

So, I settled in to wait. I kind of hoped she'd give me a fashion show, but no such luck. One of my shoppers had been hovering for her, but I sent them away. She'd turned down every single offer of help she'd been given. Our people were good. A number had asked her.

When she finally came out, she'd changed into a pretty sundress that was as simple as it was lovely. It was a honey-gold color that should have washed out her pale skin, but instead it seemed to make her glow. She gave a little start when she saw me, but I held up my hands.

"I was done, so I was just waiting for you." Then because it was the truth, I told her, "You look beautiful in that."

A hint of shyness seemed to come over her as she glanced down and then up again. "Is it hypocritical of me to want to pick up a couple of things?"

After rejecting all of the clothes his people had picked out? "No," I answered her honestly. "You said you wanted to pick out your own things. Will you be offended if I buy them for you?" And even if it tasted like fucking ash on my tongue, I continued, "If you like, I'll make sure you have the receipt and you can pay me back later."

"If you'll take me by a bank, I can pay you back today."

My eyebrows climbed at that. "If you withdraw..."

"You asked me to trust you," she said, before I could finish the thought. "Trust me that I won't do anything to alert my family to where I am."

Well, if that didn't open up a whole other topic of questions, I didn't know what would. However... "Done."

The relief and the pleasure twinning in her expression went straight to my dick and he woke right the fuck up to say hello. My dick and I needed to have a very long conversation about wanting and having. Cause no matter how much we wanted, we'd both be better off if we didn't have.

Her, too, I suspected.

As it was, she really only had picked out a few things. A couple of pairs of jeans, two shirts, one button down and one pull over t-shirt, the sundress, a leather purse that looked like it could double as a backpack, a new pair of soft cotton sleep top and shorts, as well as a pair of boots that looked a great deal like the motorcycle boots I'd ordered for her. The leathers and the boots were in *my* closet at the moment, since her negative reaction to the others made me wary of giving them to her.

Still, she added a second dress to the stack, this one another daytime dress, and it was very Bohemian with an oversized loose skirt and a banded waist. She'd look like some kind of fortune teller or pirate queen when she put it on.

And I could hardly wait.

Once we finished, I took her to the bank she requested and while it killed me to wait, I walked her inside and settled in the lobby and didn't follow or listen to anything she said. It took her less than fifteen minutes, and she returned with a spring in her step and a smile on her face.

When I offered my arm, she hooked her hand onto my elbow without questioning it. I was on point the whole way back to the car, keeping my eyes out for anything that might jump out at us, but so far—it was a normal, sunny day in the city and we might as well be any couple out to get some things done.

She counted out—in cash—the three hundred or so I'd spent on her clothes, and I had to bite my tongue when she held it out. The moment I accepted it though, she smiled and seemed even happier.

"Thank you."

That soothed my battered ego and pride. I wanted to be the one taking care of *her* and she apparently wanted to be the one taking care of *herself*. I couldn't really fault that.

"You're welcome." Maybe I should have kept my mouth shut, but I had to ask. "Get everything you needed?"

The grin she favored me with was wide and warm. "Yes. Perfect. Ready for our next stop."

That was it. Nothing more. Curiosity ate me alive. It took physical effort to keep my mouth shut and not ask. In fact, I was so focused on that, I didn't mind letting her pick the music or think about what the hell my next stop was until I pulled up outside the titty bar.

Shit.

"Oh," she'd said with a real laugh. "I've always wanted to go inside one of these." And the little snot was out of my car before I could stop her.

Goddammit.

Too bad Jasper wasn't here. I deserved another damn punch.

LET'S DANCE

EMERSYN

My flight landed mid-afternoon. As much as I dreaded deplaning and heading to my uncle's place, the one upside was he'd texted to say his own trip had been delayed and he wouldn't be home for another two days.

Maybe his plane would crash.

One could hope.

Or one would if one thought there was any chance of it.

Shaking off the melancholy, I focused on the fact that I had forty-eight hours until I had to see him. I'd done every-thing I could to put off this break that would send me home. The last time, however, he'd told me flat out that he would revoke the permission that allowed me to continue with this particular company, if they couldn't get their scheduling shit together.

That would bring me home permanently.

Better a two week stint in Hell than a full relocation. I could survive two weeks. I just had to keep my chin up, my smile in place and...

I stumbled mid-step at the sight waiting for me on the other side of the door letting us out from the gates to baggage claim. I swore we locked eyes at the same moment because she began to jump up and down waving. I barely noticed the two hulking shadows behind her—though hulking might be rude.

Lainey would laugh.

In fact, she was, as I hurried through the doors, Lainey yelled, "Hurry up, bitch! We've got things to do!"

My carry-on bag hit the floor as Lainey slammed into me with a hug. It'd been over two years since we'd seen each other last. Our schedules had been shit for making it happen. I still sent her birthday presents and she did the same. We talked as often as we could manage and texted the dumbest shit all the time.

"I missed you," she said with a laugh, and I squeezed her back, trying to desperately halt the tears burning in my eyes. Her keepers hung back, but I met Adam's gaze briefly. He surprised me with a nod as Ezra swooped forward to grab my bag from where it had fallen.

"What are you doing here?" I asked her. More stunned than anything else.

"I busted out of school. You think my bestie is gonna be this close and I'm not going to come and see you?"

Pulling back, I stared at her. "I have to go..."

"Not for a couple of days. Isn't that what you said? He's away on business and no one is there but the staff?"

Well... that was true.

"But what about the staff?"

"Tell them you decided to spend a couple of days training since he wouldn't be there. We'll get you there before he gets home." Lainey squeezed my hands. "Please?

You have no idea what I had to do to get these jackasses to agree to this plan."

Ezra snorted. "Pretty sure you didn't ask."

"Or do a damn thing," Adam said crisply. "But we're not staying in the airport. Do you have other luggage, Miss Sharpe?"

"Her name is Emersyn," Lainey chastised him. "Don't be such a formal douchebag."

She'd mentioned getting more frustrated with him, more because she'd been seeing less and less of him I thought, but again, I was not going to offer that insight. Besties hated together. It was a rule.

"But I haven't told him he can call me Emersyn," I reminded Lainey. The earlier dread having all but burned away under the fierceness of her smile. "And yes, I do have a bag."

Adam nodded once. "Then let us collect that and go."

They weren't kidding about getting out of there. Lainey and I stood, arm in arm, catching up on everything while we were waiting for the bags to come out. Ezra found mine before I could even point it out and when I frowned, he pointed to the dancing shoes on the luggage tag.

Oh.

Fair enough.

"Ignore them," Lainey instructed as we headed to where a car waited for us. A limo, and Lainey climbed right in, dragging me with her. The driver took my luggage and placed it in the trunk, then Adam and Ezra followed us inside. "We're staying at the Lewis, the rooms are not booked in *any* of our names. It's private, exclusive, and open to members only. You have to know someone who knows someone to even get an invitation."

I didn't ask which of them had that offer.

"We've got a suite all to ourselves. We'll go in like movie stars, faces hidden and shit, then we'll go straight up to our rooms and if you're feeling it, we can go out dancing tonight at the ColorBox."

Seriously, she was racing through all of it and I could barely keep up. The excitement in her eyes and her voice were contagious though.

"Do I want to know what the ColorBox is?"

"An obnoxious club that most people of fine pedigree wouldn't be caught dead in," Adam said, in a damn near bored tone. "You're more likely to catch fleas than attention in a place like that."

"The music's good though," Ezra said with a grin in my direction. "The drinks aren't half-bad either."

"The only drawback to the whole thing is I had to promise to not go anywhere without one or both of them," Lainey admitted. "But they promised to not be wet blankets the whole time. Also, Ezra can really dance."

"It's true," Ezra said.

Adam made some kind of grunting noise and I had to bite the inside of my lip to keep from laughing at the glare he shot the other guy.

"But you two can dance together, just no bumping and grinding with the rabble."

Okay, that was funny, and a laugh escaped before I could stop it. I shot an apologetic look at Lainey, but she seemed to be finding a laugh of her own. "We do not *bump* and *grind* with anyone, thank you very much." Then she gave me a damn near conspiratorial wink, before she added, "But I have heard the guys who frequent there are hot as hell. Hopefully they can dance as well."

The matching negative growls that came from both

guys had me collapsing into Lainey, laughing my ass off. She snickered and then flipped the boys off.

"Don't get your panties in a twist," she snarked. "I'd rather make out with Emersyn than some strange guy."

"I'd pay to watch that," Ezra offered and then flinched as Adam punched him.

I raised my eyebrows as Ezra rubbed his arm, Adam had barely missed hitting his face with that strike.

"Said I'd pay to watch it, not that they should do it."

But Adam looked so coldly furious, I tucked my arm through Lainey's and tried to slide back into the seat. I did not envy Ezra when they were alone.

Adam was pissed.

"Ignore them," Lainey said with a sigh. "I do. Besides, for the next forty-eight hours it's you and me, Em. We're gonna have a great time. We'll call it our birthdays and Christmas all at once."

I had no idea how she could possibly ignore Adam, but she was right. It was kind of like my birthday and Christmas all at once. I planned to soak in every single moment of it.

Granted, my sixteenth birthday was a while away, but we could celebrate early.

24

EMERSYN

Of all the places Liam could have brought me on his "errands," a topless bar never even made my list of guesses. After pushing myself at the store to look at clothes and just *look* at them, not imagine what anyone else would say or why they would say it.

Don't think about dressing for an event or a place, just myself. It took time, and more than once, I'd felt kind of physically fucking ill over it. Then I found the first top that I'd liked and after that a pair of pants. Bit by bit, I just wandered through, not really looking and at the same time absorbing all of it.

The sundress I'd picked for myself, and currently wore, made me think of Lainey. It reminded me of her smile and how bright and hopeful it always made me feel. If I told her, she'd laugh her ass off at me. I totally took a picture of the dress and myself in it, then fired it over to her on the app that encrypted the messages but also erased them after they'd been seen.

I hadn't had time to check it to see if she'd seen it yet. I'd wait until later. The fact that Liam not only took me to the bank but let me handle the business without following me or listening in had me damn near giddy.

When I told Jasper that Liam had been great, I'd meant it. This? This went above. He didn't like not knowing, that information was clear as day in his expression. But he hadn't pressed me for more on the bank stop or for what happened that day Vaughn came over.

The sun warmed my back as Liam caught the door before I could open it and he gave me a long look. His eyes were hidden behind sunglasses, but then so were mine. I had to tilt my head back to meet his gaze. They were all so much taller than me. What had bothered me so much in the beginning, had grown comforting.

However, my thoughts and our position flashed me back to the moment his lips connected with mine. The carnal demand and heat that had flooded me at the connection. I'd literally spent my day with Vaughn, fucking and talking, then fucking some more. My pussy had been sore, almost irritated, and bruised after so many rounds, and one kiss from Liam had sent a damn near rejuvenating flush of warmth between my legs.

Then...

"What?" Desperate to not follow that thought to its conclusion, I reoriented myself to where we were and what we were doing. "Or are we not going in here?"

That would be such an epic bummer. Particularly because I really wanted to sneak a look inside. I'd heard all about topless bars from some of the other dancers. Some of them had even worked a few, or done shows where they'd gone naked in Vegas.

I'd never been allowed to go to anything like that, but it

fascinated me. Not the sexual nature of it, but the difference between the women who just shook their asses for dollars and the actual performers who took over the stage—clothed or not.

"You're seriously excited about this?" Why did he sound so surprised?

"Yes. I wasn't kidding. I've never been to a clothing-free show or a topless bar. I've always wanted to go."

His eyebrows skyrocketed over his sunglasses.

"Oh, get your mind out of the gutter," I snarked and smacked his chest. "Dancing is dancing. Some performers just work nude. I knew a few of them over the years. I want to see their style and how they work the stage. It's not always about sex, you know."

"Yeah," Liam grunted as he pulled the door open, letting the pulsing music inside wash out in a wave. "You keep telling yourself that, Hellspawn."

I would have flipped him off, but I was too busy pulling my sunglasses off to let them adjust to the much dimmer lighting inside. The interior smelled a lot nicer than I expected, to be honest. Though, that might have been judging the interior by the exterior. While it looked like some ugly blocky building from the outside, the interior was far nicer.

There were three stages, one large one that included a runway out to a pole in the very center of the place, then two others forming a triangle with that one. Smaller platforms, but each also featuring a pole. There was a ledge-like table around each platform and chairs pulled up to each one. Beyond those, there was an actual bar with far more comfortable seating, then booths and lounge looking areas.

I pivoted to look at something, as Liam caught my arm and turned me around, before clasping my hand in his and setting off across the bar. I had to take two steps for his every one, but I was excited. There really weren't that many people in here, a few customers for the most part and the music shifted as a new dancer strutted out onto the center stage.

Liam got in the way, and I leaned around him to keep watching. I swore he muttered something very impolite, before he nudged me to climb into a booth. I picked up the skirt so I could walk around the circular booth bench on my knees. I made it about halfway, when he tapped the table and I glared at him for interrupting the show.

Hands raised, Liam smirked, then pointed at the table and mimed drinking. Oh. I shrugged. "Get me whatever," I told him and dropped to sit on the seat while the girl on the stage—who was dressed in a mock tuxedo and what had to be five inch stilettos, strutted to the music.

She had good rhythm, I'd give her that. The song she'd chosen wasn't one I knew. The beat though, damn it was nice and I was tapping my foot to it. I barely noticed when Liam slid a cold bottle of beer in front of me, or when chips arrived at the table.

The dancer had stripped down to just a thong and her breasts were out and bouncing. I winced at a couple of her moves, cause no one's boobs liked those kind of moves. Still, she was working the pole and *that* got my attention and held it.

Unfortunately, while she definitely had the leg strength, she didn't have it in the abdominals. Beautiful woman, but her breasts got in the way, and she couldn't quite control her motion. Not that her audience minded.

A flash of movement in the corner of my eye caught my attention as the waitress leaned down and into Liam. She was all but pressing her breasts into his face. He put a hand on her hip and then gave her ass a pat, before he said something in her ear.

She laughed, then flashed me a look that bordered on hostile, before she rubbed her breast against his cheek again, then walked away. What the hell was that about?

If she wanted Liam, she could have him.

Course, that would require him wanting her, too. The way he picked up his bottle of beer and took a long drink before he glanced down at his phone without once following her movement, said he wasn't interested. The bluish-white light from the phone illuminated his face. Whatever was on his screen irritated him.

The first dancer finished her set and another rocked out to some Pink, that I definitely knew, and I almost whooped for her. She wore a red teddy, red stilettos, and had this midnight black hair that gave her both a look that was sensuous and innocent.

Holy crap, she could move.

The waitress came back and this time, she brought food. Liam passed the plate around to me and I stared at the salad. It had a lot of protein in the form of shredded hard boiled eggs, bacon crumbles, dice and grilled chicken as well as ham. The rest of it was cheese, lettuce, tomatoes, avocado slices and cucumbers.

Lots of protein and veggies, no dense carbs. I grinned at Liam, but he was talking to the waitress. There was another plate in front of him, a burger in a lettuce wrap with grilled tomatoes and what looked like broccoli. No carbs for him, either.

Ha!

The waitress had perched on the end of the booth and she and Liam were talking by whispering into each other's ears. Though to be fair, with the volume of the music, probably the only way for him to hear her. A fork had come with mine, all rolled up fancy in a cloth napkin.

Somehow, I didn't think everyone got this treatment, and I started studying the bar while Liam and his waitress got cozy. Though to be fair, she was the one doing all the touching, he kept his hands to himself, and his gaze flicked away from her regularly and not toward the dancers but the other customers.

I speared a bite of my salad and divided my attention between the dancers and Liam. The waitress's attention on him began to grate when she kept rubbing against him or putting her had on his thigh and he did *nothing* in response. If anything, he seemed to be enduring the contact, even if he was talking to her.

When I'd ticked off five minutes of her molesting him, I reached for something on the table and accidentally knocked his beer bottle over so it spilled all over her.

She gave a little shout and leapt out of the booth.

Oops.

The hostility in her eyes took up residence on her face as she glared at me. "You little bitch," she swore and wow, I heard that *loud* and clear over the music. Guess they didn't need to whisper in each other's ears after all.

Liam patiently handed her the cloth napkin that came with his silverware, and had already righted the spilled beer.

"Just refill the drinks after you've cleaned up," he said, and his voice was pure ice. "Don't ever call her a bitch again or your ass is fired. Clear?"

Pissed was not the word for her, but she glared at me one more time, all venom, then stalked away. "Probably wouldn't be a good idea to drink whatever she brings back." I bet she'd spit in it.

Mine at least.

He snorted softly. Without warning, he slid a little closer to me and settled his arm on the back of the booth behind me and his lips were right at my ear. I went completely still at the first teasing brush of his breath. "If you wanted her to go away, Hellspawn, you just had to ask."

Pfft. I scoffed aloud and then looked at him, though I had to lean back a bit because we were too close. "If you wanted her to keep pawing you, look more interested next time."

Shock flared in his eyes, and I gave him a little shove away from me with my shoulder. To my surprise he took the hint without me having to repeat it. The waitress returned with our beers and Liam took a drink of mine pointedly, to show me they were fine.

At least she didn't stick around after that. He was back to his phone again and I was halfway through my salad. The next couple of dancers didn't hold my attention, so I tracked the dark haired girl. She was on one of the two smaller stages and she had almost perfect form on the pole. Envy and curiosity flooded me in equal measures.

By the time I finished my salad, she was done and Liam leaned in and said, "I need to go meet with a couple of people. I won't be long or far. Stay here." The last two words were a direct order that chafed until he added, "Please."

"Okay," I said, offering him cooperation. Was I curious about his business? Yes. But like he'd not said anything about my bank trip or asked me for details, I would show him the same courtesy and respect.

"Thank you, Hellspawn." Then he pressed a kiss to my

forehead. "I'll try not to be long. I'll also send a different waitress over if you want anything else."

Two beers really should be my limit, I was already more relaxed than I'd been in a while. I kind of wanted a cigarette but I could wait. I smiled because the new waitress idea was really thoughtful. Liam crossed the club and vanished through a set of doors near the bar—with the waitress I'd dumped the beer on.

Ugh.

Well, I guess maybe he had been interested in the molesting. I wrinkled my nose. Maybe he was firing her. I should in no way take any joy in the idea of some girl losing her job, but she irritated me.

Before I could focus on that too much, the dancer I'd been enjoying earlier, sauntered out from doors I hadn't seen by the stage. Oh, hell. I grabbed for my bag and pulled out some bills.

When I held them up, she met my gaze with her own. Intrigued from the looks of it, she adjusted course to my table, and I moved around the side a little.

"You are not my normal clientele," she told me rather bluntly as she settled a hand on the soft curve of her hip and studied me. Honestly, she was one of those really beautiful women and I loved the way she seemed so comfortable in her own skin.

"Probably not," I said with a grin. "But you have amazing technique. The work on the pole? That's competitive level and beyond."

She bit her lower lip at the compliment, and I held out a pair of twenties. The guys around the place had been tucking ones into her g-string, or at least what I thought were ones. I wasn't going to touch without permission, and she glanced at it then at me.

"Lap dances are five minutes, no touching at all. I can touch you. You cannot touch me." The explanation had my eyebrows lifting.

"Does that mean you'll stick around to talk for a minute?" Because I figured that was code for the only way she could linger, because there were a couple of guys trying to get her attention.

"Pretty much," she murmured, as she swayed a little closer. "You all right with a lap dance?"

"Never had one," I admitted. "But I won't touch and I'd prefer to keep the contact to a minimum."

Understanding filled her smile and she nodded as she made a little twirl motion with her finger. "Swing your legs out here, sugar, let me dance straddling them. It'll put on a good show and we can talk."

I followed her directions and as promised, she moved to straddle my thighs but never once did our skin make contact. Moving to the music, she had perfect control her body followed the musical cues like any other highly trained dancer.

"If you have questions, sugar, ask them now and then slide that twenty in right here..." She arched her back and rolled her hips. It was a lot of sex simulation, which I got, and right here was where she held the side of her thong out a giving a shadowy peek of her cunt if I'd been interested. I wasn't.

I tucked the bill into place. "Is this part time for you? Are you in between bigger gigs?"

She chuckled. "It was about a year ago when I started here," she admitted, grinding the air a few centimeters above my thighs. "But I was also knocked up and the contract..."

"...says you have to maintain a certain body weight and

figure. There's also a morals clause." It made me gag to even think of the last one.

With one hand on the booth back next to me, she dipped so her chest was at my eye level and let out a little sigh. "Pretty much. I was fired the second the lines turned pink and I wouldn't abort the baby. Fuck the director and his wandering fucking hands."

I grimaced. "That sucks." I'd known a few dancers that happened to. The fact it nearly happened to me.

"It does, but it doesn't. I have a little girl, she's five months old and absolutely perfect."

"Congratulations."

"Thanks. The guys here let me work right up until my due date. Believe it or not, there are fuckers in here who tip even more for a baby bump when I'm lap dancing."

I don't know which of us made the worse face, but she threw her head back and laughed.

"It's good. It let me afford taking six weeks off after she was born and my roommate is my best friend. She looks after her during the day when I work, cause her job is at night."

"Oh." Childcare probably would cost otherwise. I tucked another twenty into the other side as she mimed running her head over my hair as she kept rocking her hips. "I can't imagine that would be easy to be away from her."

"It's not, but I make good tips here. Even better now since that sexy fucker you're dating bought the place and kicked all the gangbangers out."

Sexy fucker...

"Liam owns this place?"

It made total sense and still stumped me in the same breath. I didn't bother to correct her about the dating thing.

"He does and he's amazing." Real admiration filled her

voice. "All the dancers got raises, so it's not just tips making us money, and he promised that anyone putting in thirty hours a week would get healthcare. They never offered us that before. It's like a fucking gift."

I was so happy for her. Bending backward, I snagged my bag and drew it to me as I straightened. My new friend gave me an appreciative look. "You've got moves."

"A few," I admitted. "Been a while since I've been on a stage."

All at once she straightened up as I slid her another twenty. I'd taken out less than a thousand, so I needed to be careful, but she had a baby and was working here instead of a show or a circuit.

"You wanna hit the stage here?"

"What?" I glanced around and it hit me that even though the music was on, no one was on the main stage. There was only one dancer at one of the other pole tables. Two others were doing lap dances like... "I'm sorry, I should have asked your name."

She'd finished dancing and backed up a couple of steps to give me space. "I'm Ria," she told me. "My stage name is Jasmine."

"That's pretty," I said and held out my hand to shake hers. "I'm Emersyn."

"Nice to meet you Emersyn, got a stage name?"

I laughed. Yeah, that was my stage name and if she'd been on the circuit, she'd probably know it so I just said, "Syn, obviously."

"Perfect. C'mon, we're low on dancers in the mid-week because a bunch of the hard drug users quit over the you want to work, you get clean policy. A couple of the others are in rehab."

Bag in hand, I glanced around the club, but Liam was

nowhere to be seen. He said he'd be nearby, so maybe he had a meeting in the back. I wasn't leaving the club. so I was technically staying put.

I scooted out to follow her. Backstage was just like every other dancer's dressing room I'd ever been in. "You don't have to strip," Ria said as she led me over to a rack of clothes. "I'm a bit bigger than you and girl, did you skip the tits line? I haven't been that flat since junior high."

I snorted. "Not enough body fat, it happens."

"Fuck," she said with a sigh. "Truth be told before Carmen, that was me. Flat boobs, flat abs, no ass. Now I'm all boobs and a little bit of ass."

I cracked up at the description. "You're beautiful."

"Sugar, you do not need to sweeten me up. Save all of that for the big man. He deserves good things." Her admiration of Liam was such a pure thing, and I kind of wanted to know everything he'd done, but she pulled out a dark little number and held it up to me. "Whatcha think?"

I studied the outfit. I'd worn similar before. It was a skintight, body mesh. It covered all the important parts, but it looked like you were wearing nothing but some body paint.

Up close, it was clearly *not* paint, but still...

"I don't really want tips," I said, and she laughed.

"They'll toss it up on the stage if you won't go to them. If you want to get out there and dance, I can get you six to eight minutes of all the freedom you want. Just tell me what songs you'd like."

Decision made before I really thought about it, I told her the music I'd like and shimmied out of my sundress. I hadn't been able to wear a bra with it anyway and this thing would show panties, so I put those in my bag with the dress then pulled the outfit on. I might have objected before, but the clean, fresh-washed scent of it promised it hadn't been used.

Ria vanished for a minute, then came back and she showed me a locker where I could put my bag and shoes. I set the lock numbers before securing it.

"You good with going barefoot? The stage is pretty clean, but it's not that clean."

"I'll be fine," I promised her. While she wore a gorgeous layer of cosmetics, I didn't bother. First, I would rather use my own stuff and second, I wasn't here to impress anyone but myself.

The songs I'd picked were ridiculous, but they were fun songs. Songs Lainey and I had danced to at a club when we were fifteen and playing hooky from our lives.

"You're up," Ria said with a wicked grin. "Knock 'em dead."

I slid to the edge of the stage to wait for my musical cue. It was dark, the lights hadn't come up, only the dimmer lights around the bar were on. The best part, no one else was on a table or a pole. This would just be me.

All at once, my breathing fell to where it should be and I closed my eyes. This was just another stage in another city with a faceless audience—well—one face I knew, but I couldn't let that distract me.

As soon as the whistling began in the dark, I took the first step and then the next. The beat struck and I followed where the rhythm took me. Somewhere came applause, but it faded as I began to spin and switch leads as the music picked up the beat.

Everything vanished, leaving me alone with the music, as I did a roll over and then landed. One leg up and then I took the beat's increasing pace to run the half dozen steps and then I was on the pole.

I danced my feet against the air, muscles keeping the rest of me steady, like I was actually pacing myself. Then I hooked my upper leg and let go with my hands as I spun. There were shouts and more applause as the song ended and I slid into the splits.

Laughter eddied up through me. I lifted my chin, awareness of the lights and the people and a pair of steel blue eyes locked on me punched through the haze.

Then the next song began, and I blew a kiss to Liam before I did a back bend and pushed up onto my hands before flipping back to my feet. There were bills on the stage, but I ignored the money. This music was about having fun and I was enjoying the hell out of it.

This time when I hit the pole, I went from a back hook spin into an armpit hold. When I went from a basic invert to a crossknee layback, I locked eyes with Liam again, he was standing right at the edge of the stage, and I swore he looked like the top of his head was going to blow off.

I got it, this wasn't what we were here for, but it was fun and I was loving it. I tried to convey that with a look before I rolled myself upright. My muscles were a little pissed with me. I'd been lazy as fuck too much lately and if anything told me I needed to get my ass back to work it was this.

At the same time, I was riding the thrill and this time when I finished, I dropped down so that I was face to face with Liam and I grinned.

He blew out a breath and then hauled me off the stage out of the pool of ones. There were whoops and whistles and catcalls, but all of that faded the moment he slammed his mouth down on mine.

Back arched, I groaned into his mouth. This was—perfect. It was everything I wanted and the dance to boot.

The possessiveness in his kiss held me still, but I darted my tongue out to dual with his and when he fisted my hair, I returned the favor.

Finally, he dragged his head up and looked down at me. I wasn't sure which of us was breathing more raggedly. "Hellspawn, you're gonna be the death of me."

I wouldn't.

I promised.

Inside.

With care, he slid me down his body to set me on my feet and there was no mistaking the erection tenting his dress pants or the hunger in his eyes. "I need to get dressed," I told him.

"Go," he whispered. "Then we're out of here."

As much as I didn't want to explode the moment, I hurried back to the changing room. The sundress felt like almost too much to have on with my overheated skin. Ria was waiting with a bottle of water and a wide set of eyes.

"Please don't," I said when she opened her mouth.

"Then it is..."

"Don't ask." I licked my lips as I shimmied into my panties and then held out the outfit to her.

"Keep it," she murmured. "It really doesn't fit me anymore and your secret is safe." She mimed zipping her lips. "But you're fucking amazing."

"The money out there," I said with a grin, before I pulled my bag over my shoulder. "That's for you."

She blinked. "I..."

"For you and Carmen." Then I was hurrying back out, because I had to tell Liam his dancer knew who I was but she wouldn't tell. Maybe I was being an idiot to trust her, but I did. Liam was waiting for me right next to the door to the changing room. Gone was the heated eyes and the hungry expression. All that remained was a stony exterior.

"What's wrong?"

"We need to go," he said, cupping my elbow and guiding me through the bar. As we passed one of the tables there were two guys unconscious on the floor, well one was. The other was groaning and rolling from side to side. I glanced from them to Liam.

"Did you...?"

"Yes."

"Do I want to..."

"No."

We were at the door, and he pushed it open and took two steps out before something hit him and it slammed into his chest and sent him staggering into me. We went down together and then the whole world blew up in a hail of bullets and screams.

STRAIGHT SHOOTER

KELLAN

The drive to Browning seemed to drag. In the passenger seat, Doc glared out the window. We should have told him. We also should have known his release had come through. The attorneys we paid for should have notified us.

Or maybe Raptor had instructed them otherwise. In all fairness, none of us had talked to him in months. Jasper had made the treks weekly, with the rest of us alternating. Either we went with him, or separately.

Fuck, I had a headache.

Doc's phone buzzed as I followed the exit for the prison.

"He's clear," Doc said. "They let him out of the gates, he says he's walking and we should keep an eye out for him."

Where the fuck was he walking...?

Then I just shut up that line of thought. Milo had spent the last three years in controlled, caged environments. I would have started walking too. While I didn't need heat or a ticket, I accelerated.

We found him ten minutes later, doing exactly what he

said, walking up the road with a jacket over his shoulder and his face turned up to the sun, even if he squinted. I swung the car in a U-turn, so I could pull off onto the shoulder of the road to get him.

Goddamn, he was wearing the same jeans and shirt he'd had on when they'd arrested him. He'd never had a chance at bail and he negotiated a plea so damn fast, we'd barely had time to deal with the fallout. Now here he was—Milo, the guy who'd been planning since the day I met him.

While the clothes might be the same, the man inside them—

I didn't even manage to say his name before his fist lashed out and slammed into the side of my face. My sunglasses cracked and went flying as I staggered back toward my car and hit the hood.

"What the fuck, Milo?" I growled and I blocked the next shot. But he was fast as fuck, and I took a kidney shot and another fist to my jaw that clacked my teeth together so hard, I tasted blood and swore I cracked one.

"Enough," Doc ordered, as he dragged Milo off of me.

No, not Milo. The cold, raging fury in those eyes was all Raptor. I spat out blood and though he wasn't struggling, he still strained against the grip Doc had on him.

"One, I'm not seeing you get hauled back to jail for some stupid fucking fist fight," Doc growled, and then he yanked Milo off his feet, holy shit. One minute Milo was up and the next he was down on his knees, his arm in a lock. "Two, calm the fuck down. We got here as soon as possible and I told you the first chance I had. They would have too, but you haven't exactly been reachable."

A muscle ticked in Milo's jaw as his gaze fixed on me. "Where is my sister?"

The snarled words struck even harder than his fists.

"She's safe," I assured him as I rubbed at my jaw. Fuck he hit like a truck, and my eye was already beginning to swell and tear. "Let him go, Doc. He has a right to be pissed."

Doc stared at me like I was stupid, but I shook my head at him then focused on one of my oldest friends and brothers. As soon as Doc let him go, Milo closed the distance between us and gripped my shirt so hard one of the buttons popped off and the fabric began to tear.

"Explain." One heated and hostile demand as he glared at me.

So I did. I told him about the show. About driving her. How Vaughn and Jasper got in to work it so they could be close and how I kept an eye on her. But we all saw it. We all saw how hurt she was and the closer we got, the more we saw. I edited some of it. I didn't need him blowing his top right here on the side of the highway.

The whoosh of air as cars passed us didn't seem to matter. Milo kept his grip on me and his gaze so laser-focused, he wouldn't miss a single twitch if I had one.

"Jasper made a call," I told him. "She was hurt and hurt bad. I won't lie, I fought him on it. Vaughn did too. But he didn't trust the people at the show to look after her and he didn't want to leave her alone in a hospital without backup or cover. So, we took her to Doc. Then we took her back to the clubhouse where *we* could look after her and protect her."

Even if my jaw and eye were throbbing, I held his gaze.

"It was the right thing to do."

Suspicion crept into eyes that had never been this icy or empty when he wasn't confronting a threat. Not sure how I felt about being perceived as a threat. "You said you argued against it."

"I did." No lie. I had. "I was wrong. Jasper made the right call. Even if we didn't grasp it fully then."

"Grasp *what?*"

"Tell him," Doc said. "Or I will."

I cut a look past Milo to Doc. All at once, Milo released me and took a step back then glared at Doc without turning his back on either of us. "Tell me, now."

Doc folded his arms. "Calm your shit down."

"Don't—"

"Calm your shit down. You're no good to anyone, least of all *her* like this." The flex of muscle in Doc's jaw was hard to miss or how his lips flattened. He hadn't known before, and when he found out—man he'd been as pissed as Milo was right now.

"Her dance partner was abusing her." I almost said rape. But some things—some things a brother didn't need to know. We'd dealt with the problem. Sparrow deserved some privacy. She didn't want to talk about it, or at least she never had with me.

Milo clenched his fists and then dropped his chin, his whole body stilled and I got it. He was leashing his anger. While he got his shit together, I met Doc's gaze. The dislike in his eyes was easy to read but I shook my head. We weren't telling him about the rape.

Fuck my life, Doc just nodded once. A curt, short nod that conveyed agreement and "no shit" at the same time. Of course, it shouldn't surprise me, Doc had been fantastic with her from the beginning.

While Jasper might have been the first to see the abuse, Doc recognized the trauma.

Finally, Milo lifted his head and he seemed "calmer," though I would use that word lightly. "I want to see her."

"I know," I told him. "We'll take you to her. We'll take you home."

That sounded really fucking good.

"If I haven't said it," I told him. "It'll be damn good to have you back."

This time he accepted my hand and hauled me forward. The hug was brief but heartfelt, then he pulled away. Goddamn, he'd put on some muscle. "It's good to be back. I'm also fucking starved. Let's stop for burgers on the way back..."

I grinned then stopped when my jaw and lips protested at the movement. "I know a place."

"Tell me about her," he ordered as he climbed into the backseat of the car. That was a difference, but when I met Doc's gaze over the top of the car, I let it go. Usually Milo rode up front, but...if he wanted the back, then he could have it.

"She's a great kid," Doc began, as I got the car started. "Stubborn as hell. A fighter. Attitude for days. She reminds me of another punk I know. She doesn't take shit from anyone. Every day she's been with these assholes she's gotten stronger. They're good for her. So keep that in mind when you see Vaughn," he glanced over his shoulder, "and Jasper."

Holy shit, had Doc just said we were good for her? I wasn't altogether sure whose side he was on. None of us had been, even if he hadn't been an enemy, we could be certain he was still a friend or an ally.

But now? Maybe Milo wasn't the only one coming home.

Finally.

25

KELLAN

I took the corner at speed and ignored the waving fists of the pedestrians and the horns of the people behind me because I didn't use my indicator. Fuck them.

"Dude, I want to get there alive." Vaughn had one hand braced on the dashboard and the other clamped on the oh shit handle. Not that he raised his voice or sounded remotely panicked.

"You will." I kept my gaze on the road, flowing in and out of traffic. The others were behind us and none could keep up with me. Right now, I was less concerned about that than getting to the damn bar.

When word reached us, we'd been too far away. Tracking down the source of who had been hijacking our shipping lines and routes proved to be one bad lead after another. Worse, we took another damn hit while we chased a bad trail.

Now...*this.*

"Slow it down," Vaughn ordered, but I'd already taken

my foot off the gas. Flashing lights filled every inch of the parking lot. A pair of ambulances were parked not far from the building and firetrucks arrayed so they could put out the fire. Or already had, based on the lingering smoke above and the charred edges of the roof. There were men up there checking it—with pickaxes, nice.

A cop tried to wave me around and I locked eyes with him. The guy had a familiar face. His expression tightened but I didn't back down or move on. I was going into that parking lot or leaving the car right here. His choice.

Vaughn was reaching for the handle when the guy waved me in, and I cut the wheels and pulled in. I didn't bother with finding a parking spot, just found an empty space and then we were both out and moving.

Chaos reigned. The noise of radios, people crying, dozens of voices talking, some shouting, the hammering on the roof, the swish of water, and the rumble of the engines added to the cacophony.

I was on my way across the parking lot heading straight into the heart of the mess. The front walls of the bar were littered with bullet holes. There was no mistaking that kind of damage.

"Molotov cocktail?" Vaughn muttered and motioned toward the roof. We moved together, he was a half-step behind me, and I knew why. It let him watch my back.

"Maybe." I wasn't going to assume shit until we got a good look at it ourselves and right now, the fucking roof on that bar could cave in for all I cared. I needed to know...

"Dove," Vaughn exhaled and I swore my heart remembered how to beat. I caught sight of her a split-second after he did. She was in the shadow of one of the ambulances, a suit jacket wrapped around her shoulders despite the heat. I tracked my gaze over her, looking for any signs of injury.

There were flecks all over her bare legs beneath the skirt, but I couldn't tell if that was torn skin, dirt, or blood.

All three added fuel to the simmering fury in the back of my head. From this angle, she looked fucking furious and was clearly arguing something. I followed her line of sight and found Liam sitting on the back of the ambulance while a paramedic looked at him. He had his shirt off and a bullet proof vest lying on the bed of the ambulance next to him.

The cluster of blue-black bruises center mass looked like they would fucking hurt and just poured gasoline onto the pyre I planned to build for the mother fucker who went after one of ours. Relief swarmed Liam's expression when he glanced past her to us, and he caught her hands and tugged them until she finally turned.

Blood speckled her face, and there was...fucking blood on her dress. It was a pretty yellow sundress or something, with a crimson stain smearing it from the elastic bodice down to her mid-section.

A moment later, I had an armful of Emersyn and I caught her to me and held her tight. Vaughn paused only long enough to run a hand over her hair. "You got her?"

Not letting her go either. "Taking her back to the car." We needed to get her out of here before anyone really noticed her. Sooner or later, everyone present would need to be questioned. "Check on Liam, see what he needs." The others would be here soon enough, and if I could get her in the car and out of here before they saw her dress, we might avoid more bloodshed in the immediate aftermath.

"On it." Vaughn brushed her hair again and then went. I tried not to focus on how she felt or how fucking much I'd missed her. Despite the insanity spilling out around us, she settled something inside of me that had been teetering since the confrontation with Milo on the side of the road.

From where we stood, I studied the lot. A coroner was pulling a gurney through the door with a body on it, already bagged up.

I tightened my hold on Emersyn, gradually growing aware of the hard shape of a gun at her abdomen under the dress and pressing against me. A shell casing gleamed in the sunlight next to a yellow placard with a number as some tech took a picture of it.

"Come on, Sparrow," I said, tucking her under my arm and turning her to where I'd left the Challenger. Under the jacket was also a small backpack sliding off her arm, so I caught it before it hit the ground. "Let's get out of here."

"We can't leave him..."

"We can," I said as I guided her toward the car. Her steps dragged just a little, but I settled for coaxing rather than ordering, or just picking her up, no matter how badly I wanted to do both. "Vaughn is with him. Vaughn will stay with him until the others get here."

"They're coming?" That was when she turned her head up to look at me. Fuck, her pupils were blown, and I slid my hand to her wrist as I got her moving again. Her pulse raced and her skin was too cool. Cool and clammy.

The jacket.

Bless you, Liam. Another car ripped into the parking lot, just as I got her into the backseat. Rome and Freddie were both out of the backseat of that car, with Milo and Jasper leaping from the passenger and driver's seats, respectively.

We didn't have time for politics. "Freddie," I called after I whistled. "Get over here." He didn't even hesitate, jogging over toward us. Despite all the stress of late, he'd been holding it together for the most part. "Backseat," I told him. "Keep her warm and calm."

He frowned and then ducked down. "Boo-Boo, baby!

Long time no see." He was already climbing in and nudging her over easily, before wrapping an arm around her. "Did I miss the invitation to this big blowout?"

I shut the door and refused to roll my eyes. Milo glared at me. "She's fine," I told him. She wasn't quite. But she would be. Right now we did not need the war of the Hard-head-igans playing out in real time. "Deal with this. I'm taking her to the clubhouse and I'm calling Doc so he can give you verification. But we need her off the street."

Reporters were showing up, news vans, and I'd already spotted one chopper. Big shootings in the middle of the day were actually unusual. One of the things we'd done as we exercised control and grew it, was minimize this kind of shit.

Rome glanced at me. "Don't leave yet. Two minutes."

I nodded and he set off toward the ambulance.

Jasper fidgeted hard but he'd finally given me a nod, then followed Rome. No running alone. Rome kept flouting that damn rule, but if we could keep eyes on him, we were. This was his brother in the middle of the shooting. Instead of following though, Milo moved to the back door.

I readied myself to catch his homicidal ass if he flipped, but inside the car, Emersyn was lying down with her feet up on the back door across Freddie's lap. That put her head right where Milo had opened the door. I spared them a look and the fact Freddie had covered her up with the jacket.

A cut on her cheek was the only thing visible, besides some nicks and scrapes on her bare feet.

Where the hell were her shoes?

Sliding into the car, I got it started as Milo said, "Are you okay?"

"Liam got hurt," she answered him in a voice that was a little stronger than the threadier tone she'd had earlier. I caught Freddie's eye in the rearview mirror and he gave me the faintest of nods. "We were leaving and then there was this god awful noise and suddenly he fell backwards like something hit him and he crashed into me. I tried to keep him up..."

"Shh," Milo murmured, and the knots in my gut eased some. His calm response didn't mean he was calm, but he had it together. "Liam's going to be fine."

"You didn't—"

"He had on a bullet proof vest, Sparrow," I said before Milo could offer up anything. "Bad bruises. But he'll be okay."

"Bruises still hurt. And then there was so much noise and people were screaming."

Freddie's whole expression turned troubled.

"I'm sorry you had to go through that," Milo said quietly. "Liam will be fine. Vaughn, Rome, and Jasper are with him right now. We'll look after him."

Something tightened in my chest at that last sentence. It had been a long time since we were a "we" with Liam, but over the last few weeks one thing had become apparent to all of us, whatever Liam had said when he left, that hadn't been the reason. He and Milo were too tight, and Milo trusted him with Emersyn.

Neither were in a sharing mood, but maybe it was time to call them out on that shit, too.

"Jasper hates Liam."

"Liam saved your life, pretty sure Jasper will appreciate that, Boo-Boo. And if he doesn't, they'll just beat each other up. Nothing new." Freddie made it all sound normal, but she made a sound of disapproval.

"Shut up, Freddie," Milo growled.

"Leave him alone," Emersyn argued and I had to bite back a smile. Rome was already on his way back to me.

"I'm used to it, Boo-Boo," Freddie soothed as Milo sighed.

"It's going to be fine," Milo told her. "I promise. Now, listen to Kel and Doc, I'll see you soon. I love you." Rome opened the door and slid in, as Milo pressed a kiss to her forehead and then he closed the door. He nodded to me and jerked his head.

Thank you.

Rome clicked his seatbelt into place. "Liam is fine," he said over his shoulder. "Probably cracked a rib or two."

"That's not fine," Emersyn argued, and this time I didn't hide my smile. She sounded *pissed*.

Didn't bother Rome too much, he just shrugged. "You danced with cracked ribs. You were fine."

"Did you really just throw that back in my face?" she demanded and Freddie coughed. Poor kid, his face was red from trying not to laugh.

"No. Just facts," Rome stated like it was the simplest thing in the world. "He doesn't like fuss. You don't like fuss. Both of you need care. Both of you are getting it."

"Someone shot at him. That's not *fuss*."

He appeared to consider it. "Fair. Are you mad at him?"

"What?"

"Are you mad at him?"

"Yes," she answered and followed it quickly with, "No." Every word grew stronger and as I made my way out of the parking lot, I avoided the cop who let us in and cut down one of the alleys behind the place, to come out on another street.

They hadn't shut it all down yet, and we might need to grease some palms.

"Both is good," Freddie commented. "That means he'll have to work hard to make up with you and you can enjoy his efforts."

She groaned. "That's terrible."

"No," Freddie argued. "It's logic. Also, if he's making it up to you, that could involve presents and cool things. You should milk it."

"I agree," Rome offered and I glanced at him, but his expression was placid. "Liam will want to."

"He doesn't owe me anything," Emersyn countered, ever the little contrarian. I kind of liked that about her. "He saved my life, if anything I owe him."

"Never tell him that," Freddie and Rome said at the same time.

"Why?" Poor thing was so mystified.

"Because protecting you is something we've all sworn to do, Sparrow," I explained before it could get any more confusing for her. "He's going to blame himself for putting you in harm's way and before you argue that he didn't, he most certainly fucking did."

"Agreed," Rome tacked on. "The choice of locations was not ideal, nor well thought out."

"I hate you all," Emersyn proclaimed.

"Even me, Boo-Boo?" Freddie practically pouted. "But I'm your favorite."

"Not if you agree with them that this was Liam's fault."

Oooh, those were fighting words. Rome had his phone out and showed me the message. He'd told Doc to meet us at the clubhouse for Emersyn. I nodded. The stronger her voice sounded, the more confident I grew that she was fine. Rattled definitely, but physically fine. I had a feeling someone's nightmares would be on point tonight.

She needed to not be alone. Maybe Milo would finally

give in and let her stay at the clubhouse with us—or we could just damn well overrule him. I liked that idea more and more.

"Well?" It took me a minute to realize what she was asking.

"I don't disagree with them," Freddie said. "That's not the same thing."

"It's totally the same thing."

"Nope. It's not. I don't disagree, and while I don't, that does not mean I automatically agree with them."

"How does that even work?"

"Oh," he sounded delighted. "I'm so glad you asked. They think Liam took you to a bad place and put you in a bad spot, more or less, right?"

"More or less," I answered when Rome stayed quiet.

"Great," Freddie said, warming to his topic. "I do not necessarily agree he took you to a bad place—first of all there are some excellent dancers there and I've had a couple of really excellent blowjobs out behind the joint."

Oh, for fuck's sake...

"Really." Oh, her tone held so much dry warning in it and Rome's lips curved.

"Absolutely." Freddie had never met a red flag he wouldn't charge right past. "So, blowjobs, good time, not a bad place. See what I'm saying? You being there? Not a bad idea. They're dancers. You're a dancer."

I flexed my hands on the steering wheel. We were almost to the clubhouse. We could make it without me strangling Freddie, even if amusement seemed to linger on Rome's face.

"Continue," Emersyn suggested.

"Right, so, if it's a bad place and Liam took you there, then their logic says Liam put you in a bad spot. But it's not a bad place, ergo you may or may not have ended up in a bad spot, that may or may not have had anything to do with the location. Maybe it was Liam, he's such a charmer and the girls all love him, but he left a trail of some hot jealous pussy behind him if you know what I mean."

I swore under my breath and tried to not focus on what Freddie was saying because it was giving me a headache.

"I'm following." Yeah, red flag Freddie. Danger Freddie Dunlap, danger!

"Right, so maybe it was one of those hot pussies being all jealous that he's got your perfect pussy now—"

I almost slammed on the brakes, but it was Rome twisting in the seat that had Freddie backpedaling.

"Not saying he has had your perfect pussy, of course." Oh look, Freddie remembered he liked breathing. "Right?"

Was I the only one straining to hear her response? The idea of her and Liam fucking was not high on my list of mental visuals that I needed. Her and Vaughn I'd already made my peace with, 'cause that was a done deal. Same with Jasper. Liam? I mean, it was possible, I supposed.

"That's none of your business." Damn.

"Damn, so mean to me—*anyway*—my point is, we don't know who did what to whom. Maybe it was just a bad coincidence you guys were walking out that door at the same time as someone started firing."

Thank fuck, there was the warehouse. I had scanned our surroundings and our tail all the way back. There was a rat outside and he ran for the door as I pulled up. The roll door went up without me having to touch the control. I spun the car and backed us in, sparing Freddie a look.

"So, there you have it. I don't disagree with them. But I don't *agree*, either. Two totally different things."

"Uh huh," she said with a groan. As soon as I got the car parked and the roll door lowering, I twisted in the seat.

"Give me the gun, Sparrow. Tell me where you got it."

Rome paused on getting out of the car as Emersyn wiggled under the jacket, before she sat up and Liam's coat fell to her lap. She held out the Glock toward me.

"Liam asked me to keep it for him."

"I'll make sure he gets it back," I promised as I checked the magazine. It was empty a few bullets, and from the smell, it had been fired very recently. "Did this burn you?" It had to have been hot when he gave it to her.

She shook her head.

"Make sure Doc checks, okay?"

Then we were all climbing out. Rome circled the car and got to her before I could. Freddie snagged the jacket as Rome looked her over. "Whose blood?"

She swallowed. "A waitress's. I tried to help her but... she died."

Fuck.

None of us said anything. There were rats moving around one of our trucks and offloading the shipment. They were out of earshot.

"It's not your fault, Starling," Rome said.

"He's right," Freddie agreed, circling the car to join us. "It's not."

"I know," she admitted. "But I really didn't like her and now she's dead."

"Well," I said slowly. "That sounds complicated. But not liking someone doesn't automatically get them killed. Trust me. If that was the case, this world would have a lot fewer assholes in it."

The corners of her mouth tipped up and when Rome opened his arms, she folded right into him. The feeling of the donkey giving me a solid fucking kick again was hard to miss. But I refused to be jealous of Rome or any of my brothers.

Just—no.

A door slammed and I turned, blocking Rome and Emersyn automatically, even as Rome turned her away. Doc strode toward us.

The look on his face was far from friendly.

Oh joy. What the fuck did we do now?

DUET

ROME

With care, I aimed the spray paint can as I added the finer detail. The canvas for the work was larger than anything I'd attempted before. It had taken me several nights of slipping out after bed check. The guys would cover. They always did. Especially if I didn't make it back in the morning before the first alarm. I didn't always make it to school some days, either.

The texture of the color worked, the gray offered a more opaque shadow. It had taken some practice to get the feet in the right positions. The nights I'd had to scrape away some mistake and start again pushed at me.

I wanted it to be perfect. I could see the series in my mind and translating the detail to the canvas I'd chosen challenged me. New materials, a new way of painting actually. Hooking myself by a rope and then climbing over the edge of the building to move around the side of it, also meant when an area was drying, I had to move to another part.

In truth, I worked from the outside in, like the puzzles Liam used to build. I could almost see the imaginary lines creating the sometimes oblong shapes, with bulging ends or half-cupped circles waiting to be joined together.

The moment the idea came to me, I knew I could do this. The rumble of his motorcycle carried easily through the darkness. I kept my attention on getting the feet. The series had begun with the little girls in different ballet poses or steps.

First position. Heels together and arms cupped in the front.

Second. Feet apart, heels pointed at each other and arms spread out like a t.

Third. One heel in front of the other, right arm up, hand curved with the left arm extended.

Fourth. One step forward from third position, heels still facing each other. Left arm up, hand curved inward while the right arm curved out with hand on side.

Finally, fifth position, right leg in crossing in front of the left, toes pointed away with the feet parallel to each other and arms raised. It was the most brutally uncomfortable position.

It had taken me hours to match each one, until I understood the motion. Each little girl at the bar had their hair pulled up into tidy little buns, their tiny bodies clothed in pink leotards and floofy tutus. Another textural lesson.

But this last girl, she didn't fall into line, if anything she danced away from the others and her eyes were on the mirror and it was the girl in the mirror I worked so diligently to complete. The darkness of the eyes, the way the light hit from a window off the edge of the painting and the shadows her feet cast as the light sparkled around her.

A spotlight, but also a ray in the darkness. The little

dancer had one foot up and seemed ready to spring into action. Again and again, I'd reworked her until I'd found her. She'd hidden from me, as though she didn't want to be seen in the light, but I needed to see her.

So I compromised, I painted her but she lacked the smiles of the others. Where they wore smiles of accomplishment, she seemed almost stern by comparison.

Focused.

Determined.

Nothing would stop her.

The motorcycle's engine cut off as Liam glided up to where I'd parked the bike I'd "borrowed" to get all the way over here. I'd put it back on my way back to the group home. At night, though, the ten-speed was a lot faster. It gave me more time to work. The scent of coffee drifted up, along with sugar, and I finally glanced away from the work and back to the dark alley.

A cooler breeze rushed against my sweaty skin and I appreciated the change in temperatures. If it was too humid, the paint might take too long to dry properly. Painting on brick meant layer after layer to make sure it soaked into the porous material.

Liam stared up at me as he sipped his coffee and then motioned to the thermos. "I brought plenty, and the cinnamon toast you like."

I chuckled. A bribe. Walking backward, I used my feet for balance as I studied her, she was almost there. Almost done.

Almost ready for me to leave her be so she could...

"Why isn't she with the others?" Liam asked. "Don't they have to practice together?"

I glanced at the other dancers. Their mirror images weren't quite as sharp as hers, but that was because their focus was elsewhere, their eyes elsewhere. The movement and the motion was there, but her...

Meeting her gaze in the painted mirror, I sighed. "She doesn't want to be with them." Then I moved and shifted the rope in my harness so I could begin lowering myself, walking down the side of the building until I reached a point I was clear to jump.

After pouring me a coffee, Liam passed me the cup and I took a drink. It was hot, almost too hot. Despite the fact my muscles were fatigued and sweat coated my body, the drink was perfect. I needed the boost. When he held out a bag of food, I dropped to sit on the ground where I could study the work. First light would be soon.

I always noticed the imperfections then and I'd know what to fix the next night.

"How do you know?" Liam settled on the ground next to me, his jeans almost too clean, too new for this alley and I probably should have sat somewhere else, but this was fine.

"I just do." The toast wasn't as hot as the coffee, but it was crunchy and the center was soft, compared to the edges and the crisped faces that melted on my tongue, like they'd been coated in sugared butter or something. The first bite forced me to close my eyes to process the taste and the sensations. My stomach growled, wild hunger digging its claws into me.

Devouring the toast, I washed it down with the coffee. I was starving. Then I couldn't remember if I had gone to dinner the night before or not.

Something else sweet clouded the air and grew more cloying as I finished the toast and it no longer competed. In the alley where the only other smells came from, a puddle at the end which had gone stagnant and some old dumpsters who carried decades of refuse infused into the metal, this scent *really* didn't belong.

Not saying a word, Liam finished some sandwich he'd been eating. A broad smile had settled on his face. "I got more food if you're still hungry," he offered and motioned toward the bike. That sent another waft of the too sweet, cloying scent to coat my mouth. I tried to wash it away with the coffee. It was like gum on a shoe, it didn't want to dislodge.

Finally, I leaned toward my brother.

It was him. "Why do you smell like perfume?"

A wild laugh escaped Liam. "Bro, I'm glad you asked. You focused on me and not whatever is going on up there?"

"She's fine where she is. Why do you smell like perfume?" I repeated the question. Ms. Stephanie wore perfumes, but hers were lighter, more citrussy to me. This was definitely not that.

"Just want to be sure, because I have been *dying* to talk to you about this."

Liam didn't die to talk about anything. He did his thing and I did mine. Hyperbole was something he used when he wanted to build up the drama. I waited, hoping if I just kept my nose on my coffee, I'd get rid of the scent. It didn't belong here.

"Sex," my mirror said, "is, pardon the pun, *fucking* awesome. Remember I told you about getting my dick sucked?"

Vaguely. He'd gone on and on about coming all over a girl's face. How great it had felt. I could do the same thing in the shower, and I didn't have to worry about cleaning someone else afterwards. Still, Liam waited for my response to continue, so I nodded.

"Let me tell you, pussy is even better than we thought.

Hot, tight, and goddamn you can *feel* her all fisting around you, and that my brother, is way better than your hand."

"Does it always smell like that?" I made no effort to disguise my distaste and Liam snickered.

"She likes to smell good, and on her, it smells great."

"It's not so great on you," I advised him. "You should shower and burn the clothes."

"Fuck you."

I shrugged.

"Anyway," he continued having lost none of his cheer. "She let me go down on her a few times now and she's got a power suction for a mouth. Fuck she can get me off in five minutes or less. But last night—" He went on and on about the different ways he'd played with her and coaxed her out of her clothes. "It's a game," he admitted. "She was no virgin, but I didn't care. It's about the chase, but when she's bent over in front of you and you've got your hands on her hips and you can fuck into her as hard as possible—you have got to try it."

Oh. That was why he was giving me all the details. "No, thanks." I rose to clean up my mess and gather up my gear and supplies.

"No thanks?" Liam bounced up to his feet and followed me. He was helpful, so I didn't mind the closeness. "Rome, man, you have got to let me hook you up with a girl. This girl, another girl, but fuck I can't be the only one who likes this. Get your dick sucked just once and it'll change your life."

I paused after shoving the last can of paint into the bag, and stared at him.

"I've got your back," he promised. "I'll find you a good lay, perfectly clean, someone who won't be clingy, too. I mean this chick last night..."

Definitely, no. I shook my head. "I don't want a girl," I informed him and went back to what I was doing.

"You don't want a girl?" I swore he repeated it three times before he shook his head. "Rome, man, come on—" He hesitated a second then straightened. "Well, fuck." It wasn't until I faced him again and caught his gaze briefly that he continued. "More interested in a guy then? I mean, I know some guys who apparently suck dick real well…"

"Why would I want a guy to suck my dick?" If I didn't want a nameless, faceless girl, who smelled of cloying perfume to suck my dick, I couldn't see a guy doing it.

"Well, just checking," he said, frowning. "If you're into dudes, it's cool. Just—keep in mind they better treat you right or I'll fucking kill them."

That made me smile. "Do you want a guy to suck my dick or do you want to kill him?"

"Ha. Ha."

Still, he didn't leave it alone, going as far as to follow me to secure my ropes before returning to the alley as the first rays cut across the city. This building was east facing, so that helped. But it was blocked by another, so the light was slow to reach out and touch her.

Like the light in the painting, it knew better than to try and catch her. What did they call those things? Fireflies? Yeah, fireflies in a jar. Even with air holes it seems cruel.

"You're serious about me not setting you up?" Liam asked finally, as he leaned against his bike and I pulled my shirt back on. At least I'd cooled off.

"Yes. I don't want anyone sucking my dick."

Another sigh and Liam cut his gaze up at the wall. "She doesn't want to be with the others."

"No." I almost wished she'd make a face in the mirror, but she didn't. Her posture perfect, she held the pose that was utterly different from the other girls, up on her toes straining with her arms above her.

Tiny.

Peerless.

Isolated.

But when I looked in those eyes, I saw...

"Rome," Liam groaned and gripped my shoulder. "If you change your mind. Girl. Guy. Both. Together. Whatever. Let me know. I'll help set it up."

Shaking my head, I bumped him with the shoulder he gripped. He let me go while I slung on my backpack on my way to the ten speed. "I don't need any of that."

"You sure?"

Bike upright, I straddled it and glanced at my mirror. So alike, but he lived one side and I lived on the other sometimes. "Yes."

"Sure, like she doesn't want to be with the others?" Liam confirmed motioning to the painting. No mocking scorn echoed in his voice. He was serious. He wanted to understand.

I couldn't ask for more.

"Yes." Then I kicked off with the bike and headed away.

"You're an asshole, Rome," Liam called after me and I shot him the finger over my shoulder. His laughter followed as I picked up speed until the rumble of his motorcycle revving up drowned it out.

26

Someone trying to *kill* Liam was not how I wanted to get back to the clubhouse, nor how I got to see Doc again. Or any of them really. Doc pulled me into the office where they had a medical kit and lights. The others crowded in after us. When Doc fixed them with a rough look, Kellan didn't blink. He crossed his arms and leaned back against the wall. Rome damn near mirrored his exact pose.

Why did everything have to turn into a fight? I locked eyes with Freddie for a second and he winked before he folded his arms and settled himself in the exact same pose as the others. The twinkle in his eyes was new, but not the lazy smirk on his face.

"Oh for fuck's sake, just shut up while I do this then," Doc said by way of dismissal and turned his back on them as he faced me. "How you doing, Little Bit?"

"I'm great," I answered, probably in the driest tone I'd ever been able to muster. "You?"

Lips pursed, he cast his gaze skyward for a second. "I deserved that."

"Hmm." I didn't disagree. I was also not setting Freddie off by saying it. "I'm not shaky anymore." I held my hand out to demonstrate. "Nor am I freezing." Which was good, because Rome had Liam's jacket and Freddie had my backpack.

"That's good. Hop up on the desk for me. Any injuries you're concerned about?" Doc always spoke in such a soothing tone when he went clinical. That, in combination with his respectful distance, had more of my nerves settled.

"Mostly cuts. There was a lot of glass and little splinters of stuff. Liam took the worst of it."

"And the blood?" Like the guys, he zeroed in on the blood soaking my dress. I felt so bad for the waitress I'd dumped the beer on. Granted, I hadn't wanted her to keep molesting Liam if he didn't want it, but I'd never wished her dead.

One minute she'd come toward us, and the next pink mist exploded as a bullet went through her throat. I tried to stop it but...

"Hey," Doc murmured, as he eased the blood pressure cuff onto my wrist and urged me to hold it up against my chest. "You still with us?"

"There was a waitress," I told him. "I can't quite get the look of her eyes out of my head. I tried to help her. Liam said she was gone, but I had to try." I shook my head, trying to dispel the reel playing over and over in my head. It was also why my hands were stained. "It's just—she's dead, so this is all hers."

"Okay." Doc blew out a breath. "Let's start with your hands. I want to go over every part of you that you got blood on."

"What?" But Kellan overrode my question with a, "Why?" as he pushed away from the wall.

"Because of the risk for infection, and in specific blood borne ones," Doc answered, focusing on me. I groaned, but he lifted my chin with one gentle gloved finger "You're going to be fine."

Gaze fixed on his, I glanced down at my hands and legs then at him. "Can we wash this off in here or do we need to go up to my room?"

"We can do either, where would you be more comfortable?"

Considering the fact the guys were like a wall of stone —well Kellan and Rome seemed to be, Freddie just grinned. He looked better, and for that I was glad.

"Let's go to my room, so they can figure out what's going on." I was feeling better, and I slid off the desk. Doc didn't retreat fast enough, so that meant I had to squeeze past him. "And then they can give us some privacy to talk."

Yes, I said it as a statement, but I hope my expression conveyed what I wanted it to. That I needed to talk to Doc alone.

When I held out my hand to Freddie for my bag, he said, "I can carry it..." But Rome plucked it out of his fingers and nodded.

"I'll carry it up. Freddie can send one of the rats for food. Kellan and I will check on Liam and the others."

Everyone stared at him.

Honestly, I *stared* at him. Rome was not one for issuing commands. He'd given instructions and offered guidance, but orders?

"What?" He glanced from me to Kellan then to Freddie and and Doc. "Kel would have said the same thing."

"Right," Kellan said slowly, the skepticism practically rifling the word.

"Only *he* would be taking her up," Freddie said. "And *you* would be staying with me."

Rome shrugged, then held out his hand to me. I looked at the blood then him, but he just took my hand and laced our fingers together. He didn't wait for the others to comment, just guided me out.

"Um..." I said trying to keep my voice down, cause the rats were still there and oh...my least favorite of them all stood directly in front of us, like he'd been right outside the door. I dug my nails into Rome's hand almost reflexively.

Rome stared at him. "What?"

"Just came to see if we're ready to move the trucks." He might be talking about trucks, but he was staring at me.

No, he was staring at my chest.

"Keep looking at her like that, J.D.," Kellan advised, as he joined us and suddenly blocking me from the rat's line of sight. I shivered, because it was like I could still feel him looking at me.

Freddie draped a leather jacket over my shoulders and I glanced at it, then him. He was down to is a white t-shirt and jeans. He also had a knife out. The blade snapping out then vanishing again.

"Really," Freddie said. "Keep doing it. Jasper and Rome haven't beaten the shit out of anyone in the last twenty-four hours, I'm sure they could use the stress relief."

The jacket helped.

"Look, guys, she's got blood all over her, but I didn't see shit. Just gonna go finish with the trucks and wait to be told when I can piss."

"You should probably clear which hand you can use to touch your dick with," Doc added from behind me and that had me twisting to look at him. He didn't acknowledge the glance, if anything he kept his gaze fixed. "Now get out of the way."

Rome gave my hand a squeeze of warning before he set off, Freddie and Kellan stayed behind, and Kellan whistled before he yelled for someone named Shaun.

Yeah, I didn't want to know. I hurried inside as Rome guided me in and then I was in the clubhouse and on my way up the stairs. Guilt raked through me a little that I relaxed the closer we got to "my" room. While I'd spent weeks bitterly complaining about it, I'd never been more happy to see the room.

After setting my backpack on the bed, Rome turned and cupped my face. He studied me, locking on my eyes and I went still under the survey. Doc walked in behind me and moved toward the bathroom, but I couldn't pull my attention from Rome.

"Will you be all right? Or do you need me to stay?"

If I wasn't all sticky with blood and kind of all over the place, I'd have kissed him for that question. Oh—fuck it. I rose up on my tip toes and he bent his head almost automatically. The kiss was almost chaste, but he pressed his lips to mine and we just held there for the longest moment.

Finally, I settled back on my heels. "I'm safe with Doc."

Even if he knew parts of this story or there were things we needed to talk about, that was a truth that resonated with me. I was starting to think I was safe with all of them.

He nodded, then stripped off his shirt and set it on the bed next to my backpack before reclaiming Freddie's jacket from me. "I'll be back. There are still some things in the dresser." The muscles along his arms and chest—everything rippled as he moved. It had when he painted shirtless, too.

"Rome?" I really did *not* need to be thinking with my cunt right now. But I swore my pussy spasmed at the flame in his blue eyes.

Stopping in the door, he glanced at me.

"Will you check that Liam is still all right?" Right. That was what I wanted to say, in that husky a voice.

A smile touched his lips. "Liam is fine."

"You're sure?" That sounded better.

One nod. Then he left, closing the door softly behind him.

In the bathroom, the shower turned on and I finally turned to confront the guy who'd been too busy to see me lately.

"Shower," he said before I could open my mouth. "Let's get all of that blood washed off. It will also give me a better idea of if there is anything we need to—"

I peeled the sundress down. One of the straps had snapped earlier, but the fitted top hadn't budged. A part of me mourned the dress. I'd genuinely liked it, but more of me mourned the waitress I hadn't liked.

The explosion of sound. The raw fear in her face. Then one moment she was standing, the next on the floor, blood sprayed out behind her in a vee and even more bubbling out of her neck. The fixed way she'd stared at me.

"Breathe, Little Bit," Doc ordered, the warmth of his hands closing over my icy ones pulled me back to where we were. My room. The clubhouse. The shower. The dress was off and it dangled from my hand. With deliberate care, Doc took it from me then set it aside. "Right here," he continued. "Eyes on me."

I lifted my lashes and met his dark gaze and swallowed. "I'm okay."

"Of course you are," he agreed with me. "That's why

we're breathing together." He'd pressed one of my hands to his chest, over his heart, and he spread his own against my chest. The warmth just highlighted how cold I was, and I started shivering. "You're fine," he repeated. "Inhale slowly, count to four, then hold for two and exhale for four. Do it together?"

He made it sound like the easiest thing on the planet. It was. Breath control was vital to what I did. So why couldn't I? I choked on trying to hold even a little bit of air and Doc tapped two fingers against my chest.

"Again, inhale," he commanded. I took in as deep a breath as I could. "Slowly." He tapped those two fingers.

Thump-thump. One.

Thump-thump. Two.

Thump-thump. Three.

Thump-thump. Four.

Hold for two.

Thump-thump.

Thump-thump.

"And exhale."

Over and over for the next five minutes, until I wasn't choking on trying to take a breath and my heart stopped racing. At some point, I'd leaned my head against his chest and he'd shifted his hold to wrap an arm around me. Could a person be burning up and freezing at the same time?

"You good with getting in the shower now?"

"Want to get in there with me?" It was a weak offer, I would have turned me down if I'd heard someone invite me in that same wobbly voice.

"Little Bit." The note in his voice ordered me to look up but I didn't want to see the rejection, not right now, but at the same time, I took a deep breath, squared my shoulders and stopped being a baby. I couldn't fall apart just because she...

And right now, I couldn't focus on her. I didn't even *know* her. Why was this stuck in my head? Ignoring that, I met Doc's gaze.

"You're tempting on a good day," he told me without hesitation. "I'd like nothing better than to just take care of you right now."

Oh.

"But that's not what you need."

That single flare of hope died an ugly death.

"What you need is to wash off the blood. Then we do the exam, then we talk. Good?"

"What if I don't want to talk anymore?" I shook my head before I was even finished speaking. "You know what. Ignore that." I sucked in another breath, it wasn't as hard to control my breathing now. "You're right. I need a shower. I need to not see her—this blood on me. Then you can do what you do."

I stepped away from him and squeezed past to get into the bathroom proper. Peeling off the panties, I grimaced at the sight of the blood staining the hem and what looked like fine soot...

Doc took the panties from my hand and what might even be sexy in any other context, just got lost as he studied the hem. "This looks like gun powder."

I opened my mouth, but he lifted my panties to sniff at them and I swore my body went haywire. My pussy clenched, my nipples went tight, but my heart hammered and I went cold for an entirely different reason. I damn near fell in the tub as I twisted away from the sight and dragged the curtain to hide me as I slid under the water.

Hands braced against the tile, I could barely feel the

sting of heat against my flesh. The quiet from beyond the curtain elongated as I stood there, motionless under the water as it soaked my hair flat and ran in bloody red rivulets down until I reached for the soap and began the process of washing.

"Little Bit," Doc said slowly, and I swore it almost sounded like he sat down. Maybe he did. The toilet was right there, but I kept my gaze fixed on my hands. "There are all kinds of trauma. What happened to you today was definitely traumatic, but I don't think it comes close to touching some of what you've been through."

The moisture in my mouth dried up. I got the soap in between each finger and around the nail beds. I spent a long time on that, before I went to wash the blood from my chest. I couldn't say how long that took before Doc sighed.

"If you ever need to talk...I don't know if I'm the right guy."

That wasn't what I expected him to say.

"I will listen to anything you want to tell me. And I promise you," he continued. "I swear to you, nothing you tell me will ever go to the guys."

"Nothing?"

"Nothing." He sounded almost pained to say it that way. "Loyalty is something all of us understand. But I meant it. What you tell me, stays with me. I'll take it to my grave."

The water was clear and my heart wasn't racing anymore, so I dared a peek around the shower curtain. Doc sat on the toilet, elbows braced on his knees and his head down. The muscles in forearms seemed to flex and I swore it looked like he kept himself still.

"You don't want to keep things from them." It wasn't a question.

"No," he confessed. "The bridges I burned with some of them may never be rebuilt, Little Bit. But that's not on you to worry about. I'm a grown man. I know exactly what I'm offering you."

"Jasper..."

"Will deal," he finished for me. "So will Milo."

I snorted. "He's so angry at everything."

"Well, so are you, in your own way."

"I am not."

"One trauma survivor to another," he murmured, and his gaze trapped me in place. Until this moment I hadn't felt naked or vulnerable with Doc, but something in his eyes told me he saw far more than I wanted *anyone* to see. "You are angry. You're just much better at containing it, redressing it, making it look or sound like something else. I admire that about you."

Another shock.

"But don't pretend with me, Little Bit. You don't have to and I'd really rather you didn't."

"There are some things that I just can't talk about." Couldn't. Wouldn't. Never desired to.

"That's fine, I don't like it," he said. "But I'll accept it. Just don't lie or pretend it isn't there."

"How do you..."

He shrugged. "You accept people for who they are and what they are capable of sharing and you work on building trust. It took me a long time to learn it again, too." Another grimace. "Maybe I'm still having to learn. Maybe I'm figuring out that holding back all this time wasn't the right thing to do. I don't know. There are things I'd never dream of talking about and yet, I almost want to tell you."

I turned off the water and he rose, snagging a towel to hold it out to me. "Why me?"

He let out a soft laugh, one that tasted and echoed with disbelief, before he trailed his knuckles down my cheek. "That's the million dollar question. Not one you need to worry about right now. Let's take a look at everything and see what we're dealing with. I do want to do blood work on you and I do want to do some general tests. It's advisable anyway."

"Okay."

Surprise flickered across his face. "Okay?"

"I trust you." It wasn't surprise this time, but genuine shock as he straightened, and the hand that had fallen away from my face, he raised it to cup my cheek. My hair dripped and there was still steam in the air.

"Who are you?" he asked.

It was my turn. "I think that one is the billion-dollar question, Mickey."

His eyes softened at his name.

"One I hope you can help me find the answer to."

FUCKED UP

JASPER

Standing in Kellan's room and *hearing* her soft cries had been one thing. I don't think my dick has ever been so hard or my vision so red. It took effort to not slam the door open and charge in there. But I had to know. I had to *see* it with my own eyes, so I opened it and the sight staggered me even more than the soft words between them.

I wanted to kill him.

Vaughn had *my* girl and he was *fucking* my girl and they were whispering loving words and soft caresses and she was so gone on him and all I wanted to do was *kill* my brother.

Rage and I had been constant companions locked in an unhealthy, toxic relationship, or that was what all the counselors had tried to tell me when they took me aside after fights. Rage was my father. Rage was watching my mother die. Rage was losing the ability to even cry for her.

Rage was Raptor in that fucking prison.

Rage was that fucker Eric putting his hands on her and hurting her.

Rage was the fact that danger kept coming for her.

Now Rage had a target—a face and a name—and it wanted to beat Vaughn bloody.

I left.

Not just the room, but the whole clubhouse. I didn't slow until I was in my car and I accelerated for the exit before the door had even rolled up. The tires screamed against the concrete. I swore the door grazed the top of my car.

I didn't care.

The tight turn as I left gave me a scrap of control. Then I caught sight of Doc in my rearview mirror and I swore his expression filled with pity.

Raw fury punched through me.

I didn't want his fucking pity.

I ignored traffic laws, lights, and everything else. Later, I'd be grateful for the lack of people on the sidewalks as I hit the access road for the highway and floored it.

The speedometer raced over three digits as I whipped through the traffic. My vision narrowed down to the field of what was in front of me. Everyone else could fend for themselves. I avoided other cars, switching lanes and cutting around them.

My blood boiled and my knuckles were white on the steering wheel. I smoked half a pack of cigarettes and barely noticed the taste. It wasn't until my car and I were practically prowling down a lazy suburban street in the town of Wimberly that I allowed myself to relax the rigid control. Despite being an hour away from Braxton Harbor, it was everything Braxton Harbor would never be.

It was quiet.

Picturesque.

Soft.

Filled with families.

Dreams.

Homes.

It was the kind of place the unwanted were never found. No, we were shuffled off to the cities. Wimberly was a cut above and they didn't pretend otherwise.

Despite the hour and the darkness, when I pulled into the driveway—the porch light turned on and the front door opened, though the screen door remained closed. Lights were on inside, too. It was her way of telling me to just come in.

Once I had the car in park, I leaned my forehead to the steering wheel, eyes closed, and tried to get a grip on the demon in my DNA straining at the chains binding him in place. Never had the locks I put on him been so tested.

My father's voice was as clear to me right now as it had been all those years ago.

"Fucking pussy boy. Crying over a girl. Kill the fucker who touched her and then teach her a lesson. Make sure she understands her place. Or are you just going to sit there and cry like a baby? What kind of fucking man are you anyway—"

I slammed my fists against the steering wheel and cut the engine, before throwing myself out of the car. It was too fucking silent out here. Too quiet to drown him out. Night birds called to each other. The air cool, but nowhere near as chilly as it was in the city.

Lighting another cigarette, I paced away from my car. Then back. Up and down the driveway as I burned through one cigarette, then lit another from it before I discarded the old and ground it under my boot.

"Weak. Pathetic and weak. Just like your whore of a mother..."

Fuck him and his voice.

"The belt is where you start. Then the palm. Then the fist. And if your whore won't behave, then you can..."

"Shut up. Shut up. Shut up." I chanted the words under my breath, wish my cigarette was a joint and that I had brought weed with me or something. A bottle of Jack would do it. Just get him out of my head.

The smell of alcohol on his breath as he peered down at me. The spittle that flew from his lips. *"Stop crying for her, you little pussy. We don't cry for whores. She was weak. She made you weak. Pussy is for fucking and for serving. Nothing else. She betrays you, kill her."*

I had no idea how long I paced up and down the driveway or how many cigarettes I killed, until I saw the growing stack by my car door. I needed to clean those up. It wasn't until I crouched to clean up my mess that she spoke. At some point, she'd come out onto her porch and just sat there in the swing—her house had a porch swing that was so perfect for her. I couldn't even resent it.

"Do you want to talk about it?" The soft invitation carried over the neatly trimmed yard—though there were more than a few weeds in it. The punks we paid to keep up on it when we couldn't get out here hadn't been doing their job. I'd get them before I left.

"No," I said as I straightened with a handful of cigarette butts, my fingers smeared in ash. I probably smelled like that pile of used up, burnt, and discarded refuse. "Yes."

I couldn't look at her yet. I needed to get the locks secured once more and the demon back in his cage. He destroyed everything he touched. Poisoned it.

Look at me.

"Well, you can come sit with me and we can talk out here, or you can go upstairs and wash off the ashtray smell and come back down for something to eat in the kitchen."

When I didn't answer, she rose and I finally noticed the mug in her hand.

"I'm going to make another pot of tea." The moment our gazes locked, Ms. Stephanie smiled. That smile hadn't changed. Not once in the nearly twenty years I'd known her. It still made me want to ask her for a hug. "Don't ask for beer. I won't give it to you."

A laugh escaped me, it was hollow and more than a little brittle at the edges, but still a laugh. "I'm legal now."

"No," she informed me as she stood at the door. "You're all still my boys. None of you are old enough to drink, because that just means those gray hairs I keep finding are the real thing. So, tea or hot cocoa. You choose. But *when* you come inside Jasper Horan, you take a shower and don't forget to hose that ash off my driveway. Please and thank you."

"Yes, ma'am."

Another smile escaped as the screen door rattled closed behind her. I dumped the butts into the trash, then hosed off the driveway. I stripped off my shoes before I went in, and I went straight up to the guest shower. There was already an old t-shirt of mine and some sweats that I'd left behind before, waiting for me.

When I made it back to the kitchen, she'd taken up residence at the little table in her breakfast nook. She had a pair of glasses on as she read on her Kindle, and she glanced at me over the top of them when I came in. "Much better."

Before she could rise though, I waved her back to the chair. I had gotten some measure of control back by the time I got out of the shower. Like hot soap and water could

wash me clean. "I'll make the cocoa." I knew where everything was.

"Oh, I'd like that." Another smile. "You can tell me
what's bothering you, too, please."

Fair.

It was why I'd come here, right?

"I fucked up..."

27

After the shower, I sat in a towel while Doc went over my legs with not only a light but also these magnifying glasses that he perched on his nose. It left me torn between hilarity and kind of turned on. Doc could rock glasses, even they did hyper magnify his eyes when he glanced up at me.

"It's okay," he murmured. "You can laugh. You're having to put up with me touching you."

Something he'd asked for permission prior to inspecting my skin for even the slightest open wound. The caress of his fingers along my thighs, knees, and calves was not something I objected to at all. If anything, my cunt had all but returned to pulsing in anticipation every single time he skimmed my thighs.

This was death by contact.

And seriously, I was here for it.

"Your legs are perfect, Little Bit," he said and the huskier note in his voice made me smile. Because when he straightened there was a definite bulge in his pants I hadn't seen earlier. "I need to check your chest now."

"Okay." I dropped the towel, so it pooled at my waist. Sitting on the little counter didn't quite put me at his height, but close enough. "Before you ask, yes you can touch my breasts."

I didn't add any caveats to that invitation. Doc wasn't going to take advantage—not in this situation. He was so damn clinical, if not for the way his voice roughened, I'd assume he wasn't anywhere near interested in me as I was in him.

The scary thing, was how much I liked his attention and how much I'd missed it. Those thoughts kept doing circuits in my brain. When he cupped my right breast, my nipples pebbled into violently stiff points and I closed my eyes.

It was with the lightest of touches that he traced his fingers over my breasts, looking—again—for any open wounds. The heat flushed me, spread upward from my belly and then down again. I swore my pulse was a physical thing between my legs.

The sensual torture—clinical or not—continued until he'd examined every inch of my skin. The warmth of his breath teased me and I tightened my grip on the counter to keep from just pushing my breasts up and begging him to suck them.

Something.

Going after what I wanted—it was like winning a series of campaigns in a war I'd spent so much time on my back foot, that I craved these victories.

Vaughn's passion.

Jasper's rough kisses and soft words.

The passion-drenched and quiet moments with Rome.

The dangerous invasion of Liam's kiss, that for just a

little while had burned a path into the encroaching darkness and forced it back.

Freddie's and Kellan—I wanted all of them. Slut or not. Whore or not. Whatever, I wasn't going to label it. Not when...

"Hey," Doc's voice gentled, as he glided his hand up to my throat and for a moment, I truly did forget how to breathe. I opened my eyes to find him right there, his lips an agonizingly close to mine. "Where did you go, Little Bit?"

In trying to escape his nearness and the profound effect it was having on my libido, I only succeeded in squirming against the towel. The faint roughness teased my soaking cunt and there was nowhere near enough friction.

"I want you," I admitted. I wanted him—all of them—in a way I'd never wanted anyone before. I liked their touch. Craved it. Looked forward to the little ones, the arm around my shoulders, the knuckles against my cheek, the way Mickey's huge hand seemed to hold my whole throat and I melted against that contact.

"Oh, Little Bit," he whispered with a sigh, every single word a kiss denied, as his lips brushed tantalizingly closer. "I'm way too old for you and you've got those boys all down there fighting to be your champion."

"I want them, too," I confessed. No lies here.

"I'm glad." He stroked his thumb over my pulse point, and I tried to roll my hips against the towel to alleviate some of the need, but all it did was leave me frustrated. "You need to come don't you?"

My heart thudded in my cunt, my ears, my fucking neck where he touched me, and I swore even in my lips. All of me, so desperate for him.

Not trusting my voice, I nodded and Mickey glanced down. "Take off the towel, Little Bit." He never stopped stroking my throat while I shifted, wiggling until the towel was a memory on the floor. "Spread your legs."

Hunger raked through me. Raw desire. With his hand on my throat, I had to stay where I was, but spreading my legs as wide as I could, put my soaked pussy on display.

Mickey let out a rush of air that teased me and I swiped my tongue over my lower lip. "Freddie's right you know," he said softly as he reached for my hand and I surrendered it immediately. "That really is one of the prettiest pussies I've ever seen."

I wanted to preen. He liked...

"Flushed so red and inviting," he continued, as he moved my hand to my core and without once actually touching me, pressed my fingers to my clit. It was swollen, hard and even the faintest brush of my nails sent me squirming again. "Look at me, Little Bit."

I dragged my gaze up as he cupped his hand over mine, trapping my fingers against my pussy. Glasses gone, all I could see were his eyes and the heat in them scorched me,

"Make yourself come," he ordered, and I curled my fingers and began to do a slow, but steadily increasing, ring of circles around my clit. My hips arched forward. "Ride your hand," he whispered. "Imagine it's Vaughn on his knees for you."

The groan that came out of me wasn't human.

"Or maybe it's Jasper, pinning you down and burying his face in your cunt. Has he done that? Has he fucked you with his tongue? Have any of them?"

The combination of his words and my fingers had me so close. Mickey's fingers were right along mine, following every movement. I was so close and then he caught my hand and stilled everything.

Fuck. I wanted to cry.

"You didn't answer my question."

My breath came in these fast little pants and my pulse raced. The only places Mickey actually touched me was my neck and my hand. Yet his nearness seemed to fill the whole room.

"What was the question?"

"Have any of them fucked you with their tongue?" The quiet demand sent another spiral of need through me.

"Yes. Tongues. Fingers. Pierced dicks. Not pierced dicks." The words fell out of me in a rush.

"Good girl," he whispered and then he moved my fingers for me, faster and faster. The tension coiled so damn tight, I arched my hips upward and when I would have pulled back as the first wave hit me, Mickey didn't let up with my fingers, and the moment I opened my lips to scream he slammed his mouth down on mine.

He swallowed every sound as he made me come. I drenched my fingers and his, and still he sent me spiraling again. When it almost stung it was too much, he let go of my hand and broke the kiss. The last sweep of his tongue was a lingering reminder of how he tasted.

Like more.

So much more.

Shudders rippled through me, my nipples ached from their neglect and at the same time, laziness spread out from my core, softening my muscles and easing the tension in my spine.

Not once had I looked away, even when I wanted to, I couldn't when Mickey's gaze was like this prescient thing digging in my soul. So, when he slid all three of his fingers into his mouth to lick them clean, I damn near came again.

"Better?" he rasped out.

I nodded slowly. "But I still want you."

He closed his eyes briefly, then he dragged me right off the counter, arm banding around my waist as I automatically hitched my thighs to his hips. The kiss this time was all demand. He devoured my mouth. The thrust of his tongue conquered and his body ground into mine, as he pressed me back against the wall.

The roughness of his jeans against my clit detonated me all over again and he sucked the sounds from my mouth until I all but collapsed against him.

"Sometimes," he whispered. "We can't have what we want, Little Bit. No matter how badly we want it."

My heart shredded because he retreated behind his professionalism and settled me back on the cold sink counter. I was both replete from orgasm and desperate for so much more.

"Mickey," I managed as he retreated as far as the doorway. The very obvious wet spot on his jeans had me licking my lips. "Sometimes we can."

I'd never wanted anyone the way I wanted all of them. Admitting it, even silently to myself, was—dangerous. Wanting was not something I'd ever let myself do. Not when all I could be was a threat to what I wanted.

But these guys...

"Little Bit, you're killing me." He almost laughed, but there was a distinct lack of humor in his eyes. "You're fucking perfect and if you were anyone else, I'd already be balls deep in that cunt of yours until you forgot those boys existed."

Fuck me. I wanted to beg.

"But I'm the guy who carried you, as a baby, into the system. I found you. I looked after you. I—took you and Milo in. I encouraged him when he wanted to let you go when the

Sharpes came calling. So, you're you, Little Bit. You're you and I had a hand in that. And as beautiful as you are and as much as I —well the age difference was bad enough before. Now? Milo's like my kid brother. You're his baby sister. You're...you're an old soul in a baby's body." I didn't think he could crush me. "Wanting you is wrong. Wanting you is like wanting a child. I can't want this with you, Little Bit. I'm sorry."

I was wrong.

Mick—Doc finished checking me over and then, at my request, took the blood sample. He promised to run it against Milo's, though he insisted he already knew the answer. I couldn't respond to that. Not when his words kept playing on a loop in my head, sharing reel time with the look of the dead waitress's face and the heat of her blood on my fingers as I tried to put pressure on the wounds.

When he was done, I walked out of the bathroom nude and dragged on clothes in a hurry. I'd never been embarrassed before. Bodies were just bodies. No, I was bleeding from wounds they couldn't see and I wanted to keep them hidden. Most of the things I had access to were the guys clothes. Rome's shirt. I had no idea who owned the cut off sweatpants, but at least I could tie them on.

"Little Bit..."

Doc's voice followed me as I picked up the backpack and left via Kellan's room. The concrete in the hall was cold against my bare feet. I had no idea what happened to my shoes.

Had I been barefoot when they got me from the club?

Downstairs, I found the guys gathered in the kitchen talking. Well...arguing really. They were yelling.

Okay, to be fair, Milo was yelling.

At Liam.

Liam zeroed in on me as soon as I walked in. Relief swam in his eyes as he gave me a once over and I gave him a little smile. He looked better. Like me, he seemed to have showered and he had on Rome's clothes. I recognized those from one of the times we went painting.

"You still haven't told me what you were thinking by taking her to a topless club. And stop eye-fucking my sister. There's enough dick in this room already trying to climb into her pants." Milo's words penetrated and I broke eye contact with Liam to stare at my "brother,"

There wasn't time to respond, verbally or otherwise, Liam struck so hard and so fast I swore the crack of bone on bone as his fist slammed into Milo's jaw ricocheted around the room. I flinched, I couldn't help it, and then two arms twined around me and pulled me back against his chest.

Rome.

I didn't even have to look.

"That is not processing." My words sounded ridiculously loud in the dead silence that followed that hit. Milo half crumpled against the counter. He didn't drop, but his knuckles were white where he held it.

"No," Rome agreed, tightening his grip. "He deserved that."

"Yes," Jasper said, shocking the hell out of me as he moved to stand next to us. "He did."

Liam didn't pursue the attack, if anything, he just stood there and glared icy daggers until Milo finally straightened. Blood trickled from the corner of his mouth and from one nostril. The marks of a healing black eye were still visible on

Liam. Jasper's face was a roadmap of arguments played out in blood and violence. Reaching into the fridge, Kellan—who didn't seem to have visible bruises anymore—pulled out a beer and popped it open before offering me the cold bottle.

"You okay, Sparrow?"

"I'll live," I told him as I accepted the bottle. His fingers lingered on mine and he nodded.

"Good. Do you mind going out to the living room or better yet, up to your room?"

"Or the studio," Vaughn suggested. "Food will be here shortly and we'll bring it to you."

"You want me out of the way because there's going to be more arguing."

"Didn't say that," Kel told me, though the rueful smile confirmed my supposition.

"Is the argument about me?"

"Yes."

"No."

"Partially."

"Dove..."

"Maybe."

"No fucking maybes about it," Liam spit each word. "This has been all about her from day *one*."

Milo met his glare with one of his own, and it was the first interaction between them I'd witnessed where they weren't in agreement, or at least on even footing.

"Liam's right."

"I'll be damned," Vaughn said as he winked at me. "You've done the impossible, Dove."

"Someone write it down, we'll need to remind him he said it." Kellan's dry observation sent laughter, albeit uneasy laughter, through the rest of them.

"Right, well, if it's about me. I'm not going anywhere." I patted Rome's hands on my stomach and he let me go. On tip toes, I kissed his cheek then glanced at Jasper. "Do you have your cigarettes?"

Because right now, I desperately needed something to do and drinking beer wasn't enough.

He pulled the pack and the lighter out. After handing me one, he waited until it was between my lips before he lit it. The whole time I could *feel* Milo's stare boring into me. Only, he wasn't alone. Doc stood in the doorway to the kitchen, there but not, and I met his gaze briefly before I looked away.

Nope. I couldn't deal with Doc's rejection right now.

Just. No.

Instead, I looked toward where Milo and Liam were still in a stand-off. He glared at my cigarette, so I took a long draw on it. Keep pushing it, I willed him. Piss me off.

Give me something to fight right now.

"Fine," he ground out. "You can stay but you don't get to say anything."

I snorted. "Like you fucking listen."

His pained look raked guilt through me, but I refused it purchase. Just like I refused to deal with Doc or anyone else right now. If Jasper and Liam could get along, then I would content myself with that.

Two hours later, I had to admit. I really regretted my decision. We'd adjourned to the living room and instead of the furniture, I'd sat down with my back to the wall. Freddie had dropped down to sit right next to me.

"Solidarity," he whispered, and I bumped his shoulder. While Jasper, Liam, Rome, and Vaughn arrayed themselves near, they were still focused on the argument with Milo. Unsurprisingly, Doc backed Milo.

Color me shocked.

Kellan hadn't said much, instead, he'd listened to all of them make their cases, which basically boiled down to "what do we do with Ivy" while they dealt with the "big secret problem" that they alluded to in conversation. I'd finished the beer and another cigarette

I'd even eaten the burgers when the food arrived. At least mine was wrapped in lettuce, and I could have kissed whoever ordered it for me, but they were too busy deciding what to do with me.

Staying here was out of the question. Milo wanted me at Liam's. Provided Liam didn't take me to any more strip clubs. "Like I've never seen breasts or cunts before," I'd muttered, and while Rome grinned and Jasper flat out laughed, Milo hadn't been thrilled.

Around and around they went, including alternating who stayed with me so I would "always" have a guard.

I was so sick of this discussion. We weren't getting anywhere. Jasper and Vaughn wanted me here. Liam seemed to want me at his place, or at least didn't mind it, but refused to cage me. Rome was fine with either option, save locking me up.

"You thinking what I'm thinking?" I murmured to Freddie, because while he hadn't jumped into this discussion, he had been sitting here with me. Kellan had weed somewhere, and there was a roof, and I could go for getting high right now. Every muscle in my body hurt, but that was nothing compared to my heart after Liam collapsed. After the waitress died. After Doc called me a child and informed me that he couldn't want me.

Wanting me was wrong.

Yeah, skip.

"No." Freddie didn't even look up from his phone when he answered.

"How do you know you're not?" I elbowed him. The distraction would do us both good.

"I was thinking I wish I could go back in time and have sex with my seventh grade math teacher. She had the most amazing tits. They were like twin globes—you know those world globes we had in classrooms? Each of her boobs were fat and round and she wore these bras that just put them right there for you to want to touch. I want to go back in time and just fuck the hell out of those tits." Freddie looked at me. "Is that what you were thinking?" Then he blinked. "I mean, your tits are great. Don't get me wrong. I like boobs and that pussy of yours—fuck me."

"Freddie!" Every single one of them shouted.

"Yeah, yeah," he said as he leaned back and shot me a wink. "Shut up, Freddie."

And I just burst out laughing. "Please don't ever shut up."

"Don't worry, Boo-Boo, I won't. Promise."

The laughter turned purely into giggles and I leaned my head against his shoulder. As much as I wanted to get high or something, taking Freddie would be bad for *him*. Still...

"How hot was she?" I asked in a low voice as the others resumed their regularly scheduled *What do we do with a problem like Emersyn* discussion? I was half-tempted to just take my backpack and go. I had the money for a hotel.

Maybe the time apart and the space would do us good.

Except, I wasn't an idiot. There was danger all around me, what happened earlier proved it. It also proved I needed to decide, and soon, if I was willing to keep risking their lives.

Freddie offered me his phone and showed me a picture.

This woman had been his teacher? She was—stunning. And he wasn't kidding about her breasts. Mine were—non-existent by comparison.

"Sexy, right?" he tucked his cheek to the top of my head and I nodded a little.

"I'd do her," I offered. Solidarity.

"Oh fuck," Freddie whispered. "Give me a minute with that image, Boo-Boo. I think you just became more perfect."

Another soft laugh escaped me and when I caught Milo staring at me, I raised my eyebrows. He sighed and everyone went quiet.

"Emersyn," he said slowly, and I could almost hear the self-correction from Ivy. I appreciated that. "What do you want to do?"

JUMPING

LIAM

Dressed in a suit, I sat in the back of the courtroom. Milo instructed the others to wait. Let me be the face for now. Jasper's colorful opinion still rang in my ears. Then again, the mottled bruising on my knuckles were a sign of my equally colorful, if brutal response.

We both needed to burn off some steam. I wished I could have said it helped. As legal proceedings went, this one was dry and boring. Then finally they called Milo's case and brought him in. His dark-eyed gaze found mine. Dressed in a button down and slacks, he'd skipped the tie I'd sent him, though the suit jacket fit perfectly.

"All rise..."

Twenty-five minutes later, it was over. Twenty-five minutes to accept the plea bargain as agreed on between the District Attorney's Office and Milo's court appointed attorney. I'd hired a better one, he'd fired them and went with whomever he got from the public defender's office.

I had no doubt Milo had been the one to strike the deal.

None whatsoever. When the judge told him he had to allocute, the last fragment of hope I had for him *died*. Milo William Harris Hardigan had been sentenced to three years without a chance for parole or earlier release before the completion of his sentence.

However, if he faced any other indictments, they would be handled individually and not impact the details of this particular deal. Did he understand? He did.

I didn't.

In other words, if Milo faced any charges *unrelated* to this one, he would have to undergo another trial and that could add what? More to his sentence. God. Fucking. Damn. It.

The judge alternated between scolding and reasonable. The eighty-something-year old geriatric had no patience for perpetuating the myths of violence and that zip code determined fate. He told Milo in no uncertain terms he could do better and should.

Not that he lightened the sentence one whit. Court adjourned and Milo glanced back at me as he rose and turned his back for the officer to secure him with handcuffs once more. Then he jerked his head at me.

As I approached, I heard Milo ask the officer—politely —if we could have a moment with his attorney. The man nodded. "Keep it brief." Then he stepped back to give us a modicum of privacy.

"Don't talk," Milo ordered. "Just listen." My teeth clicked together as I clamped my mouth shut. "It's time. Make the break, make it clean and go."

Fuck.

"I know you don't want to. I don't want to have to ask this of you."

But he would and I'd do it.

"Tell no one." What went without saying was "except Rome." He didn't have to say it and I didn't have to hear it.

Lying to my brother wasn't an option.

"They aren't going to take it well." Understatement of the year. Though his attorney had already packed up and left, there were still a few in the courtroom, most of them with business of their own, but I was well aware that *he* could have someone else here, observing.

For that, I kept my expression neutral.

"That's fine. The more pushback you receive, the better. It needs to be clear you can't be a double agent anymore." No names or details. "Jasper may never forgive us."

"Then we live with it." Those were the last five words I said to him before they took him away. My phone—*the* phone—rang as I exited the courthouse. Unsurprising. I didn't even make it to the steps.

"How did Hardigan pull that off? He used a public defender." Rage coiled like a dangerous snake in his words, poised for a lethal strike.

"Damn good question, sir," I responded. I'd honed this role for years, practiced until it was a second part of my skin. "He declined the attorney I sent him and then must have negotiated something for himself. He's smart enough to have pulled it off." Fuck his majesty and everything else about him.

I had to *betray* my brothers for this plan to work and they wouldn't know, all because this control freak fuck had *tests* for me to complete and an absolute fucking hard-on for destroying Milo and the other Vandals, for who the fuck knew why.

"For now," I continued as though trying to cover my own ass. "He is out of the way. Without him, the Vandals will be without a leader."

"You could step up into that role..."

"Yeah, unfortunately, not." I slid into my car and started the engine with a push. The soft growl as she snarled awake helped soothe my soul for what I had to say next. "They know."

"How?"

"Pretty sure Milo figured it out. So, I'm cutting my losses and getting out before they have time to act on it." That wasn't his majesty's plan. Too fucking bad. At the moment, the King could choke on it. We'd been playing this game of chess for far too long and I hadn't moved up high enough. Yet.

Instead of anger though, he merely sighed. "Very well, probably better to not burn you any further. I will have more tasks for you. Let me know once you're secure."

Great.

"Congratulations on achieving knighthood."

I froze. That was definitely a promotion from Rook. Even if we were all his pawns in this game.

"Your brother?" he continued as I backed out of my slot. The phone had gone to hands-free mode, the distortion of his voice was even worse over the speakers. We hadn't even been able to find a voice print match and I'd sunk money into it. Whatever he used was good.

"I don't know." I lied. I did know. Rome would stay with them. "He may stay. He may come with. Either way..."

"Yes, yes. If we touch him, you'll burn us all to the ground. We have a deal, you and I. One I have given no one else."

Right.

"However, if you get him out of there, then we can wipe the others off the map and be done."

No comment. Even if I had to say something.

"Understood."

The call ended and I flexed my fingers on the steering wheel. At the next red light, I switched phones. I just sent one message.

It's time.

28

Sparrow chose to go back to Liam's. Of all the things I'd have bet on her saying, the words, "I want to go back to Liam's," didn't even make the top ten. What should have solved the hostility in the room only redirected it.

Weirder still had been Jasper's response. "You sure, Swan?"

Her nod had settled him, and that was that.

What the actual fuck had happened to all of them? Milo now looked like he wanted to object. Freddie seemed puzzled and disappointed. Right there with you buddy. Vaughn wasn't happy either, but he accepted her response without argument. Rome didn't care, why would he? Where she went—here or there—he could easily follow.

Still, watching her leave *with* Liam and not challenging it, had been difficult. Doc's quieter, furious response had been more intense than any of ours. But I'd get answers. Without the audience.

I gave her twenty-four hours to bounce back from the shock. Twenty-four hours while I added new GPS tags to the last of our trucks. I tagged the cargo trailers, the rigs, and the tires. There was a bonus one I'd added to the hydraulics in case they did more than just "switch" out the rig or the trailer itself.

Milo had asked me to talk to my sperm donor. We had eyes on him. His history in trafficking wasn't lost on me. While Milo didn't want to ask me, he had, and I'd told him I'd think about it.

There wasn't much I wouldn't do for my brothers but talking to Jonathon Warrick required opening old wounds buried beneath decades of scar tissue. I'd kept my distance from Warrick *and* his family. A choice, to be certain, but one I'd never questioned before today.

When I should be making those arrangements, I texted my sparrow instead.

Me: *You free today?*

Her: *Yes. Liam's not up for more training yet, despite what he says.*

I snorted at the description.

Me: *If he says he can do it. He'll do it.*

Her: *Why does that not surprise me? Doesn't matter. He left. Said he had a meeting.*

Fine.

Me: *Get dressed. I'll be there in twenty.*

Her: *Anything special?*

Me: *Comfortable.*

It took me way less than twenty minutes to get there. But I took the extra time to get it together. I had to make a couple of circuits of the block to ensure no one was watching Liam's. When I was certain, I skipped the parking garage, which was for residents only, and parked on the street.

Before I could even get out of the car though, Emersyn had opened the passenger door and slid inside. She set her backpack on the floor at her feet.

I glared at her, even as her smile hit me in the chest like a punch. "Don't even start with me." After snapping the safety belt, she leaned over and brushed a kiss to my jaw. "I stayed *inside* while you circled the block and stayed out of sight until you *parked*."

"Dammit, Sparrow," I swore. "It's not that simple. We still don't know who wants to hurt you." All of that had gotten lost with the mounting threats now approaching from multiple directions.

"No one knows where I am," she argued. "Disappeared, remember? Kidnapped. Held in a room for weeks, then in the clubhouse, now my new 'pied-à-terre' up there. And I'm even *disguised.*"

Snorting, I reached a hand over to wrap against the back of her head. Yes, she had on a baseball cap and sunglasses with her hair pulled back in a ponytail but... "Sparrow, I'd know you fucking anywhere."

This close, there was no way to miss her nostrils flaring as her breathing quickened. It had been the most natural thing in the world to bring her to me. I wanted to kiss her— then she closed that gap, pushing herself toward me, and our lips connected.

The world narrowed to the softness of her lips where they massaged mine. A single tentative brush of her tongue against my lips had me groaning. Wrapping her ponytail around my hand, I tilted her head so I could hunt down the sweet flavor of her tongue.

Coffee. Mint. Bacon. And chocolate. All of that, and something indefinable yet utterly her, pulled me down. If she were a siren sent to tempt me to bash my boat on the rocks and then surrender my life to her, this would be how I went.

The softest of moans filled the interior of the car as I nibbled and sucked on her lower lip. A deep desire to see her naked and blindfolded, while also bound to my bed so I could spend hours pleasuring her until she was putty, filled me near to bursting.

A horn blaring into the morning blasted through the haze of wanton lust, and I opened my eyes to find her own blinking back at me slowly through the sun glasses. "You don't run out to meet any of us," I said slowly, dragging my brain up from my dick, because fuck me it wanted her naked and riding my cock right here in this car. I wanted the scent of her beaten into the leather. "No arguments on this one, Sparrow. It's not just your enemies that might be a threat, but ours."

When the flush infusing her cheeks paled, I wanted to kick myself. I stroked her soft ponytail as I released it.

"That last thing we want is you hurt," I explained gently. "No, not just for Milo, Sparrow. So let that thought go, that the only reason any of us care is because of him. We might have started that way, but that's not what brought you to us or why I'm here today."

Then, because I needed to stop being distracted, I made myself release her and jerked the car into traffic. It was a lot smoother than it sounded. My baby accelerated swiftly and easily.

"I didn't think it would hurt since I stayed inside." The quiet response from the passenger seat sliced at me.

"We scold you because we care," I damn near tripped on

that last word. "You know that. So why do you keep pushing all of us? What can we do to ease that up?"

Releasing a humorless laugh, she shook her head. "I've reconciled myself to staying hidden. It's not a bad idea. And I was there when those bullets started flying..."

The way her voice went small just pissed me off.

"...while I know you guys are used to some of that, I'm not. But I am doing my best." The protest pulled a reluctant smile from me.

"Sparrow, no one is saying any differently. You've stood up to things I've seen grown men shit their pants at. From ambushes, to sabotage, to personal attacks. Don't think for a second, we don't see how strong and capable you are. It's not you we're wrestling with. The world—it's a darker place than you realize."

Derision filled her snort. "Sooner or later, you guys will stop acting like I came from a glittery world of light and kindness. I know just exactly how damn dark the world is."

And now we were fighting. Fuck. I flexed my hands on the steering wheel. Then I abandoned that because I broke it, I needed to fix it. Holding my hand out to her, I didn't put it on her leg or try to take her hand.

When she slid her hand into mine, I relaxed and gave her a gentle squeeze. "I didn't come bust you out to yell at you or have a fight, Sparrow. I'm sorry."

"No," she said, with a sigh. "I am. All of this is taking me time to get used to, and I want to complain and rage against the restrictions. I don't want to be caged."

"We don't want to cage you."

She snorted.

"Okay, fair," I admitted. "How about this, *I* don't want to cage you."

"Better." Then after a moment, she asked, "Why did you come to get me?"

"Can't I just want to see you?"

Laughing, she squeezed my hand. "Of course, but in all the time I've been at Liam's, you haven't tried to see me."

"Hey," I protested. "No one was supposed to go and see you."

"Right, because Milo the DICK-tater..."

Fuck my life, she made him sound like a poorly constructed tater tot, and it was killing me not to laugh. Did she not know that she sounded like every little sister I'd met—ever?

"...didn't want me seeing any of you."

"A, that's fucking hilarious." No point in lying, particularly when I was already chuckling. "B, Milo is definitely one of my best friends, more, he's my brother..."

"Better yours than mine," she muttered, but there was something in her voice. Putting a pin in that for now, I'd pursue it with her later.

"That *said*, Sparrow. None of us are going to let him make unilateral decisions where you're concerned. Nor are we going to back him making them *for* you, unless it's a matter of life and death." I tried to keep it matter-of-fact.

"Like the other day at the club..."

"Exactly, we came and got you and removed you before you could be questioned or identified." I fucking hoped, anyway. So far, what news coverage there had been, focused only on intensifying gang violence in a city where crime had been steadily increasing. Nothing about her, not even a sideways view of her.

I'd bet money Liam arranged to buy the footage. There were just too many damn people present.

"I get it," she said quietly. "And I'm glad you're not

letting him make every decision." Irritation flaked off every single word with the way she ground them out. "This may sound weird, but I like you guys. Most of you anyway and...I feel like we were getting to know each other and bam, he's back and everything has changed."

"Everything is always changing." Advice I was confident in giving her. "Look, you may have had steady parents and family, but you traveled with your show extensively. You were always changing cities, venues, companions—and by companions, I mean drivers, not anything else."

"The drawback of not knowing how," she pointed out. "Most of the time, I didn't even know what city we were in."

"Exactly," I continued, as I followed the side road toward an old industrial area. "So, you're familiar with adapting, Sparrow. Life with us—it's always about adapting. We learn that pretty quick in the system. If you can't adapt..."

We owned about a third of the buildings now with bids on two more. But nothing was open back here, no one worked, not even security. Which meant huge empty parking lots and wide open road.

"What happens if you can't adapt?"

I sighed as I pulled to the middle of the lot and put the car in park. "Switch with me for a second," I told her, before I unbuckled my seatbelt and slid out of the car. By the time I circled around to her door, she hadn't moved and stared at me with a look of pure bewilderment.

It was adorable.

"Kellan." I hadn't realized how much I craved to hear the sound of my name on her lips, until this moment. "I don't know *how* to drive."

"I know, Sparrow. That's why we're here. Today is driving lesson one."

It took willpower to not laugh as she ripped her sunglasses down and stared at me. "Are you shitting me right now?"

"No." I kept it simple. "This car is my baby, I would never fuck her around like that, much less you. Now—get in the driver's seat. Come on. We've got stuff to go over."

Another long moment where she stared at me, searching for something, and then a wild grin lit her up and she wiggled out of the car. I couldn't move fast enough to escape the clamp of her hands on my cheeks or the way she tugged me down. Then the hot, wet kiss competed with the sun for how fast she inflamed every single one of my senses.

The contact didn't last near long enough, because she was already racing around the car to climb into the front seat. Savoring the taste of her on my lips, I settled in the passenger seat. With care, I moved her backpack into the backseat, on the floor behind the driver's seat.

Excitement seemed to bubble off of her. Excitement and a sense of happiness I hadn't seen in so long, I hadn't realized how empty and cool her smiles had been, when compared to the ones she threw at me now.

For a split-second, she was every bit the arrogant, playful, and flirtatious girl I'd been driving, but she was also so much more. "Be as excited as you want, but listen..."

Like she was in the kitchen and the garage, she was very responsive to following my lead—or in this case, my orders. How responsive to commands would she be in bed... and all at once that image of her sprawled, tied up and locked in place with her legs spread, unable to hide any reaction from me, filled my head.

Later. It was both a promise and a plea to myself.

First, we went over the basics like what and where everything was. She didn't complain about how thoroughly we went over everything. Nor did she complain when I made her repeat everything back to me. I wanted to be absolutely certain she had the best foundation, before we actually got four thousand pounds of steel and vehicle involved.

When she started the car, went through all the lights and processes, I couldn't have been prouder. She had to adjust my seat for her much shorter legs, but we played with it until she was comfortable.

For most of that first hour, she'd been attentive, responsive, and perfectly submissive to each request. If I kept thinking about sex, not only would we never get out of this parking lot, we may never get out of the car.

And I refused for the first time we fucked to be in a car. I could afford to show her care, dammit. Then again, stripping those pants off of her, or better yet if she'd worn a skirt then I could just...

"So, we ready to do this or what?" The question burst that little fantasy, but only because there was zero chance she knew what I was thinking. Lowering her sunglasses, she studied me. "You're flushed. Are you feeling okay?"

"I'm fine," came out a little more strangled than I intended, but she laughed.

"Please tell me you're not imagining fucking your seventh grade teacher and her amazing globe-like breasts."

"Definitely not my seventh grade teacher, and your breasts are perfect for licking and sucking. I bet I could get an entire one into my mouth." And damn, if I didn't want to try.

Also, I'd literally just said that aloud and Emersyn

stared at me, mouth forming a little 'o' that would be perfect to fuck.

"Well," she said, swallowing before she shoved her sunglasses back into place. I knew the feeling. Control did not feel all that accessible at the moment. "I meant—are we ready to try driving itself?"

"I don't know," I murmured because I really didn't trust my voice and I rubbed my thumb against my lower lip to keep from putting the theory of her breast in my mouth to the test. "What are you ready for?"

The loaded meaning wasn't lost on her, and the sunglasses came off and so did mine. She didn't shy away from my gaze, not once. "I'm ready for a lot of things," she admitted.

"Just things?" Why was I pressing this?

"Am I ready for you?" I had a feeling she wasn't asking me that. "I want to be, but..."

"You're already having sex with my brothers," I said. "I don't care. That doesn't make me want you any less. Fuck, if anything, I just want you more. Fresh from one of their beds looking hot, fucked, and swollen like you did that day in Vaughn's room."

She shuddered and her nipples made an appearance against her t-shirt. Yeah, I was pretty sure I could get the whole thing in my mouth.

"But that said," I pressed on and gave my dick a very unpleasant squeeze to distract it, all the while aware of the way her gaze tracked with my hand and how she focused on the hard as fuck erection straining the denim. "We're here to teach you how to drive my car. Lessons for how to ride me come later—and they're extra."

"Extra?" Archness added a distinct lift to the huskiness of her response. "How much was the car lesson?"

Fuck—with an opening like that? I unsnapped my seat belt and leaned across to pin her to the driver's seat. No words, no talking, fuck barely any breathing, as I kissed her. I demanded access with my tongue and she opened to me, letting me sweep in and taste every inch of her. I had a gentle hand on her chin, then I slid it down to her throat.

The contact on her flesh, I kept light. No squeezing, but also no allowing her escape. I kissed her until she trembled and shook and only then did I lift my head. "How wet are you right now, Sparrow?"

Her thighs pressed together but not fast enough. Her shuddering swallow satisfied some deep predatory instinct I barely recognized. "Soaking."

"Good." I ran my tongue over my lower lip again, then hers. "Consider 'that' the cost of today's lesson."

"We haven't even started the car."

I chuckled softly. Because no, we hadn't. Also, so fucking proud of her for not taking the deal at face value. "The cost covered the whole day, whether you drive it or not."

"Uh huh and when can I get on the highway?"

"Depends on what you're willing to pay—"

"Right...you're a fucking tease, Kellan."

It was my turn to laugh. She sounded so disgruntled. "Don't worry Sparrow, I'm sure you'll find some relief. Who knows—maybe I'll send a Hawk over to find you after."

That earned me a smack on the chest and a flash of excited grin she couldn't hide. Why was I offering to let one of my brothers fuck her instead of me?

Because we're going to earn it. Some dark part of my soul whispered. *Sparrow is going to come to us. She'll fly right into our arms and our bed.*

The old adage of *if you love something, let it go* floated

through my mind and I smiled. I could let her go to the others. Let them slake the desire and need I'd just incited. Then I'd do it again.

And again.

Eventually, it would be my bed she was in...

Pinching off that thought, I focused on her. "Let's start the car."

Another giddy laugh, though there was definitely an undercurrent of desire zipping through the air. "I still can't believe you're gonna teach me to drive. "

I waited until we'd gone over hand positions on the wheel, gears, and accelerator versus brake and the clutch.

"As for why I'm teaching you, I want you to have every skill you need. Driving is an essential skill. It gives you a way out. Jasper is probably gonna take you to the range if he hasn't already. You said Liam's teaching you how to fight. The others are all trying to teach you different things, share different parts of ourselves with you."

It wasn't that we wanted her in a cage.

No, we wanted her to be able to cage anything that came at her.

"Ready?"

"Yes!"

Our beautiful bird had been prey for too long.

No more.

When we were done, she would be ready for anything. Even if I had to survive the grinding of gears and lurching as she learned.

It would be worth it.

TRUTH

EMERSYN

Everything hurt. It was incredibly hard to move or dance or act like everything was normal. I'd pushed past pain before, but the first day in rehearsals after...

"Emersyn," the director called, and I went still. He never talked to me. Not really. We had choreographers, costumers, and even my she-bitch-of-a-chaperone, Marta, whom we communicated through. But for the most part, the director rarely spoke to me directly.

Like, ever.

My stomach bottomed out and I swore I was going to throw up. How I managed to walk across the stage to where he waited without collapsing, I had no idea. If possible, it hurt even more.

"You don't look good," he said, his tone dismissive. "Not the routine, that's fine. You look ill. Go see the doctor."

"I'll be fine," I assured him. I never saw the doctor for the company, other than to provide the notes and records from our private doctor.

"You're *not* fine." He swept his hand out as though encompassing all of me and I flinched. I hadn't meant to, and the apology was right there on my tongue. "You're shaking, you're pale, and you are sweating way more than that simple routine demands. If you've picked up the flu, it's not the end of the world, but you go see the doctor and get cleared or you are out."

No.

"I'll go," I said. Marta wasn't here, she was probably sleeping off one too many drinks from the night before, and that was fine. I didn't want her as an audience anyway. The doctor was set up in her own room. The show kept a physician and nurse on staff, as well as a masseuse. Take care of the performers being the theory.

The doctor was a very nice woman, or at least she always seemed to be. Jane Chapman, the doctor, glanced up when I came in, and her polite smile fell away to concern. Almost immediately she was on her feet. Thankfully, she was alone.

"Hey," she said by way of greeting as she reached over to take my wrist. My pulse hammered too fast. I knew that. "You just got back, right?"

"Yes ma'am," I admitted. The two week break that I ended up with my uncle. I wanted to die. "Just a little tired."

"Right." She flipped a sign on the door and closed it to mark she was with a patient. "Let's take a look. Go behind the partition and get out of the dance clothes and into the gown."

I didn't want to change, but I didn't want the director to boot me either. So, I stripped it down and pulled on the too thin hospital gown. I didn't want to be this exposed.

She was very nice, keeping up a gentle chatter as she went over me and my symptoms. What hurt. Where it hurt.

When she palpated my stomach, I swallowed the groan, but I couldn't hide my expression.

As soon as she got to my thighs, however...

"Emersyn," she murmured and the real horror in those words made me want to curl up into a ball and die. The rest of the exam was so humiliating and it didn't matter how kind she was. There was hemorrhaging. And there was a tear of the perineum and she needed to put a couple of stitches in.

She used a numbing agent and it helped. Fuck, that hurt more than I'd realized. Well...it also explained the blood. My period hadn't started and at the last doctor's checkup, he said it was normal because I was so small. Or something.

Only after she'd finished and helped me to sit up, did she pull a chair up and say, "Who hurt you?"

"No one." It was such a lie.

"You just came back from two weeks with your family, right?"

I closed my eyes. "It must have been something—" I tried but I couldn't come up with an excuse. Not for the bruises on my thighs or the very distinctive bite mark that had been left on the inside of my thigh right, where it joined my hip.

He'd done that the very first night and it was slow to heal.

"If someone is hurting you, you can trust me. Let me help you."

The tears wouldn't stay hidden and my throat hurt. Everything about her beckoned to me to just *trust* her. She was a doctor. They couldn't tell anyone, right?

So I did. No names. Just—what happened.

Not once could I look at her as I spoke and finally, I asked if I could get dressed.

"Of course. You're taking the next couple of days off, then only light work for another four or five after. The stitches will dissolve on their own, but let's heal that tear and the rest of you."

"But the show—"

"Will be fine and dancers get injured all the time, the director doesn't need to know why."

"Thank you," I whispered. Once I was dressed again, she gave me a hug and a small prescription bottle.

"These are for the pain, they'll also help you sleep. I want you to talk to a counselor, too...and we'll figure it all out, okay?"

The bottle clenched tightly in my hand, I nodded. I went back to my dressing room and retrieved my dance bag. The numbing agent was still helping. A lot. My car service picked me up and took me back to my hotel, where I spent the next three days sleeping.

The pills she'd given me were perfect. I didn't feel anything at all when I took them.

Four days after I spoke to her, Jane Chapman died in a car accident. It was all over the company. Everyone was shattered. She'd been so well liked.

After that—nothing changed. It was like I hadn't told anyone. Except now I had a bottle of pills that would numb me if I needed it, and the show's new doctor was more than happy to refill it when I explained it was for an as needed basis, without any explanation.

29

The next week flew past. Every day, as promised, Kellan came to get me for a driving lesson. So far, I'd actually managed to not destroy his gear shaft and I'd been able to drive circles around the industrial buildings.

I wasn't ready for the "road" yet, but soon, he promised. Every single day, I paid for my lessons with another kiss. Seriously, I was getting the better end of this deal. His kisses were drugging and addictive. They utterly destroyed my concentration and usually left me squirming in my seat.

But it was only kisses. Nothing more. He didn't touch me, except to occasionally cup my face. It was sweet and hot and distracting. I also didn't go down to meet him at the street anymore. Even if it made me crazy, I waited for him to come up.

Once or twice, Liam had been there when Kellan arrived to take me for my driving lesson. He tried to invite himself along, and Kellan just grinned.

"Sure," he'd agreed so readily, I'd been surprised. "When's your next self-defense lesson with her?"

Liam *scowled*. Flat out, glared at him. "Fine. You teach her to drive. I'll take care of the fighting."

That was that.

As for fight training, I'd been reluctant to try and hurt Liam while he was so bruised. But the fourth time he flipped me on my back and pinned me, something tore loose and I'd struck back. I got my legs around him and twisted, even as I forced my wrists to go limp and then slid out of the hold.

"That's my girl," he'd grinned as I had him on his back, my hand raised to strike. "Just like fucking that, and if you see bruises on someone, you aim for those. It'll hurt more."

"You're such an ass," I scolded him, even as I tried to catch my breath. I did not like to be held down like that and he fucking knew it.

"You're not a coward," he retaliated. "Or a mouse. You're a goddamn fighter, Hellspawn. Don't forget it. That means you fight dirty and you fight hard and you do what- ever you have to."

"You're not my enemy."

"For the moment." That warning was like a slap of icy water in my face. Suddenly, the last place I wanted to be was straddling his chest, but he gripped my hips before I could move. "Stop. Think. I'm not saying I'm your enemy."

I narrowed my eyes at him. Ever since the shooting, he'd blown hot and cold. But I hadn't slept alone once. If Rome didn't show up, I woke up to Liam in my bed. One night, he'd just put me in his and told me to stay there. I hated it, but I also hated the nightmares that had haunted me all week.

The last thing I saw in my mind before I went to sleep

was the dead waitress. I woke up screaming too. Rome or Liam would wrap me up and stroke my hair and tell me it was all okay.

"But enemies can look like friends, Hellspawn. They can look like allies. Until you are one hundred percent certain about someone, you never give them your back and you don't hesitate. Because if someone is trying to hurt you— they aren't your friend."

How right he was.

Still, I'd tried asking about the club. But he wouldn't tell me anything. Not with regard to the waitress who died or anything else. "Don't focus on that." Yes, it was the night-mares, I got that, but that wasn't the only reason I wanted to know.

When I finally demanded to know if the dancers were going to be okay while it was closed, he'd given me a puzzled look. "I'm paying them for six weeks, probably not quite as much as they'd make in tips, but enough to cover their bills. Their jobs will be there when they come back. Don't worry, Hellspawn. I take care of my people."

One thing he did struck me as odd though. Well, I supposed it should be the one thing he didn't. We never discussed the dance that led to him ordering me off the stage or the kiss we'd shared before the world went side-ways. Honestly, I had no idea if I liked that or not. With all the other insanity they seemed to be trying to shield me from, I didn't want to tip the balance.

Freddie texted daily. Rome, I saw often. Kellan came by frequently and it was rare that I didn't see Liam. Jasper had been very absent, but Kel only told me that Jasper was with Milo.

There was another absence, since I'd chosen to go back to Liam's, Milo had merely agreed and I hadn't seen him since. Mickey had only texted me to say he was bringing the results over. I thought that meant he'd come to see me.

He hadn't.

The results had been left with the doorman and sat unopened on the dresser in my room.

Vaughn had managed to come by a couple of times, but he needed to be available for the guys. He promised they were all safe and told me nothing else.

Secrets.

Lies.

More secrets.

At least they were being honest that they had secrets, I supposed. As for my dance studio, that had been off limits for the last four days. No arguments. I made up for it at the gym when Liam took me to train. I finally figured out he owned the place. It was why we could go whenever we wanted, and it was always emptied out just for us.

Under that gruff, steely exterior was a man who truly did care about the people around him, from his community to his employees, to his friends.

The Vandals were still his friends. They couldn't prove it to me otherwise.

The phone rang and I glanced up from where I'd been stretching and rolled to my feet. So far, the only people who called on the landline was the doorman or the security in the lobby.

I checked the caller ID and yep, it was the lobby. "Yes?" I asked when I answered.

"We have a delivery down here. Would you like us to hold it or have them bring it up?"

Delivery. "What kind of delivery?"

"One moment, ma'am." The phone muffled.

Liam didn't want me to open the door to any deliveries.

I could authorize them to bring it up, but have them leave it at the door. He'd received a couple for him while I'd been alone. I'd just taken the boxes to his room and left them without comment. While I didn't ask, he certainly didn't tell.

"The gentleman said he's brought three glazed, three chocolate covered, a half dozen with sprinkles, and the salted variety you requested."

I couldn't help the grin spreading across my face at that description, or the fact I wanted to laugh in delight. "Please, send him up."

"Yes, ma'am."

The call disconnected and I half-bounced, skipped over to the door and watched through the peephole. It was a couple of minutes before the elevator dinged open and a delivery man stepped out. From his blue "uniform" to his cap, he looked like every nondescript deliveryman I'd ever seen. As promised, he was carrying a large white box.

Then he faced the door and pair of amused gray eyes twinkled. He'd trimmed his beard, but his bruises seemed to have become a thing of a past. Excitement flooded me as I doubled back to the security panel and entered the code. I opened the door to find Jasper grinning wide as he held up the box.

"Donuts for the lady?"

The smell of them was almost as delicious as Jasper himself. I took the box from him and stepped back so he could slip inside. Without opening the box, I slid it onto the table and then turned. I couldn't really tell who reached for who first, but I wrapped my arms around him and yanked off the cap as his mouth claimed mine.

His tongue sought and demanded entrance. I sucked on it as his beard rubbed against my cheeks. The closer trim was soft as hell, but I found myself missing some of the thickness. The weight of his erection pressed through his uniform and he walked the three steps to the dining room table and shoved everything back so he could perch me on it.

Head lifted, Jasper eyed me. "Missed me, Swan?"

Dragging the zipper on his uniform down, I grinned at the t-shirt beneath it, that looked to be all but spray-painted on his muscles. He shrugged it off his shoulders and when I teased my nails under his shirt, he dragged that up and off and then I was staring at the wall of muscle.

Fresh bruises marred his skin in places and there was a bandage over his side. I traced my fingers from one mark to the next as he pushed my thighs apart to get closer to me, but I locked my legs around him and held him back just a step.

"It's fine," he whispered. "I promise."

"How many stitches?"

"Just five."

"That's not fine, Jasper," I informed him.

"Can't even feel them," he assured me, as I went for the button on his jeans and loosened them. I caught him watching me as I gave him a careful nudge back and then hopped off the table. I kissed every bruise as I lowered the zipper on his pants.

Making no move to stop me, Jasper murmured, "What are you doing?"

"Hmm, delivery promised me the salted ones that I liked." I dropped to my knees as I dragged his jeans down, along with the form fitting boxer briefs he had on. His cock was already hard and extended. The vein beneath it pulsed and the musky scent of him was something I'd missed.

Had it really been weeks since our night?

I wrapped my hand around him, swirling my thumb over the tip as I began to suck one of his balls and then the other.

"Fucking Christ," Jasper swore and his hands slammed down onto the table. Then I began to lick up his shaft, teasing that vein and I swore his dick grew even harder. Another strangled noise escaped him, and I smiled as I alternated between licks and sucking kisses until I reached the tip.

I lapped at his slit like it was a lollipop and when I met his gaze, his pupils had almost swallowed the gray. Need burned in those eyes. Jasper had said he loved me. Those words echoed in my mind as I opened my mouth and swallowed him against my throat.

Another litany of swear words escaped him as I began to move. This was what I'd wanted to do for him since that night, but he'd said no or not yet, and then he'd pounded into me until we saw stars together. But here he was, letting me do as I wished, and I thrilled at his every response. I cupped his balls and began to stroke him and used my free hand to add to the pressure on his cock. I couldn't quite get all of him down my throat, but I was trying.

Strain bulged at the muscles in his neck and the tick in his cheek. He hadn't touched me yet and I was already soaking for him. Still, I kept up the pressure, licking and tasting. The salty drops of precum were perfect. Loosening from his dick with a bit of a pop, I grinned up at him.

"Jasper," I whispered. "You can fuck my mouth if you want to."

I worried a bit for the wood of the table as the muscles in his arms flexed. "Swan, I don't know if I can be gentle."

"And you know I don't care." How many times did I have to tell him this?

"But I do," he said and with a hand that trembled, he smoothed it over my hair. "So, you can suck me off because you want to, but please don't ask me to risk hurting you. I can't do it."

I melted. "I won't. I'll never make you do something you don't want to do. I promise." Then I stroked his cock once more before I said, "Do you still want this? Or do you want..."

"You can have me any way you want," he promised, and I swirled my tongue over the head of his cock once more. Maybe if I could show him that he could handle it, that I could—so I sucked him back into my throat and kept my eyes focused upward. I deepened the thrusts, bringing tears to my own eyes as I increased the speed and the friction.

His hips gave an involuntary jerk and then another, and I took my cues from the intensity in his gaze and the way his whole body seemed to coil. An elongated fuck escaped him and he came, slamming his fist against the table as the first hot splash of cum flooded my mouth.

I had enormous control over my gag reflex, but the rush of salty fluid almost choked me and I loved every fucking minute of it. When he sagged, shaking, I kissed his cock and then leaned back and licked my lips.

"Swan," he said in a ragged tone I'd never heard from him before. "I hope you're ready for what comes next."

He didn't explain, merely picked me up off the floor. My dance shorts hit the floor along with my panties. I was tugging off my dance tank even as he set me back on the table. The wood was cold against my ass.

"Jasper this is..." The rest of the sentence died unspoken as he pulled up a chair, hooked my legs over his shoulders and buried his face in my cunt. What he meant by next, was a storm of orgasms, as he all but devoured me.

This was Liam's table, some distant part of my mind protested, but my body was having none of it as I ground my cunt against Jasper's face. When he wasn't thrusting his tongue into me, he was sucking on my clit. A ragged scream tore free as I crashed from one orgasm into the next. Jasper was relentless and I flailed a little, it was like I couldn't control anything.

The world narrowed down to the loving tribute he paid to my pussy, and I bucked up against his mouth and each time he would let up just a little to let me calm down, he would run his hands over my breasts, teasing and tweaking the nipples. I was so damn gone on this.

"Jasper—" I couldn't breathe. "Fuck. Fuck, Fuck."

"With pleasure," he teased and rose. My legs trembled and the respite was welcome. Sweat soaked my skin and Jasper's whole face glistened. Then he hauled my ass along the wood before slamming his dick home and I came with another scream. "That's it," he encouraged me as he thrust deeper. "Come for me again."

I didn't think it was possible.

I was wrong.

Eventually, he relented and gave me a break. He sat in a chair with me sprawled against his chest, my legs hanging down either side of him as I straddled his lap. His cock was still inside of me and we were a mess of fluids. Sticky. Sweaty. Perfect.

Trailing his fingers up and down my back, he let out a long sigh. "I didn't think I'd have this with you again," he admitted.

"Sex?" I wasn't firing on all cylinders at the moment. Boneless. Replete.

Safe whispered a little voice in the back of my mind and I had to agree with it. Dark and dangerous as these guys might be, that sense of safety just grew the longer I was around them. Safer than I'd ever been, except when I was with Lainey, and that had always been a risk.

"Yes, brat, sex. I never thought you'd fuck me again." The dry tone just made me giggle and I finally managed to lift my head and meet his gaze. "No," he continued in a more solemn voice. "This—trust from you. I thought I'd broken it and lost you when we came home to Milo being there."

"It sucked," I admitted. "Not going to lie, and I still can't wrap my mind around it. Part of me thinks you should have told me, but I know I wouldn't have believed you."

With care, he brushed the hair back from my face. "Do you believe us now?"

"That you're sorry I found out that way?" Yes, I played dumb, but then closed my eyes for a minute. Naked or not, I could handle this. "I believe you believe it. I believe—part of me wants to believe it. I'm terrified that it's true though."

Concern filled his expression. "Why?"

So many reasons. "Can you tell me what's going on with the Vandals? What has all of you so worried and busy?"

Part of me wrestled even with asking. Did I want to know? The simplest answer was yes. I wanted to know because... I wanted to help. Not that I had any idea how.

"Yes, there's a lot going on," he said slowly. "More than I can tell you right now. No, it's not because I don't trust you. I do. But it's safer for you not to know. Someday—someday I hope soon, we'll have it sorted and then I can tell you. Trust me?"

Maybe I was insane to say yes, but I nodded. "I trust you." I had even, when I wrestled with the idea of the lie and the betrayal. "I just want to help."

"You help every day just by staying safe. Fuck, my beautiful swan, I do not know what I would do if something happened to you. When we got word of that shooting..."

"I'm fine," I reminded him and leaned back a little so he could see me. "See, the only bruises I have are from training and they aren't even that bad. Liam took the worst of it. Not only from the first shots, but the ones that came after and he was covering me—he protected me."

Jasper cradled my face in his large hands and then pressed the gentlest of kisses to my lips. "I'll be sure to thank the son of a bitch profusely and let him have the first hit next time."

I laughed. "You two are awful to each other."

"It is what it is, but he protected you. And you seem to like him." The last few words sounded a little distasteful to him.

"I do like him," I admitted. "He doesn't treat me like I'm going to break." Which was more important than I'd realized. "He's also showing me things, like how to break a man's thumb and to get out of a hold if someone a lot bigger than me has me pinned."

He'd been showing me a few other tricks, too. Some of which I couldn't actually imagine doing to another human being, but I wasn't going to not try to learn it all.

"Fine," Jasper grunted. "Two hits and I won't hit him first—for at least a week."

I rolled my eyes, but it was a concession and I kissed him. "Thank you."

"You're welcome." His voice tightened as I squeezed his cock, he was waking up. Though he'd almost slipped free, there was no mistaking the thickening pressing against my swollen flesh.

"Doc—sent me the blood test results."

"And?" One syllable. One question. No judgment.

"I haven't opened them." Admitting that made me feel a little small.

"Milo would cut off his arm before he hurt you, Emersyn." The gentle certainty was kind, especially considering Milo's reaction to him when we came back. "If I know anything about love at all, it's from watching him love you."

"I've only ever known one person who loved me without conditions or expectations." I didn't mean to say it, but it came out that way.

"Well now you know more," he said with the kind of certainty I wanted to grab hold of and never let go. "Though I'm curious about this other person."

"Maybe I'll introduce you someday."

"I'd like that." The fact he kept rubbing my back made me sleepy but also just—loved, and we could have sat at this table like this the rest of the day but it couldn't be comfortable. "You want to tell me what happened with Doc?"

"What?" That question seemed to come out of left field.

"You are usually soft with him and glance at him for things, but at the clubhouse the other day, you wouldn't even look at him."

Oh.

"Did he do something...?" He let that hang there but I shook my head.

"A lot happened with Doc, but I can't tell you yet." Using his own answer earned me a mock scowl. No, he didn't like it, but there was no anger in his eyes. "No, before you ask—I don't want to talk about that."

He sighed. "Fine, one more question, then I'm going to spread you out on this table again. I'm hungry for some pretty pussy."

"Oh, just some?"

That earned me a pinch and I laughed. "Funny girl."

"I can be."

"Agreed." Then he sobered. "Why did you come back here? To Liam's? Why not stay at the clubhouse when—"

The door behind him opened and I glanced up to find Liam walking in. He didn't even look all that surprised, considering I was impaled on Jasper's dick and naked. "Get dressed, Hellspawn. We have a lesson."

"Fuck that," Jasper answered for me. "We're a little busy."

"With your bare ass on *my* dining room chairs," Liam said with a snap. "Not that anyone asked you. Let's go, Hellspawn. I'm sure you can finish bouncing on his dick later. He's been here for hours, if he hasn't gotten you off by now, he isn't going to."

"Like you'd know," Jasper retorted, then glanced at me. "Right. Keeping it nice. I've managed to pull about a half-dozen orgasms out of her. I'll happily give her a few more." He flexed his hips upward and seated himself deeply again. I gripped his shoulder as a gasp escaped.

One thing I'd been discovering between Jasper and Vaughn, when they came back for seconds or thirds, I was so much more sensitive.

"And as excited as I am not, Hellspawn and I have a deal."

We did. I kissed Jasper lightly. "Sorry, he's right..."

With a groan, Jasper gave me a little lift off his dick and a rush of wetness slid down my legs. It really should have embarrassed me that not only Jasper seemed fixed on the cum dripping down my thighs, but so did Liam. "I'm going to grab a quick shower."

Jasper licked his lips. "Take your time, I'll sort this out with Liam and go along..."

"The fuck you will," Liam said. "You can put your dick away, get dressed and get out. The doorman was concerned that the fucking deliveryman came up and didn't leave."

I winced. "I'll hurry."

But I wasn't a factor in this conversation anymore. They were glaring at each other as Jasper took his time standing and pulling up his pants. Fuck, he hadn't even taken off his shoes.

As fast as I was, it still took me about fifteen minutes to clean up and get dressed in fresh clothes. When I came back out, Jasper and Liam were cutting at each other verbally.

At least it wasn't fists.

That seemed good.

Thirty minutes later, we still hadn't left and they were still fighting.

When we hit an hour, I texted Vaughn for rescue. I didn't think either of them would stop. They were trying so hard to push the other into taking a swing. Or maybe they were just enjoying the fight. Either way, I was done. Vaughn answered a couple of minutes later that he was at work, but give him a few and he'd come and get me.

It was another hour before Vaughn got there, he texted me he was outside and I told him I'd be right down.

Rising, I snagged my backpack and headed for the door.

"Where the hell are you going?" Liam demanded, as I opened the door.

"Out," I said, glancing from him to Jasper and back. "Clearly you two have some issues you need to work out and Vaughn is downstairs waiting for me. I won't be alone and you'll know how to find me."

They were still staring at me, slack-jawed, when the

elevator arrived. I blew them a kiss and stepped inside. As soon as the doors closed, I sagged back against the wall.

I flipped a mental coin on who hit who first as soon as I was out of sight.

My money was on Liam.

PREY

No one at the group home even batted an eyelash when I disappeared anymore. The guys covered for me, they always did, but even the gatekeepers at the door just looked the other way when I left.

I always came back.

It took time to find the right canvas and after a week, I'd found the highway underpass below 40th and Warrington. It was deep in the old industrial center that had been gradually changing. Old buildings were being purchased, repurposed, and turned into lofts above with shops below.

Gentrification was the word.

Liam thought it would be cool if we got one someday just for me. A place I could paint and have all the room I wanted.

I didn't need a building for that. I had a whole city of them. But Liam liked to dream and I liked that he did.

It took time to get to the location though and even on my bike, it could take up to an hour depending on when I left. But I'd found a faster route and it shaved fifteen minutes off my ride, which gave me more time with the underpass.

Dark, the few and far between street lights, didn't penetrate the shadow under the bridge. So, I had to do a lot of work from memory. I'd duct taped a flashlight to the top of a helmet and used it to give me a better view.

Every night for a week, I'd spent every hour I could manage under this bridge. The birds took time and depth to get their feathering right, particularly in the form they would be in when I finished. I never started in the same place I left off. Each night, a new bit of it would come to life. An arm. A leg. The wings unfurled. Some with them tucked close. The swirl of birds coming to life...

A glass bottle skated over the asphalt, the tinkling noise carrying in the dark silence of the night, louder than the hiss of my cans of spray paint. The muttering of a profanity followed, only to be cut off abruptly. Nothing changed my actions, I finished the section of wing I'd been working on and then took a step back, as though studying it.

The noises in this part of town had grown very familiar over the past week. Skittering bottles and hushed steps didn't fit. Old Martin and Jefferson Two Blades were the only pair who made regular use of the underpass. Homeless old drunks with issues I didn't understand.

I always left them food or cash when I came to work. It was their place. They left me alone and I did them the same courtesy. They were also over at the shelter two blocks away, having scored beds for the night 'cause they wanted to shower.

So, I *had* been alone under the bridge.

Even the tension in the air shifted with the new arrivals.

Multiple.

Moving with stealth. Or attempting it.

Setting the paint can down, I crouched toward my backpack to switch out what I was using and turned off the flashlight. Eyes closed, I let myself get used to the sudden darkness swallowing me and crept away from my spot on silent feet.

Unlike my guests, I knew every crevice in the broken cement. Step on a crack, break a mother fucker's back. Kick a stone, die alone. Strike first, avoid the worst. There were a few dozen others. Jasper and Liam used to make them up on the fly.

But they were good lessons.

Lessons that kept us alive. Three steps to my left and then I was behind one of the concrete columns that served as one of the bridge's piers. Once there, I closed the bag silently then slid it on.

I carried a knife, but I needed to know if they were armed or not. Fists would be faster. Once my backpack was secure, I crouched down to listen. Keeping my eyes at the ground, kept me from being blinded when light suddenly flooded the underpass.

"Spread out," a male voice ordered. Someone checked the magazine on their gun. The slide and clip back into place was almost as loud as a gunshot. "Alive, fucknut. They want him alive."

I did not have to extend the same courtesy. My phone vibrated in my back pocket. But I ignored it. If I turned it on, the light might give me away.

"Alive only means breathing, right?" A new voice. This one came from farther away.

"Stop fucking around," the first guy ordered. "He was just here. If Four hadn't hit the damn bottle..."

"Mac didn't mean to..."

"Numbers, Jackass." Flesh pounded flesh and a grunt of pain followed. "No names."

Still, they weren't venturing closer.

The report of a gun was loud and ricocheted off the walls around me, much like the bullet that sparked on the concrete abutment and flung off to bounce again.

"What the fuck are you doing?"

"You said alive," came a new, deadlier voice. There was the threat. "You didn't say not bleeding. Flushing him out."

Then a half-dozen guns went off, and I kept pressed my fingers inside my ear a split-second before the noise rose to deafening. Sparks. Bouncing bullets. Violent noise. Something hot sliced over my side, but I said nothing and ignored it.

The firing stopped almost as soon as it began.

The vibrating in my pocket had stopped. With care, I glanced around the edge of the column. Five men, more like shadows I couldn't make out, were backlit by a set of headlights.

I didn't see the sixth. From where they were to where I was, I couldn't move without being spotted.

A shoe scuffed to my left and the sixth man came around the column, but he didn't look down.

Not before I came straight up, grasping his wrist where he held the gun. One hard uppercut slammed his teeth together. Then I smashed his gun into his face. His nose erupted in a bloody spurt and he dropped to the ground. It was over in ten seconds. Now I had a gun.

"Did you hear that?"

"We all heard that."

"Where did it come from?"

"Shut up." The first voice growled. The one who'd given

the order to spread out. I appreciated them talking though, it told me how far away they were.

Another gun went off, farther away still and one of the headlights popped. The shattering of glass startled them and I glanced out to see them turning away. Without hesitating, I aimed for the other headlight and fired.

The gun would deafen me briefly, but I had a mental snapshot of where everyone was and I was already running as we plunged back into darkness. Across to the other side, behind another concrete pier for the highway. Bullets flashed in the darkness. I stayed low, tracking where the flashes went off.

They didn't move from their positions.

Stupid.

Two of them let out shouts and then the firing from those positions stopped abruptly.

"Fuck," the pissed off one who'd started firing in the first place swore and I tracked by his voice, arm steady and fired low. Two shots in rapid succession. He screamed.

The sound was that of a wounded animal braying and I was already rolling and moving away in the darkness. My eyes were adapting to the dark, I could make out the motion of indistinct figures, two stationary, one on the ground and a fourth one approaching at a run from behind the car.

He would go for the guy on the right. He *always* went for the guy on the right first. So, I went for the guy on *my* right. We hit at the same time. His managed to fire a gun but was down, a moment later, the brutal snap of a neck echoing as I choked the life out of mine. He clawed at my arms but I didn't let him go, and eventually even that fight went out of him and he was down.

"You're late," I told Liam.

"Answer your phone next time," he snapped back.

A groan and a curse pulled our attention. Liam had his phone out, flashlight on and walked over to the guy on the ground. He was bleeding—heavily. His kneecap looked to be almost gone and his face was ashen under the light.

Liam pointed his gun at him. "Name?"

"Numbers," I said. "Mac's dead, he was four." This guy wasn't Mac. This was the one who wanted to flush me out.

"Name," Liam repeated, not looking away from the guy on the ground.

"Fuck you," the man swore, spittle flying.

Liam stepped on his bloodied knee and the man howled in agony. I pulled out my own flashlight and scanned the area. The first guy I'd only knocked out. But he was dead when I got to him. Probably one of the bouncing bullets.

Two had torn into his back and a third took off the side of his head. Too bad. Turning away, I stared at my painting. Bullets had dinged it. Chipping away at paint and concrete alike.

It would be a while before I could come back and fix it.

Another scream came from the guy, and then Liam fired his gun. Right into the other leg.

"Last chance. You still have fingers, wrists, elbows and shoulders. I'll put a bullet in every single one." Every word from my mirror was a cold promise. I rejoined them. At that rate, he would need the gun I collected. "Name who sent you and you die quick. Keep his secrets and you die in agony."

"Fuck you."

"Not polite enough." He pinned a hand with his foot and shot off the guy's thumb.

Shock had to be keeping him from feeling it too much

cause he was still awake, but the blood loss would kill him sooner or later.

It took two more fingers before he finally said, "The King sent us. The King. We're just pawns. This was our pledge...just wanted him. Alive."

"Understood." Then Liam made good on his promise and put a bullet in his head. The night was awkwardly silent and despite all of the noise, not a single flashing light anywhere. My brother turned to me and frowned. "You're bleeding."

"Scratch." I waved him off. "You're in danger." I knew who the king was supposed to be.

"No," he said with a shake of his head. "This was a test. He wants leverage. It's time he learned what I'll do."

I nodded. "Need help?"

"No." He gripped my shoulder, then lifted my shirt to look at the wound. "That's more than a scratch."

"They're dead. I'm alive. It's a scratch." I held out the gun. "Took from the guy back there. He's dead too."

Liam nodded. "Go back to the group home. Do me a favor, stick close to the guys for a few days while I take care of this."

I couldn't come back here for a while anyway. I glanced at my painting again.

"Sorry, brother."

"I'll fix her." Later. "What message do you want to send?"

"Touch my brother and I'll burn his world down. Starting with these corpses. Now go."

"I can help."

"Not this time."

"Stubborn," I pointed out.

"Fuck you," he retorted. "Go."

I was almost to my bike when he called, "Next time answer your fucking phone."

I just flipped him off. The ride back was uncomfortable. My side really burned, the pain radiating by the time I got to the group home.

Milo and Jasper met me at the door and got me in quiet. They also insisted on looking at my wound before they woke Vaughn up. He waited for me to shower then cleaned it, stitched it and put a bandage over it.

"Don't worry," Vaughn told me. "We can tattoo it later. It'll be bad ass."

I wasn't worried. But I liked the idea of a tattoo.

What I didn't like was the tenor of fear in Liam's voice about them coming after me. I just had to make sure no one ever took me. I wouldn't let them hurt him that way.

Ever.

30

Vaughn hadn't been kidding about ducking out of work to get me. Instead of going back to the club-house, he took me to the ink shop where he worked. Best. Distraction. Ever. The whole building he worked in was gorgeous. It might be a squat little strip mall with a cracked asphalt paved parking lot, where the white lines for the slots were so faded they might as well not be there at all, but the building itself was a splash of wild color and life amidst a gray and gloomy backdrop.

Inside, it was everything I imagined a tattoo parlor would be. Dark, comfortable lounge area at the front with black leather sofas and chairs. There was a gorgeous fish tank full of colorful little buggers. The art on the walls—so many designs to look at. Vaughn chuckled as I paused at every single one to look at them.

"Like those, Dove?" he asked and I grinned.

"I love them. I've always wanted a tattoo...but you know I wasn't old enough and then there were the costumes and the one time I got a temporary, I swear Marta had an aneurism."

"The stuffy old battle axe bitch?" He leaned against the wall and folded his arms. The indulgent expression on his face warmed me from head to toe.

"Well, I would never have said that to her face. But yes, her." I sighed a little. "She was my chaperone. In charge of making sure I did my homeschooling and that I didn't get into any trouble."

"The cunt was shit at her job."

I shrugged. "It wasn't her job to like me or be my friend." I paused at a whole frame filled with different sayings. "Spoiled brats like me, who are indulged by the world around them, need a firm hand, and that was her. She was also paid to make sure I didn't make friends."

"What the fuck?"

I winced. I hadn't quite meant to share that part, but still... I glanced over to find him scowling.

"I knew you didn't hang out with any of the other dancers, except the prick, and even him you were avoiding." Yes, by then, I had been. The year before?

"Eric was kind of my fault," I admitted. "He wanted me, and he was sweet for a while. And I thought I could have something of my own."

Cupping my neck, Vaughn pulled me from the picture to face him. For such a huge man, he was infinitely gentle. "Nothing about that prick was your fault."

Head tilted back, I sighed. "I led him on..."

"Dove, I don't care if you stripped down and sat on his face until he couldn't breathe. When you said no, it was done. When he hurt you the first time, it was done. It didn't stop him from fucking every other girl in that show."

That, I also knew about.

"It's done now."

"Right." He stroked his thumb along my neck. There were people talking in the back and the girl sitting at the reception desk didn't even look over at us. It was kind of nice to be so anonymous, where the only person who saw me was him. "Tell me what tattoo you want and I'll do it right now."

"Really?" Surprise fountained through me. "Right now?"

"Hell, we can do it any time you want." Then he slid his hand from my nape to my face. "No one else is putting a single mark on this skin except me."

I raised my brows.

He chuckled. "Fine, no one else is inking this skin except me. I can handle you with Jasper or Rome, but outside of the Vandals, no one else."

"What about Liam?" Because he'd kissed me twice now...

"I don't care what the rest of those assholes say or what plan Milo has up his sleeve, Liam never stopped being one of us." Then he leaned down and brushed his lips against mine. "Doc counts too."

An ache opened up inside of me at that, and I gave a little shrug. "Doc doesn't want to want me. So no worries there."

"Doc can be an idiot sometimes," he murmured, then gave me another kiss before turning me around to rest with my back to his chest. "What do you want, Dove?"

There were so many options. "Would you choose for me?"

"You don't want to pick your own?"

"I want them all," I admitted. "But I also want it to be special. My first one should be..." Pushing the next words out took real effort. "I've lost out on so many firsts. I want this one to matter. If you pick it for me cause I asked, and you do it—then I get to decide and you'll make it special."

The lump in my throat hurt and the words left behind an ashy residue. Trust was hard.

"Come on," he whispered and guided me back to a room. He unlocked the door and inside it was so—

"Wow." The walls were one long mural of art and there were birds in every part of it, flying, diving, some just sitting proud and watchful, but it was what was in the birds —the skyline of the city. "Rome."

It wasn't even a question.

"Most of it." He stroked his hand down my back, as he nudged me over to the chair. "I helped with the design, then let him loose."

That sounded wonderful. "I love watching him paint."

"It's something else, right?"

I perched on the chair, set my backpack down and nodded. Vaughn moved around the room, setting stuff up and then nudged the door closed. Some of the others had been open in the hall and you could hear the buzzing of their machines, but I hadn't been looking.

"It really is," I said, torn between studying the wall and studying him. Everything about him should terrify me. Huge hands. Big muscles. Built so solid. Yet, he was so fucking gentle with me, his touches felt good and they never hurt.

Facing me, he studied me for a long moment.

"What?" Curiosity swelled up.

"Do I get to decide where to put it?"

Fair question. I chewed on my lower lip. "I want to be able to see it, but—I have to be able to hide it too."

"So, something only your lovers will know," he

murmured more to himself than me, and I shivered. My lovers.

He was right. I had more than one. "Yes please."

"Take off your shirt for me, Dove?"

I raised my brows.

"If I do it, I'm going to keep going until I have your cunt out, so I can lick up every juice I know you have to have soaking you."

Holy shit, my pussy clenched at the description.

"And I'm not fucking you here. Your moans and orgasms are not for public consumption."

Another wash of heat went through me, but I stripped the shirt up and over. The bra I had on was just a sports one, more because I got hot when Liam and I did fight training than because my breasts really needed it. Though they had gotten a little bigger lately.

Clearing my throat, I motioned to my bra. "On or off."

He ran his tongue over his lower lip and all I could think about was doing the same. "On," he said with a groan then shook his head. "But you're coming back to the clubhouse tonight and you're sleeping in my fucking bed, or I'm staying with you."

"Deal."

That decided, he had me settle back in the chair and he laid it down. "If at any point you need a break or you want to just take a moment, you tell me." The order settled into my bones. "We have all day and all night, Dove. No rushing this."

"I adore you," I whispered, and he shot me a look. The sheer pleasure in his eyes made me happier. I should tell him more often.

"Right back atcha, beautiful." Then he went to work, he used something to clean my belly, in fact, he was focused on my belly button and my abs. I focused on staying relaxed, but it kind of tickled. "So, Marta was your chaperone," he said. "Why weren't your parents ever with you on the road? Don't they get into that kind of thing?"

"Sometimes. But they're very busy and have business and Mother has all of her charities and functions. In the beginning they used to come to the shows, but as I got busier, so did they."

"Huh." He blew across the coolness on my skin from the cleaner and I shivered. My nipples pebbled up so tight they ached and considering how deep inside of me Jasper had been earlier, I shouldn't be this wound up. "That's fucked up. Then again, we came to every show we could when you were nearby."

I swallowed at that. "All of them?"

"As many as we could. Tickets weren't cheap, sometimes we could only get enough money for Milo to go, but he never missed one. This is going to sting a little, ready?"

At my nod, he turned on the machine and it began to hum. The sting was there as he went to work. It was like a light knife carving into my flesh, but it didn't *hurt*. I'd known real pain. This was just an irritation and not even that. Not really.

This was me getting something I'd always wanted, from a man I adored, and that knowledge flooded my system.

"I was really close with my mom," Vaughn said as he worked. "She was the best person ever. But she'd been diagnosed with cancer before I was even born. They told her not to have me, she told them to go fuck themselves."

A laugh escaped him.

"Probably not in those words." He was so intent on what he was doing. "But she was great. Every day was an adventure. Even when she got so sick she couldn't get out of bed. I'd sit there and read to her, like she used to read to me. We were a team. Somewhere along the way, I was doing more for her than she could do for herself. I was always a big kid, and it was a blessing."

He glanced up at me and I nodded. "Because you could help her."

"Yep. Lots of kids that age, they're super scrawny, but I wasn't and I could lift her and carry her if I had to. But she kept getting sicker." A sigh escaped him, and tears burned in my eyes. "Whatever they were doing wasn't helping. One night, she sat me down and told me what was going to happen. That she had to go to hospice and we'd done our very best. The next day was when I met Ms. Stephanie."

I couldn't stop the tears that escaped and I swiped at them.

"Mom—you'd have liked her," he told me in a certain voice. "She would have loved you."

"I wish I could have met her. She sounds amazing. I can't imagine my mother reading me a story, much less..."

The machine's whirring paused and he looked at me. "Your parents suck."

I laughed, because oh my god, those words. "They love me, I think—in their own ways. They're just not demonstrative. They buy me things, make it possible for me to pursue my dreams."

"They let you go when you were eight, to grow up around strangers with a bitch for a chaperone and no friends. Sorry, Dove. They suck."

Yeah.

They did.

"They tried," I said softly. Not sure if I meant those words for him or for me. To be honest, "I just don't think they knew how to be parents." There were times when I was almost certain they hadn't wanted me, but I'd been an obligation but now...

Now if those test results said Milo was really my brother, a fact I'd already begun to accept, and I had been adopted, then they must have wanted me at some point, right?

"They weren't perfect," I admitted. "They were never there when I really needed them. Then I learned to not need them, and it was better. I think they'd care if something happened to me. I saw on the news they were still looking."

"Right," he agreed, head bent to his work. "Nothing says love like a quarter of a million for any information leading to locating your whereabouts."

I supposed.

"Dove," he continued. "I'm sorry they sucked. You deserved a hell of a lot better. That was what Milo wanted for you. What—they all wanted for you. But we aren't what has happened to us."

Another pause as he glanced up and the near topaz brown of his eyes held me riveted.

"We're just not. Losing my mom and going into the system sucked, but I found a family in my brothers. Orphan isn't who I am—it's just—a part of my past. We get to choose who we want to be. No one else. Just you. Just me."

"I kind of love that—but I don't always know who I am or who I want to be. Just that I had to get away and stay far away."

His hand was cool against my side as he dabbed the tattoo to take care of the welling blood, before returning to it. "When I look at you, all I see is beauty, grace, and a ferocious need to survive."

"When I look at you," I answered. "I see strength, kindness—and dedication to those you care about. I see safety and...power. All of it in this gorgeous package of tattooed skin and muscles, that just make me want to bite you."

"Soon," he said with a wink. "You can bite me all you want."

A shiver raced through me. It took him only a few more minutes and then he was done. My first tattoo, and when he held up the mirror so I could see, more tears escaped.

Head up was written in a half circle above my belly button in the most gorgeous script.

Wings out was written below it, forming a circle. It was —beautiful. There was a falcon launching from the t on *out* and it curved upward, keeping to the circle, while on the left side there was a hawk diving.

Hawk and Falcon.

They were perfect.

"What do you think?"

"I think I want to go back to the clubhouse and..."

His grin grew. "One sec, Dove, let's get you all set up so this heals." His fingers were so gentle as he cleaned it then applied this ointment, before covering it. "Thank you," he said after he helped me get back into my shirt and gave me a kiss.

"For what?"

"For sharing your first with me."

My heart squeezed so tight at that, and I bit down on his lower lip just like I'd been wanting to for a while. "Thank you." Because I had my first tattoo. My body. My choice. My gift to us.

"Vaughn, I need you."

He cleaned up in record time and then we were out of the parlor and back in his car. Even the sting of the tattoo across my abs didn't dissuade me. I wanted to be with him, and I wanted his cock right now.

The three-minute ride back to the clubhouse seemed to take forever. Thankfully, no one seemed to be around when we got there. We were all over each other as we got to his room, shedding clothes and going for lingering kisses in between every touch.

Vaughn sprawled on his bed and beckoned to me. "Come sit on my face, Dove. Give me that pussy."

If I hadn't already been soaked, that would have flooded me with wanton need. As it was, the dampness was already beginning to trickle down my inner thighs. I crawled up the bed and straddled his face.

"Hello, beauty," he murmured and then speared me with his tongue. With gentle hands he guided me into grinding against his tongue, teeth, and lips. Alternating between long sucking pulls on my clit, he drove me right up to the edge. The door to his room opened with a light knock and I glanced over my shoulder.

Rome stood framed in the doorway. He came the rest of the way in and locked the door.

"Hi," I greeted him, almost breathlessly. It was hard to focus with Vaughn tongue fucking me.

"Starling." He moved up to the head of the bed. When he knelt we were face to face and I swore it just spurred Vaughn harder and he pressed two fingers inside of me.

I dropped my head, trying to fight the sensations spiraling out. Rome brushed his fingers under my chin and lifted it.

Fuck. Fuck.

His beautiful face seemed to swim as the coiling tension drove me to madness, and then Vaughn sucked my clit against his teeth as he curved his fingers inside of me. The effect detonated my orgasm and Rome captured my lips with his, as I began to cry out.

He swallowed, licked and sucked every sound right from my lips. It was an echo of Vaughn's tongue inside of me. The kiss and the orgasm went on and on. I caught Rome's hand and moved it to my breast. He toyed with the nipple gently and then trailed his kiss down to suck it against his teeth. The sting just added to the feeling.

"Shift," Vaughn ordered as he lifted my boneless body and urged me to turn over. "Hands and knees, Dove. Look up at Rome."

That was not a hard command to follow. Even in the low light of the room, the way his eyes glittered filled me with want.

"Fuck her mouth, Rome," Vaughn said. "She likes the taste of cock, don't you Dove." He kept his hands at my sides, stroking over my hips and then down the back of my thighs.

"Yours," I admitted. "I like yours. I like Jasper's" Then I stared up at Rome. "Can I suck you off?"

The question triggered action and Rome shed his clothes, stripping all the way down until I could see even his gorgeous—oh my fucking god—it was tattooed. There was a dancer on his dick. Behind me, Vaughn held still, just stroking my hips, as I lifted a hand to touch Rome's cock.

"May I?"

"For you," Rome whispered and it sounded like a promise. Vaughn kissed my lower back, and I swore he was both teasing and soothing me in equal measure. It was me—he'd had me tattooed on his dick. It was me in the silks, back arched, legs up, in mid-flight.

I stroked every inch of the thick tattooed skin and then traced my tongue over the tip. He gave a shudder and slid his fingers into my hair. With the lightest of tugs, he pulled my gaze up to his again.

"Open your mouth, Starling—tell me if I need to stop. I've never done this before."

Shock flooded me, but there was no time to ponder because Rome thrust his dick against my throat, pushing deep until I was gagging on him. In the same moment, Vaughn thrust into my already swollen pussy and the combination of his piercings and the strength of his thrusts, tumbled me swiftly toward orgasm.

I rocked my hips back, flexing and squeezing at the monster dick that stretched me, all the while I concentrated on Rome. He wanted the control, and the speed, and I gave it to him.

Sucking hard, I ran my tongue over Rome's cock as he shifted around, thrusting deep and hard, sometimes backing off and then going again. He was looking for what he liked, so I changed how I licked and sucked until he let out a harsh guttural sound.

There.

Fuck, I could barely think as Vaughn pounded into me and Rome rocked his hips, his thrusts growing more forceful. Every single one pushed him into my throat and I convulsed around him. That was what he wanted, and I gave it all. There was a bit of a pop every time he pulled free, and then I cupped his balls and both of his hands were in my hair.

"Starling..." A warning, but I didn't need it. I could feel him throbbing. The precum left a salty taste in my mouth and then he came, and the transformation of heated lust and focus to wonder and release, was the most beautiful thing I'd ever seen.

I swallowed every drop, damn near choking as Vaughn intensified his thrusts. Lit up from the inside, I was incandescent with pleasure. Spent, Rome eased from my mouth and dipped to kiss me, long and hard. He chased the flavor of himself around my mouth as I moaned with Vaughn's every deep push.

"Play with her clit," Vaughn said in a guttural voice, as he peeled me away from Rome. With ease, he lifted me until I was on my knees, my back to his chest and my legs spread for Rome to see where Vaughn vanished inside of me.

It was one of the most erotic things I'd ever experienced, having Rome watch us. Then he trailed his fingers along my over sensitized flesh. The sensations were overwhelming and colliding. He teased my nipples, leaving me ready to beg for more. Then he kissed around the plastic covered tattoo and when he reached my cunt, he teased his tongue against my clit, then began to lap at me and from the way Vaughn jerked and thrust, he was catching him too.

And that was it, I was gone. Flying. I came, and Vaughn let out a shout as he flooded me with his release. Rome continued to lap at us as Vaughn collapsed on his back with me sprawled on top of him.

"Rome," Vaughn said in a breathless, wrecked voice. "You don't have to lick my cock man."

"It's in the way," was Rome's only response, before he buried his face against my cunt and began to suck at my clit in earnest. It was too much, I began to spasm and thrash. They pinned me between them and I swore, Vaughn was getting harder the more I squeezed around him and the next rush not only made me see stars, but it shattered everything.

I was in a million pieces scattered amongst the stars, blissed beyond all measure.

I never wanted it to end.

Ever.

INTERROGATION

MILO

The cops sitting across from me wore the unfriendliest of expressions. They weren't playing good cop, bad cop like they did on television. They'd been bad cop all the way. I'd been in the box for over fifty hours. They'd let me piss once.

That was fine.

It wasn't like they gave me much in the way of hydration. I could sit here another fifty.

"You could make this easier on yourself," the first detective said. With male pattern balding in full effect, the sides of his hair were almost clown length.

"Has anyone ever told you that Bozo is not a good look on anyone?" I kept my tone mild, but to be honest, I was curious. "You could make life easier on yourself if you looked at shaving that off or at least trimming it up."

His eyes went flat and hard. "We have you dead to rights. You and Burns had a huge falling out over your girlfriend. You threatened to kill him. We have four witnesses who have given us statements to that effect, and he was found with his dick stuffed into his mouth."

"Sounds unpleasant." Again, I kept it neutral. I'd asked for an attorney, as was my right, and they were "working" on it. In the meanwhile, we kept up this little farce where they were talking at me, rather than questioning me.

"You know what happens when the lawyers get here," his partner said, going for sympathy. He really shouldn't bother. Bloodshot eyes, faint tremor in his hands, and a hint of jaundice to his skin—I knew an alcoholic when I saw one and he'd been stuck in here too long.

Sucked to be him.

"We can't help you anymore."

"You might want to pop a breath mint," I suggested. "The whiskey you drank on your break earlier is pretty cheap and you probably spilled some on your tie, cause I can still smell it."

Mouth compressed, he glared at me. "Look, you little punk, we know you did it. You know you did it. You can come clean now or..."

A knock on the mirror shut him up. He slammed his chair back and his partner followed him. I leaned back in mine and stretched my legs. They still had me handcuffed to the table. The uniformed officer who came in said nothing as he took up a stance next to the wall.

Now we began the hang out and wait game. Fine. I rolled my head from side to side, then leaned forward to stretch my back, before working out to lay my head on my arms and doze.

It was a vulnerable position, but fuck I was handcuffed to the table anyway. Dropping into a light sleep came easy. Sleep when you can, stay aware of your situation, and patience. These were all skills I'd cultivated.

I got maybe ninety minutes, when the officer cleared his throat and I flicked my eyes open to find the doorknob moving. Good man, even if I didn't dare acknowledge Officer Titus.

He'd be well rewarded later.

The man who came in looked like he'd tripped over the sixties, landed in the seventies to pick up that ill-fittted suit, before he rolled all the way down to now. Cream of the crop.

"I'm Mr..." He paused and flipped the file in his hand and nearly dropping his briefcase. "Hardigan's attorney. If you'll step out please, Officer."

Titus nodded, then gave me a brief look over the attorney's shoulder. His opinion wasn't any higher than mine.

Alone, the attorney set his things down and said, "Take whatever deal they are offering you. If we go to court, you're going to need an ironclad alibi. If you don't have one, you'll do twenty-five to life."

"Good to know you've already figured this whole thing out." The dry comment earned me a glare. I was getting very good at that.

Flipping open the folder, he pushed it toward me. "Sworn statements. Two affidavits. Video footage of you and the victim in a full on brawl at a Southside bar that spilled into the streets, and at least one bystander was injured."

"He tripped trying to video us with his phone," I pointed out. "Just to be clear. No one actually touched him, he was just a klutz."

"Right, klutz or not, they can link his injuries to you and this Burns fellow." He flipped to the next page. "The autopsy shows he took a severe beating, so severe it left internal injuries. If someone hadn't strangled him to death, he probably would have died from them."

While I didn't evince any real interest, I did look at the pictures. Burn was a fucking wreck of a man. Even his face was swollen and distorted. The beating I gave him wouldn't have done that.

Those injuries were also numerous and discolored, which meant peri-mortem. Hard to bruise too much or swell when the blood stopped flowing.

"I'll admit, most of this is circumstantial," the attorney said. "But they do have one witness who will swear, in court, that you detailed exactly how you would kill this guy and why."

I met his gaze and waited.

"They won't tell me who. Just that she will receive protection and once court proceedings begin, I'll be able to get that information during discovery. But Mr. Hardigan, you have known gang affiliations. You've had run-ins with the law before, they've got a sheet on you."

"All petty stuff and most of it when I was a juvenile and sealed. That makes it inadmissible, unless it directly relates to the crime and they can prove it to a judge. This doesn't."

Frowning, the man eyed me. "You're well-versed"

"I like to read. I'd also like to eat and have some water. We're coming up on fifty-two hours. In twenty, they have to charge me or let me go. And your name would be nice."

"Shit," the man swore. "Martin. Martin Russell." He went to hold out his hand for me to shake, but that was hard when I was still shackled to the table. "My apologies, Mr. Hardigan. And wait—you said you've been here for fifty-two hours?"

"That's a guesstimate." I shrugged. "It doesn't matter.

Twenty or so they charge me or have to let me go, but I've gotten to piss once, and they haven't provided a meal."

"I'll take care of that and I'll get you arraigned immediately." He checked his watch "Judge Fraser is taking cases tonight. He's a bag full of dicks, but he can't stand police misconduct any more than he can gangbangers."

"Ask him how he feels about college students."

Surprise flickered in his eyes.

"And yes, I'm enrolled. I currently have a 4.0 at State. Eighteen credits from graduation."

"You're pre-law." His expression turned downright tickled. "Mr. Hardigan, I apologize. I came in here and gave you shitty advice. I'm going to take care of that right now."

He left with a spring in his step and I slumped back in the chair. If they didn't let me take a piss soon, I might whip it out and see if I could paint their mirror with it. That would be entertaining.

The door opened again, and I glanced up expecting to see Titus, not another suit, considerably younger and wealthier from the look of him. Warning bells went off, but I didn't shift my position.

"Mr. Hardigan, my name is Dominic Walsh, I'm not an attorney yet. Nothing you say to me is privileged. So don't say anything at all. Take the deal they offer you. Plead guilty to manslaughter in defense of another. The victim raped your girlfriend. He damn near killed her."

I said nothing but the handcuffs bit into my wrists.

"If you fight this, the prosecution is going to receive incontrovertible evidence that not only did you do it, but she helped you."

My jaw locked.

"She's the witness they're using against you. The one you told exactly how you would kill him. What they aren't telling you was that there were drugs in his system, he was unconscious when he was killed. Incapacitated. The fast-acting roofie was out of his system, it doesn't have a long life in the blood stream."

I saw exactly where he was going with this.

"There's more. They'll start going after the Vandals, one by one. Freddie Dunlap is the easiest target, but Jasper Horan and Rome Cleary would be the next most likely. Do you see where I'm going?" He paused a beat then said, "Don't answer. Take the plea, tell them you'll allocute to it and the why. It means you'll have to stand in court and tell them you killed him and exactly how. I can get you everything you need to know."

He blew out a breath then checked his watch.

"I'm out of time. Take the deal. There are players at work here that want you dead and off the board entirely. This would be a setback, but not one you can't overcome. If you take the deal, you'll have help."

Then he was gone.

Thirty minutes later, and after Titus took me for a bathroom break and some water, a third suit walked in

His name was Walker Remmington, he'd been sent by Liam.

I sent him away.

"Officer," I said, not looking at Titus. "Tell them to get the district attorney in here. I want to make a deal and I want it in writing."

Walsh had told me the one thing I needed to know. I wouldn't put any of them through it. I could survive three years and it would keep all of them safe.

31

EMERSYN

I stayed at the clubhouse. More, I didn't leave Vaughn's bedroom. Even better, they didn't leave either, save the one time Rome went to find drinks and Vaughn went for food.

It was while Vaughn was gone that I had to ask... "Did he tattoo your cock?"

Rome smiled. "He showed me how. But I did the work."

"Can I?" He'd pulled on sweatpants when he went to find us water. Lots of water. There was beer too, but I didn't want to numb anything. I also hadn't bothered to get dressed. I was too busy soaking up the fact they were so relaxed with each other.

Another first for me. At least another willing first, and I wouldn't let any other memory have this place. In fact, I shuttled it into a dark box in the back of my mind and bolted it shut. He pushed his sweatpants down and released his semi-hard erection.

"How—how did you do it?" With care I stroked my

fingers over the image. I couldn't believe he got me on there like that. It was definitely me. I couldn't even process what it meant to me.

"Carefully." There was almost a sly grin when he said that, and I laughed at him. "I would get hard and then do it piece by piece. It takes time and the pain would soften me up again. I'd heal, then think of you, and continue."

Oh my god.

"Would you like to suck me off again?" The genuine curiosity in that question threw me. "Liam told me once I would love it, but until you, I never wanted to try."

"Rome, you did this—a long time ago. You had to have."

He shrugged. "It was for you. Always you."

And if that didn't damn near break me. Then, to hide my tears and the dangerous emotions threatening to burn me up, I began to stroke his dick up and down, slow and steady. He smiled.

"That is nice. But I like your mouth and throat more."

Chuckling, I gave him what he was asking for, and began to slowly suck on the head of his cock while I stroked him. He hardened almost instantly.

"Yes." Rome ran a hand over my hair. "That. Faster and deeper."

I cut a look up at him the first time he bumped my throat and the blissed expression on his face sent tears streaming down my cheeks.

"Come," Rome beckoned. "Sit on my face, let me taste you again. Without Vaughn inside you. Just me." If that wasn't enough to make me almost spontaneously come again... I shifted on the bed and he moved so that I was fully on his face and those fingers and lips began to pull me apart. I focused on giving him the best fucking blowjob, I could.

I wanted him to have all the pleasure. His shout was my only warning before the first splash of cum hit my throat, and I milked him for every drop. After a moment, he resumed his tonguing of my cunt and then he was fucking me with his mouth and his fingers. When he gripped my ass in both hands, I stiffened and lifted my head.

All at once, I locked eyes with Vaughn and he knelt there cupping my face, as I rocked my hips against Rome. The pressure of his fingers so close to my ass—

"You're safe," Vaughn reminded me and wiped some of the cum from the corner of my mouth before he kissed me. Little kisses, soft kisses, like butterflies. "Careful of her ass, Rome. Gentle. Dove is uncertain."

All at once, Rome's grip on me lightened and he massaged my ass. I was so close, and this was so sweet and... "I don't mean to..." I whispered.

"You're safe," Vaughn repeated. "No one will take anything from you anywhere, until you are ready, if you ever are. I am perfectly content to fuck that cunt of yours and that mouth. Fuck, I'll come in your hand."

The words and Rome's hard suction on my clit sent another orgasm spiraling through me. And rather than being finished, Rome just lapped up all the wetness until I was a shaking mess.

Then and only then, did Vaughn make good on his word. He flipped me over and fucked me until I saw stars, and this time when I blacked out, I didn't wake up until morning, sandwiched right between them, their naked bodies wrapped around mine.

It was heaven.

Until I met my brother's gaze where he stood just inside the doorway.

My brother.

I closed my eyes.

"Can you get dressed, please?"

I nodded once.

Vaughn swore and he flung a pillow at Milo. "You don't fucking let yourself into my room, Raptor."

Milo didn't say anything, he just turned on his heel and left. Eyes closed, I lay there for a long moment.

"I'll deal with him," Vaughn said. Which was nice, because after the last twenty-four hours, my cunt hurt in all the right ways and I was one long sensual bruise. Even my abs ached.

Tattoo—right.

"No," I said finally, opening my eyes to find Rome watching me. "I need to talk to him." Needed to stop running away from it. No, I hadn't read the results, but there were too many similarities, too much truth. If it turned out we weren't siblings, that might actually break me.

"Do you want us to go with you?" Rome asked and I kissed him. "No, I'll be okay."

I showered alone, because honestly my pussy really did hurt. Not in a crippling way but yeah—we were closed to dick for a bit. The guys found clothes for me, and Vaughn checked my tattoo, putting fresh ointment on it before I went down.

Milo was in the kitchen drinking coffee. I paused in the doorway, studying the man in an unguarded moment. For all that he'd seemed like a brute, there was a gentleness to him. An intensity I didn't understand.

"I'm sorry," I told him and he glanced at me.

"For the sex? You're an adult, Emersyn," he said it with wrinkled nose of distaste. "I don't have to like it, but you really can fuck whoever you want."

"Thank you. Both for the permission and the coffee." I took the mug he pushed my way and couldn't resist a bit of the snark, still. "And no, I'm not sorry about the sex. I'll never be sorry about them." Any of them. Sitting down, I took the chair nearer to him rather than opposite. "I'm sorry I don't remember you. I'm sorry I struggled to even believe you."

"But you do now?"

"Yes," I told him before I took a sip of coffee and turned the whole idea around in my head. "And no."

"Helpful," he countered with a hint of a smile. "Care to clarify?"

"Doc did the blood test."

"He told me. Gave me a copy too."

Of course he had. "I didn't open mine."

Milo frowned. "Why not?"

"A part of me is terrified it will be true. That my parents have lied to me my whole life. That—the things I've gone through. The things that happened—so much of it could have been avoided. Maybe it would have changed. I don't know. If it's true, then the lies are going to bury me."

"Nothing," he told me in a growl, "is ever going to hurt you again."

How much I wanted to believe him. How much I wanted to hold onto the hope and the safety they offered. *That* terrified me even more than if it were true.

"You said a part of you was terrified it would be true. What about the rest of you?"

"That it won't be," I admitted. "Your guys have all looked after me—you have—because you think I'm your sister."

"I know you are." He shifted in his seat and pulled out

his wallet. I thought he was going to show me the picture again, but he pulled out was a single sheet of paper.

Test results.

Positive match.

Close family match. The percentages and graphs were all a bunch of numbers, but positive match were the words I focused on.

Milo Hardigan was my brother.

I had a brother.

"I'm sorry," he told me, and I glanced at him through the film of tears in my eyes. "I know you were scared it was true."

"Why didn't they tell me?" Why keep up the lie? Why did they let Uncle—or was that why they let him? Did they know? Or did they not care? I always thought they didn't know. I tried to tell them once, but the words wouldn't come and they were in a hurry.

"I don't know," he said honestly. "Maybe they didn't want you looking for your roots and finding out where you came from. They're wealthy and they're powerful. Blood-lines mean a lot to them."

Yes, they did.

How many times had Uncle Bradley called me a Sharpe?

I shook my head as I kept staring at the paper, the thoughts tumbling over and over like a drunk hamster on a broken wheel.

"Tell me about our mother," I asked more than demanded. "I know you tried to once but..."

"You weren't ready to hear it," he agreed. "Let's make some breakfast while we talk."

"I'm good at three things so far," I warned him.

His laugh made me smile. "Show me what you can do, kiddo. I'll see about teaching you some more."

While I worked on the pancakes, he made the eggs. He told me about our mother. About her drug addiction and how when he was younger, he didn't understand. Then she OD'd on a bad batch and that was that. He did his best to look after me, but it was a while before anyone noticed. Then Mickey came and we were in the system.

Some of the stories he told were hilarious, but as we carried the plates to the table, he mentioned, "I never admitted who our father was. I didn't want them tracking him down."

"Is he still alive?"

"Don't ever look for him, Ivy," Milo said then grimaced.

I covered his hand and he stilled. "It's okay. You can call me Ivy. Everyone else calls me a bird or a Boo-Boo or a demon from hell. Ivy's kind of refreshing."

Milo laughed. Really laughed, head thrown back and eyes alight with joy. When I squeezed his hand, he returned the affection. Sobering, he said "But I'm serious. Don't look for him. He won't be an ally or friend. He's the worst. A drug dealer. He wanted to take me and leave you with her. He never wanted you."

That should probably hurt, but considering I really hadn't known about the man's existence prior to now and being *wanted* wasn't necessarily all it was cracked up to be, I just nodded.

"That came out badly."

"It's fine," I assured him. "Really. I still wish—well, no I guess I don't. If they'd adopted you too, I don't think you'd have liked it very much."

I'd have had an ally, though. Or maybe Uncle Bradley would have gotten rid of him, too.

That was my answer. That was why they hadn't adopted Milo. "I really don't know what to do with having a brother. You keep acting like you get to decide for me. That you have control of my life."

"Our world..."

"Milo, no. The world is dangerous. Believe it or not, I know that. I'm not an idiot. I might struggle with some things and not understand all the players on the board but shutting me out isn't solving anything. I told you, I won't be caged. If you want to be my brother—then let me be your sister."

I thought it odd no one came to join us. Then again, maybe they were letting us talk. We circled the conversation around to my performances and a little to his schooling. When we alighted on his time in jail, he shook his head. "Not yet, Ivy."

"You think I'll hate you for it."

Pushing the plate away, he said, "I pled guilty to manslaughter. I pled guilty to killing the man who raped my girlfriend."

Horror crawled through me.

"I thought it was the right thing to do. I didn't want to put her through any more hell, and I didn't want them looking any closer at the Vandals. The plea bargain kept me from a longer sentence."

I swallowed.

"The only drawbacks were, I couldn't help you. I couldn't help them. I couldn't help her."

"What happened?"

"That—is a story for another day." He met my gaze. "They put me in jail for killing a man. That's the long and the short of it."

"For killing someone who deserved it." I shrugged. "Not going to hate you for that." How could I? I sure as hell didn't hate Jasper and the guys for killing Eric.

Or for the punks at the park.

Or the guy at the shop.

Or the people Liam had fired back on at the club.

I actually hoped he'd killed some of them.

When Milo reached out, I met him halfway and locked my hand with his. "Be patient with me?" I asked. "This is still...new."

"I've waited almost 18 years, kid, I can wait a hell of a lot longer if I have to. You couldn't get rid of me when I had to change your shitty diapers or when you wouldn't sleep or when you would throw blocks at my head. I can wait this out."

I laughed, "Charming."

"You totally were," he agreed almost solemnly. "But I want to get to know you again. I want you to know me. And —hear me out—while it's still not safe for you to be here full time, we're working on making it so you can come back when you want to."

That was a lot.

It was more than a lot.

While it seemed we'd crossed miles over breakfast, the journey ahead was so much longer. Vaughn paused in, before he had to go to work and checked the tattoo on my stomach one more time. Milo opened his mouth and when I stared at him, he shut it again.

"Fine, I can still think it though," he warned me, and I grinned.

"Right back atcha, big brother."

The words flowed right off my tongue and Milo's smile —he didn't look quite so fierce and dangerous. Milo took me back to Liam's after I said goodbye to Rome and made plans to play video games with Freddie. He was downright bummed that he hadn't woken up until I was leaving.

Liam was in a mood when we got there. His place also smelled violently of lemon polish, and there was a chair missing from the table. I kept all smartass comments to myself. We really shouldn't have fucked on his table.

"I need you to stay in today," he told me after Milo left and I showed him my new tattoo. That gave him pause and he grinned. "Vaughn does good work. But seriously. I need you inside and to stay put. Don't answer the door and don't take calls from the doorman today."

"If this is about yesterday..."

"It's not," he said. "I've got meetings today and I might be unreachable. I'll feel better knowing you're here and secure. So, promise me?"

"I promise...but can I convince you to bring home pizza for dinner?" Because oh I had a craving, and I was starving, even though we'd just had breakfast. Probably all the extra calories I'd been burning.

"Done."

I grinned and started to turn away, but he caught me, spun me around, then kissed me until I couldn't breathe and my heart hammered in my ears.

"Be a good girl for me, Hellspawn." Then he was gone, and I was still trying to form coherent thoughts, much less sentences.

I did my stretches and a lighter workout, largely because I was sore. Eventually, I curled up on the sofa and turned on the television. I wanted to check a few more movies off my list and maybe take a nap.

Instead of porn, it looked like Liam had been watching the news.

And there I was, in full color with the news banner listing how I'd been missing now for almost nine months.

While the FBI and law enforcement seemed to have given up, they switched to an interview with my uncle.

Hot ice flashed through me as the camera focused on him.

"We have new leads. The family will never give up looking for her. My sister-in-law is beside herself in grief and my brother had a minor heart attack last week."

My heart squeezed.

"While he is recovering, I am committing every resource I have to finding her." He looked right through the camera, and I swore I could feel his gaze on me. "It's time to come home, Princess. I will find you. I promise."

I would have thrown the remote at the television, but it cut away to other bounties and rewards being offered. One from the Reed family was substantial, so was the one from the Benedict family. All in all, it factored into the millions from all sides.

Grabbing my phone, I texted Lainey through the app and checked it repeatedly until she answered me.

Her: *Don't worry. It's all appearances. Though Adam seems determined on the subject and Ezra is unbearable. I haven't told them. I've told no one. I have your back. If you need me, just say where and when.*

The message vanished. Then another appeared.

Her: *What do you need?*

Me: *I don't know yet. But if he is getting close, I'll use what you sent me*

Her: *You better let me know where you are.*

Me: *I promise.*

Maybe I should tell them. Tell them all why I didn't want to go back. Why I didn't dare.

But the moment I told them—they were at risk.

Jasper. Rome. Kellan. Vaughn. Freddie. Even Liam and Milo, especially Milo, it would hurt him so badly.

They would go after my uncle.

I closed my eyes. As much as I loved the idea of him dead, every other person who had learned the truth died or disappeared.

I couldn't let that happen to them.

No, I just needed to stay away.

Emersyn Sharpe needed to die.

32

EMERSYN

After the last message between Lainey and me vanished, I closed the app. Then stared down at the phone. The news had moved on to other things. The crime wave in Braxton Harbor. The continuing investigation into the shooting at the topless dance bar.

There were more stories. Car jackings. Two robberies. A truck full of illegal immigrants. That took the conversation in a different direction. Most of it made me sick. And I had to wonder if this was what had them so preoccupied. The sharp rise in crime and collateral damage was a concern.

When they switched to the police chief and the mayor, I turned it off. It all sounded kind of horrible. The phone rang in the kitchen, breaking the sudden silence, and I jerked. Heart racing, I tried to catch my breath as it kept ringing.

Liam didn't want me to answer.

So I didn't.

Ten minutes later, the elevator dinged in the hallway

and I climbed to go and look. I'd never seen Liam's neighbor, if there was one. The doorman appeared with a package, he set it down in front of the door and knocked perfunctorily before making a note on his phone. Without another look at the door, he boarded the elevator and I waited a full five minutes after he was gone before I opened the door.

It wouldn't be the first time I retrieved a package for him. Only it wasn't for him.

It was addressed to me.

Someone sent me something here.

The only people who knew were the guys. I hadn't even told Lainey where I was. Phone on the table, I slit open the envelope.

Pictures fell out of it. Dozens of pictures.

Kellan and I at a driving lesson. Rome and I on the street. That was months old. That was when he took me out for the first time. Pictures from Kellan's shop, Vaughn's tattoo place—the hotel where Jasper took me.

There were pictures of all of the Vandals too.

Every single one of them down to Freddie. In each shot, the crosshairs had been painted over them.

The last picture was the worst.

It was Milo in a prison orange suit and his fists were bloody and his face bruised.

A single sheet of paper accompanied the photos. My stomach curdled at the message. Come home or else.

Most of the pictures were from the last week. Most, but not all.

He had to be close. I hadn't even looked to see where he was during that news broadcast, but it had been the *local* news.

I'd just found my brother, I couldn't let my uncle hurt

him. Clearly, my uncle knew about him. Knew where I was, too.

How long had he known? How long had he been this close?

I sank into a chair and stared at the images. Then the letter, and covered my mouth with my hand.

If I stayed, they would protect me. They would fight for me. What had Jasper said? They'd die for me, too.

No.

No one else died for me. No one else got hurt.

My heart squeezed in my chest so hard, it hurt with every beat. I gathered the photos up and tucked them into the envelope again. If I could burn them...I would. For now, I carried them back into the bedroom and packed them into a bag.

I wanted to take their shirts with me, but I didn't dare.

He would already be in a mood. The sting on my abs reminded me of what Vaughn wrote.

Head up. Wings out.

I could do this.

I could protect them.

Rome's bear sat next to my bed. I picked it up for one last hug, and pressed a kiss to its head before I put it back.

They saved me.

Now it was my turn.

Only when I was ready to go did I look at my phone again. I couldn't just disappear. My thumb floated up and down the list and I finally chose Freddie.

"Boo-Boo!" He answered on the first ring. "Guess what I'm doing?"

"If it's your former teacher, you wouldn't be answering the phone."

He snorted. "You don't know that. I can multi-task."

A laugh swelled out of me. "Well, for her sake, don't answer the phone if you get to fuck her and for mine, don't tell me who you're fucking while on the phone with me."

"Deal," he agreed. "Feel free to dirty dial me any time. I'd love to hear you come."

Another giggle escaped. Freddie really could make me laugh even now. "Look..." I sobered and let out a heavy sigh.

"Nope."

"What?"

"Nothing good comes from a sigh like that. What's wrong, Boo-Boo?"

"I have to go home." The words were ash in my mouth. "It's time."

"Well fuck, come on. Need one of us to pick you up? I've missed having you here."

I would not cry. I refused. "Not to the clubhouse, Freddie. To my..." I hated what I was about to say so much. "To my real home."

"You don't want to do that," he argued. "I know you don't."

"My mother is sick." Not a lie. "My father had a heart attack." I still couldn't believe that. Was it true or a lie to lure me out?

Worst of all why did I care?

"Boo-Boo, don't do this." All traces of humor were gone from Freddie's voice. "I mean it. Don't. Let's get the others. We'll talk and make a plan. Milo's the best planner ever...."

"Freddie stop," I said softly, and he went silent. "Thank you for wanting to do it, for making me laugh and for being you. But I have to do this. I need you to tell everyone this was my choice."

I hated myself more.

"I don't want you to go."

"I'm sorry."

"Wait for me. I'll be at Liam's in no time..."

"Thank you for caring. I'll call when I can." Which would probably be never. Hanging up on him was the worst feeling ever. I thought I understood the pain, but saying goodbye *hurt*.

I left a note for Liam. Short and to the point. But I couldn't stop the tears falling as I wrote the lies about needing to go and wanting to be back with my family now.

I wiped them away and took the elevator to the lobby. On the trip down, I put myself back together. I pulled Emersyn Sharpe out of mothballs, she didn't quite fit anymore. Hard and jagged edges cut into my soul. The too brittle exterior chafed.

But it was safer behind that wall. That distance.

The car waiting for me didn't surprise me.

The driver just opened the back door and I slid inside. I didn't look back. I couldn't. I held onto the bag. Not the one with the ID and cash Lainey had set up for me. I left that hidden in Liam's place.

I might need it eventually.

The driver said nothing to me, though he did make a call. "Yes, sir, I have her. She was exactly where he said she'd be."

He.

Someone had just made a lot of money.

Good for them, I supposed.

I hadn't brought my new phone with me either. I'd left that with my bag. I wanted Uncle Bradley to have nothing to connect to them.

Memorizing the numbers had taken a minute, but I'd committed three to memory.

It was all the time I'd had.

Flash of movement outside the car caught my eye and I stared at the motorcycle and rider pacing us.

Liam.

Dammit.

I closed my eyes and looked away. The driver said something under his breath, and suddenly we accelerated. But no matter what he did, the bike followed us. When he jerked and took an unexpected exit, the bike shot past. We'd turned too fast for him.

It wasn't long before we were on an airport road. They all looked the same and the driver glided through one security gate followed by another.

Private airfield.

He pulled all the way up to the plane that sat with its engines idling. The driver came around and opened my door. I didn't say anything when he took my bag, just climbed out. The twenty or so steps from the car to the stairs of the plane seemed to take an eternity.

A shout behind me had me faltering mid-step. "Don't do it!" I glanced back as soon as I was at the stairs. Liam was outside the gate and security was swarming him.

His expression was hell. "Hellspawn!"

Stop, I whispered silently. Just stop.

Turning away, I climbed the stairs.

The door behind me was already closing and the pilot instructed me to take a seat. The cabin's only other occupant watched me as I took a seat opposite him. Clicking the seatbelt on echoed, even as the plane began to move.

"Welcome home, Princess."

Emersyn and the Vandals will return in Dirty Devil.

To keep up with Heather and all her series join her reader's group:
Https://www.facebook.com/groups/HeathersPack/

AFTERWORD

So, yeah—that happened.

You probably need a minute, so I'm going to sit here while you curse my name. Pretty sure they will be printing the buttons with #TeamMadAtHeather on them, if they haven't already.

Still need a few more minutes to digest that?

Fair enough. I've got time. Get some water, take a breath, walk it off and come back.

I know in the very beginning, I promised you a happy ending at the end of the story. Well, we have a while to go before that end. While I always knew this is where Ruthless Traitor would end, I wasn't prepared for it any more than you were.

It's important to recognize that in Vicious Rebel, Emersyn made a choice to go back to the Vandals. She made the choice to stay there. In this book, she fights a battle with her brother to stay with the Vandals. She fights her own doubts. Her own fears.

The Vandals, Liam included, help strengthen her. They help her fight back and reclaim herself even if they aren't one hundred percent sure of the battle she is waging. They know part of it. As much as she chose to go back to them, it was her choice to walk away—to protect them now.

They mean more to her than her own safety. She cares. Are you terrified for the next book? I am and at the same time, I know this journey is far from over.

Hang in there and feel free to drop into the Pack or the Spoiler group to yell at me.

xoxo

Heather

ABOUT HEATHER LONG

I *love* books. Not just a little bit, but a lot. Books were my best friends when I was growing up. Books didn't care if I was new to a town or to a class. They were always there, my trustiest of companions. Until they turned on me and said I had to write them.

I can tell you that my own personal happily ever after included writing books. I've always said that an HEA is a work in progress. It's true in my marriage, my friendships, and in my career. I am constantly nurturing my muse as we dive into new tales, new tropes, new characters and more.

After seventeen years in Texas, we relocated to the Pacific Northwest in search of seasons, new experiences, and new geography. I can't wait to discover what life (and my muse) have in store for me.

Maybe writing was always my destiny and romance my fate. After all, my grandmother wasn't a fan of picture books and used to read me her Harlequin Romance novels.

Friends to lovers, enemies to lovers, friends to enemies to lovers, you name it, I love them and love to write them. I started with Earth Witches Aren't Easy, the first in the Chance Monroe trilogy, but my characters and I have traveled a long way since I created that urban fantasy world.

One of the series I hear my readers recommend the most is the Untouchable series followed in quick succession by the Vandals, and that just delights me. No lie, whenever one of my readers brings up my wolves, I do a little a fist pump.

I'm active on social media, and I love hearing from readers. Feel free to tag me with a question about any of my books, or just say hi!

Follow Heather & Sign up for her news and updates:
www.heatherlong.net
TikTok

ALSO BY HEATHER LONG

82nd Street Vandals

Savage Vandal

Vicious Rebel

Ruthless Traitor

Dirty Devil

Brutal Fighter

Dangerous Renegade

Merciless Spy

Always a Marine Series

Once Her Man, Always Her Man

Retreat Hell! She Just Got Here

Tell It to the Marine

Proud to Serve Her

Her Marine

No Regrets, No Surrender

The Marine Cowboy

The Two and the Proud

A Marine and a Gentleman

Combat Barbie

Whiskey Tango Foxtrot

What Part of Marine Don't You Understand?

A Marine Affair

Marine Ever After

Marine in the Wind

Marine with Benefits

A Marine of Plenty

A Candle for a Marine

Marine under the Mistletoe

Have Yourself a Marine Christmas

Lest Old Marines Be Forgot

Her Marine Bodyguard

Smoke & Marines

Bravo Team Wolf

When Danger Bites

Bitten Under Fire

Cardinal Sins

Kill Song

First Chorus

High Note

Chance Monroe

Earth Witches Aren't Easy

Plan Witch from Out of Town

Bad Witch Rising

Her Elite Assets

Featuring:

Pure Copper

Target: Tungsten

Asset: Arsenic

Fevered Hearts

Marshal of Hel Dorado

Brave are the Lonely

Micah & Mrs. Miller

A Fistful of Dreams

Raising Kane

Wanted: Fevered or Alive

Wild and Fevered

The Quick & The Fevered

A Man Called Wyatt

Going Royal

Some Like It Royal

Some Like It Scandalous

Some Like It Deadly

Some Like it Secret

Some Like it Easy

Her Marine Prince

Blocked

Heart of the Nebula

Queenmaker

Deal Breaker

Throne Taker

Lone Star Leathernecks

Semper Fi Cowboy

As You Were, Cowboy

Magic & Mayhem

The Witch Singer

Bridget's Witch's Diary

The Witched Away Bride

Mongrels

Mongrels, Mischief & Mayhem

Shackled Souls

Succubus Chained

Succubus Unchained

Succubus Blessed

Shackled Souls (Omnibus)

Space Cowboy

Space Cowboy Survival Guide

Untouchable

Rules and Roses

Changes and Chocolates

Keys and Kisses

Whispers and Wishes

Hangovers and Holidays

Brazen and Breathless

Trials and Tiaras

Graduation and Gifts

Defiance and Dedication

Songs and Sweethearts

Legacy and Lovers

Farewells and Forever

Wolves of Willow Bend

Wolf at Law

Wolf Bite

Caged Wolf

Wolf Claim

Wolf Next Door

Rogue Wolf

Bayou Wolf

Untamed Wolf

Wolf with Benefits

River Wolf

Single Wicked Wolf

Desert Wolf

Snow Wolf

Wolf on Board

Holly Jolly Wolf

Shadow Wolf

His Moonstruck Wolf

Thunder Wolf

Ghost Wolf

Outlaw Wolves

Wolf Unleashed